S0-BBM-424

THE WEDDING CRASHER

THE WEDDING CRASHER

A Novel

MIA SOSA

THORNDIKE PRESS
A part of Gale, a Cengage Company

Copyright © 2022 by Mia Sosa.
Thorndike Press, a part of Gale, a Cengage Company.

ALL RIGHTS RESERVED
This is a work of fiction. Names, characters, places, and incidents are products of the author's imagination or are used fictitiously and are not to be construed as real. Any resemblance to actual events, locales, organizations, or persons, living or dead, is entirely coincidental.

Thorndike Press® Large Print Romance.
The text of this Large Print edition is unabridged.
Other aspects of the book may vary from the original edition.
Set in 16 pt. Plantin.

LIBRARY OF CONGRESS CIP DATA ON FILE.
CATALOGUING IN PUBLICATION FOR THIS BOOK
IS AVAILABLE FROM THE LIBRARY OF CONGRESS.

ISBN-13: 978-1-4328-9762-8 (hardcover alk. paper)

Published in 2022 by arrangement with Avon, an imprint of HarperCollins Publishers

Printed in Mexico
Print Number: 01   Print Year: 2022

This one is for my readers.
I appreciate every kind message,
every shout-out,
every emoji-filled review.
Thank you for choosing to spend time
in my fictional worlds; I'm honored.

CHAPTER ONE

THE CARTWRIGHT HOTEL
WASHINGTON, DC

SOLANGE

There's only one rational explanation for what's happening in this stairwell: I'm cursed.

Yes, I'm being dramatic. Yes, the drama's guaranteed to escalate from here.

I'm in this predicament because my cousin Natalia, a cosmetologist by trade, called me at the last minute and begged for my help with, as she put it, "providing white-glove makeup services" for a wedding at the Cartwright. What even *is* that?

My other cousin Lina, the wedding coordinator for this swanky boutique hotel, has instructed me to keep a low profile. She would never admit this, but I'd bet money she's worried that my alarmingly effective most-men-are-trash pheromones will change the outcome of this highly anticipated affair.

So fine. I'm happy to hand Natalia

7

makeup brushes or wipes or whatever and keep out of sight. Except she assigned me an additional duty — asking for a broom and a dustpan — and I figured I could snag a few extra vials of courtesy moisturizer for my ashy hands if I just went down to housekeeping myself.

Damn my cheap ass to hell.

I should have purchased the lotion from the hotel spa and continued on my clueless way. Instead, I'm now rooted to the landing between the second and third floors, intruding on a private moment between the bride and a man who *isn't* the groom.

"You don't love him," the man says, his blue eyes overly bright and his tie askew. Then he reaches up to caress her face.

The bride, a vision worthy of any wedding magazine layout, steps back, easily dodging his attempt to touch her. "I never said I did."

Good Lord. She's not even denying the accusation? If my mother were here, she'd gasp, place a hand across her forehead, and say, "Que escândalo!" She'd be right too. Because this? This is an *epic* scandal.

"Then don't do it," the man urges. "You'll regret this for the rest of your life."

"Give me another reason not to go through with it. One that counts."

He gestures around them. "Where the hell

is all of this coming from, Ella?"

She paces in the small space, twisting her perfectly manicured hands and mumbling incoherently, her face scrunched up in distress. Several beats later, she stills and takes a steadying breath. "I'm in love with you, Tyler. The question is, are you finally ready to admit your feelings for me?"

Holy shit. Is she serious?

Not-the-groom closes his eyes and says nothing, giving her the answer she wasn't hoping for.

The nosy part of me wants to watch what happens next; the sensible part of me knows I can't stand here forever. *Think, Solange. Think.* Okay, okay, I suppose I can pretend to be oblivious to what's unfolding and slink past them. Since the bride's makeup was already done when I arrived, Ella and I haven't crossed paths, so I could make myself scarce in the dressing suite, and she would never know her secret's been compromised. Or I could tiptoe back to the door on the third floor. Considering they're totally engrossed in each other, I may be able to leave undetected.

I eye the stairs, then turn my head and stare at the door. Decisions, decisions. *But hang on a minute.* I didn't do anything wrong. This is the bride's mess, not mine.

And I want that fucking lotion — it's magical. Plus, I need time to plan my next move.

Because the apparently unlucky groom isn't a stranger. Not exactly. Dean and I haven't met yet, but he's the best friend of Lina's boyfriend, and loyalty to my cousin (along with basic decency) dictates that I consider whether to disclose what I'm witnessing.

A loud gasp signals that the choice of how to extricate myself from the situation is no longer mine, however, and when I glance back at the duo, two pairs of wary eyes are gazing at me.

Thankfully, I'm quick on my feet. "Sorry to interrupt, folks," I say, giving them a jaunty salute. "I understand the need to sneak away just before you say 'I do.' My husband and I had sex literally ten minutes before we tied the knot." I'm not married, but I *can* lie to someone's face when the occasion calls for it.

To my relief, the tension in the bride's body recedes, as if she's determined I'm not a potentially hostile friend of the groom. Her unrequited crush, meanwhile, rubs the back of his head and barks out a laugh.

"It's so hard to stay away from him, you know?" she says. "Just an hour more and we'll be in each other's arms for our first dance." Playing the role of a bride flirting with her intended, she gives him a coy smile and tugs on the lapels of his suit jacket to draw him close. *Is he a wedding guest, for heaven's sake?* Then she winks at him, the faint blush blooming across her dewy cheeks conveniently enhancing her performance.

Wow, she's as talented an actor as I am.

I wave off her apology and graze the wall until I reach the first step that will lead me to freedom. "No worries. Enjoy and congratulations." When I'm three steps down, I add, "I wish you all the best." Why? Because it's in neither my nor the groom's interest to reveal what I really think about this situation. Not yet, that is. I'll just grab that broom and dustpan — oh, and the free hand cream, of course — and find Lina. She'll know how to handle this.

But when I return to the bridal suite (without the damn lotion because the hotel stocks it in a locked cabinet), Lina is nowhere to be found and isn't answering my SOS text. Worse, the ceremony's due to start in minutes.

"Where have you been?" Natalia asks as she dabs powder on a middle-aged woman's chin and forehead. "I asked for the broom fifteen minutes ago." She looks at my reflection in the mirror and raises an eyebrow.

11

I'm fidgeting. She notices.

Natalia twists her upper body — a significant feat given that she's eight months pregnant — and leans in my direction so only I can hear what she says next. "Everything okay? You look like you've seen a naked ghost with a humongous schlong."

I roll my eyes and puff out a short breath. Natalia frequently speaks in the tongue of her ancestral land: a frat house. "Uh, I'm not sure. It's just that I saw the bride when I went downstairs and —"

The woman in the chair jumps up, dodging Natalia's hands as my cousin tries to blot the woman's face. "Ella's downstairs? But why? She's supposed to be here putting the final touches on her makeup."

Actually, from what I could tell, Ella's shooting her shot with another man. To Ella's presumptive relative, I say, "I'm not sure, exactly. Maybe you should check on her?" I eye Natalia and mouth, *I need to talk to you. Outside.*

She nods, but then Ella sails into the suite and parks herself right between my cousin and me, several tendrils of her blond hair having escaped the intricate topknot she's chosen as her wedding-day hairstyle. "I've got a bit of shine, but we don't have a lot of time," the bride says to Natalia. "Could you do a quick refresh?"

Natalia activates her professional mode. "Of course."

Before Ella drops into the chair, she slides a troubled gaze in my direction. "And who do we have here?"

"This is my cousin Solange. She's *pretending* to help me today."

I give Natalia a dirty look, then add for Ella's benefit: "I'm also on the groom's side."

Ella swallows. "I see." Then she fans her face. "Is there someone who could get me some water? I'm feeling a little parched."

I point to an impressive display of snacks — and *bottled water* — on a table a few feet away. "There's some right there."

"I'm partial to sparkling, actually," Ella says, giving me a tremulous smile. "Helps to settle my stomach, which for obvious reasons is doing a number on me today."

Natalia grins at me sheepishly. "Would you mind, Solange? Maybe ring room service?"

"I tried calling in the hall," Ella says quickly. "They're not answering."

"The café on the mezzanine level, then?" Natalia asks.

Oh, I see what's going on. Ella *wants* to get rid of me. I'm probably the only thing standing between her and the marriage she's hoping to enter.

Gripping the chair handles, Ella leans over and pins me with a feverish gaze. "I understand you don't have any dog in this fight, but that sparkling water would be just the thing to calm my nerves. It's my big day, and I'm out of sorts." She shakes her head as if to clear it. "I don't do my best thinking under circumstances like these. Can you find it in your heart to do me this one small favor?"

Dog in this fight? Out of sorts? Not her best thinking? This woman's really something. Using just a few carefully selected phrases, she's telling me to back off and keep quiet about what I saw. And maybe I should. Still, I can't help making a plea for her to do what's obviously best for everyone involved: call off this wedding.

"Are you *sure* this is what you want?" I ask.

"It . . . it is," she says, her voice breaking.

"It's not too late to change your mind, you know."

"My parents would say otherwise. Besides, I've made my choice."

We stare at each other for a long moment, then I puff out my cheeks and exhale.

"Fine," I tell her. "Every bride deserves to

14

get what she wants on her big day. Even if it isn't readily available. I'll see what I can find."

She gives me a shaky laugh, then twists around and relaxes against the seat back. Gah. I'm officially drained. A half hour more and Natalia will release me from my duties.

Just get the damn water, Solange, and move on with your life. Intending to do precisely that, I stalk to the door of the suite, then, with a last glance at my cousin, who's squinting in my direction, I walk across the threshold and resist the ever present urge to meddle in someone else's business.

When my phone buzzes in my pocket, I pull it out and see a text from Lina:

Sorry. The cellist got lost on her way here. Needed to get her settled. What's up?

I type a quick reply as I walk to the bank of elevators: *never mind. we're good*

Lina: K, great. The ceremony will be starting soon. The groom should be on his way, then Jaslene will come get the bride. Is everyone all set up there?

Me: think so. might want to check with Natalia to be sure

She texts a thumbs-up emoji.

15

Before I can respond in kind, a person slams into me, and I drop to the ground like I've been KO'd in a championship bout. Figures. If there's one thing I'm good at, it's falling on my ass with verve and panache.

"Fuck, I'm so sorry," a husky voice says above my head.

I blink a couple of times and open my eyes. Whoa. The white man leaning over me isn't your average Joe. Nor your average anything. On the contrary, he's off-the-charts handsome — so much so that I imagine his facial features competing daily for the title of best body part.

"You're no match for me," his plump lips say to his strong jaw.

"The hell I'm not," his jaw retorts. "Everyone knows I'm fucking irresistible when the big guy strokes me."

"Pipe down, you two," his hazel eyes tell them. "When we gaze at a woman for longer than three seconds, she's a goner. Try to top that."

There's a tiny patch of scarred skin above his left eyebrow. It's the money shot (the basketball kind, that is), and it adds a hint of mystery to his impeccable appearance.

"People dig me the most, though," the scar boasts in a seductive tone. "Because it

16

suggests he spends his days poring over spreadsheets and his nights kicking ass in a dingy boxing gym."

"You're all great," I say.

Out. Loud.

A touch of pink on the apples of the man's cheeks tells me he's noticed my blatant perusal. "Are you okay?"

"I'm fine. You're fine. We're all fine."

Not-your-average-Joe smothers a laugh and clears his throat, then offers his hand. "Here, let me help you up."

I take it and allow him to pull me to standing. Jesus, he's tall. The man eclipses me by at least five inches, and I'm taller than the average woman. And now that I have my bearings, I notice the black tuxedo and dirty-blond hair: *This* is the person Lina gestured to when I asked her to point out the groom.

"I apologize," he says, the flush creeping up his cheeks deepening a shade. "I'm a bit distracted today."

"You're the groom," I say.

"Yep," he says, nodding.

"Dean."

My mastery of obvious facts is breathtaking. Truly.

"Two for two." He gives his head a quick shake. "Should I know you?"

"I'm Solange. Lina's cousin."

He smiles, his eyes brightening in friendly recognition. "Right, right. You're the youngest."

"Only by two years," I say a tad defensively. "But to my older cousins, I'm still walking around in diapers."

Oh my God, shut up, Solange.

His smile widens (hopefully not because he's picturing me in Pampers). "If it's any consolation, Lina thinks you're brilliant."

I try not to fidget; brilliance is a lot to live up to. "I'd prefer to think of myself as resourceful and good-hearted."

"Doesn't mean you can't be brilliant too, does it?"

I tap my chin, pretending to consider his question. "Now that you mention it, you're absolutely right. I'm fucking brilliant too."

He nods in encouragement, the laugh lines around his eyes appearing just to spite me. "That's the fucking spirit."

We grin at each other — until images of the encounter in the stairwell flash in my mind and force me to remember that this man's heading to his wedding ceremony.

Honestly, I've never lamented the notion that all of the good ones are taken — lots of bad ones are taken too — but it seems especially unfortunate that I'm meeting this

18

guy today. Just in case you were wondering, Fate: You. Are. *Trash.* Because if this man were free, he would definitely rise to the top of my to-do list. Well, I'll just console myself by assuming he's bad in bed. Cutie in the streets, troll in the sheets. C'mon, it's only fair.

Dean's gaze travels over my face, then he scrunches his brow and jerks his head as though his brain needs a reset. "Well, anyway, thanks for helping out today."

"My pleasure."

I'm all smiles and pleasantries on the outside, but inside my chest is deflating like a tire with a slow leak. Truth is, the narrow hallway isn't big enough to contain the secret I'm keeping, and my lips aren't sufficiently disciplined to remain shut. It's *right there* on the tip of my tongue: *Your bride's in love with someone else. Run!*

But then Dean's phone rings, and he answers without hesitation, a shrill voice entering our bubble of conversation. The call's a timely reminder that I know very little about this man's life and shouldn't wreak havoc on it unless I'm certain it's the right thing to do.

"Dean, sweetie, that bastard posted an eviction notice on my door," the irate person on the other line says loud enough

19

for me to hear. "The judge said he couldn't do that, right? What now?"

"Hang on, Mrs. Budros."

He presses the phone against his chest so Mrs. Budros can't hear him.

"It's my client," he explains to me. "I need to take this."

"Let me guess: You're a lawyer."

"Guilty as charged," he says with a grin. "Excuse me a minute."

Pressing a finger against his free ear, he pivots away from me and strolls down the hall. "I'm back," he says to his client.

Seconds later, the elevator arrives on the floor and Jaslene, Lina's best friend and assistant, rushes out, a clipboard wedged under one arm, her gaze zeroing in on Dean. "Found him," she says into her space cadet headset. "I'll send him down right now."

Jaslene marches over and tugs Dean forward by the sleeve. "Let's go, hotshot. We don't have time for this. You're supposed to be downstairs so I can grab your bride."

Dean allows himself to be led inside the elevator, never interrupting his conversation with Mrs. Budros. Without another word, Jaslene presses a button on the panel and gingerly jumps off before the doors slide shut. Just like that, he's gone.

20

When she notices me standing off to the side, Jaslene stops short. "Are you the designated hall monitor?"

I consider Jaslene family, so she's allowed to be a smartass.

"Cute." Adopting a posh British accent, I explain why I'm loitering. "The bride has requested sparkling water, and I've been given the unenviable task of procuring it." *Eh, sounds more like a poor imitation of Count Dracula.*

Jaslene rolls her eyes. "Don't bother. You won't get it to her in time. I'll call in a request and have it sent downstairs to the waiting area."

I shrug. "I'll go back in and help Natalia clean up, then."

Jaslene pouts. "You're not going to watch the wedding? It's the first one I've planned from start to finish. I don't mean to brag, but I think I've finally hit my stride with this one."

Watching that train wreck is *not* on my agenda, which means I need an excuse. Jaslene's wearing a fitted pale blue skirt suit that complements the wedding scheme; my casual outfit would mar the vibe — or so I'll tell her. I sheepishly gesture to my skinny jeans and ballet flats. "I'm not really dressed for it."

21

"Just stand in the back," she says, waving away my concern. "Near the rose-covered trellis. You'll have a perfect view of the ceremony."

Again, that isn't a goal of mine, but if I'm honest about it, Jaslene will be hurt. This accomplishment is important to her, so that makes it important to me. "All right. I can't wait to see how it all comes together."

Lovely. Now I'll be forced to watch Dean marry a woman whose intentions are unclear. And with every second that passes, I'll wonder if I should have disclosed what I know. Like I said, I'm cursed.

CHAPTER TWO

DEAN

This is the big day, and it couldn't be more perfect.

The weather's cooperating — no small achievement given that it's July in DC — and our close friends and family (mostly Ella's) are all here in the hotel garden to celebrate this momentous occasion with us.

Max, my college roommate and best friend, is by my side, ready to hand over the ring when the officiant asks for it. Well, he's not quite ready, ready. In fact, if anything, he'll only do it grudgingly.

Granted, I never should have described this as a modern-day marriage of convenience. That soured him instantly. But it's the term Ella used as she pitched the idea of getting married, so when it was time to share the news with Max, the words just rolled off my tongue before I had a chance to consider how he'd react to them. He's a true-blue romantic; a relationship founded on mutual respect and compatible goals would never get his blessing, not unless love factored into it as well.

He leans over and nudges me with his shoulder.

I dip my head to listen. "What's up?"

"It's not too late to change your mind," he says, speaking out of the side of his mouth. "Just say the word, and I'll create a diversion while you jump over the hedges on your right. There's a clear path to the parking lot. I can hand you the keys to my car now."

I close a fist over my mouth and laugh into it. "Stop, you asshole. You're the worst best man ever. And this wedding is going to happen, whether you like it or not."

"Don't like it," he says matter-of-factly. "Just so we're clear."

"I'm aware."

Max has always been a supportive friend, but that doesn't mean he won't give me shit when he disagrees with my decisions. This is our way, and I wouldn't change it for the world. Nor will I change my mind about marrying Ella.

As I wait for the ceremony to begin, I conduct a mental survey of my life plan,

24

genuinely pleased with the progress I've made.

Step One: Pay off my student loans.

Status: Completed. Finally.

Step Two: Purchase a home.

Status: Did that last year. Not outright, but it's a start.

Step Three: Find a suitable partner and form a power couple.

Ella is an information security analyst and wants to open her own firm. Her ambition rivals mine.

Status: To be completed. Minutes from now.

Step Four: Make partner at Olney & Henderson LLP before the age of thirty.

Status: In progress. But since I'm turning thirty in November, I don't have much time left.

Step Five: Start a family.

Status: To be determined.

Now, if I could get my mother to settle in one place, I'd be golden. But since I don't set unattainable goals, that one gets slotted in the wishful-thinking corner of my brain. She's here today, with a new boyfriend I met during the rehearsal dinner. Considering I once wondered if she'd make the wedding at all, I'm counting her appearance as a minor victory.

A string quartet begins to play Pachelbel's

"Canon in D" (Ella's choice), and the rest of our small wedding party joins Max and me on the steps of the flower-adorned gazebo. Ella's older sister, Sarah, is a sweet woman who's welcomed me into the family without hesitation. Tyler, Ella's childhood friend, is another story, however. The man wears his resting smirk face proudly, and he's navigated all the events leading up to the wedding as though he doesn't give a damn about any of them. Why Ella begged me to make him a groomsman is a mystery I have no interest in solving.

The guests rise, and the woman who came into my life just six months ago appears with her dad at the wrought iron entry to the garden and takes a delicate step onto the white aisle runner. As she walks forward, she briefly gazes up at her father, a stoic man who's hard to read. He doesn't smile at his daughter, but their arms are hooked together, and his hand covers hers.

Ella glides in front of me and takes a fortifying breath. I give her a reassuring nod; mouth, *You look beautiful;* and take my place beside her. Our officiant, a friend of Ella's dad, welcomes the guests as I recite my vows in my head; we wrote our own, and I want to be sure not to say too much or too little.

As we agreed, Ella goes first.

"Thank you," she says, meeting my gaze. "For coming into my life when I needed you the most. For giving me hope for the future. For helping me let go of . . . the past. For bringing out the very best in me."

She looks so damned earnest as she says all this, which makes me feel especially shitty for noticing how often she uses the word *me*. We may not be in love, but I want this to be a solid partnership. *It's a small matter, Dean. Not everyone's a wordsmith. Focus on the big picture: You've finally found someone who's on the same page as you are about almost everything, from the importance of your respective careers to where and when you'll settle in the burbs. She doesn't expect you to love her, and she doesn't want you to lie about it either. She's a damn unicorn, so don't fuck this up.*

"I promise from this day forward to be your wife. To support your dreams. To grow *with* you and *beside* you."

Okay, that's . . . better. And now it's my turn.

"Ella, from the moment we shared a ride in the backseat of a random Toyota Camry, I knew you'd make an impact on my life. And the minute I discovered you could kick my ass in basketball, I decided we were meant to be."

That part draws a few laughs, almost exclusively from my side of the aisle.

"But seriously, everything between us is *easy,* and that speaks volumes. I like that you ask for space and give it just as freely. I like that you know who you are, where you want to go, and how you're going to get there. You impress me on so many levels. Your drive fuels mine. But more than anything, I love the possibilities of what we can accomplish together. The promise of our future. I want to do this only once, and I vow to do everything in my power to never make you question the choice you made today."

Ella's eyes are glistening, and she appears choked up by my words. She takes in a small breath and tilts her head, her gaze searching the area behind me. After a few seconds, her face falls, then she draws back and returns my stare.

She's nervous, of course. This is a major milestone in our relationship. Maybe the pressure of helping to plan this wedding has taken a toll on her. I've done what I thought was my fair share, but who's to say I shouldn't have done more?

The officiant turns to our guests. "Dean and Ella would like their friends and family to take part in their special day by answering this question: Do you support this couple as they embark on the next part of their journey?"

The guests respond enthusiastically, albeit clumsily, some simply stating, "Yes," and others proclaiming, "We do." Good-natured laughter follows, then a lone voice cuts through the chuckles and chatter and says, "I don't."

A few people gasp. Others straighten in their seats as if the ceremony *just* got interesting. I search for the source of the commotion, my gaze eventually landing on the woman I met in the hallway fifteen minutes ago: Lina's cousin Solange.

She emerges from her spot near a tall hedge bordering the garden and looks at me with regret in her eyes.

I croak out a few words, which is a miracle in itself since I'm fucking dumbfounded. "What the hell's going on?"

She ignores my question and directs her own to my bride instead: "Ella, this is one of the most important decisions of your life. It's not just about you. This affects Dean too. Are you *sure* you want to go through with this?"

Hold up. This woman, who I didn't even

know an hour ago, is trying to stop my wedding?

What. The. Fuck?

CHAPTER THREE

SOLANGE

Oh shit, oh shit, oh shit. Did I say that out loud?

My body is on fire, and the weight of the moment is pressing so heavily against my chest it's as if someone's cinching me into a corset and being purposefully cruel about it. Is this really happening? Am I doing this? Jesus, all of these guests are looking at me. *Why, why, why didn't you just keep your mouth shut, Solange?*

Because this wedding is the "before," and I know exactly how the "after" plays out. My mother had no clue my father was in love with another woman when he married her. The price she paid for that betrayal was steep: Neither her marriage nor her dreams survived it. Dean deserves better. Hell, Ella deserves better too, a fact she'd recognize if she weren't determined to get married no matter the costs.

31

What the hell is wrong with people? If you can't fully commit to a relationship, don't fucking do it. Simple as that. Yet Ella's willing to get hitched to Dean even though her heart belongs to someone who's obviously still a presence in her life.

"Ella, *please* think this through," I say once I finally muster the courage to speak again. "You *know* this isn't what you want."

The bride's eyes flood with tears, my cousin's skillful wedding-day makeup application ruined in seconds, then she turns to Dean. "Oh God, she's right. I . . . I can't marry you. I'm so sorry."

Ella lifts the hem of her dress and stumbles back up the aisle, her mother scrambling after her. Tyler throws up his hands as if to signal he wants no role in this soap opera, then jumps off the gazebo's platform and trots toward the parking lot. And Dean? He just stands there, his gaze cloudy as he braces the back of his neck.

Wearing a grim expression, Max moves to stand behind his best friend and places his hands on Dean's shoulders. With steely determination in his eyes, Max speaks in Dean's ear. The torrent of words wraps around Dean like armor, straightening his posture and smoothing his furrowed brow. The person before us isn't embarrassed by what's happened, and he's daring anyone to tell him he should be.

I certainly wouldn't. In fact, I'm now absolutely convinced I did the right thing, and that's the only reason I haven't fled the scene. The person Ella's in love with isn't some long-lost ex-boyfriend showing up at the eleventh hour and stirring up old feelings. *No, he's in their wedding party.* Which means he'll be in this couple's orbit for years to come. Just as my mother's friend (and my father's *current* wife) remained in the shadows of my parents' marriage until she stepped in to take my mother's place. I wish someone had been there for my mother on her wedding day. Maybe her life would have turned out differently. But no, she discovered the truth herself, years later, and by then she'd tied herself to him — by having me.

Too bad no one understands my ill-timed thought process. The bride's father, his eyebrows now two thick slashes of disgust that perfectly match his flattened lips, looks especially irate as he stomps up the aisle in my direction.

When he reaches me, I step back and throw up my fists, my body instinctively poised to deflect any physical contact. I know I'm the wedding crasher here, but I will kick this man's ass if necessary.

"Young lady, I don't know who you are, but this is wildly inappropriate. What's the meaning of this? You have no right to —"

"Hold on a minute, Jim," Lina says, appearing from thin air like a sorceress and stepping in front of me. "Jaslene's going to tell the guests we're taking a short break." She turns her head and directs a pointed stare my way. "While *we* sort this out."

Lina speaks into her headset as she ushers us inside the hotel, gesturing for the remaining members of the wedding party to follow suit. Her face reveals nothing, but I know my cousin: She's quietly regulating her own emotions and anticipating how to manage everyone else's.

We wait for Dean and Max to join us in a small banquet room. Unable to meet anyone's gaze, I pick at the sleeves of my top and do my best to neaten my appearance. What possessed me to wear a white blouse to fulfill my duties as a makeup assistant? Now I'm sporting smudges and splotches that make me look unkempt. I *hate* being unprepared for battle. And I'm not kidding myself either. It's going to get ugly.

As soon as Dean and Max arrive, the father of the bride rips into me: "This is outrageous, and I won't tolerate a woman with a vendetta messing with my daughter's head in a pathetic effort to win the groom for herself." He points a finger in my face as if he's scolding me. "You are going to go out there and tell these guests exactly what's going on or I'll —"

"Or you'll *what*?" I say, my voice rising to match the boiling of my blood. "I don't know your daughter. I don't even know the groom, for that matter. But I know what I heard and —"

"Stop it, you two," Lina says, her voice laced with exasperation. "This isn't helping the situation." She turns to Ella's father. "Jim, this woman is my cousin, and I can assure you that whatever you're thinking, it's way off base."

"Let me speak to Solange," Dean says. "Alone."

His commanding tone surprises everyone, all of our heads swiveling in his direction as if he's mentally brought us to heel. Gone is the friendly voice that snagged my attention in the hallway upstairs. He must be devastated. If I were in his shoes, I'd be inconsolable. To get to the stage of wanting to share the rest of your life with someone, only to discover they're not as committed to the relationship as you are? That's a soul-crushing blow he may never fully recover from.

Lina looks between us and nods. "Fine. Let's give them a minute."

Dean and I remain in place. Everyone else shuffles out of the room. Everyone except good ol' Jimbo, that is. Instead of leaving quietly like the others, Ella's dad storms out, barking into his cell phone to complete the picture of a pissed-off father of the bride.

When the door clicks shut, I exhale deeply. "I'm sorry, Dean. I know what I heard, and I thought you should know."

He gazes at me, his expression wary. "What did you hear? And when did you hear it? Before or after we met in the hallway?"

I swallow hard, absorbing the apparent implication of his question: If it was before, I could have saved him the embarrassment of standing at the altar and discovering his fate in front of their guests. How do I explain this so he'll understand? *Just be honest, Solange.* "Before. I didn't think it was my place to say anything, though. Figured it was possible you wouldn't care." His eyes go wide, but I forge ahead. "Then I heard your vows. You told her you wanted to do this only once, and her immediate reaction was to look past you. To someone who's obviously still in her life. She *wanted* that man to stop the wedding. When it was clear he wouldn't, she was willing to marry her second pick. You. Did I do the wrong thing? Should I have kept quiet?"

As soon as I ask those questions, I want to snatch them back. Dean isn't obligated to absolve me of my guilt. I made what I thought was the right choice, and I need to live with it, no matter how he responds to the news.

"We're in an open relationship," he says flatly. "That explains why it wouldn't have mattered."

My stomach drops. *Fuuuuuck.* I should have kept my nosy mouth shut. Now I've made a mess of things, and it wasn't even warranted. "Oh, Dean. I'm so sorry." My eyes well with tears. "I owe you and Ella a million apologies, then."

"Solange, relax. I'm just messing around."

My knees buckle, and the tightness in my chest unfurls. I place my hands on Dean's shoulders and lightly shove him away. "What is wrong with you? This isn't funny."

He pulls me within inches of his body and wipes a thumb under my eye just in time to catch a teardrop. "No, it isn't, but you're tying yourself in knots over this, and this is *my* time to be overly dramatic. Stop stealing my moment, dammit."

I stare at him, unsure what to make of his reaction to the train wreck he's just experienced. Is this a guy thing? Has he been conditioned to think men should appear unflappable even in situations as catastrophic as this one? "Wait. You're not mad?"

"I'm disappointed, but I'll survive. It's complicated, okay? Now, before we get too far ahead of ourselves, tell me exactly what you heard."

Oh God, why? Maybe if I pretend that I'm not here, he'll go away. I squeeze my eyes shut and freeze in place. Failing to sense any movement around me, I open one eye and peek at my surroundings.

"Solange, I can see you."

"No, you can't."

"*Yes*, I can," he says, a thread of humor in his tone.

Is this real? Is he really unbothered by everything that's happened?

"Solange, I need to know. You're probably the only person who'll tell me the unbiased truth."

Okay, well, when he puts it that way, how can I deny him? Maybe if I stick to the facts, I'll be able to get through this. Meeting Dean's gaze straight on, I blurt out the highlights. "Ella was standing on the landing between two floors. He —"

"Tyler."

"Yes, Tyler. So Tyler was telling her not to do something. Not marry you, I guess. Said she would regret it." I wring my hands. "Then she said she loved him. And she asked if he was finally ready to admit his feelings for her. He didn't respond. I didn't hang around much after that. Is this enough to get the picture?" My voice is strung tight; one good tug and it'll unravel. "I'm not lying, Dean."

"I believe you. I have no reason not to." He runs both hands through his once perfectly styled hair and drops his arms in defeat. "What a mess."

Wanting to comfort him, I step forward and gently caress his forearm. He looks down at the place where our bodies connect, his eyes narrowing on that spot as if the answer to this wedding-day conundrum can be found there. Realizing I have no right to touch him, I jerk my hand away. "Sorry. I didn't mean to overstep."

I'm apologizing for much more than invading his personal space. I hope he knows that.

"Don't worry about it. I appreciate your concern in all of this." He draws his shoulders back, erasing any sign of the dejected stance he held moments ago. "I should talk to Ella." Blowing out a long breath, he unknots his tie and lets it hang around his neck. "I have to go." He strides to the door and opens it. Before he leaves, he turns around, then tilts his head as he studies me. "Are you going to be okay?"

Am *I* going to be okay? What an odd thing to ask. I should be the least of his worries. Giving him a shaky smile, I motion for him to carry on. "I'll be fine. Go do what you need to do. And, Dean —"

"Yeah?"

"If there's anything I can do to help, Lina knows where to find me."

"I think you've done enough," he says, his lips quirked up in a playful grin.

Groaning, I pretend to stab a dagger through my heart.

"Kidding," he says, bowing slightly as he backs out of the room. "I can handle it from here."

He's right: I'm just the catalyst; the rest is up to him.

Once he leaves, I drop my head and heave a deep sigh. That. Was. Awful.

When I look up again, Jaslene's standing at the room's threshold, eyes narrowed, clipboard drawn, as if she's readying herself for a gunfight at the O.K. Corral.

Jaslene may be sweet, but she's no pushover. Her vibe is a delightfully terrifying blend of "kill 'em with kindness" energy and "I'll cut a bitch" swagger.

She enters the room and closes the door, her gaze locked on me the whole time.

Jesus. I can't catch a break today.

DEAN

I find Ella pacing in the bridal suite. She's kicked off her shoes, her hair's down, and the area beneath her eyes is a kaleidoscope of smeared makeup. As soon as the door closes after me, she stops short.

"That was unexpected," I say, shoving my hands into the pockets of my slacks.

She hiccups before she answers. "Oh God, Dean, I'm so sorry. I made a mess of everything, and you're the collateral damage. Please know I never meant for it to turn out this way."

I cross the room and sit on the couch, motioning for her to join me. She regards the gesture suspiciously, as if my politeness could only be a ploy. But Ella should know me better than this. Then again, neither of us knows the other all that well, it seems.

"Ella, I'm not upset. I just want to understand."

She hikes up her dress and pads over, then arranges a shitload of fabric as though she's tussling with a parachute before she finally settles next to me.

"So tell me about Tyler."

She leans forward and places her elbows on her lap, her face crumpling. "We've been friends forever."

"*Only* friends?"

She nods. "Yes, I promise. But I've been in love with him . . . well, forever. I thought I'd gotten beyond it. Thought I could marry you and forget about him. When he confronted me today, though, I felt certain that we were finally on the same page, and I just *knew* he was ready to confess his love for me. Spoiler alert: We aren't, and he isn't."

I sigh on the inside since there's no point in making Ella feel any worse than she already does. But yeah, she had a good thing going, then turned her world inside out for someone who won't return her feelings. I'm not mad at her. She's obviously free to do and think what she wants. Still, I thought we had an understanding — that what I was offering was enough — and I'm disappointed by her sudden change of heart. Couldn't she have figured this out before we did that registry shit at Crate and Barrel? The memory of the way that sales associate directed all her comments to Ella still pisses me off. Hell, I can appreciate a tasteful place setting just as well as the next person.

"So if this was how you were feeling, why'd you walk down the aisle anyway?" I ask.

Her gaze hits the floor. As if whatever she's going to say — or can't say — is too foul for her to face.

Holy shit, it's uglier than I thought. "You were bluffing, and he called you on it."

She lifts her chin, wiping at her tearstained cheeks. "Yes. No." She throws up her hands and shakes her head. "I don't know."

"A tiny part of you hoped he'd stand up there and stop the wedding. Is that it?"

Before she can answer, someone knocks on the door of the suite.

In the hall, Lina calls out, "Ella. Dean. May I speak with you for a moment?"

Oh, right. We're in the middle of a fucking wedding, and the guests must be wondering what's going on. I heave myself off the couch and open the door.

Lina pokes her head in. She looks from me to Ella and grimaces apologetically. "I need to know what to tell the guests. If you want me to stall . . ."

Stalling would be useful if there were a

chance we'd get beyond this, but there isn't. When Ella and I agreed to marry, we also promised to be honest, to always be considerate and respectful of each other. She's been holding out on me, though. And even if she's willing to suppress her feelings for Tyler now, she may not be able to later. Where will that leave me? I'd rather not find out. The point of all this was to build a strong foundation from day one, not start our marriage on shaky ground. "I think it's fair to say the wedding is canceled," I tell Lina. "Wouldn't you agree, Ella?"

Ella covers her face with her hands and nods.

Lina steps inside. "I'm sorry. Jaslene and I will take care of informing the guests. Don't worry about anything here. My team will deal with the vendors. I'll follow up with you both — separately — early next week." With a last concerned look in my direction, she withdraws from the room, and Ella and I are alone again.

"I'll leave you to change," I say.

"What are you going to do next?" she asks.

It's an absurd question. Reminds me of those old TV commercials when the winning quarterback of the Super Bowl would answer that he was going to Disney World. "C'mon. It doesn't really matter what I do

44

next, does it?"

She chokes out a sob, then says, "I hope we can remain friends."

"I'm not so sure that's a good idea, but I do wish you well. And I hope you find what you're looking for."

"Please know that I didn't mean to hurt you."

"I'm a big boy. I'll be fine." And it's true. I care for Ella. Envisioned a future with her too. But if she isn't meant to be a part of my life, I can't do anything to change that. "Be good to yourself." I stroll out of the suite, my head still spinning. In the span of an hour, this day has gone from sixty to zero. Fuck.

Actually, I *do* know what's next.

Revised Step Three: Get wasted.

Status: On it.

"Drinking won't help you feel better, Dean."

I'm slouched over in the corner of the hotel bar, nursing a Macallan on the rocks, and someone's here to mess with my buzz. I look up to see my mother, her lips pressed together and her expression leery.

"Mother."

"May I join you?"

I gesture to the stool beside mine. "Be my guest."

She lowers herself onto the seat and raises a finger to get the bartender's attention. Once she's ordered — an uncharacteristically sedate club soda, of all things — she swivels around to face me. "I'm sorry this day didn't turn out the way you expected."

"Not your fault."

"I'm not so sure about that."

"What's that supposed to mean?"

She sighs. "It's just . . . Don't take this the wrong way, son, but Ella isn't the person I imagined for you."

I draw back and meet her gaze, flinging the tip of my tie behind me. "Why not? She's intelligent, driven, beautiful, charming."

"You're not really saying much," she says, barely containing her grimace. "That's a checklist."

"Checklists are a successful person's handbook. Don't knock 'em 'til you try 'em."

"I'll pass," she says on a chuckle. "I'd rather let my heart lead the way."

As usual, I refrain from pointing out the obvious: Her heart's been a consistently unreliable navigator for years. If she can't accept that fact by now, she never will. My mother can erase her past all she wants, but I was there too.

Surprising me, my mother does something she hasn't done in years: She combs her fingers through the front of my hair as if she's attempting to arrange it neatly, then she ruffles it. "I know you think it's important to always stay on track, but that doesn't mean you can't give yourself the space to fall for someone too. I want you to experience it all, Dean. That moment when the person you love walks in a room and you get this warm, fuzzy feeling in your chest and all you want to do is run over to them and hold them tight? Don't knock *that* 'til you try it."

"That warm, fuzzy feeling in your chest is fickle and clouds your judgment. Makes you indifferent to things that should be red flags. Convinces you that it — and only it — matters when we all know on some rational level that will never be the case. It's the reason Barnett married Amber even though he was worried about her cosmetics credit card and the student debt she hadn't been making any payments on."

She looks at me quizzically. "Who're Barnett and Amber?"

"They were on this reality TV show on Netflix called *Love Is Blind*. The experiment was to date people without seeing them in person first. They would hang out in these

47

solitary pods and . . ."

My mother's brows snap together.

I gesture as if my point isn't worth our time. "Anyway, a bunch of people were talking about the show at work because it's been picked up for a second season, so I was curious. Doesn't matter. You get what I'm saying."

"Sort of, but as usual, you have it all figured out in your own head."

Something about her tone makes me think she didn't mean that as a compliment.

"And if I know you," she continues, "you'll regroup and be back on the straight and narrow path in no time. I just wanted to let you know that Harvey and I are hopping in the RV and going on a road trip. A little hiking in the Olympic Peninsula, then a visit to Lake Crescent. We leave tomorrow morning."

"What does Harvey do again?"

She rolls her eyes, plainly wanting me to register that she's annoyed by my question. "He's a retired airline pilot. Has a good head on his shoulders. Treats me well."

I've heard that phrase so often in reference to her boyfriends, all of whom eventually become ex-boyfriends, that I'm starting to wonder if she knows what it actually means to be treated well. All the disappoint-

48

ments, the crying, the willingness to uproot her family for a new guy only to discover he's just not that into her. She remembers none of it. But I do. And I will not be doomed to repeat her mistakes.

There's something to be said for being led by pragmatism. Case in point: Ella and I didn't contort ourselves to fit into each other's lives; we just slotted into place. And now that we're no longer together, we can slot the hell back out without much fuss. That's not Melissa Chapman's way, though. Never has been, never will be.

Thing is, I want my mother to be happy, but it's clear to me that she's searching for happiness in the wrong places; Harvey and Lake Crescent are just her latest destinations. Maybe this time it'll finally work out. For my mother's sake, I certainly hope so. But I'm not holding my breath. Not even for a second.

"Enjoy yourself," I say, knowing from experience she wants some semblance of my approval. "And be safe. Try to avoid being featured in a *National Geographic* documentary as a cautionary tale. No selfies with black bears, okay?"

She smiles and throws an arm around my shoulders, giving me a light squeeze before she stands. "Take care of yourself, Dean."

"Always do," I say, forcing a smile.

I don't mean it as a dig, but her face goes pale anyway. I suppose a guilty heart perceives blame even when it isn't warranted.

CHAPTER FOUR

SOLANGE

Yesterday I crashed a wedding and rode an emotional roller coaster dealing with the aftermath. So today I'm desperate for maternal affection — and snacks. The absolute best place to get both is Rio de Wheaton, the Brazilian grocery store and café my mother and her two sisters operate out of a strip mall in Maryland. Lately, it's become a Sunday ritual of sorts too: I gorge on free food and soak in their attention, then my mother and I volunteer together at my neighborhood's community garden.

When I open the shop's door on Sunday afternoon, I spy my mother muttering to herself, her brow knitted in concern as she wipes the top of the salgadinho display case. "Mãe, what's wrong?"

She immediately straightens and relaxes her expression. "Everything's fine. A lot on my mind, that's all."

"Filha, fecha a porta," Tia Viviane says as she whizzes past me without pausing. "You're going to let the flies in."

I scoot inside and close the door behind me. "Sorry! I should know better."

If my mother and her sisters were each one of the seven dwarves, Natalia's mother, Viviane, would be Grumpy; my mother would be Bashful; and Lina and my cousin Rey's mother, Tia Mariana, would be Happy.

With mischief in her big brown eyes, Tia Mariana puts her hands around her mouth and addresses the Brazilian regulars loitering in the café section. "If you're planning to get married, don't invite this one to the casamento." She cackles through her next words. "Ela dá azar."

Oof. I can't argue with her there. Just yesterday, I was thinking the same thing. But knowing you're a magnet for bad luck and having your aunt declare it in front of everyone are two entirely different annoyances. Shaking my head, I pretend to tap her with a magic wand. "Go to sleep, Ruthless Dwarf."

"What does that mean?" Tia Mariana says, peering at me suspiciously.

I ignore her question and move around her so I can say hi to my mother — and get to the snacks.

Because she knows her daughter, Mãe has already opened the case and is waiting with steel tongs in hand. "O que você quer comer?"

"Coxinha de frango e empadinha de queijo."

She places the savory morsels on a paper plate and hands it to me, a folded napkin tucked between two fingers. We make the exchange smoothly, as if we've done this a thousand times; considering my slight obsession with salgadinhos, we probably have. I groan as the intense garlic aroma wafts around me, then I squeeze my eyes shut when I bite into the coxinha. Yeah, sex is good, but this perfectly seasoned chicken wrapped in golden fried goodness *never* disappoints. Bonus? You don't even have to engage in conversation with anyone to enjoy it.

My mother, her deep brown curls peeking from under a silk kerchief, sets the tongs down and shifts items on the counter for no apparent reason.

"So what's with the long face and nonstop movement?" I ask between hearty chews.

My mother's always been a nervous Nellie around people she doesn't know; she's rarely this fidgety around me, though, which

53

means something must be up.

Tia Viviane zigzags across the aisle to our right as she places items on the store shelves. "Might as well tell her, Izabel. She's going to find out eventually."

My mother grits her teeth at her older sister, then takes my arm. "Come. Let's sit."

Oh God. We talked two days ago. What the hell happened in the interim?

We claim a small table in the corner of the café, our chairs positioned so we're facing each other. Since the unease in my gut is messing with my appetite, I set aside my snacks and reach for her hand instead. "Whatever it is, we'll get through it together. I promise. Just tell me."

She nods. "Okay. This is what happened: Lina told Mariana about the wedding yesterday, then Mariana went on WhatsApp and told the family in Brazil about it. So they called, and we were all on the phone, and we got to talking about all the kids and what they've been up to. Lina and Max. Natalia and Paulo and the pregnancy. Rey and his latest boyfriend. So Cláudia started yapping about how you're never going to settle down, and somehow I told her that you were seeing someone and that it was getting serious." She drops her head. "I'm so sorry. I don't know why I lied, but she was being such a metida about it, and I just wanted to shut her up."

I let out a shaky breath, and my stomach unknots. Jesus, is *that* all? I'm never getting back the year of my life she just took from me. But now that I'm no longer imagining the worst, I can focus on easing my mother's guilt. It doesn't surprise me that our cousin Cláudia teased her on the phone; over the years, I've overheard my mother and tias talk about our wonderful family overseas, and Cláudia's name has come up quite a bit. As far as I can tell, she's the outlier, the traditional relative, the one who thinks her cousins are questionable role models because they're all single moms.

Cláudia couldn't be more wrong. My mother's example has taught me to be uncompromising when it comes to love. She refused to put up with my father's bullshit, and I, too, refuse to tolerate men who can't or won't give me one hundred percent of themselves. No more men who treat relationships as a game of "the commitment is lava." If I'm all in, they should be all in too. Luckily for me, despite a few false starts, I can spot an emotionally unavailable man from a hundred paces. *Not in a hat. Not cuddling cats. Not even if he's gorgeous will I fuck with that.* So what if this means I haven't had a steady partner in ages? I know my worth, and I'm not letting anyone diminish it. One thing's clear: Not being in a relationship is better than being in a bad one. Because one bad relationship can change your life forever.

Still, I know Cláudia's criticism is a sore spot for my mother, so her decision to tell a little white lie makes sense in that context. It's innocuous enough — especially since I hardly ever interact with Cláudia at any rate.

"Don't worry about it, Mãe," I say, picking up my plate again. "It's no big deal. In fact, it's already forgotten."

"But that's not all," Tia Mariana singsongs a little too cheerfully from her spot near the beverage case.

I stare at my mother, waiting for an explanation.

"Well, uh," she says, her gaze settled on the area behind me. "Cláudia and her family are coming to visit the first full weekend of August — her husband has something for work in New York — and she asked if they could meet the person you're dating when they're here." She slumps against the chair. "I wasn't thinking, and I said yes. Que confusão!"

What a mess, indeed. But I'm *not* going to make my mother feel bad about it. It's

56

against my three-part code: Help others to the best of your abilities, never do anything half-assed, and *always* honor thy mother. The latter principle is absolute. This woman was dealt a shitty hand when she hooked up with my father, a man who was in love with someone else from day one and treated my mother like a consolation prize. After he left, she and her two sisters raised me and my cousins, making tons of sacrifices along the way. So I have no patience for anyone or anything that threatens my mother's well-being.

"Mãe, don't feel bad. You actually didn't lie." I give her a small smile. "I *am* seeing someone, and it *is* getting serious."

She gasps. "You are?"

I shake my head and give her a playful wink. "No. But see? I can *pretend* to be dating someone while our cousins are visiting. I even have the perfect person to play my partner."

"Who is he?" she asks, sagging in relief.

"Could be a 'she,' Izabel. Or a 'they,' " Tia Mariana observes.

I whip my head in my aunt's direction, and she laughs.

"What?" she says. "Rey and I talk about these things."

My mother waves her sister's comment

away. "It makes no difference to me. I just need it to be convincing."

"I'll ask Brandon to do it," I say, wanting to rein these two in.

Her eyes grow as wide as a semitruck. Yes, my closest friend and roommate is going to be shocked to discover that he and I have finally admitted our love for each other and are now dating. Luckily for me, Brandon is an aspiring actor and always game for a bit of improv.

She claps her hands. "He's perfect! Brandon's a good boy."

"Exactly. So whenever Cláudia and the family visit, I'll be sure to bring him around. Then you can tell them later that it didn't work out."

Honestly, that's the general trajectory of my real relationships anyway. Turns out vowing never to pursue emotionally unavailable men significantly reduces my options. Who knew?

Remembering the premise of the latest romance novel on my nightstand, I can't help wondering whether this could be the start of my own love story: friends to lovers with a side of fake dating. Nah. Considering my track record, a happily-ever-after like that is about as likely as my meeting a shape-shifting bear in line at my neighborhood Dunkin' Donuts.

"I'm so glad you're not mad about this," my mother exclaims, beaming at me as if I'm the best daughter in the world. "Ha, I'll even be able to tell Cláudia you two are serious enough that you're living together." She winks at me as if we're co-conspirators. "No one needs to know that you and Brandon are *just* roommates. Que maravilha!"

Seeing my mother happy again is exactly what I hoped for.

Pesky problem. Easy solution. Check and check.

"Now," she says, her demeanor noticeably more relaxed than it was a few minutes ago. "Tell me what's going on with the school. Have they offered you a job yet?"

Oh boy, here we go again. I've tried to explain the situation a million times, but she only registers the parts that fit her vision for my future. My position with Victory Academy was never meant to be permanent; it's a condition of the fellowship that funded my graduate studies. And sure, it's been an amazing experience, but my year in DC is a rest stop, and I don't want my mother thinking otherwise. "Mãe, please don't get your hopes up, okay? They're not obligated to give me a job. In fact, money's so tight, it's almost guaranteed they won't have the budget to bring someone else on." Maybe if I say this a dozen more times, she'll finally accept that it isn't going to happen. "Besides, I have an excellent opportunity to go back to my old job if I want to." Returning to BFI, a nonprofit that coordinates volunteer home construction for low-income families in America and abroad, would be a no-brainer; I'd get to travel all over the country, and as the organization's workforce development coordinator in the United States, I'd be doing precisely what I trained for.

"But Ohio's so far away," she says, frowning. "And your whole family's here. What if you need me, filha? What if you meet someone and have kids? I wouldn't be there to help you."

Peering around us as if I don't want anyone to eavesdrop on our conversation, I lean over and thread my fingers through hers. "So I'm not sure how you're going to react to this. I mean, it's breaking news, and it might be too much for you to absorb. See, there are these things called" — I hunch down and lower my voice to a whisper — "airplanes, trains, and phones. You can communicate with people living in other states and even visit them if you want to."

Disentangling our hands, she rolls her eyes at me, then flicks my forehead. "Você é uma sabichona, mas eu te amo."

My mother always switches to Portuguese when she's essentially calling me a smartass. "I'm just kidding, and I love you too." I glance at my watch, then gather up my trash. "Ready to head out?"

"Soon. Let me use the bathroom first." She unties her apron as she stands. "I can't wait to see what the area looks like without all of the weeds."

The community garden we're working on together is in its infancy, so it would be more accurate to describe it as a plot of land we're still preparing for planting. I asked my mother to help, hoping she'd develop enough of an interest in it to continue after I'm gone. More than anything, though, I'm treasuring our mother-daughter bonding time.

"The space is really coming along," I say. "Wish I could hang around long enough to see everything grow."

She pats my arm before she heads off to the back of the store. "You'll still be here, filha. I can feel it in my bones."

No, I won't, but she's obviously not ready to accept the inevitable. Which means my mother's in for a rude awakening at the end of the summer. But it can't be avoided. Because she doesn't deserve to live her life in the shadow of someone else's mistakes.

CHAPTER FIVE

OLNEY & HENDERSON, LLP
WASHINGTON, DC
ONE WEEK LATER

DEAN

News flash: The first day back at work after your wedding is called off sucks.

If I didn't know any better, I'd worry that my job is in jeopardy. But I *do* know better, and this walk of shame across Olney & Henderson's main floor is just a necessary rite of passage when you're the focus of office gossip. By now, everyone knows that I didn't get married while I was out on vacation. They also know why.

In an environment like this one, where people are openly and secretly cutthroat, it's crucial to give your colleagues as little ammunition as possible. Understanding this, I chose to invite only two people from Olney to my wedding: my assistant, Ginny Sloane, and Michael Benitez, a junior partner two years senior to me and the only person here I consider a true friend.

Michael spread the breakup news at my

request, the canned message we jointly put together meant to eliminate anyone's inclination to ask me for details. But I'm sure Ginny filled in the gaps with her own colorful commentary; hence, the office scuttlebutt.

So far, there's no snickering. But I see several sets of wide eyes, and so many people are clearing their throats as I pass them, you'd think everyone in the whole damn firm is dehydrated. Fuck me, this is going to be painful. It's not that I care what they think; what bothers me is that they're thinking about my personal business at all.

After running the gauntlet, I sit at my desk and take a deep breath.

Within seconds, Michael swoops into my office and closes the door. "Heads up before we go into the morning meeting: The EQs are wondering if they should take some work off your plate."

The EQs, or equity partners, are at the top of our law firm's hierarchy. Unlike Michael, who's a non-equity partner, they actually own the firm and make the important decisions — such as which senior associates they'll invite to join their ranks.

I take a sip of coffee as though I'm unconcerned by the intel. Nothing could be further from the truth, though. "Why did that even come up?"

"As expected, the canceled wedding hit the rounds," Michael says. "They're thinking you're probably bummed about it and need a little time to regroup. Olney said she wanted to be more sensitive to associates' needs. Per usual, Henderson doesn't give a shit. He also complained that you've been doing a bunch of work for that pro bono clinic at Georgetown, and if anything, that stuff should go first."

Christ. We're six weeks away from partnership decisions, and this is the state of play: Olney thinks I'm emotionally distraught-;Henderson isn't impressed with my workload. They're looking for go-getters, dealmakers, and client magnets, not people who need their hands held when a romantic relationship goes sour, or worse, people who don't pull in their fair share of business. "As much as I hate to admit it, Henderson's right. I'm fine. And they *shouldn't* give a shit about my private life. One way or another, I'll make that clear to them."

"Well, you may get a chance to do just that," Michael says with a sly smile.

"You're so fucking shady, and I appreciate it with every fiber of my being. What do you know?"

He scoots to the edge of his seat and leans

forward. "A couple of months ago, a head-hunter contacted us about an associate who's considering a lateral move to the DC area. Her name is Kimberly Bailey. Word is, her partner is interviewing for artist-in-residence programs in the DMV area. Bailey's a dream candidate: top-tier law degree, law review, a federal clerkship, 30 Under 30 in *Atlanta Law Magazine,* the whole shebang. She's the fish we never expected to catch."

That's an understatement. Lawyers with a pedigree like Kimberly's don't usually leave their firms, not when partnership is on the table. But a relocation, especially for family reasons, is a solid justification that doesn't raise red flags with prospective employers.

Michael gives me a Grinch-who-stole-Christmas grin. "There's more, though. The headhunter didn't mention this, but Henderson knows from his own sources that her father is Larry Bailey, general counsel of Baxter Media Group."

Holy shit. Baxter Media is *huge,* and I know exactly where this is going. With numerous television, newspaper, and advertising properties all over the country, Baxter Media must generate *a ton* of legal work. One of their flagship companies, SwiftNet, is a major internet service provider with headquarters right here in DC. For a firm like ours, which has branded itself as the lawyer's law firm, snagging a client like Baxter Media could keep the lights on for a long time; recruiting Kimberly Bailey would be the logical first step in that process.

"We're going to bring her in for a round of interviews," Michael explains. "And unless she runs naked through the halls, I think it's fair to say we're going to offer her a job. But she's also looking at other firms, so Olney and Henderson want to make sure we come out on top in the end."

"How do they expect to guarantee that?"

"By showing her a great time when she and her partner visit the DMV. They'll be here for the next couple of weeks, and she's asked to meet with senior associates during that time. Apparently, she joked that it was the only way she'd get the real scoop on the firm's culture."

"She's right," I say, nodding.

"The partners know this too. But they don't think the usual fancy dinner is enough. They want to offer an insider's tour of DC. 'Do whatever it is young people do,' is how Henderson put it. All expenses paid."

"Damn, they didn't bother with any of that when *I* interviewed."

"Can your dad give the firm millions of

dollars in business each year?"

I don't even know where my father is, but I doubt it's anyplace good. "I'm guessing not."

"Exactly," Michael says. "This is big-league stuff here."

Knowing exactly what's at stake, I rub my hands together in anticipation. "So, in other words, I need to get in on whatever they're planning."

"Let me put it this way: If you manage to lure Kimberly Bailey to the firm, the part-ners will be so far up your ass you'll need an enema to flush them out."

I stare at him blankly. "This was all good news until you said that."

He shakes his head at me. "Focus, Dean. You want to be the master of your own fate? Well, here's your shot."

"All right, all right. Thanks for having my back."

Michael salutes me. "Admittedly, I'm do-ing this for my own benefit too. It's hard hanging around with those folks. They're stodgy as hell, and they wouldn't recognize an innovative idea even if it was delivered in wrapping paper that literally said 'Innova-tive ideas inside.' I need you to get your ass in gear and join me."

"I plan to, and I'm on it."

A quarter of an hour into the Monday Morning Meeting — capitalized because it's very much a specific phenomenon at Olney & Henderson — I sit in one of the chairs reserved for associates that frame the perimeter of the room and wait for the opportunity to snag the Bailey assignment.

"Final order of business," Sam Henderson says from the head of the partners-only conference table. "Senior associates, we're looking for one of you to work on an after-hours assignment. Non-billable. Any takers?"

Henderson is in typical form; everything's a game to him. This must be the Kimberly Bailey assignment, but he's testing us to see who's willing to take on an extra project. No associate with a sense of self-preservation volunteers for anything that doesn't count toward their minimum billable hours requirement, so most associates' gazes fall to their laps. Not me, though. Thanks to Michael, I know this will be a relatively easy task with the potential for great rewards.

I shoot up my hand. "I'd be happy to."

Peter Barnum, an Ed Sheeran lookalike who's as close to a nemesis as I have at the firm, shoots up a hand as well. "Me too."

Henderson looks between us. "Dean, I

don't think —"

Olney clears her throat, eliciting an eye roll from Henderson.

"Come see me after the meeting, then," he says to us both.

Ten minutes later, Peter and I arrive at the threshold of Henderson's office. Our boss's assistant, who only works for Henderson, ignores us.

"Peter."

"Dean."

"Heard about the wedding," he says matter-of-factly. "Can't win 'em all, I guess."

What an asshole. Everything's a competition to Peter, and I suspect he thinks of me as his fiercest challenger. "That's actually one of the nicest things anyone's ever said to me. You're a stand-up guy."

Peter lacks even a shred of self-awareness. First case in point: He's wearing a baby-blue polo with an upturned collar. Reminds me of the arrogant pricks I used to ring out in the dorm commissary as part of my work-study job at Penn. Second case in point: He actually smiles at my comment — as though I've just given him a compliment.

Thankfully, Henderson's assistant deigns to acknowledge us and waves us back. When we enter, our boss nods and gestures for us

70

to sit in the guest chairs facing his desk. "Dean. Peter. I'll make this quick."

True to his word, he gives us a rapid-fire rundown of the assignment, then he turns his gaze to me. "Dean, I envision this as a welcoming committee of sorts. Ms. Bailey and her partner are interested in asking about work-life balance, housing in the area, firm dynamics, and the like. I figure this might be something right up Peter's alley. He and . . ."

"Molly," Peter offers, looking like an overeager puppy desperate to be petted.

"Yes, that's right. Peter and Molly just purchased a home in NoVa, so they may be a better fit for this."

Henderson's a smart man. He wouldn't dare say outright that I'm not a good fit for the task because I'm unattached, but the implication is there just the same. It truly burns that I'm in this position. If Ella had stuck to her end of the bargain, I would be a shoo-in for this assignment. Instead, I'm scrambling to make myself relevant. And sure, I *could* try to persuade Henderson to disregard my newly single status, but I know he's looking for any reason to box me out of opportunities whenever Olney isn't around to run interference. Henderson's considered me a threat ever since a major client dropped him from a trial team because they wanted me to handle the case on my own. Embarrassing for Henderson, sure. Still, I didn't orchestrate that shitshow, so this personal vendetta is uncalled for. If he'd just give me a goddamn chance, I'd do a bang-up job of selling Kimberly Bailey on both the firm and DC life. Unfortunately, Henderson doesn't *want* to give me a chance, and now he has a decent excuse for his decision.

Michael's crass prediction flashes in my brain. On the eve of associate evaluations, what could be better than having my bosses so far up my ass that I'd need an enema to flush them out? Metaphorically speaking, of course. I'm already on shaky ground with the firm, which means I *need* this assignment. Without it, I'm unlikely to turn things around to make partner by thirty, and if I don't, what the hell was the point of never deviating from my plan for success all this time?

A woman with curly hair and chocolate-brown eyes immediately comes to mind, and my solution tumbles out effortlessly, pure adrenaline fueling my pitch-perfect delivery. "Sir, I didn't bring this up earlier because it didn't seem relevant, but since you mentioned wanting these outings to be with our significant others, now's an appropriate time to tell you that I'm in a serious relationship with someone, and I think she'd be a real asset to our effort to recruit Kimberly Bailey."

"Bullshit," Peter coughs into his hand.

Henderson cocks his head. "You're in a serious relationship? Less than two weeks after you canceled your wedding?"

I chuckle and massage the back of my head. Shit, my ears are burning. *Don't pass out, Dean. Don't you fucking dare pass out.* "It's definitely an unconventional turn of events, I get it, but the short story is that the woman who stopped my wedding is a longtime friend. And, well, I'll just say that once the dust settled after the ceremony, we realized we'd been suppressing some pretty big feelings. She's known me longer than I've worked here, and we've shared a condo for years, so she really is qualified to speak to what she's observed about my lifestyle as an associate firsthand, and what's even better is that she knows DC inside out. Anyway, I think she'd be more than happy to join us."

"What's her name?" Peter asks.

He's trying to box me into a corner. *Well played, Peter.*

"Her name's Solange Pereira."

73

Peter narrows his gaze on me but says nothing.

Henderson knows I'm more charming than the sack of potatoes to my right. I mean, Peter unironically brags that he "bagged" his wife as soon as he told her he'd graduated from Harvard — a moment he describes as the dating equivalent of a mic drop. Skin-crawling stuff, really. Once Henderson considers Peter's insufferably douchey upturned collar, his choice will be clear.

But then Peter adds, "You mentioned Bailey's partner is looking at artist-in-residence programs, right? Well, Molly's dad is an art professor at NYU. It's a superbly teed up icebreaker."

I clench my jaw so hard I'm probably at risk of rupturing a blood vessel somewhere.

Henderson snaps his fingers. "You both should do it. The more, the merrier. I think you two would strike a good balance. Keep the other one on his toes. It'll feel festive. Engaging. Besides, I need you to be candid, but not *too* candid. What better way to ensure a light muzzle on your honesty than to have you keep tabs on each other?"

Fuck, fuck, fuckity fuck. It's bad enough that I just forced myself to fake a relationship, but now Peter's going to be watching my every move? This is bad. Really fucking bad. But I'm pinned against the ropes, and there's no way out that won't damage my already tenuous standing with Henderson.

It's okay, Dean. You're a fighter. And you know how to execute a plan. Think of this as the biggest assignment of your career, and you'll excel in it like you always do.

Still, that little voice in my head is begging me to heed the warning signs. Given the stakes, I choose to ignore it.

Somehow, I need to convince Solange to go along with my scheme.

Somehow, we'll need to convince Peter that we've known each other a long time and that we live together now.

Somehow, I'll need to pretend this woman is my partner even though I know nothing about her other than that she's blessed with great hair and possesses nerves of steel.

Henderson drums his hands on his desk. "I'll send you the dates Ms. Bailey is available once I have them. Keep me apprised of your plans."

I stand up awkwardly, a bunch of chaotic thoughts rattling around in my brain and messing with my equilibrium. What if Solange refuses to help me? And even if she says yes, what if we do a shit job of pretending to be a couple? What if Peter finds out

I'm lying and rats me out to the firm?

Stop, Dean. There's no point in second-guessing yourself. You can't do anything about it. I draw up straight and square my shoulders. "Thanks for the opportunity, sir. We won't let you down."

Outside Henderson's office, Peter shakes his head. "I don't know what the hell you were thinking back there, but I know a con when I see one."

"Believe what you want, Peter," I say, my head down as I type a quick text to Lina. Solange did say her cousin would know where to find her if I needed her — and I definitely need Solange now.

Peter shuffles off without another word.

When I'm sure he's gone, I take a deep breath. Will I live to regret this? Probably. Am I committed to seeing it through anyway? Damn right I am.

CHAPTER SIX

SOLANGE

I reread Dean's succinct text inviting me for breakfast for the hundredth time, then scan the Instagram-approved coffee bar to confirm that he hasn't arrived yet.

It's a bright place. Too bright. White walls, gray floors, teak furniture, with a few strategically placed potted plants serving as the only pops of color. A social media influencer's dream location from which to influence and shit.

What's more, chalk-written motivational quotes cover a plethora of surfaces, encouraging the shop's customers to fully realize their best selves:

Be kind to yourself.

Smile and the world smiles back at you.

Seize the slay. That one's certainly a choice.

And my personal favorite: *Here, coffee is a must; talking isn't.*

The rush of folks getting their first cup of weekday java has passed; what's left are the diehards, those who treat coffee as sustenance, and they are my people. I wait in comfortable silence, sipping an overpriced special blend and observing the happenings around me.

Minutes later, a woman hunched over her laptop at a neighboring table straightens in her seat, her eyes widening at something — or someone — in her field of view; instinct tells me that Dean is the something or someone who's captured her attention.

As if on cue, he appears at my side and gestures at the other chair. "Hey, Solange. May I?"

I give him a friendly smile. "Of course."

"Thanks for agreeing to see me," he says as he settles in his seat.

"It's the least I could do . . . considering."

He pulls out a packet of travel-size disinfectant wipes and cleans the table. "Bear with me. I worked on a case about sanitizers last year, and I'll never be able to see a non-porous surface in the same way again."

"Okay, Dexter."

He stops wiping and gives me a blank look. "I'm *not* a serial killer."

"That remains to be seen. Now I'm extra glad we met in a public place."

78

"You're a trip," he says, his lips twisted in a half smirk.

A barista swoops in and places a mug on the table; she winks at Dean before she walks away.

"You're a regular?" I ask.

"I am."

"How very hip of you."

He grins. "I called ahead and placed my order when I realized I'd be running a little late. Made sure to ask if you had a cup."

"Oh, well in that case, how very ordinary and considerate of you." I point at his mug. "What the hell is that anyway?"

"A nonfat soy latte with an extra shot, one pump of honey blend, and caramel drizzle."

"I think I hate you right now."

This time he smiles widely, his eyes crinkling at the corners. "Do you need anything else? Want to order food? They make great pancakes."

"No need," I say, lifting my mug. "This regular-ass coffee is enough."

I want to focus on whatever has brought us together, but I'm distracted by the man's buttoned-up appearance. I bet he'd never survive even a few hours on a BFI construction site; dirt under his fingernails is probably listed as an allergen in his medical records. "Does your firm frown upon business casual?"

Furrowing his brow, he peers down at his clothes. "It's permitted, but this is my style."

"Ah."

Admittedly, it's a dapper vibe. His tie is knotted expertly, and the way his collar falls, I imagine he uses brass stays to achieve a perfect neckline. I glance at his wrists, unsurprised to see that a half inch of his shirt cuffs is visible beyond the sleeve of his blazer. Freshly shaved, and without a hair out of place, Dean very well could be your average uptight asshole. Nothing I've seen of him so far suggests that he is, however. Well, the elaborate coffee order is a yellow flag, but I'll reserve judgment on that one since I'm *very* particular about how I prepare eggs, and most people don't understand my fussiness on that score.

Anyhow, asshole or not, the vibe is working, because I can't help picturing us roleplaying a scenario in which he *is* an uptight jerk and I spend an evening making him pay for his assholery by undoing him completely: shirt unbuttoned and rumpled, hair mussed and on end, and my discount drugstore lipstick smeared across his expensively cologned jaw.

Yikes, Brain. Not helpful. This man was all set to marry someone less than two weeks

80

ago; he's absolutely off-limits — and so not your type.

I crack my neck in an effort to clear my head. Lina says it's a disgusting habit, but it's what I do when I need to regroup, and it isn't hurting anybody. "So, what did you want to talk to me about?"

Dean draws in a deep breath and releases it slowly. "I think I may need your help after all."

"I'm listening."

He dives into a long and convoluted explanation of a career crisis; with each new wrinkle in the saga, my jaw drops a fraction, until it finally hits the floor. When he's done, I stare at him.

"Hello?" he asks as he leans over and waves a hand in front of my face. "Blink once if you're still with me. Blink twice if you're in distress."

I widen my eyes and blink them so furiously that I'm experiencing a strobe light effect behind my lids. This is bananas. And there's *no way* we can pull this off. "What the hell were you thinking?"

He sighs and runs a hand down his face. "Nothing smart, that's for sure. And look, I'm not going to sit here and try to convince you that my plan isn't wild. It is. But I've been working my ass off for eight years so I

81

can make partner. Recruiting this person is the kind of major coup that could seal the deal. I *need* this chance."

"Don't you think that's a problem? Shouldn't working your ass off for eight years suffice?"

He pauses, as if my point had never occurred to him, then says, "In an ideal world, sure. But this is the law firm world. You're only as valuable as your last big client or lucrative case. This has the potential to accomplish both and —"

The barista appears again. "Would you like another cup?"

Dean gestures to his mug. "Still working on this one, thanks. Solange?"

"Nope, still good sipping on my coffee with twenty pumps of nothing."

After the barista leaves, Dean rolls his eyes at me.

"Do you do that often?"

"Do what?" he asks, tilting his head.

"Roll your eyes. It's charming."

"My coffee order really upset you, didn't it?"

"It did," I say, unable to keep the grin off my face.

"Can we get back to the matter at hand?" he asks.

"Your ridiculous idea to pretend we're a

couple? Sure." I set aside my mug and lean forward. "Why does it have to be me? You could ask *anyone* to play the person who interrupted your wedding for a very good reason and saved you from a lifetime of pain and disappointment."

He draws back and frowns. "You're overstating what you did."

He's wrong. My mother is proof of that. She poured her heart and soul into her marriage and got almost nothing in return. Someday Dean will recognize the world of hurt he avoided by not marrying Ella. In the meantime, I'm not here to convince him of my virtue. "Okay, that's fair. Marrying a person who's in love with someone else is a minor inconvenience in the scheme of things. But my question still stands: Why me?"

"Two reasons," he says as he adjusts his tie.

I'd love to see that tie wrapped around his head as he wades in a public fountain after a few too many drinks. I snort at the thought.

"What's funny?" Dean asks.

"Nothing. You were saying?"

"The two reasons it has to be you. One, Olney & Henderson is a gossip mill, and my assistant attended the wedding. I can't risk getting too far afield of the actual truth without potentially compromising this whole operation."

"It's an operation now? Good grief. What's the other reason?"

"I identified you by name."

Shit on top of shit with a dollop of shit on the side.

He reaches over and places his hand over mine. Damn, it's silky soft. In embarrassing contrast, my hands are still sporting scratches from this weekend's community gardening project.

"I'm not asking you to sign over your life," he says, his eyes pleading with me not to reject him outright. "I just need three nights; depending on your schedule, maybe time for one daytime get-together too. And we're only talking about a two-week window at most. Maybe a spur-of-the-moment outing if she returns for a second round of interviews. I *know* you don't owe me a thing. And I'm definitely in a bind of my own making. But if you could find it in your heart to do this, I'd be so fucking grateful. Frankly, I don't have anyone else to turn to."

Crap. He said all the magic words, and I didn't even need to coax them out of him. He's in a bind, and he needs my help. He doesn't think I owe him this, but he's asking anyway because he's desperate. I can't say no. It's not in my nature to turn down someone in need — and that's especially the case when the person has been through a heartrending experience like Dean has. Not to mention, I had a part in everything that went down, even if he agrees that it was for the best. But we need to establish a few ground rules before I commit to this farce.

I slide my hand out from under his; he flinches as if he just remembered we were touching.

"I have several conditions," I say.

"Okay. Yeah. Name them," he says, his voice shaky — with relief, maybe?

"Number one, I will not pretend to be someone else. There lies disaster. The only role I'll be playing is as your girlfriend."

"And roommate," he adds.

I shake my head in exasperation. "Yes, that too. But *as* me.

The current me. Not an idealized me. It's bad enough that I'll be spending my free nights with a bunch of lawyers. That's like scheduling a root canal, a Pap smear, and a mammogram all in one day. I'm not adding an extra layer of hell to that by pretending to be Ella 2.0."

"Who?"

"Your ex-fiancée, Ella. Remember her?"

He thinks about our exchange a bit, and a corner of his mouth lifts. "Yeah, I remember her. And I absolutely agree on that point. That goes for me too. I want to be as up-front as possible about everything except the fact that we're not really dating."

"Okay, good. Number two, any physical contact beyond a touch here or there, or a hand on the lower back, *if any,* will be initiated by one of us *only* if it's clear the other consents to it."

He loosens his tie. "Definitely. I wouldn't want to make you uncomfortable." Then he stares into his mug as he strokes his jaw.

I take in a deep, calming breath. Perhaps I should make that a rule: He can't touch his jaw in my presence. Okay, now I'm being weird.

"Should we agree on a safe word, then?" he asks. "Not in the usual sense, but maybe an inside phrase that will let us know it's okay to kiss a cheek, for example. A *face* cheek, I mean."

I drop my head and cackle, then try to compose myself before I speak again. I'm only half successful at the effort, though. "The fact that you felt you had to clarify which cheek you meant is cause alone for me to abandon ship. Let me be absolutely clear: Ass cheeks are off the table."

He slides down into his chair and covers his face with a single hand. "I know. Dammit, I know. Give me a break here. I've never done something like this."

That makes two of us. But this will be excellent practice for fake dating Brandon when Cláudia visits early next month. If I can pretend to date Dean, a virtual stranger, then faking a relationship with Brandon, a man who's known me since high school, should be relatively straightforward.

He peeks between his fingers. "So, about that safe phrase . . ."

"It should be something that doesn't feel forced," I point out. "How about the person giving consent says, 'You can't help yourself, can you?' As if they're teasing the other person. It's the kind of statement that could precede physical contact, and it sounds natural to my ear."

"Yeah, that works," he says, nodding.

So far, so good. I'm crafty. He's reasonable. We might actually get out of this mess unscathed. "Another thing: You're going to have to be flexible about the schedule for these outings. I cannot move an already-planned weekend trip to Vegas with my roommate."

"When's that?"

"Second weekend in August."

"Okay, we should be done by then. Not a problem."

"Also, my weeknights aren't always free."

"Work conflicts?"

"Exactly."

He draws back and frowns. "I don't even know what you do for a living."

"I'm teaching adult education and empowerment classes in the afternoon and evenings."

"Like for the GED, you mean?"

I nod. "Yeah, that and a job readiness course."

"Lina said you went to graduate school."

"I did. I took this job in exchange for getting my master's degree fully funded."

"Nice. You left school without being saddled by debt." He tucks his hands under his chin and looks at me wistfully. "What's that like?"

"It's weird, actually. I'm incredibly grateful, but sometimes it feels too good to be true. I'm waiting for someone to tell me it was all a clerical error and ask for the money back."

Dean releases a deep sigh and sags against his chair. "I took out a staggering amount of loans for law school, so in my mind, working for a firm was a given. I'm not sure I would have taken the same path if I'd finished debt-tree." He gestures as if to dismiss the subject. "Enough about that. Tell me, what's next for you? After the fellowship ends, I mean."

I resist the urge to ask him what he would have done differently, since he plainly doesn't want to talk about it. Maybe another time. "I'm considering a position coordinating adult training for BFI in Ohio."

He leans forward a fraction, his eyes flickering with interest. "What's that?"

"Building Futures International. Think of it as Habitat for Humanity on steroids. The beneficiaries are all reentering the workforce, so they get housing assistance *and* career counseling. I'd be overworked and underpaid, but I'd get a lot of responsibility — mostly because they'll be overworking and underpaying me." I shrug. "Anyway, if that doesn't feel like the right choice, I'll figure out something else to do. As long as I'm helping people, I'll know I'm on the right track."

"When do you have to decide?"

"They're giving me until the end of the summer."

"I must admit," he says, straightening in his chair, "I'm fascinated by how relaxed you are about it. I wish I had that gene. I'm all thumbs if there's no plan." He plucks at the cuffs of his shirt. "Anyway, we'll have to figure out how to spin that."

I bristle at the suggestion that my career decisions need to be spun in any way. I'm not floundering; I'm just considering my next steps carefully. And if Dean thinks my background isn't impressive enough for his lawyer friends, he can shove it. I narrow my eyes at him. "What do you mean by that?"

Maybe it's the hard edge to my tone, or maybe he can smell the I'm-fully-prepared-to-kick-your-ass aura surrounding me, but he immediately puts up his hands in surrender. "Whoa, whoa, whoa. I'm not an asshat, you know. All I meant was, there's no one-size-fits-all way of approaching career choices. What works for one person won't necessarily work for someone else. My point *unrelated* to that is, if you're committed to not lying about your background, *and* one of your job prospects might take you out of the state, we need to figure out how to explain that so it doesn't raise a few eyebrows. It'll probably come up in conversation."

I unclench my fists under the table. "Oh, okay. I see what you're saying. You may keep your balls, then. And yes, we can work on that too."

"Great," he says, his voice overly cheerful. "And thanks for letting me hold on to my balls. I've grown attached to them over the years."

"You're welcome," I say, winking at him.

Despite his stodgy appearance, Dean seems like a fun guy. I'm beginning to think spending a few nights pretending to be his girlfriend won't be a hardship. "Okay, so the next thing isn't a condition. It's just something you need to know about me: I don't do anything in half measures. I'm either all in or all out. If you want to do this, we're going to have to put in the work. Real stuff too. Names, poignant memories, idiosyncrasies, the whole nine yards. I'm not showing up on several dates with you and embarrassing myself. I'd never sign up for something like that."

This bit of news seems to energize him. He rubs his hands together and bounces his shoulders as if he's dancing in his chair. The image doesn't compute, so I tilt my head in an attempt to put the world back on its proper axis.

"That's *exactly* what I wanted to hear," he says, then reaches behind him, pulling out a folder from his messenger bag. "It means you'll take this seriously, and that can only be a good thing." He slides a file across the table.

"What's this?" I ask as I peek inside and leaf through the contents.

"Think of it as a primer on me. For fun, I'm calling it the Dean Dossier."

"I already have double D's. I don't need yours too."

A dash of pink stains his cheeks. I should control my urge to throw him off-kilter, but the man just handed me a five-page, single-spaced biography, along with a clear envelope containing a mishmash of photographs from various periods in his life. Can anyone really blame me for not curbing my wiseass tendencies?

"I drafted a form for you too," he continues. "Which I can send as soon as you give me your email address. Just fill it out and return it to me when you have a moment."

My eyebrows snap together so quickly I may have given myself a permanent unibrow. As surreptitiously as possible, I trace a finger down my forehead to check. "You're serious?"

"Why wouldn't I be?" he asks, looking genuinely confused. "You said you'd be willing to put in the work." He points at the folder. "That's your study guide."

Wow. Just wow. This guy's something else.

I hold up the Dean Dossier in one hand. "Are you telling me everything I need to know about you can be found in here?"

Dean shakes his head. "Well, not *everything,* but enough to throw Peter off our scent. He's going to try to poke holes in our story. That" — he points to the folder — "will make it harder for him to accomplish his goal."

Sections of the dossier are separated by Roman numerals. One section is titled "How We Met." Another is titled "Dean :The Early Years." It's as though I'm preparing to enter an amateur Witness Protection Program.

My eyes bulge when I get to the "Interesting Facts About Me:The Highlights" section. I can't help it. "You try to avoid saying the word *Houston*?"

He blushes. "An ex-girlfriend lives there. It's a long story."

I'm not touching that one. "And you spent part of your childhood in Delaware?"

He nods. "Yeah. Why do you seem so surprised?"

"I didn't think anyone actually lived in Delaware. Except for the Bidens."

"So much hate for the tiny state," he says, his lips pursed in mock offense.

"Settle down, 40 Cent. No need to get so

defensive." Scanning the next page, I try to imagine Dean assembling his life into a PowerPoint presentation. Who *does* that? "You've included all of your social media handles too. How thorough."

Detecting none of my snark, he smiles proudly. "If we're supposed to be dating, we should follow each other on at least one of these accounts. Instagram, probably. And post a pic or two for some realism. Everything you need is there."

I toss the folder onto the table. "Fine. I'll read it. But faking a relationship is going to require more than just reading our histories and being mutuals on Twitter. We're going to need to get comfortable with each other. Finish each other's sentences. Be playful and loving. That requires acting, not just reading."

"I'm prepared to do that too," he says. "Impersonating a man in a real relationship is a strength of mine."

I give him a blank stare.

"Too soon?" he asks.

"Definitely."

"Duly noted," he says. "Seriously, though. I know I'm asking a lot of you, and there are no words to express how much this means to me. You've been a bright spot during an admittedly rough time."

Rough seems like an understatement. Which reminds me: We're going to need to talk about his breakup with Ella eventually. A close friend and roommate would know the backstory. Still, I'd much prefer to end this coffee date on a high note, so I simply say, "I'm glad."

"And if there's anything I can do for you in return, just say the word."

Now *there's* an intriguing offer. Although it obviously wasn't the impetus for my saying yes to his harebrained scheme, having Dean indebted to me may nevertheless come in handy someday. But surely he doesn't mean *anything.* "How about a million dollars in my bank account by close of business tomorrow?"

He chuckles. "Anything except that."

"Then how about an IOU that I can cash in when the time's right?"

"Deal." He pulls out his wallet and places a credit card on the table. "So when would you like to get started on putting in the work, as you called it?"

"I'm available this weekend. I'm thinking we should visit each other's homes. You can learn a lot about someone by seeing them in their living space. Besides, if we're supposedly roommates, I should get a sense of your neighborhood and the layout of your

95

place, right?"

He nods as he chews on his bottom lip, then says, "I like the way you think. Text me the times you're available. I'll be in the office most of the weekend, but I'll take a break whenever you need me to."

"All work and no play makes Dean a dull boy, you know."

As soon as the words leave my mouth, I know they're the wrong ones. I may as well be twirling a lock of my hair and batting my eyelashes.

Unbothered by my flirtatious dig, he trails a finger across the scar above his eyebrow and gives me a lopsided grin. "Don't let my meticulous appearance fool you. I'm never dull when it counts."

Oof. I don't appreciate that information. At all. In the hands of someone with a dirty imagination like mine, it's titillating. And Dean very well knows what he's insinuating, which makes him dangerous. While I may have some unfinished business to sort out this summer, being this man's rebound is *definitely* not in my plans.

I rise from my chair, internally tugging at the net Dean's thrown over me. I'm doing him a favor. Nothing more. Better to remember that and be on my way. "I'll see you this weekend. Come prepared to tell me everything I need to know about Dean Chapman that *isn't* in the dossier."

"That'll take more than a weekend," he calls after me.

"Too bad," I call back. "That's all you're going to get."

Chapter Seven

DEAN

Saturday afternoon, I'm sitting in my office prepping for an appearance in one of my landlord-tenant clinic cases when I get a text from Max:

I heard.

It's been two days since Solange agreed to be my fake girlfriend. I'm surprised it took him this long to start poking his nose into the situation.

Me: Heard what?

Max: About you and Solange. The scheme. Shit like this never works. Lina and I know.

Me: I don't have a choice. I fucked up. You know what making partner means to me.

Max: Right.

Me: This isn't a game, it's my future.

Max: I know.

Me: It's only a few fake dates.

Max: Make sure it stays that way.

Me: Okay.

Max: I mean it, D. You do not want to get on Lina's bad side.

Me: She has a good one?

Me: Kidding.

Max: Line. Crossed. I'm kicking your ass the next time I see you.

Max: Listen, I don't know the details, but I know Solange doesn't need your brand of bullshit.

Me: What the hell. I'm an honest guy.

Max: Says the man who just agreed to fake a relationship.

Me: Honest about my feelings, asshole.

Max: Semantics, dude.

Me: Are you done?

Max: Yes.

Me: You have nothing to worry about. Check in when you have something useful to say.

Me: Are we still on for basketball tomorrow?

Max: Yeah.

I toss the phone and my reading glasses on the desk, then massage my temples, the eyestrain from staring at a computer all day finally getting to me. Now's as good a time as any to make my way over to Solange's. Taking a quick tour of her apartment and eating carry-out together at mine sounds like an ideal way to spend the evening. I'm glad Solange suggested we do this; it reassures me that we're equally committed to the success of our ruse.

As I pack up to leave, I can't help smiling about our conversation at the café. She's a bright woman. Confident. Takes pride in her convictions. Deploys her sarcasm with the skill of a seasoned trial lawyer wooing a jury. And she's definitely a good sport for helping me out. But in the end, Solange has a wanderer's soul, and she's obviously still finding herself. Can't wait to see what she does when she finally figures out her place in the world.

At this stage in my life, I'm looking for someone just as goal-oriented as I am, a person who knows what they want and is well on their way to getting it. Without the baggage of being in love with someone else, of course. So as much as I hate to give Max credit, he's absolutely spot-on about this: There is no point in blurring the lines with Solange. Good thing is, I'm not inclined to anyway.

"Well, well, well, if it isn't the guy who's

trying to steal my girlfriend."

The Black man at Solange's apartment door looks me up and down as a dozen thoughts crash into my head at once: *What the hell is going on? I thought Solange wasn't dating. How is our pretend relationship going to work if she's with someone? Did Solange tell him about our arrangement? And how is his goatee so damn perfect? There isn't a single blemish on his dark brown skin. Does this man even eat sugar? Should I dodge and weave now or protect my jaw and back out slowly?*

The stern expression on his face slips, and he grins at me. "I'm just fucking with you, man." He gestures for me to come inside and puts out his hand. "I'm Brandon. Good friend and roommate. Occasional fake boyfriend when she needs me."

The tension in my muscles dissipates. "I'm Dean," I say as we shake hands. "Good to meet you."

Just when I think the situation's clear, he plants his legs wide and glares at me. "Full disclosure, though: Between us, I'm secretly in love with her, and I'm not happy about this little game you've drawn her into. Sounds like you're using it as an excuse to get close to her."

It's a standoff, and I have no idea what to

do next, so I meet his gaze and wait.

"And . . . scene." He shakes his head, his mouth twitching in amusement. "Again, I'm messing with you."

Solange strides into the room from down the hall, an empty laundry basket in her hands. She's wearing a light blue dress that hugs her curves, and her feet are bare. "Brandon, they asked you to work an *emergency* shift for a reason. Get your ass in gear."

Brandon swipes a wallet off a table in the foyer and tucks it into the back pocket of his jeans. "True, indeed. My patrons and their alcohol-induced confessions need me stat."

Solange flicks her gaze upward as if to warn me against being fooled by her friend's melodrama. "Brandon's a bartender and aspiring actor who isn't ready to live in New York. That should explain a lot." Lifting the basket, she adds, "I put my clothes away in your honor. Otherwise, I usually treat this as my dresser for the week."

She doesn't say hey, or hello, or anything, and for some reason that omission eases my nerves. If she's this casual with me now, imagine how she'll be after we actually get to know each other. It also suggests she isn't worried about our scheme, and I could use any extra bravado she has to offer. I place my hands over my heart and bat my eyes. "I'm flattered."

Solange and I smile at each other. It gives me the opportunity to look at her. *Really* look at her. Without the spectacle of a canceled wedding in the forefront. Without the prospect of her saying no to my pretend-relationship proposition ratcheting up my anxiety. There's so much to admire too: Her eyes are the kind of brown that feels sumptuous — like the center of one of those molten lava cakes you're advised to order even before you've had the entrée because it takes thirty minutes to prepare. And that hair. It's everywhere. Big curls in different shades, from caramel to walnut; they deserve their own zip code, and I'd fucking live in it if I could. Now, I don't dare stare at her mouth — feels too intimate — but I do register her high cheekbones and the smoothness of her brown skin. Ironically, Max's warning prompts me to think about leaping over the lines I claimed just an hour ago I had no intention of crossing. Who would blame me? Not a goddamn person, that's who.

A throat clears, snapping me out of the moment. Oh, right. The roommate's still here.

"I'm out, people," Brandon says, a knowing grin suggesting he can easily guess where my head's been. "I'm covering for someone who's running late, so I'll be back soon. Just in case you need to sync your activities with my whereabouts."

Solange purses her lips at Brandon, then dismisses him with a wave. "Tchau."

"Good to meet you, Dean."

"Same, man."

After Brandon leaves, Solange crams the laundry basket in a standalone utility closet by the fridge, using her backside to ram the door shut. "Can I get you anything? Water? A beer?"

"I'm good for now, thanks." I spin around and study her space. "You know, we're practically neighbors."

She nods. "I saw that in the dossier. The backstory is that Brandon's parents own a couple of properties in the district. This is one of them."

"Now *that's* a sweet deal."

"Yeah, *especially* considering my salary." Her eyes suddenly grow wide, and she points in my direction, backing away slowly. "Oh my God, what are those?"

"What?" I say, holding up my arms and scanning the area around me.

"Are those . . . jeans? I thought you only

wore button-downs and slacks because they're more your" — she makes air quotes — " 'style.' "

I tilt my head and flatten my lips. "Really? Right when I was beginning to like you . . ."

She wrinkles her nose and gives me an impish smile. "Just glad to see you know how to be casual. I'll be good from now on, I promise." Expanding her arms wide, she adds, "Okay, so this is my place. Feel free to inspect everything except Brandon's room and my underwear drawer. Any questions, ask away. I'd shadow you around the apartment to make sure you don't steal anything of value, but there isn't much that falls in that category."

"Where should I start? Bathroom?" I give her a wicked grin. "Your medicine cabinet?"

"Jesus, Chapman. That's a little forward, don't you think? You haven't even taken me on a date yet."

"Apologies. Bedroom, then?"

"That's more like it," she says with a wink.

I was kidding before. I'm not *beginning* to like her; I *do* like her. She's unassuming and witty, and I can't stop smiling at whatever happens to tumble out of that gorgeous mouth.

No.

It's just an ordinary mouth, dammit.

She racewalks down the hall, then opens a door with a flourish. "Ta-da. Welcome to Casa Solange."

I stand at the threshold and take in the space. Fuck me. It's sexy as hell. The focal point is the queen-size bed, which is framed by a floor-to-ceiling headboard upholstered in midnight-blue velvet. Nothing is sleek; it's just texture and more texture. From the fuzzy blanket at the foot of the bed to the three-dimensional metal wall art above her dresser. But there isn't much else here. A few flat U-Haul moving boxes are propped up against her closet; they're a reminder that her furnishings are probably sparse because it makes it easier for her to pack up and head off to her next destination.

Looking for an item to distract me from the allure of Solange's bed, I settle my gaze on a photo collage on the opposite side of the room. "What's that?"

"Just some photos of people I met during my travels," she says in a detached tone.

I point inside. "May I?"

She swallows, then shrugs her shoulders. "Be my guest."

I'm not sure why I'm drawn to the collage. Maybe it's because I think it's going to give me some insight into Solange's personality beyond the information she sent me.

106

Now that I'm close to it, I can see that Solange is in every one of them. Looking relaxed and content. With people of different ages and racial backgrounds. All smiling proudly. "They're wearing hotel uniforms."

"Yes," she says, appearing at my side, her arms crossed over her middle. "They're the folks who clean the rooms. Or the bellhops who bring up people's bags. When I was a child, my mother would always task me with finding out the name of the person who was responsible for cleaning our hotel room. Before we checked out, she'd leave a tip, and I'd leave a note, usually consisting of a terribly drawn picture and a thank-you scrawled across the page. 'We can't forget the people who work in the shadows,' she would say. She cleaned houses herself when she first came to the U.S., so I think she knew how important it was to be acknowledged, and she certainly knew the value of an extra few dollars in her pocket."

"Then you started taking pictures of these people on your own trips?"

"Yeah. Whenever I visit a new place, I take tons of pictures. Of beaches. Of beautiful sunsets. Or mountain ranges. Or even a fantastic meal. All in an effort to capture my experience. One day, I realized what was missing: the people who make the bed or bring you towels or do a million other tasks we take for granted. So I started capturing them. With their permission, of course." She shrugs again. "Just something I do."

It's a tic of hers, I now realize. Whatever follows that shrug is important, but she doesn't want to let you in on that fact. I also realize something else: Solange may be unsure where her future will lead her, but being a good person is her moral compass; that's a level of success some people never reach. "It's incredibly considerate, and it speaks volumes about you."

"I'm a messy bitch sometimes, so don't get too carried away," she says, her tone playful again.

"Definitely noted," I say, wanting to lighten the mood as much as she apparently does. "You know, it's not the eyes that are the windows to your soul, it's the stomach. Let's see the kitchen next."

She gives me a shaky laugh as she nods her assent. "Sounds good."

I make small talk as I follow her down the hall. "Miracle Whip?"

"Gross," she says over her shoulder.

"Mustard?"

"Only on a soft pretzel or a Cubano."

"Ketchup?"

"Of course. It's a base."

"What the hell for?"

"Mayo, ketchup, and garlic. Whip 'em together and you have the best dip for yuca fries or tostones."

"Gross."

She stops short and stares at me over her shoulder. "I will kick you out of this apartment for that kind of blasphemy."

"Delicious, then," I say, rubbing my stomach.

We reach the kitchen, and my gaze immediately homes in on the dozen or so small appliances that sit side by side in the compact space. "Think there's enough on that counter?"

"Hush," she says, grinning.

"Why all the coffee gadgets?"

She grimaces, turning her nose up in disgust. "Brandon swears by his Keurig, but I like to prepare my coffee the old-fashioned way." She opens a cupboard: One shelf is crammed with mugs, the middle shelf houses K-Cups organized by flavor, and the top shelf holds a dozen red boxes labeled "Pilão."

"What are those?" I say, pointing to the boxes.

"That's the coffee my mother and tias sell at Rio de Wheaton."

"The place they've been running since

109

2003. You and your cousins did homework there after school."

She raises a brow. "I see someone's been studying the Solange Dossier."

"I have."

Gleaned a lot from it too: a year abroad in Argentina during her senior year; a stint as a census field worker on both coasts after college; next, two years at Building Futures; then, graduate school and this DC placement to fulfill her fellowship. In that same time, I've had one and only one job — as an associate at Olney & Henderson. Some people plant roots; others sprinkle seeds and let others tend to the growth. Solange seems to be in tune enough with herself to know she's more suited to the latter. I admire that about her.

"Well, if you've been a diligent student," Solange says, "you also know my mom and tias are my suppliers for just about any Brazilian product I want." She closes the cupboard. "But for your purposes, the key is this: I like my coffee strong. Black. No sugar. If we're at dinner and you pour creamer into my cup, I won't drink it."

"That's important," I say, pretending to jot that tidbit in a pad. "And just so *you* know, I like mine sticky and sweet. The more caramel drizzle, the better."

She stares at my lips, as if she's having trouble processing my words, so I wave a hand in front of her face, and the movement appears to clear the mental fog. She blinks twice, then shakes out her arms and says, "Sounds like a cinnamon roll, not a beverage."

"Okay, you know what? Your animosity for my coffee preferences is getting out of hand. Hasn't anyone ever told you it's rude to yuck someone's yum?"

"I'm a fan of swallowing, so no. Plenty of people seem to enjoy when I yuck their yum, actually."

"Are we talking about the same thing?"

"Probably not," she says, holding back a smile.

I jam my thumbs into the front pockets of my jeans. Jesus, my head's spinning. "Honestly, I can't keep up with your brain. Just when I think our conversation's headed in one direction, you take a sharp turn."

"It requires some getting used to, I'll give you that." She tilts her head and studies me. As if she's sizing me up. Then she snaps her fingers. "I have an idea! We should go out. To a bar."

Spinning, spinning, spinning. "I thought you wanted to head over to my place."

She dismisses my question with a flail of

her hands. "We can do that later. For now, though, I think it would be wise to get in some practice. In an unrehearsed scenario. We're not going to have dossiers or the benefit of a script for any of these outings with Kimberly Bailey, so we should get comfortable winging it. Somehow I don't think that's one of your strengths."

She's not wrong. That my first instinct was to make up a sketchy story about my canceled wedding is proof alone of that. Besides, spending time with Solange isn't a chore. So, yeah, if she wants to simulate a night out on the town to help us work out any kinks, I'm all for it. I look down at my attire. "I'm probably not dressed for what you have in mind, though."

"This place is casual. You'll fit right in."

"Let's do it, then."

Practice is a good thing. And given what's at stake, I appreciate that Solange is willing to put in this extra effort. Besides, it would be better to stumble through our performance now than when it actually matters. I mean, how much trouble can we get into in a bar?

CHAPTER EIGHT

SOLANGE

Dean and I weave our way through the crowd at Sip City, one of my favorite nightspots on U Street, and step up to the only area along the twenty-foot-long bar that isn't occupied by a patron. Brandon wordlessly slides us two stools from behind the counter, and Dean wastes no time setting them down so we can stake our claim on the space.

It pays to have friends in important places.

The crowd is thick, a riot of disparate conversations buzzing around us, punctuated by an occasional cheer coming from the karaoke room nearby. Although the clientele's diverse, as is often the case in DC, the clusters of friends hanging out are more homogenous.

"Okay if I leave you alone for a minute?" Dean asks, his minty breath warm against my ear. "I need to use the restroom."

I try not to shiver — and fail. "Sure."

Dean draws back. "Are you cold?"

"I'm good," I say, not meeting his eyes and adjusting my cropped cardigan so it covers my shoulders. "There's a draft above us, I think." *And it's sending your highly potent pheromones my way.*

"Okay," he says, tapping the bar rail. "Be right back."

"Should I order you anything?" I ask before he goes.

"Water's fine for now."

Of course it is.

As soon as he's gone, Brandon sidles over, dragging a dishrag over the countertop.

"Water for Dean and a Blackberry Jam for me," I tell him. "And thanks for holding a spot for us."

"Why the change in plans?" he asks.

I lift my butt off the stool and lean over, not wanting anyone else to hear us. "Dean's kind of stiff."

"Sounds promising," Brandon says, lifting an eyebrow as he prepares my drink. "I fail to see the problem."

Rolling my eyes, I push him away. "*Around me,* I mean. It's like there's an outline in his head for everything, and if you don't fit into the right section, he doesn't know what to do with you. We came here to practice

114

being a couple in public." I spread my arms and bend at the waist as if I'm taking a bow. "A bit of Method acting, if you will."

Brandon sighs. "That's a common misconception about the Method — that actors stay in character throughout the time they're filming a movie or something, but really it's about using your own life experiences to better understand your character's situation. The Strasberg approach —"

"Brandon."

"Yeah?"

"You've gone over this many, *many* times before."

"Right," he says, shaking his head, then looking around and finally acknowledging the patrons clamoring for his attention. "Well, practicing makes sense." He fills a glass with water and sets it next to my cocktail. "Duty calls."

I swivel my stool around and survey the crowd. I'm searching for a couple. Preferably one that isn't averse to public displays of affection. It doesn't take me long to find one sitting at a prime table in the corner. They're both white and dressed for a night out on the town. Dark hair. Dark eyes. Late twenties, maybe early thirties. Very *Vampire Diaries.* The guy's arm is loosely draped over the woman's shoulder, and she's tucked against him as she nuzzles his jaw. Several empty cocktail glasses are scattered in front of them.

"I'm back," Dean says as he slides onto his stool and swings around so that we're facing in the same direction. Water glass in hand, he asks, "What'd I miss?"

I lift my chin. "Those two snuggling. At three o'clock."

"Yeah. What about 'em?"

"Let's go over there and introduce ourselves."

"As a couple?"

"Exactly. They seem totally into each other and don't mind who knows it. Should be easy enough to strike up a conversation. I'll take the lead."

I'm already out of my stool and grabbing my drink when Dean says, "Why am I not surprised?"

"Heard that."

"I assumed you would," he says, his voice laced with amusement.

I stop short and pull him close, then slip my fingers through his. God, whatever cologne he's wearing smells amazing. It's crisp and citrusy and hits my nose in the same way peppermint hits my tongue: like a burst of energy that recedes quickly and lingers in this satisfyingly muted state. Dammit. Why couldn't he smell like funky gym socks — or a teenage boy's bedroom? Now that I think about it, I suppose those are similar odors if Rey's childhood grooming habits are any guide.

I give Dean's hand a playful squeeze, then stroke his jaw. "Someone's feeling sassy tonight, I see. Keep that same energy as we talk to these two, okay?"

"I'll do my best," he says, his chest rising as he takes a small breath, then releases it slowly. I suspect I'm not meant to see the effort, but I notice it just the same. Well. My touch affected him. Isn't that interesting?

No, Brain, it's not interesting at all. What the hell is wrong with you? The man recently experienced a painful breakup and needs space to recover. You couldn't custom-design a man more emotionally unavailable than this one, so get those non-platonic thoughts out of my head right now.

The woman straightens in her chair as we approach, her eyes widening in interest.

"Hey," I say, careful to make eye contact with them both. "The bar's packed, so we were wondering if you'd mind sharing a table."

They exchange a glance, then the man slides the empty cocktail glasses off to one

117

side. "We don't mind at all. Join us."

"I'm Brynn," the woman says. "This is Jaxson."

Her tone's welcoming, and her partner's wearing a half smile. We sit across from them, Brynn to my right, and Jaxson to Dean's left.

"Nice to meet you, Brynn. My name's Solange, and this is my boyfriend, Dean."

Now that only a few feet separate us, I'd put their ages at closer to midthirties. There's an air of sophistication in their demeanor, and our arrival didn't appear to unnerve either one. They're secure in their relationship, it seems, or maybe just confident in each other's tastes. I peek at their hands and notice they're both wearing gold bands.

"Are you guys married?" I ask, leaning in so I can be heard over the music pumping through Sip City's surround speakers.

"We are," Brynn says, placing a hand over Jaxson's. "Ten years. What about you two?"

"Just dating," Dean says as he casually rests his arm on the back of my chair.

Just? Oh dear. We've got our work cut out for us. And sweet Jesus, he looks so proud of himself too. *Look, Ma! I'm pretending to be her boyfriend!*

Suppressing the overwhelming need to

throw some serious side-eye at Dean, I add, "Um, what he means is that we're not sure marriage will ever be a goal for us. We're comfortable with the way things are."

"Ah," Brynn says, nodding. "It's certainly not for everyone. Are you from the area?"

"I'm a transplant," Dean says. "But I've been here long enough that I consider it home." He looks over at me. "And Solange grew up in Maryland."

He's saying the right words, but the delivery is sterile. As if he's running a finger down a page of my dossier, refreshing his memory, then answering. We're going to have to work on that.

"Jaxson and I are from Austin," Brynn says. "Figured we'd take a trip to DC for some sightseeing. Our hotel concierge recommended this place when we asked for an unpretentious spot to hang out for our last evening here."

"Good choice," I say as I sneak a glance at Brynn's husband. "It's a favorite among the locals, which says a lot."

Jaxson's gaze bounces between Dean and me. I get the distinct impression that he's assessing us. Or maybe I'm just misinterpreting his broody vibe. Either way, it's unsettling. I'm considering how to draw him into the conversation when he rises from his chair and throws a few bills down. For the tip, presumably.

"I'll be right back, friends," he says. Before he leaves, he drops a kiss on Brynn's forehead.

As soon as he's gone, Brynn leans forward and clasps her hands on the table, her eyes glinting with excitement. "So, Solange and Dean, would you like to spend the evening with us?"

Um, what?

Oh.

Oh shit. Are they . . . ?

Dean furrows his forehead and chuckles. "Isn't that what we're already doing?"

She traces her finger across the rim of her (empty) glass and pops her lips.

Cringe.

"Back at our hotel room, I mean," she clarifies. "All four of us."

Yep, they're swingers. Which is *totally* fine. But Method acting is one thing; Method *fucking* is quite another. *Nice, Solange. You really know how to pick 'em.* I bet they're pros at this, too, because I'm beginning to think Jaxson's abrupt exit was meant to ensure that their proposition and my and Dean's response to it would be as nonconfrontational as possible.

Recognition dawns on Dean's face, and

120

his eyes nearly fall out of his head. "You mean . . ."

"Thanks for the offer, but we'll pass," I squeak out as I jump to my feet and pull Dean up by his sleeve. "We're not part of the lifestyle, and I think our relationship's still too new for us to explore something like that. Isn't that right, sweetheart?"

Dean settles a splayed hand on my back and gently presses his fingers there. "Right. Exactly. That's just what I was going to say. Precisely that."

Dear Lord, he's terrible at this. So terrible it's actually endearing.

Brynn isn't at all surprised that we're not interested in their offer, though. "Such a pity, but I understand. Sorry for any misunderstanding. It was great meeting you."

"Same," I say, giving her a half-hearted wave. "Hope you and Jaxson get home safely!"

We speed-walk back to the bar, where Brandon's waiting, his raised brows suggesting he's eager for a rundown of our fake dating exploits.

"How'd it go?" he asks.

"We got propositioned by a couple of swingers," I say flatly.

Brandon pumps his fists in the air. "Success!"

Dean barks out a laugh. "I guess you could call it that. Seriously, did that just happen?"

"It's not unheard of in here." Brandon peers at Dean more closely. "Are you sure you don't want anything stronger? Tequila, maybe?"

Dean begs off. "Tequila's my Kryptonite." He holds up his glass. "I'll stick with this to be safe."

"Fair enough," Brandon says, glancing at me. "Well, holler if you need anything." And then he walks off.

"I have another idea," I say.

"No, no, no," Dean says, crossing his hands over his chest and lifting his nose in the air. "Moreover, hell no. Whatever it is, I'll pass. My tender sensibilities can't handle any more of your ideas."

I bump his shoulder, secretly loving that he's loosening up around me. It'll give what I'm about to say more impact. "Oh, c'mon. Hear me out. You'll like this one."

"Fine," he says, rolling his eyes. "I'm listening."

"Let's just . . . talk. And ask the burning questions that never made it into our respective dossiers. No faking. No lying. Just realness. How does that sound?"

"You're being reasonable," Dean says, giving me a crooked smile. "What's the catch?"

There is none, really. He's a good guy, and I'm interested in his story. And if learning more about him helps to make our fake chemistry more convincing, there's no downside, is there? "No catch or ulterior motive. I'd just like to get to know you."

He lets out a shaky breath and bumps my shoulder. "I'd like to get to know you too."

I scoot over to face him, then trace the small scar above his left brow with my index finger. "Let's start with this beauty. How'd you get it?"

His eyes go wide, and he takes a tiny sip of air.

I drop my hand and pretend not to notice. Because what else is there to do?

"My first pool accident," he says. "I was twelve."

"You're a swimmer."

He nods, his thumb absently swiping at the condensation on his glass. "Used to be. Had dreams of training for the Olympics and everything."

"Why didn't you?"

"My mother and I moved around a lot. I was never in one place long enough to make a team and stick to it." He throws up a dismissive hand. "Wouldn't have mattered anyway. Very few people are good enough to

123

compete at that level. And the odds of qualifying are slim to none. Like a tenth of a percent slim to none. But when you're a kid, you dream about shit like that. Well, I did, at least."

He tells himself that it wouldn't have mattered *precisely because* it very much mattered to him. And still does, I think. Someone who didn't care about his prospects wouldn't have bothered to calculate the likelihood of making the Olympics. "Were you good?"

"I was."

There's no conceit in his voice. It's simply what he knows to be true — and I believe him.

"Do you still swim?"

"Not as much as I'd like to." Suddenly he straightens. "My turn."

"Go for it," I say.

"Of all the places you've visited outside the United States, which one is your favorite?"

"That's easy. Brazil. I'm not sure I can do it justice, but if there's a place with more natural beauty, I haven't come across it. Plus, there's an energy there. It's the spirit of the people. Their joy for life. Their national pride. It's something to witness. Here in America, it's just my mother, her sisters, and my cousins. We're a small family. But there? My relatives get together and suddenly dozens of people are smoking meats in a makeshift brick oven in someone's backyard. It's wild. And when I'm there, I feel even more connected to my mother. Makes me realize how scary it must have been to leave the only home she'd ever known and go after her piece of the so-called American dream here."

"Your mother and aunts sound like amazing women. Is someone writing all this down? For posterity?"

"Lina is," I say, nodding. "She's the historian. Family trees, recipes, even juicy gossip."

"Nice," he says. "I haven't traveled outside the country much. Not unless it's for work. But I'll add Brazil to the bucket list. You're an excellent ambassador."

"Maybe I'll even agree to be your tour guide someday."

He gives me a "yeah, yeah, sure you will" smile that irks me a bit. Mostly because it isn't at all difficult to imagine doing just that. We'd have tons of fun too. Dean letting loose on the streets of Rio would be a hoot, and I would get as many incriminating photos as I could.

I take a moment to survey our surroundings. The crowd's thinning, but the folks who remain are getting loud and boisterous. Not my idea of a good time. Still, I don't want to cut our conversation short. We haven't even talked about Ella, and I'm itching to ask about her. I begin to speak, then snap my mouth shut. Is it too soon?

Dean notices my hesitation and opens the door for me. "I'll take 'topics that may be difficult to broach but that you desperately want to discuss anyway' for a thousand dollars, Solange."

"Oh, thank God," I say, exhaling in purposefully overblown relief. "Okay, let's see. Here's your clue: You were all set to marry this person just two weeks ago, until a nosy interloper stopped the wedding."

He pretends to press a clicker in his hands. "Who is Ella Smith?"

"Correct. Well done. So, uh, tell me about her. Because I'll confess, I'm perplexed by how well you seem to be handling the breakup."

He faces me and nibbles on his bottom lip as he considers my question. It's one of his habits, and I *hate* it. If he had crusty lips, I'd tell him to have at it, but no, Dean's lips are plump and look pillow soft. The plump-lipped bastard.

"What?" I prod.

126

After several pensive beats, he says, "I'm going to be honest here, and I hope you won't judge me too much."

"Go on."

He rakes a hand through his hair and lowers his chin. "Ella and I were only together for six months, and we didn't love each other. Our intended marriage was meant to be a means to an end. For the both of us."

This time I open and close my mouth like a ventriloquist's puppet as I gather my thoughts. Now it all makes sense: Dean's low-key reaction to canceling his own wedding, his eagerness to recruit me for his fake dating caper, the ease with which he turned his attention to securing a promotion. "You didn't love her? *At all?*"

He rubs the back of his neck. "I *liked* Ella. That was enough for me. And for her."

With much effort, I resist the urge to wrinkle my nose. People who treat their partners as props to satisfy their own needs are *the worst.* If I were looking for a compelling reason to resist my attraction to this man — *and I am* — he's just given me one. Fixing my features into a placid expression, I pull out some cash for my drink, then rise from my stool. "Let's get out of here."

DEAN

Solange needed fresh air, so we're walking the mile and a half to my condo in Columbia Heights. It's still eighty degrees and muggy, and she's wrapped her sweater around her waist; I suppose her definition of fresh air is different from mine.

Along the way, we pass Ben's Chili Bowl, an iconic DC eatery, on our right.

"Ever been?" I ask her.

She chuckles, but the sound peters out quickly. "I'm Brazilian American. One of their signature dishes is a heaping bowl of beans and meat ladled over white rice. What do *you* think?"

"I think that was a silly question."

She smiles in agreement, but my attempt at small talk doesn't diminish the tension. We continue walking — Solange appearing deep in thought — then turn on Thirteenth Street. The air's thick and sticky, but there's a definite chill in the atmosphere — and it's coming from Solange. Just as I feared, my revelation about Ella isn't sitting well with her.

We stroll the length of two blocks before I try to draw her out. "You're judging me. About Ella."

"Honestly?" She pinches a thumb and forefinger together. "Maybe a teensy bit.

And I can admit that I'm being unfair. Just" — she throws up her hands — "make it make sense, please."

"I'm a planner," I say as if that's a sufficient explanation. In my mind, it is. To her, it's probably a non sequitur. "That's just how I'm programmed. I like setting goals and achieving them. The structure . . . it helps me stay grounded."

She nods as we stroll, her gaze trained on the sidewalk ahead of her. "So marriage was one of the goals you set for yourself."

"Yes. Along with paying off debt, buying a home, making partner at Olney & Henderson, things like that. I get that this may not make sense to you, but I know firsthand how unsettling it can be if the people supposedly in your corner can't align with your goals. Ella and I just fit. Or we did, I should say. She's ambitious. Has her own objectives. And said she wanted to support mine. A dinner with a bunch of lawyers at the firm? Ella was all over it. That was her natural habitat. And if she needed to pitch a potential financial backer in a suite at Capital One Arena? I was her person. Fun fact: I can talk about basketball with a bunch of strangers for hours. We complemented each other."

"Except for that part where she was actually in love with her childhood friend."

I screw up my face as if there's a rotten smell in the air. "Except for that. The thing is, *not* falling in love with Ella is precisely what's helped me stay on track. I can't imagine what would have happened if I'd been some lovesick chump finding out his fiancée had been stringing him along. I probably would have had to take a leave of absence just to get my head straight."

That kind of scenario is more familiar to me than Solange might realize. My own mother would mope around the house for days when a boyfriend didn't pan out. Once I hit my teens, I learned to do the cooking and cleaning until she clawed back from her latest downturn. Those were fun times.

"Your dossier mentioned one serious relationship before Ella," she says. "What happened there?"

"Carrie Sloane," I say. "We met on the first day of law school. Moved in together by the start of our second year."

We stop at an intersection, and I look around me. People are meandering nearby, and I didn't even notice. I'm focused on explaining myself. Getting it right. Because even though Solange and I don't know each other well, I care about what she thinks of me. I'm convinced that if I don't pass muster with her, I'm doing something wrong. Some people just affect us that way, I guess.

Once we're clear to cross the street, she asks, "And then?"

"She complained that our relationship wasn't growing in the way she'd hoped. I wasn't romantic, she said. Didn't tell her I loved her. Didn't sweep her off her feet and all that jazz. But I was a solid boyfriend, I thought. Faithful. Supportive. And I cared for her. None of that was enough."

Carrie wanted more than I could give her. I wish I'd figured that out before we decided to live together. It would have saved us both a lot of pain.

"Is that what ultimately led you two to end things?"

"It would have been the reason. Eventually. But before that could happen, she flunked out and expected me to move across the country with her. We were a team, she thought. And teams stick together, don't they? Well, I couldn't fathom giving up my law career for anyone. But I especially resented the fact that she expected me to. If we were a team, why was I the one who had to give something up? Obviously, she left without me. After that, I realized something important about myself: I'm not wired for romance. If two people are compatible, cool. That can be enough to make it work. But don't oversell what's happening. My mother talks about getting this warm, fuzzy feeling in her chest, and my brain immediately shuts down. I just don't see the point."

"Has it ever occurred to you that maybe you just haven't met the person you're meant to give your love to?" she asks, a tinge of exasperation in her voice.

"Has it ever occurred to you that some people aren't meant to do that ever?"

Her stride falters for the first time, then she nods. "Absolutely. You're right. And shame on me for suggesting otherwise. I've met tons of people who had no business promising to love someone forever. Kudos to you for acknowledging your own limitations."

Tons of people, huh? There's a story here. I wonder if she'd be willing to share it. We *did* agree this was the time to ask any burning questions, didn't we? "These people who had no business promising love — were they promising to love you?"

"Yup," she says glumly. "First, there was my father, who pretended he wanted to be in my life and ghosted me. Then there was Nolan. I met him in Ohio. He loved to make plans for our future, but when his stint at Building Futures ended, he asked to put our relationship 'on pause.' I don't even know what that means. Oh, and then there was the guy in grad school, Chris. Now *he* was a scammer. He said he wanted forever, but it turns out, what he wanted was a girlfriend who edited his papers and took extra-careful notes so he could miss his morning classes. Unfortunately, my bullshit detector was on the fritz when I dated him."

"I'm sorry you went through that."

She shrugs. "It's not anyone's fault but mine. I chose poorly."

"No, Solange. They were jerks, and that's on them. Period."

I *never* want to be like the men she's encountered. The kind who say whatever they think their lover wants to hear. The kind who make bullshit promises, then balk when someone relies on them. I grew up with those guys. My mother and I had our lives upended by those guys too. I'll be damned if I become one of them.

She taps me on the side; apparently, I've been silent too long. "I'm not scarred by any of this, and there's no need to feel sorry for me. If anything, it's helped me figure out what I *do* want. So, yeah, it's all good."

"Just in case it isn't abundantly clear, I

133

don't play games with my partners. I'm always up-front about what they can expect of me. Probably explains why it took me this long to find someone who shared the same outlook. Or said she did."

Wide-eyed, Solange stops midstroll and grabs my sleeve. "You mean there aren't droves of women in the twenty-first century willing to enter into a marriage of convenience to further their ambitions? I'm shocked, I tell you. Absolutely shocked. Still, it's your life, so carry on, my emotionally mature friend. Carry on." Her phone rings, and she checks it. "It's Brandon. Give me a sec."

I stroll beside her as she speaks to him. Then we pause in front of the Tivoli Theatre, a DC historic landmark, its bright lights bathing the intersection with a soft yellow glow. Or maybe that's pollution. Yeah, that's definitely pollution. Despite the smog, the area's still buzzing with passersby and people dining outside along Fourteenth Street.

"I swear, dude," she says to Brandon, shaking her head. "One of these days, I'm not going to be around to save you." A pause, and then: "Yeah, yeah. I'll be there as soon as I can."

Solange glances around, then taps on the

screen. "Sorry about that. His coworker finally showed up, so he's heading home, but Brandon being Brandon, he forgot his keys. Needs me to let him in." When she's done fiddling with her phone, she looks up at me. "My ride should be here any minute. Rain check on the tour?"

"Sure," I say. "I can send you photos of the layout of my unit. That should be enough to field any questions about" — I make air quotes — " *'our'* place."

"Good thinking." Treating me to the loveliest lopsided grin, she bumps into my side. "Listen, getting back to what we were talking about: If your philosophy on relationships works for you, it's not my place to judge. Really."

I release a shaky breath. Even though Solange now understands the nature of my and Ella's relationship, she hasn't dismissed me completely. She's showing me more grace than I'm used to. And that should be enough, right? I don't need Solange's permission to be who I've always been. We can respect each other's differences and still work as a team for the next two weeks. Positioning myself for partnership should be my main concern anyway.

A dark sedan pulls up beside us and the passenger-side window slides down.

Solange leans over and looks inside the car. "Gabriel?"

The driver nods.

"This is my Lyft," she tells me. "Thanks for an interesting night."

"Yeah. That's a great way to describe it: interesting."

I survey her features in the lamplight, taking in the way the shadows seem to adore the planes of her face. There's truly no angle at which this woman isn't alluring. I'm irritated with myself for noticing.

She gives me a slow smile. "We made good progress today, you know."

It's been a roller coaster of an evening, but on balance, I'd have to agree. "We certainly did. Almost scored a foursome, too."

"Let's keep that between you, me, and Brandon," she says with a wink.

"Deal." I shove my hands into my back pockets. "So, about Tuesday's main event . . . What if I pick you up at the school? That way, I'll be familiar with it before we meet with Kimberly Bailey."

"That works," she says. "I'll text you the info. Good night, Dean."

"Good night, Solange."

I watch her go, then my brain starts messing with me. What if the call from Brandon

136

was planned? An excuse to cut the evening short because she just isn't interested in spending any more time with me than she absolutely needs to? No, Solange doesn't strike me as the kind of person to play games like that. Besides, what does it matter? We're two people brought together under unusual circumstances. Heading in different directions but with a common purpose for a finite period. I can't forget she's doing me a huge favor, and there's no need to overthink every interaction. We just need to pretend we're in love. For four outings. With a chance at partnership on the line — and an irritating colleague hoping to trip me up.

What the hell was I thinking?

CHAPTER NINE

SOLANGE

"Next question: Name the three branches of government."

Inspired by my conversation with Dean this past weekend, I hum the Final *Jeopardy!* tune as I wait for one of my students to answer.

Someone yells, "Beyoncé, Kelly, and Michelle."

"True, true," I say, nodding. "The ladies of Destiny's Child definitely *run the world.*" I give them a self-satisfied grin. "See what I did there?"

A collective groan fills the room.

"Queen Bey was solo by the time she put out that song," another student notes.

Semantics. Plainly, I'm wasting my best material on them. *Eighteen-year-old ingrates.*

With about fifteen minutes left in class, Dean enters through the back door (heh) and slips into a seat — presumably to observe but actually to send me into a tailspin. Men in suits don't often catch my attention; Dean in a suit monopolizes it. It's a three-piece, too. Smiling, he gives me a small wave.

"Right," I say, tapping the top of my head as I try to stay on topic. "We were talking about branches. Political ones, not trees. Anyone remember the question?"

"Ms. Pereira, are you okay?" Layla, one of my best students, asks. "You seem off all of a sudden."

The question makes me flinch, which only proves her point. When I refocus on the current crop of candidates in Victory Academy's GED & Empowerment Class, twenty sets of eyes — a few struggling to remain open — are staring back at me.

Layla scribbles in her notepad, her perfectly arched eyebrows knitted as she waits for me to respond. From the back of the room, Dean looks at me innocently, a hint of amusement evident in the curve of his lips.

"I'm fine, Layla. Thanks for your concern. Everyone, let's take a five-minute water break and start up again at five thirty for the final bonus round."

Most of the students shoot up from their seats and rush out of the room. I stop Layla before she can scramble after them.

"Hang on, Ms. Young."

She drops back onto her chair. "What's up, Ms. P?"

"Did you get a chance to talk to your mother about my offer to give you some pieces from my business wardrobe?"

Most of the students are participating in a job fair in the fall; Layla expressed concerns about having something appropriate to wear.

Layla nods. "I did, Ms. P. Explained that you weren't thinking of me as a charity case and had extra clothes from when you were interviewing for grad school. That satisfied her."

"Good," I tell her. "And it's absolutely true. I don't need those suits, so it would make me happy to give them to someone who could use them for their own job search. I'll bring them in next class."

"I appreciate it. Thank you." She turns around in her seat and looks at Dean; after a few seconds, she twists to face me again, her knotless box braids swinging to a stop as she gives me a sly smile. "I'll leave you two alone."

As soon as the door closes, Dean removes his jacket — which does little to lessen the formality of his attire since he's wearing a vest underneath. "The school's impressive, Ms. Pereira."

The way he says my last name. Good Lord.

"There's a steady buzz in the air," he continues.

That's the sound of the vibrator I'll be using at home later this evening. It's voice-activated, and you turned it on from here.

Oh my God.

I'm a garbage person.

Stop it, Solange!

He takes a slow turn around the room, giving me a moment to collect myself. "It's as if everyone's positive energy is powering the place. Feels bright. Hopeful."

"It does, and it is," I say, straightening.

But there's room for growth, and part of my duties as a Whitman Fellow has been to make (hopefully) innovative suggestions to improve the program. My main one: Rather than continue to focus on short-term goals, Victory should roll out a new curriculum with an emphasis on mentoring and counseling district residents for multiyear success. I'm curious to know whether the school's board will accept any of my recommendations. And I feel a pang in my chest when I remember that any changes to the curriculum won't happen on my watch. "I'm going to miss this place. The students, especially."

"Is there any chance you could stay?" Dean asks. "This seems like a natural extension of your training."

"You're right about that. But there isn't enough money to offer me a permanent position here, and I'm not sure I'd want to stay in DC beyond the summer anyway." I shrug. "We'll see." Wanting to change the subject, I inspect him from head to toe, then ask, "Where's your cravat and timepiece?"

He slips his hands inside his pockets, causing the fabric of his trousers to stretch across his thighs — not that it's noteworthy or anything — then he gives me a half smile. "I left them in the horse-drawn carriage outside. My footman will make sure they're not disturbed."

Since the students are filing back in, I try to contain my laughter, but there's no use. "You seem more at ease than usual today. What's different?"

He straightens, his expression sobering. "Honestly? I think the stuff about Ella was weighing on me. Getting it out in the open is a big relief. I wanted you to know where I was coming from, and I appreciate that you didn't peg me as a bad guy."

Dean's far from a bad guy; he's just set in his ways. How he chooses his life partner has nothing to do with me. "You're fine. We're fine." I gesture to the class. "Let me wrap up so we can go charm the pants off Kimberly Bailey."

"Deal," he says, his eyes shining. "And if I haven't already said it a billion times, I can't thank you enough for helping me get out of this mess."

He's a sweet man, and my being his plus-one isn't a bother. Truth is, I want to help him get his happily-ever-after, even if the "after" simply means he secures the promotion of his dreams.

Dean should be paying me for this bullshit. Seriously.

His colleague Peter Barnum holds court at our table, his expansive gestures awkward and distracting as he explains how he convinced his wife to date him. "So then Molly says, 'Why should I go out with you?' Knowing I'd saved the best for last, I hit her with the ultimate mic drop."

"Which was?" Kimberly Bailey asks, her expression mildly curious.

"Harvard," Peter replies, pretending to drop a mic on the table.

Molly, who's a dead ringer for Anne Hathaway circa *The Devil Wears Prada,* gives us an apologetic expression. I groan.

Dean taps my foot under the table. I want to hiss at him so bad. If I had known that Peter's molecular makeup consists entirely of asshole chromosomes, I would have made additional demands before agreeing to be Dean's fake girlfriend. Not even the opportunity to dine at Rasika, where even the president probably needs a reservation, can make up for having to interact with the blowhard across the table (the naan's spectacular, though).

Barnum's last name is fitting, too, because the man is a circus clown. Molly, who's lovely, must have agreed to marry him under duress; it's the only explanation for this pairing.

I chance a glance at Kimberly and her partner, Nia. Now *this* is an adorable, well-matched couple: two gorgeous Black women who couldn't be more different in looks and personality but finish each other's sentences. Kimberly is tall, her skin dark and rich, and she's just as sarcastic as I am. Nia's petite and fair, her hair an artful arrangement of honey and red-toned locs swept up into a high ponytail, and she bounces as she speaks, as if she's bursting to share her observations because she's worried that she'll forget them. What's even more precious? Despite their long-standing relation-

144

ship, they somehow manage to look like they're still in its honeymoon phase.

I'm not sure the firm partners were thinking clearly when they put together this welcoming committee. Oh yes, it makes *perfect* sense for two white men to give a Black woman insight into what it's like to work at a mostly white law firm. Epic fail, if you ask me. Still, despite the optics, Kimberly and her partner seem to be taking it in stride.

"How about you two?" Peter asks, interrupting my thoughts and directing everyone's attention to Dean and me. "Tell us about the moment you fell in love." He leans forward and addresses Kimberly. "There's a bit of a scandal to the story." His beady eyes glitter with malicious intent. "Can't wait to hear how that all went down."

I hate Peter. Okay, *hate's* a strong word. I dislike him very, very, *very* much. Thankfully, Dean and I prepared for this question on the way over, and as we agreed then, I take the lead now. Leaning ever so slightly toward Dean, I clasp my hands together and take a deep breath. "It happened over time, actually. We'd been roommates for a while, having met through mutual family and friends who knew I was looking for a flexible rooming situation. And because I was

145

always coming and going, we were comfortable simply existing in the same space. Best part? We didn't even share the same bathroom."

It still blows my mind that Dean has two bathrooms in his unit. What I wouldn't give not to share one with Brandon. He treats my period like a string of garlic hanging around my neck, and some days I just want to fling menstrual products everywhere so he can understand how much he *doesn't* see because I'm a considerate (and relatively neat) person.

"Want to try?" Dean asks softly, sliding his plate of palak chaat closer to me.

"Yes, please," I say. I've been eyeing his crispy spinach appetizer since it arrived at the table, so I'm delighted that faking a relationship means I get to sample his food too.

Dean wipes his mouth with a cloth napkin and clears his throat. "See, I met Ella about six months ago and thought I'd found the one. But Solange was never convinced we were right together, and I ignored the warning signs. Solange said I deserved more. That I should be head-over-heels in love. I thought she was being way too romantic for her own good. We talked a lot in the run-up to the wedding. Solange forced me to do a ton of soul-searching. But I'm a stubborn guy, so I just charged forward with my plans because I have a hard time doing anything else."

Poor Dean. He's so earnest as he says this, I can't help thinking that he's noticeably skilled at telling this tale because it's mostly true. Just swap out my name for Max's, and I bet it absolutely is.

"The gag is that Ella was in love with someone else," Peter blurts out, clearly impatient to get to the juicy parts.

"Oh no," Nia says, her hand flying up to cover her mouth. "That's awful."

"You don't have to share this with us," Kimberly says to Dean. "If you want to keep it a private matter, you're more than welcome to."

Knowing that Peter's a jerk with no sense of what's appropriate in a social setting, Dean and I planned for this too.

Dean looks over at me, his eyes glowing with affection. *Well, someone's a quick study.* "It's okay. The short story is she stopped the wedding just in time. And in the aftermath" — he gently takes my hand and strokes it with his thumb — "I realized the person who truly mattered more than anyone else in the world is Solange."

What. A. Faker. I'm proud of him, though.

And slightly off-center as he caresses me. We may need another safe phrase — the kind that'll protect me from enjoying his touches so much.

"Aww, that's too sweet," Nia says, her hands pressed to her cheeks. "Inject it into my veins and keep it coming."

Molly nods along. "You two are the poster children for improbable but satisfying romances the world over."

"That's enough about us," Dean says to Kimberly and Nia. He gracefully moves his hand away from mine. "We're here to answer *your* questions. About DC. About the firm. Whatever."

Kimberly and Nia share a tender glance, then Kimberly says, "Well, as you can imagine, this is a big move for us. Nia and I found a good groove in Atlanta, but it's the right time for her to take advantage of artist-in-residence programs in DC."

Nia jumps in, deftly steering the conversation to her own interests for a moment. "The opportunities in this area are an embarrassment of riches. The arts funding here is heftier than what's available elsewhere. So I see myself staying for a while."

"*We* see ourselves staying awhile," Kimberly interjects, her mouth curving into a half smile as she surveys Nia's face. "And honestly, I'm not averse to starting over somewhere else, so long as I don't take a big hit on seniority."

"I think it's safe to say that won't be an issue at our firm," Peter observes.

Kimberly tilts her head at him. "Oh, yeah? Why's that?"

"Um," Peter says, swallowing hard and visibly fumbling for his next words. "It's just . . . you're an outstanding candidate, and your reputation precedes you."

"Well, let's hope that's the case," Kimberly says to the men. "In the meantime, I'm interested to hear what's kept you both at the firm this long."

"The money," Peter says, chuckling.

"Oh, hush," Molly says.

"What?" he asks, his gaze bouncing around the table. "I'm kidding, of course."

"For me," Dean says, "it's the quality of the work. We have one of the best communications practices in the city. I've learned a lot about media law from the partners, and they give me high-level responsibilities on major cases. You won't push papers or spend hours reviewing thousands of documents looking for the smoking gun. By the time you're a senior associate, you're working on substantive issues and regularly consulting with the firm's clients."

He's handling himself well, but I didn't study the Dean Dossier forward and backward to play the role of a potted plant. I'm fielding this one, too. "What's even more impressive is that the firm lets Dean work on pro bono cases. Even though he has no time to spare, he supervises a team of students at Georgetown who represent low-income DC residents in landlord-tenant cases."

"That's fantastic," Nia says. "Kimberly's been doing pro bono predatory lending cases for years."

"So you know how gratifying it can be," Dean says to Kimberly. "Between us, if I could devote a substantial percentage of my caseload as a partner to pro bono work, I'd take that deal in a heartbeat."

"You would?" I ask, unable to hide the shock in my voice. Recovering quickly, I tack on: "I mean, you never mentioned that to me before."

"The partners would never go for it, though, so there was never any reason to. But yeah, I would."

My jaw goes slack as I try to process this information, which, as I intend to point out to Dean later, was conspicuously absent from his dossier. If there's one trait about

Dean that rankles, it's his preoccupation with becoming a law firm partner, which I thought stemmed from a need to achieve a certain perceived status. Learning that his pro bono work isn't a résumé-building exercise but rather a sign of his commitment to helping others is enlightening. "So when you're working in the office over the weekend, it's because you're —"

"Catching up on pro bono work, yeah," Dean says.

"And the client call the morning of your wedding?"

He nods. "Also pro bono work."

Peter swings his narrow-eyed gaze between Dean and me. Then he leans forward and steeples his fingers. "I'm curious about something, Solange. What do Dean's parents think of you two as an item?"

Kimberly and Nia don't even try to hide their surprised expressions — if I were them, I'd be wondering what the hell is going on too — and Molly drops her chin as if she wants no part of her husband's asinine behavior. Beside me, Dean goes unnaturally still.

Oh, so Peter's going there, is he? *Well, let's do this, buddy.* "It's just his mom, Melissa, and she's cautiously optimistic."

He nods a few times as he considers me, a

151

fake smile plastered on his face. "Good, good. That's great to hear." Undaunted, he flattens his lips into a conspiratorial grin, as if he's inviting me to be an accomplice to Dean's downfall. "Now, you and Dean may be close friends, but I think I've known him even longer than you have. Did he ever tell you he almost flunked out of Michigan?"

I furrow my brow and scratch my temple. This attempt at feigning confusion may be over the top, but I'm having fun with it, so Dean will just have to bear with me. "Wait. That can't be. He went to Penn for under-grad and law school. Graduated with honors too. Are you sure *you* know him as well as you think you do?"

I smile into my hand, the heady scent of victory and Peter's shriveling balls wafting in the air. Kimberly and Nia share an amused glance; they seem to be enjoying the verbal volleying just as much as I am. Can't say that's the case with Dean, though. He's dropped out of the conversation al-together, and when I meet his gaze, a muscle in his jaw twitches.

I lean into him and whisper my next words: "Relax your sphincter. We've got this."

Dean drops his head, but I can see that his shoulders are shaking. *That's better.*

We continue to chat through the rest of the meal — mostly about the highs and lows of our respective careers. Unfortunately, whenever Dean has Kimberly and Nia's attention, Peter tries to usurp it.

"Would you say camaraderie is one of Olney & Henderson's strengths?" Kimberly asks, her tone playful and plainly meant to allude to Peter's ridiculous behavior.

"Generally, yes," Dean says, looking exasperated. "But we can't always pick our colleagues."

Nia snorts. "That's certainly obvious."

Peter, just as clueless as Dean said he would be, chooses that moment to tempt our guests with the prospect of another torturous outing in his company. "Kimberly and Nia, there's so much to explore here, and you should consider us your tour operators. What would you like us to arrange? A baseball game at Nationals Park? A visit to the White House? A show at the Kennedy Center?"

"I'm not sure that'll be necessary. I think we've gotten a good sense of Olney & Henderson's people tonight."

God, I hope not. If so, she's definitely not accepting a position with the firm.

Dean leans over and whispers in my ear. "Peter's being weird. We're losing them."

Again with the breath against my neck. It's so damn distracting. But also: I'd rather eat Miracle Whip in place of mayo for the rest of my life than let Peter sabotage Dean's aspirations. And that's saying a whole hell of a lot.

Before I can think it through, I exclaim: "I have an even better idea! Ever been axe throwing?"

Dean drops his head. But this time, his shoulders aren't shaking.

CHAPTER TEN

DEAN

"Axe throwing? *That's* what popped into your brain?"

For the sake of authenticity, Solange and I hopped into the same Lyft. She's heading to Sip City to hang with Brandon, and I'm heading home to get ready for an early day at work tomorrow.

The driver, Jeff, who can't be much older than the legal drinking age, must have slathered his body with cologne, so I crack open a window to air out the scent of eau de college bro.

Solange's phone comes to life, a dozen or so pings signaling an energetic text conversation on the other end. She sighs heavily, her gaze flicking upward. "Yes, axe throwing *is* exactly what popped into my mind, okay? Kimberly and Nia showed zero interest in the typical touristy things, and I figured something out of the box would spark their interest. I'm sure you'd prefer a more *refined* excursion, but those women were bored out of their minds, and I couldn't imagine another evening looking at Peter's snooty face across a dinner table. It worked, didn't it?"

The way she emphasized the word *refined* snags my attention. Reminds me of her offhand comment about not wanting to be Ella 2.0. "I don't care about being refined or highbrow or whatever, if that's what you're implying. I think Peter's an arrogant prick as much as you do."

"Then *what* is the problem?" she says, throwing her hands up in frustration.

I collapse against the backseat. "It's *axe throwing*, Solange. They're going to ask us to sign waivers. I've never *in my life* read a waiver that I felt comfortable signing. In fact, I once got hired to redo a waiver because I kept arguing with a gym owner about the shoddiness of the version he was asking me to sign. And what if someone gets hurt? The partners would have our *asses* if something happened to Kimberly or Nia. Plus, the sight of blood makes my skin crawl. I passed out at a college blood drive when I saw the plastic thingy —"

"The plastic tube?" Solange asks.

"Yeah, when I saw the plastic tube filling

up." I blow out a slow breath and rake a hand through my hair. "So much could go wrong."

I glance at Solange when I'm done. Her gaze darts to the rearview mirror, and I catch our driver mouthing, *Wow,* before his face goes blank.

Solange lightly squeezes my wrist. "Dean, relax." Her tone is gentle, as if she's trying to calm a skittish horse. "It's going to be all right. Someone at the facility will give you safety tips and show you exactly what you need to do."

"You've done this before?" I ask, enjoying her touch.

She lets go of my wrist and edges closer to her side of the backseat. "I've thrown an axe a few times, and I'm actually pretty good at it. I can even give you a few pointers. I'm telling you, Dean, you're going to love it. The first time I experienced the adrenaline rush of gripping the shaft, I was hooked."

I stare at her and swallow hard. Yeah, my brain went there.

And unfortunately, my brain's been going there all evening. Watching her eviscerate pompous Peter is the sexiest shit I've ever seen. She's just so damn comfortable in her own skin. And she makes me laugh —

enough to distract me from worrying about the possibility that we're going to get caught at any moment. Every time she spoke during dinner, I wanted to throw up a little cheer and shout *That's my girl.*

Except she isn't a girl (in fact, she'd probably pop me in the mouth if I called her that), and she certainly isn't mine. Not really. And fuck, why am I so confused?

Three more outings. With how things are going so far, maybe not even that many. That's all I need to get through. *Repeat after me, Dean: You're not the man for Solange, and she's not the woman for you; stoking this attraction is only going to complicate things. Keep it light. Keep it friendly. Keep any inappropriate thoughts to yourself.*

With that mental reset out of the way, I pat the tops of my thighs and blow out a deep breath. "Okay, I'm going to trust you on this, but let it be known, I have my reservations."

"Dean, at this point, I assume you have reservations about *everything.* There's no need to flag them for me."

Her voice lacks any inflection, so I can't tell if she's being serious or not — until she tilts her head and gives me a saucy grin. *Goddamn it.* I like her. But I don't want to. Not *this* much.

"Thanks for tonight," I tell her. "I literally could not have done it without you."

She stares out the window as the car winds its way through another DC traffic circle. "You're so welcome. It helps that Kimberly and Nia are wonderful people."

"It does."

She turns and peers at me. "And I must say, your performance skills have dramatically improved since this weekend. For a minute there, you had *me* believing you were actually smitten."

"Gold star for Dean, then?"

"Absolutely," she says with a wink.

It was all an act, of course, but I must admit, pretending to be Solange's boyfriend wasn't as difficult as I thought it would be.

SOLANGE

Sip City is the perfect place to decompress after a first fake date from hell.

"Give me every single drink in your repertoire," I say to Brandon. "Just keep 'em coming."

Brandon leans his elbows on the bar counter and taps my nose. "Will you settle for an experimental cocktail?" He waggles his eyebrows. "It has rum in it."

"Is my name Solange?"

He rubs his hands together and backs

away, a beaming smile on his handsome face.

As Brandon prepares my drink, I ignore the nosy text thread Lina started with Natalia, Jaslene, and me, and instead listen to my voice mail. Although it's not entirely unexpected, the second of two messages — the first one's spam — makes my heart sprint in my chest.

"Ms. Pereira, this is Director Cabrini at Victory Academy. I'd like to speak with you when you have a few minutes. I tried to catch you yesterday, but we missed each other."

Oh shit. What's this about?

"Come find me next time you're in," Director Cabrini says. "Take care."

He's probably pissed that I brought the class food from Rio de Wheaton earlier this week. It was a spur-of-the-moment decision, really. I just wanted to do something nice for them. How was I supposed to know the school has a rodent problem?

"It's DC, Solange. Rodents are a large enough contingent in this area they, too, should get their own representative in Congress, that's how."

"See? She's talking to herself," my cousin Lina says behind me. "I told you something was wrong with her."

160

I whirl around and find Lina and Natalia staring back at me. "What are you two doing here?"

"Lina promised me mozzarella sticks if I came," Natalia says as she struggles onto the stool next to mine. Then she drums her hands on the counter. "Let's make it happen, mulher."

Choosing to remain standing, probably to maximize her already sky-high intimidation factor, Lina folds her arms over her chest and gives me a frosty look. "You wouldn't answer any questions about your *date* on the text thread, so we decided an ambush would be the next best thing."

Natalia rummages through her purse and pulls out a snack pack of almonds. "*She* decided," she says, tossing back a few nuts. "I'm just here for the food."

"Where's Jaslene, then?"

"On her way," Lina says.

Resigned to my fate, I wave Brandon over. He hands me my drink and says hello to my cousins, then I order two baskets of mozzarella sticks. Because I know these women, I ask him to throw in a double order of fries for good measure. "Let's move to a table."

Natalia groans. "Seriously? I'm at the stage where standing takes the same effort as vigorous sex. Is it really necessary? Can't we just roll on our sides and do it here?"

"Unless you want to crane your neck for a four-way conversation, yes, it's necessary. And you're going to need to share the food."

"No, I won't," Natalia mutters.

I stand and hold out my arm. "Here, I'll help you."

As Natalia winds (and whines) her way to an empty table nearby, Jaslene rushes through Sip City's revolving door. We wave her over, and she plops down next to me.

"I'm here under protest," Jaslene grumbles, her chin lifted so high I can see up her sweetly stubborn nose.

"Oh, c'mon, Jas," I say, leaning over so our faces are close. "You can't seriously still think I'm the bad guy."

She narrows her eyes and pouts at me, no doubt annoyed with herself that she can't pretend to be upset for more than a few seconds. "No, of course not. But I can hold a nonsensical grudge with the best of them. And it's just . . ."

"It's just what?" I ask.

She scrunches her face as if she's in agony. "I worked so damn hard on that wedding — in a serious time crunch, no less — and it all went up in flames." Straightening, she collects herself, then says, "It's just going to take me a little time to see you and not be immediately reminded that a giant-ass potentially mood-killing footnote will be attached to whatever I say about this wedding whenever I talk about it."

I see her point. That's sure to be an awkward aside for any prospective client. "Fair. I can accept that."

"Jas," Lina says. "Consider this your wedding war story. Every planner has one. Remember the groom whose buddies shaved his eyebrows the night before the ceremony? That's mine."

Jaslene rolls her eyes. "Yours is quirky. Mine is dismal."

A hand massaging her belly, Natalia says, "Don't get worked up about it just yet. Picture this: Solange and Dean get married one day, and *you* end up planning *their* big day. The wedding crasher becomes the bride." Natalia throws down her hands. "Now *that* would be a fucking footnote, baby."

I cringe at the thought. "Yeah. No. Sorry to burst your bubble, but that's not happening. I'm done with emotionally unavailable men who view relationships as an entry on their résumé. That's Dean in a nutshell."

"That *is* Dean," Lina agrees. "But I'm still a softie for him. He has no interest in fall-

163

ing in love, and I don't think it's because he's a selfish guy. It's something else. Wish I knew what."

I know the tea, but I'm not sharing what he told me with this group. Dean has his reasons, and so long as he's being honest with his partners about them, I can't really fault him for elevating compatibility over love. Shit, one more bad relationship and I'll be asking Dean to send me his playbook.

Jaslene sighs. "My love life's nonexistent but not by choice."

Lina puts a hand on Jaslene's arm. "And that's okay. Relationships don't have to be the end goal."

That's what Dean said. But is it so wrong to want to find your person?

"True that," Jaslene says, nodding. "With work during the day and school at night, who has the time anyway? Maybe in the future but it's not a priority right now." She shimmies in her seat. "And I have no problem experimenting with ways to take care of myself." Her eyes widen as though she's just remembered something important. "Oh, I've been meaning to ask: Is it normal for a dildo to make you walk side to side the next morning?"

We all stare at her, then burst out laughing. *I love these women.*

A throat clears and Jaslene jerks at the interruption.

"Order up, ladies," Brandon says.

As another server carrying a large tray with our mozzarella sticks and fries stands in silence, Brandon places the baskets of goodies on the table. "I see someone else joined you, and I don't think I know them."

A flush spreads across Jaslene's cheeks before she drops her head.

"Jaslene, meet my roommate, good friend, and all-around great guy, Brandon. Brandon, meet Jaslene, family friend, wedding planner extraordinaire, and all-around Boricua goddess."

Without looking up, Jaslene puts out a hand in Brandon's direction. "I'm Jaslene. Middle name 'Utterly.' Last name 'Mortified.' "

"It's all good," Brandon says. "No one should ever be embarrassed about satisfying themselves in the privacy of their own home. Especially not someone as lovely as you."

Jaslene's head whips up, her eyes sparkling with interest. Natalia and Lina draw back, their eyebrows raised.

"Okay, Brandon," Natalia purrs. "Get. It."

"Uh, anyway," Brandon says. "Would anyone care for a cocktail?"

165

Natalia points at her swollen belly; the other women shake their heads.

"I'm not a drinker," Jaslene adds.

"I could make you a virgin," Brandon says.

She grins. "Believe me, that ship has sailed, but I admire your can-do attitude."

Brandon drops his head as he backs away. "Well, I walked right into that one." He waves with both hands. "We'll leave you to finish talking. Enjoy."

"Thank you," I singsong as Brandon and his coworker leave us. "This experimental cocktail's excellent, by the way."

"I know," he says over his shoulder.

"Back to this fake relationship with Dean," Lina says as she slides a batch of fries onto a single plate and hoards it. "How'd it go tonight?"

"I think it went as well as can be expected. He crafted a wild story, so recounting it was a distraction. Made it easier not to get tripped up on the details. And the women are genuinely nice.

I'm a little uncomfortable lying to them, but Dean and I are on the same page about making sure the stuff that really matters is one hundred percent truthful. Plus, now that the introductions are out of the way, Dean can focus on sharing the inside scoop about the firm and reeling them in."

"That's good, I suppose," Lina says. "Did you kiss?"

"No, it's not that kind of gig."

Lina nods. "So what's next?"

I dip a fry into my ketchup. "Axe throwing. This Friday."

Jaslene claps enthusiastically. "Sounds fun!"

"Fun would be fine, but uneventful is really what I'm going for," I say. "I need to finish this ruse with Dean, so Brandon and I can engage in our own fake relationship."

Lina blows out a long breath. "Do you hear yourself? Like, truly hear yourself, I mean. Because I bet if you stared in the mirror and repeated what you just said three times, Candyman would appear and tell you to get your shit together. Is fake dating your personality now?"

Jaslene slaps a hand on the table. "Wait, wait, wait. What the hell is going on?"

Lina and Natalia fill her in on Cousin Cláudia's upcoming visit while I scarf down more than my fair share of the fries.

Without missing a beat, Natalia swats my hand away the moment I reach for the last mozzarella stick. "Don't even think about it." She turns back to Jaslene. "So Solange will be faking not one but *two* relationships in the span of a few weeks."

I hit them with a smoldering gaze and throw my shoulder forward. "What can I say? I'm a popular woman."

"Fake dating isn't dating," Lina points out.

I give her a "no duh" expression. "I know."

"Do you?" she asks, her eyes narrowing. "Because it occurs to me that all this fake dating might be a convenient excuse for you to avoid the real thing."

Waving off her preposterous observation, I grab the last fry. "What would be the point of starting to date someone now? I'm leaving DC soon. Besides, it's not my fault that no one's willing to meet my exacting standards."

Lina snatches the fry from my hand. "Or maybe, *just* maybe, you make your standards so exacting to ensure that no one will ever meet them."

"Or maybe, *just* maybe, she's been holding out for someone like Dean," Natalia says.

I shake my head more forcefully than necessary. "No."

"I'm telling you," Natalia continues. "I have a good feeling about this. Scoff if you want, but when you and Dean get married, I'm doing your wedding makeup. And I'm charging you extra for getting those brows

168

under control, mulher."

"Whatever, bitch."

The nerve. Natalia and Lina don't know what they're talking about. Holding out for a relationship with someone who's one hundred percent all in isn't exacting; it's what I deserve. I'd rather be alone than be with someone who isn't prepared to love me with all their heart. I mean, the *least* I can do is learn from my mother's experience. Which means Dean is a nonstarter. Simple as that.

CHAPTER ELEVEN

DEAN

Solange: TGIF - ready for tonight? i'm excited!

Me: Happy Friday! Yeah, I'm ready. Going to send around the waiver to everyone in a few minutes. May as well fill it out before we get there. Don't forget closed-toe shoes.

Me: Still there?

Solange: sorry! i fell asleep while you were capitalizing and adding periods

Me: Cute. Later, "babe."

Solange: ugh, watch it. tchau.

I'm grinning like a fool when Henderson appears at my office door. *Danger, danger. Happiness isn't allowed here.* I straighten in my seat and throw on my poker face.

"Chapman," he says. "Just checking in on your campaign to recruit Kimberly Bailey. How's it going?"

"So far, so good, sir. They seem to already know a lot about the firm, and they've been asking lots of questions."

"That's great to hear," he forces out.

Anything pleasant takes considerable effort for Henderson.

"What else do you have lined up?" he asks.

"We're stepping outside of the box and taking them axe throwing tonight. They loved the idea."

His brows snap together. "I think it's safe to say your generation is headed in a different direction than mine. Maybe that isn't such a bad thing after all." As though he's unsure how to use his long-dormant face muscles, he slowly curves his lips into his best approximation of a smile. "You certainly seem to be doing okay."

It's the closest Henderson has ever come to paying me a compliment, and rather than lap it up the way I thought I would, I'm reminded of Solange's point the day I asked her to be my pretend girlfriend: *Shouldn't working your ass off for eight years suffice?* It should. But it doesn't. And the moment I'm no longer useful to him, Henderson will revert to his old self again.

"Was there anything else, sir?"

Henderson's uncharacteristically jovial expression slips. "Nothing else, Chapman.

Keep me updated on any developments."

"Will do."

A few minutes later, Peter Barnum darkens my door. Apparently, I'm meeting with *all the assholes* today.

"Hey, got a minute?" he asks.

"Sure," I say, minimizing the tabs on my computer because Peter's a crafty gunner who's always trying to advance his own interest and an open tab is potential ammo.

He flops onto a guest chair and leans forward, his grin too wide for my comfort. "I've been thinking: We need to elevate our efforts with Kimberly Bailey. Axe throwing isn't going to cut it. Ba-dum-bump."

I stare at him. "Is there more?"

"Well, with that in mind, I snagged us an invitation to an exclusive party in Adams Morgan on Saturday night."

"Who's throwing it?"

"A law school buddy of mine."

Oh, hell no. I'm picturing stupid-ass togas. And beer kegs. And red plastic cups strewn around a poorly lit room. Just imagining Kimberly and Nia walking across a sticky floor is making me cringe on the inside. "I'm not so sure about this, Peter. What's the crowd going to be like? Because I'm not taking Kimberly and Nia to an all-white frat party."

172

He shakes his head. "No, no, it won't be anything like that. I asked that very question because I had the same concerns and was assured it's going to be a sophisticated and diverse crowd."

Huh. That's surprisingly post-Neanderthal for Peter. Maybe he isn't as bad as I've made him out to be. "Okay, sounds fine to me."

"Great, great," he says, rubbing his hands. "I'll send you the details. There's just one thing: If you don't mind, I'd like you to send out the invitation to the group. See, the law school buddy is actually an old girlfriend, and I don't want Molly to get worked up about it."

Never mind. He's definitely a Neanderthal. "I don't know, Peter. That seems shady."

"It's not, trust me. Just send out the invite. I'm sure it'll come up when we're there, but until then, I'd rather not subject myself to the third degree. Word is, my buddy's going to announce her engagement at the party, so there really is no reason for Molly to be concerned."

Okay, that sounds harmless enough. "Fine. Send me the details and I'll invite everyone."

"Perfect," he says, jumping up. "I'll owe

you one."

Given that it's coming from Peter, I'm not expecting that IOU to be worth much.

Not long after leaving my office, Peter conveniently texts me an invite that I can pass along to the women. *How considerate of you, Peter.* I reformat it, deleting his hokey "Hey, Party People" greeting and composing my own. Kimberly accepts on her and Nia's behalf within minutes. Solange responds an hour later:

I'll go but I'm NOT wrapping myself in a bedsheet or taking Jell-O shots

I bark out a laugh. A single text from Solange and my day is already improved, assholes be damned.

SOLANGE

"Ms. Pereira, hang on a minute!"

Merda. Caught. Just a few steps more, and I would have made it to my classroom. I spin around and watch the head of Victory Academy stride toward me. He's in his forties, I think, swaths of premature gray near his temples blending nicely with his dirty-blond hair. And he's never *not* in a suit. Which immediately makes me think of Dean. Indeed, this is how I picture my fake boyfriend looking in a decade or so.

"Dr. Cabrini —"

174

He waves away my greeting. "You've been here for eight months. Please call me Greg."

"Greg it is, then. It's good to see you."

"Nice sneakers."

I glance down at my Chucks. "I'm going axe throwing this evening."

He tilts his head as though he's never heard of the activity until now. "Right." Then he raises an eyebrow, the corners of his eyes crinkling in amusement. "Have you been avoiding me?"

"Not really, no. It's just . . . I'm organizing a series of career days for my classes, so I've been super busy."

He curves his mouth into a knowing grin. "And avoiding me."

I drop my shoulders. "Is this about the lunch the other day? Because I cleaned up the room afterward. I'm happy to —"

"It's not about the lunch, Ms. Pereira. You can put that out of your mind. Your fellowship ends soon, so I wanted to get your feedback. Do you have a few minutes to chat?"

"Oh, sure. Absolutely."

We walk the short distance to his office, and I take a seat in front of his desk. He strikes a few lines on a Post-it Note, as if he's tracking his to-do list, and sits back in his chair. "So the end of your fellowship is fast approaching, and I just wanted to express my appreciation for your contributions. I also wanted to ask about your experience here. Has it been a positive one?"

"It has. The students are sponges, and the classroom is just so full of life. At first, I didn't know how the year would go. They seemed wary of my intentions. And some of them haven't received the support from teachers they deserved. But once they started warming to me, we got into a good rhythm. I'm hopeful they'll secure internships soon. With Victory's guidance, of course."

"Yes, about that," he says, reaching for a file and opening it in front of him. "The board read your recommendations. They'd like to implement several, and they hate that our budget constraints prevent them from offering you a permanent position."

I'd never tell Dr. Cabrini this, but I'm relieved the board can't offer me a job. It makes my decision to leave DC infinitely easier. Sometimes having choices just means you'll make the wrong ones. "It's okay, Greg. I have something lined up."

"Well, not so fast," he says. "I passed on your recommendations to Ms. Dotty for her input since she's our most senior staff member. She was very impressed. Said your suggestions would breathe new life into the program, and I agree."

That's lovely. Really. But what is the point of all this?

"You see, Ms. Dotty's been considering retirement for some time, and apparently reading your vision for the program convinced her that now is the perfect time for her to step aside."

"Oh God, why? Ms. Dotty's an institution."

"That she is. But here's the thing: People who become institutions bring something larger than themselves to the places they touch. Ms. Dotty is no different. And she's of the opinion that what Victory needs is your energy. She'd like us to have the opportunity to snag you while we have the chance."

I swallow hard. If this is going where I think it's going, I'll scream — internally. "Meaning . . . ?"

"Meaning if she retires now, we'll have enough space in the budget to offer you a position. And we'd task you with helping us overhaul the curriculum."

"Goodness, I'm flattered, Greg. I never imagined this would be a possibility." Truly.

"Well, we're excited to bring you into the fold. I'll need time to work out the details, but I can send you the particulars of the position next week."

"When would I need to decide?"

"Ideally, by the middle of next month. That way, we can get our ducks in a row in time for the fall semester."

One the one hand, wow. On the other hand, ugh. This is the kind of decision that could change my future. It's not one to be considered lightly. Yet with so little time to decide, that's precisely what I'll be doing. "Thank you. I'm honored that so many people have this much faith in me."

"And we'd be honored to have you. So please think it over while I finalize the specifics with the board."

I rise from my chair, then shake his hand. "Will do, Greg." Before I leave, I have to ask: "My mother didn't contact you or anything, did she? About making me a job offer?"

His eyebrows shoot up. "No, not at all."

"Right, right. Of course not." I shake my head.

Still, she's going to be delighted by this news. That makes one of us, at least.

CHAPTER TWELVE

DEAN

The warehouse facility that houses Axe & Snacks sits on a newly developed plot of land on New York Avenue close to the Maryland-DC border. It's slick and rustic at once, a feat accomplished by narrow lanes of reclaimed wood in the axe-throwing area and black-stained oak everywhere else; chain-link fences and chandeliers live in harmony here. I may not be thrilled about our chosen activity, but I can't quibble with the venue. Solange came through for us.

Thankfully, she's the first person to arrive after me. That'll give us a chance to work out any last-minute details. I catch glimpses of her as she weaves her way through the crowd, then she glides to a stop in front of me.

She's dressed as casually as one might expect for axe throwing — jeans, a navy blue fitted top, and burgundy Chucks. Yet her appearance makes as much of an impact on me as I'm sure it would if she were standing in the vestibule in a red-carpet gown. Long lines. Curves. Brown skin that looks soft and inviting. And that fucking hair. Curls and curls and curls, some of them artfully arranged around her face and parted to the side. I take a deep breath through my nose and let it out slowly, my hands itching to touch her even though I have no reason to. There's a lightness in my chest now. As if Solange's presence is enough to curb my unease about navigating this evening's sham.

"Hey," she says, her expression noticeably subdued. "Is anyone else here yet?"

"No, they all canceled."

She tugs on her ear as she surveys her surroundings. "Good, good. That's really good."

Well, something's certainly off. If there's been a constant in my and Solange's interactions, it's that she always gives me her undivided attention. "Hey, what's wrong?"

She whips her head around and looks up at me. "What do you mean?"

"I mean, I was messing with you and just told you everyone canceled, and you said that was really good."

"Sorry," she says, lifting her gaze to the

ceiling as if she's frustrated with herself. "I got some unexpected news today, and I'm still absorbing it."

I pull her over to a relatively quiet corner where there isn't much foot traffic. "Is everything okay?" I can't keep the concern out of my voice, but then I worry it'll only worsen her own anxiety. Bending my knees to meet her gaze, I try to be supportive instead. "Is there anything I can do? If you need to bow out, I can hold the fort here."

She draws back, then takes a fortifying breath. "It's nothing, really. I'm being ridiculous, and there's nothing for you to worry about. At all. Most well-adjusted people would even say it's good news, so ignore me, okay?"

I take her hand and squeeze it. "That's impossible, Solange. There's no way I could ignore you." Well, shit. That rolled off the tongue before I could stop it. "I mean . . . it's obvious you're preoccupied tonight."

"I'm fine. Thanks for caring."

"Do you want to talk about it?"

She shakes her head. "Not necessary. I'm still processing. But thanks for the offer." The sparkle returns to her eyes. "Throwing an axe through the air is exactly what I need to help me get out of my brain. I'm looking forward to this."

"I'm slowly warming to the idea." I gesture with my chin to the play area. "I was watching while I waited, and it doesn't seem all that hard."

"Don't get too cocky, okay?" she says. "We don't want to end this evening with a trip to the emergency room."

"Not going to happen." I make a big show of twisting my upper body and stretching out my arms. "I'm ready."

She flicks her gaze upward, then grabs my wrists, holding me still. "Repeat after me: I am not Paul Bunyan."

Humoring her, I take a step forward and repeat the phrase: "I am not Paul Bunyan."

"Excellent," she says, peeking around my body so she can scan the space. "And since we're still alone I wanted to mention something."

"What's up?"

"Well, this is an informal setting," she says, the pitch of her voice rising. "Which means we're going to be standing around, and I think it would be natural for us to be slightly more affectionate with each other." Seemingly unable to meet my gaze, she continues to scan the crowd. "I'm not talking full-on kissing, of course. Just . . . a shoulder bump here and a squeeze of a hand there would be appropriate. I don't

want to give Peter any reason to start causing trouble again."

I'm plainly in the Upside Down. Solange
is advocating more touching, not less, and
I'm supposed to do what? Remain unaffected by it? This is going to be torture.
"Yeah, of course," I say quickly, looking
down at my wrists, which she's still holding.
"That makes all kinds of sense."

She drops her hands and lets out a shaky
laugh. "Okay, good. We've got maybe one
more outing, I think. So we're almost at the
finish line. It's time for you to close the
deal."

My brain short-circuits for a moment.

"You went there, didn't you?" she asks,
her eyes narrowing.

"I did."

She shoves me away. "I think I hate you
right now."

"No, you don't," I say, pulling her close.
"I think you like me."

"It's all an act," she says, twisting out of
my embrace, her mouth curved into a
lopsided grin. "So don't forget why we're
here."

Ah yes, the deal. Recruiting Kimberly
Bailey to the firm. Closing "the deal" has
always been the goal. But for a moment I

actually needed the reminder. I'd rather not examine why that is.

The gathering is in full swing now that everyone's here. With any luck, I won't sever an appendage or otherwise humiliate myself.

"Are you sure you don't want to join us?" Kimberly asks Molly, her smile welcoming and wide.

Molly sets her drink on the cocktail table behind the axe-throwing lanes and shakes her head. "I have two left hands, so it's probably best if I stay right here. Go have fun."

The rest of the group turns to our instructor, Guillermo, for a few last-minute pointers.

"Hold the hatchet as you would a baseball bat," he tells us. "Step forward, lift the axe straight above your head, and release as it comes down to eye level. Step. Lift. Release. And remember, the point is not to throw it like a brick. You're looking for a single rotation. And it's all about timing."

Peter, the only person *not* wearing jeans, asks, "What about scoring?"

His competitive instincts are kicking in early. Figures.

Guillermo points to a metal bin attached to our lane's chain-link fence. "Pads are over there. Points are on the board. You can go for the blue balls on the fifth and tenth throws."

"Why are heteros so obsessed with blue balls?" Nia asks.

Solange shrugs. "That's a fair question I don't have an answer to. Personally, I'm not a fan."

Guillermo's mouth twitches — he's as entertained by Solange as I am — then he rubs his hands together. "Okay, who's up first?"

Nia bounces on her toes and thrusts a hand in the air. "Me!"

After Nia's first few unsuccessful tries, Kimberly says, "You need to bend your knees more, N." Standing behind Nia, she lightly places her hands around her partner's waist; Nia sways ever so slightly on her feet.

"Like this," Kimberly says. "Got it?"

"Yeah," Nia says, turning to lock eyes with Kimberly, her voice strained.

The chemistry between them is palpable, even when they're nowhere near each other; standing close as they are now, though, their connection is downright electric.

Not surprisingly, Kimberly takes to the sport like a pro, and much to my annoyance, Peter's relatively skilled as well. I hang back, hoping the novelty will wear off for everyone by the time I'm up, so they'll talk among themselves while I embarrass myself.

"Your turn, Dean," Solange says, cupping her mouth to announce that fact to everyone in the place. She pats my stomach in encouragement, then her breath catches. "Oh."

Earlier she suggested we touch more; I assume more flirting is warranted too, so I waggle my brows. "Felt the abs, did you?"

Her eyes flash with . . . something. Whatever it is, I'm greedy enough to want more of it.

"I . . ." She clears her throat. "I certainly did."

"It's not supposed to be a surprise, though, remember?" I whisper. "In this alternate world, you have an open invitation to run your hands over my stomach whenever you want."

She stares at me blankly, then nods. "Right. Got it."

Meanwhile, I'm grinning like a kid in a candy store. I love seeing *her* out of sorts for a change. Throwing Solange off balance may very well become my new favorite pastime. When I look up, she's staring at me, her eyes narrowed in suspicion. Dammit, she's onto me. Knowing Peter's watching our every move, I grab a hatchet, bump her shoulder, then mimic the playful wink she gave me earlier. "Wish me luck."

"You won't need it," she says, her voice low and smoky. "I have a feeling you're going to get very lucky tonight."

Damn, this woman's dangerous to my health. If she keeps talking like that, this hatchet's going to land on my big toe. With just a few words, she's got my brain scrambled. Is this part of our ruse? Or is she flirting for real? And if it's the latter, what the hell am I supposed to do with that? Shaking off the jumble of thoughts in my head, I step up to the line, get into the stance Guillermo recommended, and throw the axe.

Nia and Kimberly, who, along with Molly, are standing around the cocktail table, where a bevy of snacks and drinks await us, cheer me on. It's no use, though. The axe lands flat against the target board and crashes to the ground.

Guillermo clicks his tongue. "You released too early."

"That's what she said," Solange says under her breath.

I fake a pissed-off glare. "Stop trying to distract me."

She straightens and pretends to zip her lips.

Unfortunately, the second, third, fourth,

and fifth attempts don't fare any better. It's official: I suck at this. Still, I set up behind the line once again, vowing to give it one last try.

"Here," Solange says behind me. "Let me help." She's so close her hair grazes my arm. "May I touch you?" she whispers.

I can only nod. The anticipation alone of having her put her hands on any part of my body is making it impossible to concentrate. For a few seconds, I forget where I am and why I'm here. And before I can truly prepare myself, it happens: Her hands are on me, firmly pressing down on my hips.

"Widen your stance," she says, her breath hitching on the last word. "You're leaning forward too much." Before I can adjust my position, her hand slips under my arms and around my middle. With a gentle push, she shows me how to lift my shoulders and torso. Each place her fingers land is a hot spot, sending warmth through my veins and causing my muscles to clench. "Now try again."

A series of images flashes in my mind:

Me, walking her backward with my body.

Solange, raising her arms overhead and threading her fingers through the fabric of the chain-link fence behind us.

Me, grabbing her ass and hoisting her up.

Solange, wrapping her legs around my waist and drawing me close, then pressing her open mouth against my neck.

Christ. I wish I could tell her how I feel. That I want her. But to what end? None of this is supposed to be real, and I promised myself I wouldn't ever toy with a person's emotions.

"Thanks," I say, looking back at her.

She swallows, and my gaze drops to her neck, to the soft skin peeking out from the vee of her shirt.

"Of course," she says, her body inching forward. Then she lowers her voice so only I can hear it. "Peter's up next. It's the perfect time for you to chat up Kimberly without him interrupting."

"C'mon, Chapman," Peter yells. "Stop dawdling. Some of us want to play too."

"Like that," Solange adds, her voice tinged with amusement. "He has a knack for it."

I'm slow to connect the dots, but then it hits me: Solange is strategizing about luring Kimberly to the firm, while I'm . . . thinking about my fake girlfriend, as if *she* were the objective. *Time to get your head out of your ass, Chapman.* "Right. Good point. I'm on it." I lift the hatchet above my head and release the moment it enters my line of sight. Bull's-eye. I spin around and strut

189

like a peacock as everyone cheers. Then I guide Solange to the cocktail table, knowing my window of opportunity to engage in a Peter-less conversation won't last forever.

Molly drifts off to check on her husband, who's taking this activity way too seriously.

"Well done, Chapman," Kimberly says. "Not bad for a first-timer."

I shake my head. "Can't take all the credit. Solange is a great teacher."

Kimberly taps Solange's hand. "I've been meaning to ask you. What's it like being with him? I mean, do you see each other, or are you two ships passing in the night?"

"Hmm," Solange says. "Honestly, he's a bit of a workaholic. He's in the office nearly every day, and we rarely go out on the weekends. We haven't hung out together this much in a while. I get it: He wants to make partner. But sometimes I wish he'd jump off the treadmill. Smell the cherry blossoms, so to speak." She gives me a playful hip-bump. "I should point out that this is totally a Dean thing. Molly says Peter's always home for dinner."

I'm stunned. Save for the implication that we're a couple living together, Solange didn't tell a single lie. I *am* a workaholic. An occasional pickup game with Max at my neighborhood Y does not a social life make.

And even when Ella and I were dating, we essentially worked on separate projects at home most evenings. Solange would never put up with that shit.

Nia nudges Solange with her shoulder. "They've been talking so much about *his* work. What about yours?"

Solange gives them a crash course in her workforce development curriculum, eventually mentioning that she's hosting a Career Day event next week.

"Sounds interesting. What do you have planned?" Nia asks.

"It's totally informal. Just a day for the students to learn about various careers. I've invited people from different professions to visit the classroom and share their wisdom or whatever else they want to talk about."

Kimberly turns to me. "Let me guess. She roped you into talking about being a lawyer."

I blank for a minute but recover quickly. Figuring it would be weird if Solange *didn't* ask her boyfriend to speak to her class, I nod as if the invitation were a foregone conclusion. "You know it. There was no way she'd let me dodge that assignment."

Nia's eyes light up. "Oooh, Solange, I'd be happy to speak to your students if you'd like. I can share my own path, which was nontraditional too, so maybe it'll resonate with them?"

"Oh my God, I'd love that," Solange says, beaming. "Thank you, thank you. But it's only a few days away. Next Wednesday at five. Would that work for you?"

"We'll still be around," Kimberly says. "I have another round of interviews later in the week. But how about we make an evening of it? Maybe go to dinner afterward?"

"Sounds great," I say. "I'll fill Peter in on our plans later." He's currently pacing the width of his lane and muttering to himself while Molly tries to calm him down.

I'm all smiles about getting another opportunity to hang out with Kimberly and Nia — I thought tomorrow's party would be our grand finale — but then I realize my big, lying mouth has roped me into speaking at Solange's Career Day event. Judging by the way Solange is sheepishly baring her teeth at me, that fact just dawned on her too.

She sidles up to me as Nia and Kimberly chat on their own. She leans in so close, her shoulder brushes against my chest, then she rises on her toes and whispers in my ear. "Told you not to get too cocky, didn't I?"

Damn. Solange is just standing next to

me, but I'm wrapped up in her. The warmth of her breath skates over my skin. The coconut scent in her hair drifts around us. And her face is inches from mine, hijacking my view. It takes a herculean effort not to pull her closer, but I manage to resist the urge and instead bend to her ear. "You only told me not to get too cocky about axe throwing."

"It goes without saying: You shouldn't get too cocky about anything."

"Are you sure about that? I can think of one big reason why being too cocky could be considered a plus."

She draws back, her mouth rounding in a soft O. I appear to have rendered her speechless. Which tells me I'm crossing the very lines I said I never would.

Nice job, Dean.

CHAPTER THIRTEEN

DEAN

The good news is that Kimberly and Nia are having such a great time they begged us for a tour of the U Street Corridor, which conveniently ended at Sip City.

The even better news is that Peter and Molly passed on joining us.

The bad news is that I can't seem to focus on anything but Solange.

The even worse news is that the women just trotted off to the karaoke room, and before they left, they announced that if I dare to enter, I should be prepared to get up onstage too. But that's the kind of shit Max would do, not me.

After squeezing my way to the counter, I spot Brandon.

He points to the end of the bar, and I meet him there. Like clockwork, he slides me a stool so I can claim a space that's blessedly free of anyone on my left.

"Thanks, man."

"No problem. You look like you need to be put in the time-out corner anyway."

It's unclear whether he's suggesting I'm acting like a child, but I'm not going to press for an explanation because I'm coming to him for salvation, and I don't want to give him an excuse to refuse me. "I need tequila. Lots of it. Served as shots, please."

Brandon leans against the counter and tilts his head as he considers me. "I thought you said tequila's your Kryptonite."

I meet his gaze and give him a "no shit" expression. "It is."

He taps the bar counter with a closed fist and straightens. "Understood. Be right back."

Solange, who had a head start on cocktails at Axe & Snacks, comes out of nowhere and jostles me. "Hey, what are you doing out here?" With a glass in hand, she points behind her to the karaoke room's neon sign. "Your guests are in there."

She's being so damn cheerful. Meanwhile, I'm tamping down the urge to growl at everyone because I want something I shouldn't — namely, *her.* "Just needed a moment," I say, remaining hunched over so I'm not forced to meet her eyes. "I'll join you soon."

Brandon appears again — without my damn tequila.

Solange raises her glass in his direction, her mouth curved into a wicked smile. "This isn't one of your better concoctions, my friend."

Brandon purses his lips at her, but his eyes are noticeably brighter now that she's around. "Hey, if you can't say anything nice —"

"Then you're a bitch, and you may as well own it," she finishes for him.

They high-five and stick their tongues out at each other before collapsing into laughter.

It's clear that Brandon and Solange are close. *Really* close. They complete each other's sentences. Share inside jokes. Bump shoulders when they're standing side by side. I'm zero percent jealous of their rapport. But I'll confess to being envious of it. And it's worrisome as hell that I want to have that kind of bond with Solange at all.

"Okay, Chapman," she says, bouncing on her toes. "I'll entertain Kimberly and Nia while you consult with Brandon about whatever's troubling you." She slides her empty glass toward Brandon, spins in my direction, and taps me on the nose. "Don't take too long."

Brandon steps away with Solange's empty

glass and returns with a slim wood tray designed to hold liquor shots. "I'm guessing whatever's troubling you is Solange."

My gaze snaps to his face. The amused expression is hard to miss. "Wrong."

"You sure about that?" Brandon asks.

"What's that supposed to mean?"

"It's just that I've been watching you, and you probably didn't even realize it, because you've been watching Solange this whole time."

"Have I?" I readjust my position on the stool and massage my neck. "It's probably just a trick of the lighting."

"Riiiight," he says, setting one of the shot glasses in front of me. "Maybe this isn't my place, but you seem like a decent guy, and I know from Solange that you've had a rough time of it, seeing as you *just* broke up with your fiancée."

This conversation is making me want to fidget, and I don't fucking fidget for anyone. I'm not surprised they talked about me. After all, they live together, and he knows Solange and I are fake dating. Still, it's not knowing exactly *what* was said that makes me uncomfortable. And I can already predict the gist of what he's going to say. "Are you about to warn me not to get any ideas about Solange? Because if you are, you can

197

stop while you're ahead. The warning's unnecessary."

"So you're telling me you have no interest in her."

I take the first shot and slam the glass on the counter. "That's exactly what I'm telling you. We're platonic friends."

He laughs. "Solange and I are platonic friends. You two" — he gestures at me dismissively — "are something else. I'm just trying to figure out what that something else is exactly."

My blunder becomes apparent as soon as he attends to another patron's order: By being so adamant that he was misjudging the situation, I deprived myself of hearing whatever it is he was about to say, and now I *really, really* want to hear his take on why I should avoid Solange at all costs. I'm going to look like a schmuck, but screw it — I'll live.

When he's done ringing up another customer, I lift a finger in the air to get his attention again. "Okay, just so we're clear: You are way off the mark, but now I'm intrigued. What were you going to say?"

He twists his mouth as he watches me, as if he's both amused by my bluff and unsure how much he should disclose. Eventually, he nods to himself and shares a whole hell of a lot. "You can't half-ass anything with Solange. Not your friendship, not your opinions, and especially not your emotions. If you intend to play games, do that shit elsewhere. She deserves someone who's going to love her fiercely, so unless you think you can be that person someday, there's no point in going down that road."

Well, hell. Talk about putting me in my place. The weird part is, more than anything, I'm glad Solange has Brandon in her corner. But his warning still stings. And yeah, okay, it's the reality check I needed. "Is that why you've never made a move on her?"

He gives me a sly smile. "How do you know I haven't?"

That piece of information makes me sit up straighter, even though I know it shouldn't. I take my second shot and grimace as the tequila slides down my throat.

"Something wrong, Dean?" he asks as if it's an innocent question even though he knows damn well it isn't.

"Are you fucking with me?" I ask.

He taps my arm and nods. "I am."

"You two do that a lot."

"That's why Solange and I get along," he says, looking smug and so assured of his role in her life.

"How'd you meet her?"

"High school detention," he says. "I was a class clown. She refused to wear the gym uniform and organized a protest among her classmates. We were a match made in heaven despite our age difference."

So Solange was a rabble-rouser; that doesn't surprise me at all.

"Does she date?" I ask.

"That's a question for Solange. I'll just say this: I seriously believe if she finds herself in another bad relationship, she'll agree to marry me as her final resort." He dons this pensive expression, then glances at me before adding, "She tell you we're heading to Vegas in a couple of weeks for my birthday?"

I throw back the third shot. "I think she mentioned something about that in passing."

He taps his chin and twists his lips back and forth. "You know, it occurs to me: That could be the perfect place to pop the question." He laughs. "Friends getting married for convenience — it's what all the millennials are doing these days."

I wouldn't go *that* far, but yeah, isn't that what I was trying to do with Ella? In fact, the idea that Solange would marry Brandon because he checks all the boxes except one comes directly from the pages of my own master plan. I can see it happening, even if I know it's not the right outcome for someone who obviously wants to find long-lasting love. Still, the way Brandon's staring, I can tell he's just trying to get a rise out of me.

"Cut the bullshit, Brandon. I know you want more for Solange than that. You said it yourself: A guy only stands a chance with her if he's as committed to her as she is to him."

"You misunderstand, Dean," he says, picking up a dish towel and wiping the counter. "A guy only stands a chance if he can love her the way she deserves to be loved. Period. But no such man has ever brightened our door. And given your recent history, I doubt you're going to be the exception."

I force out a laugh. What a ridiculous conversation. "Brandon, I'm not *trying* to be the exception."

He raises an eyebrow. "Then why are we talking about this?"

That's an excellent fucking question. Because one thing I know is this: Solange and I are about as mismatched as any two people can be.

One, she's committed to helping others, wherever that may take her; I'm committed to volunteering, sure, but achieving financial security and planting roots here in DC is my primary focus. Hell, come next month, she'll probably be in Ohio, then who the hell knows where else.

Two, I'm looking for someone who'll embrace the idea of being one half of a professional power couple; Solange would be miserable attending even one of the firm events I'm obliged to attend each year, and I wouldn't want to put her through that anyway. I mean, she once likened hanging out with lawyers to getting a gynecology exam and root canal on the same day. Enough said.

Three, and most important, she wants someone who's so in love with her they'll follow her to the ends of the earth; I'm searching for a person who's pragmatic enough to accept that love doesn't always have to be the endgame.

I square my shoulders and take my final shot, welcoming the burn in my chest and the haziness in my brain. This is nice. Real nice. "Can I get another round, please?"

Brandon shakes his head. "Sorry, no. That's your fourth shot, and in case you forgot, the reason you and Solange are fake dating is because you're supposed to be schmoozing those women in there."

Dammit. He's right. Why is it so hard to focus on closing the deal, as she put it? *Because your attraction to Solange is clouding your judgment, that's why.* Well, no more. We are, and always will be, platonic friends. From here on out, I'm guaranteeing it.

Inside the karaoke room, Solange makes a show of tossing back her glass of water as though it's tequila, then slams the glass on the table. "All right, people." She points to the stage. "Who's going up there?"

Nia shimmies in her seat. "I'm game!"

Kimberly rolls her eyes. "I'll pass."

Nia isn't satisfied with that answer, however, and slides closer to Kimberly on the bench, giving her puppy-dog eyes and pouting. *"Please."*

"Ugh, how can I resist that face?"

Nia bats her eyes in triumph and throws her arms around Kimberly; they truly are a sweet couple.

"Oooh, can all three of us do something together?" Solange asks.

Nia and Kimberly nod enthusiastically, then the three women rush up to the stage, their arms linked as if they're old friends. Solange turns back and yells: "Watch our drinks, Dean!"

Wide-eyed and smiling, they sift through

the pages of a plastic binder, presumably containing their song options. Minutes later, I spy Solange and Nia conversing with the emcee, a short white guy in a black leather vest and jeans.

Solange walks up to the mic. "We're dedicating this to a friend in the audience. Dean, this one's for you."

The house lights go down, and the spotlights land on the women, all of whom are frozen in *Charlie's Angels* poses.

Shit. I don't think I'm ready for this jelly.

The music starts, and I immediately recognize the song: Ariana Grande's "Thank U, Next." When it first came out, the admins in our office played the clean version in the lunchroom as if it were their new anthem — until someone played the explicit version and the all-firm email advised that only music played through personal headsets would be permitted going forward.

Back then, it seemed like nothing more than a woman's savage (and appropriate) takedown of her exes. Listening to it now, I realize the song is about learning from your failed relationships, and I'm wondering what lesson these women think I should learn from my breakup with Ella. Doesn't matter. The main takeaway from the Ella shitshow is that I was right: Turning your life upside down over love is a fool's errand.

Still, the audience is enjoying the show, and when Solange, Kimberly, and Nia are done, several people stand and clap for them. A few customers even whistle to show their praise, and the women gleefully bask in the well-deserved attention.

The trio stumbles back to our table, laughing the entire way.

"Outstanding, ladies," I say. "Outstanding."

"Anyone else?" Solange asks, looking directly at me. "Or we could do a deep dive into the meaning of that song and how you can apply it to your own experiences, Dean."

Faced with the choice of either embarrassing myself onstage or listening to these women dissect my dating life, I ask myself a familiar question: What would Max do? The devil in my ear (who's especially fond of making a fool of me) knows the answer and prods my shoulder with a pitchfork. I jump up. "I'll do it!"

"Seriously?" Solange asks, her eyes wide. "*This,* I must see."

Nia pumps her fist. "You. Are. The. Best. Host. Ever!" She stumbles a bit, then plops onto her chair, the skin on her face and neck flushing in a striped pattern.

"I think that's our cue to leave, unfortunately," Kimberly says. "Nia's not a heavy drinker, and that flush on her skin is a warning sign. We'll see you two at the party tomorrow."

I'm glad Peter's not here to see any of this. First thing Monday morning, he'd give the partners a twenty-minute oral report on tonight's events and cast me as a villain.

After saying our goodbyes and seeing Kimberly and Nia off, Solange and I return to the karaoke room.

Solange purses her lips and gestures to the stage. "Well? I'm waiting."

Damn. She's really not going to let this go, huh?

Before I can lose my nerve, I squeeze my way to the stage and place my name on the wait list. I'm too buzzed to read the binder of song titles, so I motion the emcee over.

"I'd like to do 'Pony' by Ginuwine. The one from *Magic Mike.*"

The emcee draws back and looks me up and down. "Seriously?"

What's up with that? Do I not look like the kind of guy who will tear up a rendition of "Pony"? "Yes, seriously."

He throws up his hands as if he's backing off. "Sorry. I just figured that's a little dance-heavy."

"Don't worry about it. I can hold my own."

"You get to skip the queue, then," he says, shaking his head, a cheesy grin on his face.

I hop onto the stage and immediately zero in on Solange's husky voice egging me on.

"Woohoo," she yells from her place at the table. "Sing like you mean it."

Oh, I will. Don't you worry about that, Solange.

A spotlight lands on me, and the song's opening bars vibrate through the room. I sing the first line about being a bachelor looking for a partner. Everyone goes wild. My body takes over, buoyed along by the hum of the crowd, the fire in my belly, and the heat from the stage lights. It's as if Channing Tatum himself is in the audience and I don't want to disappoint him. A woman at a table up front walks up to the stage and slaps a dollar bill on the platform. Maybe the alcohol's messing with me, but I regard that as a challenge and accept it like the Magic Mike protégé I've always wished to be. I place the microphone back in its cradle, unbutton my shirt, and toss it into the crowd.

Then the lights go out, and Big Dean starts to grind.

SOLANGE

Is. This. Happening?

Dean is onstage reenacting Channing Tatum's provocative performance of "Pony" in *Magic Mike,* and I am enthralled. He's gyrating, thrusting, and humping like a pro, his nuanced portrayal of the troubled stripper who finds himself standing at professional and personal crossroads that threaten to . . . never mind.

Jesus, Dean has rhythm, and a very fine ass (not America's ass, mind you, but respectable nonetheless). My nipples are sufficiently intrigued by this newfound information and pucker at attention; admittedly, their standards are low these days — a strong gust of wind would also do the trick — but nonetheless, they're delighted with the upgrade.

Does Dean realize where he is? Does he remember *who* he is? Surely, he's having an out-of-body experience. Granted, the body he's in right now is uh-ma-zing, but this spectacle onstage doesn't match up with how he usually behaves in public — the man's hair is out of place, for God's sake.

Then again, he's been acting out of character all evening, starting with his flirty behavior at Axe & Snacks. That comment about having a good reason to be too cocky?

Come. On. I'm surprised I didn't burn up and turn to ash on the spot. There's only so much attraction I should be forced to fight in a single night.

I follow his movements on the stage like I'm tracking a target with a sniper's rifle. On the outside, I'm acting as though Dean's bare chest is nothing new to me, but inside I'm flailing. He's neither massive nor ripped. But he's a presence, the V-shape of his swimmer's torso making it difficult for my greedy gaze to decide where it wants to land. And who gave Dean the right to possess lats that wide? *Use those wings to fly to me, baby. Fly.*

Dean grabs the microphone off the stand and drops to the ground. Pretending the mic is a power drill, he slides up and down on his knees as he drives imaginary screws into the stage floor. He's been killing it this whole performance, but after that move, consider me murdered.

Letting out a shameless whimper, I slide down in my chair. A woman nearby uses the bar's laminated cocktail menu to fan my face.

I'm calling it right now — time of death: 9:42 P.M.

As I wait for the coroner's office to process my body, Dean jumps off the stage and his adoring fans circle him, their earsplitting cheers filling the room. After soaking up his well-earned adoration and slipping his shirt back on, he jogs up to the table and drops into the chair Nia abandoned a few minutes ago. "Was it too much?" He bares his teeth sheepishly as he waits for me to answer.

"No, it was just right, Goldilocks. I mean, what the hell got into you?"

"Four tequila shots and that Rusty Nail from earlier got into me. That's a lot of hard liquor for this little ol' body."

"And yet you were able to maintain your coordination. How lucky for us all."

Smiling, he reaches around me and swipes a napkin off the table, then pats his forehead dry. "Seriously, though, what did you think?"

"Honestly? I was distracted by the lyrics. Like, who the hell has a pony these days? Not only is it crass to boast that you have a pony, but also it's unfair to indiscriminately offer it up for a joyride." I let out a deep sigh. "Who's protecting the ponies here?"

Dean throws his head back and bites down on a laugh.

The long column of his neck is so lickable. Gah. It's time to get out of here; if I stay any longer, I'm going to end up asking him for a ride on *his* pony, and I truly doubt

I'd ever want to get off. "I think I'm going to check in with Brandon. His shift ends soon. He said he would walk home with me."

Dean sits up and his expression cools. "Of course. Sure. I need to use the restroom anyway." Then he slowly rises from the chair. "I'll see you at the party tomorrow."

I give him a goofy-ass salute. "I'll be there."

"Good," he says, nodding once.

As I watch Dean leave the karaoke room, I sway to the music, pretending I'm completely unaffected by him even though that couldn't be further from the truth. From here on out, I should be addressed as Solange of House Pereira, the Worst of Her Name, Queen of the Liars, Breaker of Vows, and Mother of Bad Ideas. I'm trying to resist my attraction for him, though. God, I'm *really, really* trying.

I drag my pathetic butt back to the main bar and claim a seat. An attractive Latinx man immediately tries to snag the spot next to mine, his gaze zeroed in on me. I'm not in the mood for conversation, so I whip out my hand to stop him. "It's taken, sorry."

"Are you?" he asks with a nod and a wink. "Taken, I mean."

Gross. As I prepare to deliver a monologue

211

on the vestiges of patriarchal values and their unfitness in modern American society, Dean slides onto the empty stool and swivels mine around so that I'm facing him. It's a lot to take in. His flushed skin. The damp hair around his temples. The way his shoulders rise each time he takes an unsteady breath. I tell myself he's still experiencing the effects of being onstage, but I know there's more to his demeanor than that.

His piercing gaze leaves no doubt that I'm his sole focus, and for a moment I forget that dozens of people are in the vicinity, the sounds of clinking glasses and raucous conversation fading to a dim hum. He studies my mouth, then returns my stare, a silent question in his eyes.

Our safe phrase tumbles out of my mouth far too easily. As though I've been waiting for the perfect excuse to use it. "You can't help yourself, can you?"

"No, I can't," he says roughly, his chest heaving as he slides his legs out to make room for me to fit between them.

I lean over and place my hands on the tops of his thighs; within seconds, Dean's kissing me. Maybe he meant it to be chaste. Just a brief meeting of our lips simply to signal to my unwelcome admirer that I'm not alone.

But that's not what this is.

Holy shit, that is far from what this is.

He traces his soft lips across mine, then angles his head to deepen the kiss, emitting a low rumble in his throat that sounds like he's begging for more. In answer, I splay my hand across his jaw and tangle my tongue with his, my ass rising off the stool to bring us even closer. There's heat everywhere. Radiating off him. Off me. Surrounding us. Dean snakes a hand around my neck and under my hair, holding me steady in a loose grip that makes me ache to stroke him. Not here but somewhere close enough that we wouldn't need to separate our bodies to get there. His fingers press against the back of my skull, massaging it, and I shudder against him.

"I feel it too," he murmurs against my lips, then he grazes my jaw with his teeth.

Oh God. My chest fills with air, like a balloon filling, filling, filling, and straining to burst, tight from the pressure of holding myself in check in a public place. This moment? I never want it to end.

But it does, of course.

Someone in the bar whoops — whether at us or the images on the large-screen TV overhead, I'm not sure. Dean and I spring apart, our breathing slow and heavy, the

213

longing in his gaze surely mirroring mine.

"One water for Dean and a Blackberry Jam for the self-saboteur," Brandon says, his eyes dancing with mischief.

In my mind, I shoot laser beams at my friend, and he disintegrates to dust. From here on out, I'm addressing him as Brandon of House Harris, the Worst of His Name, King of the Traitors, Breaker of Balls, and Father of Cockblockers.

As Brandon makes a big show of placing beverage napkins on the counter, Dean and I right ourselves, the pickup artist who started us down this path long gone.

After taking two large gulps of water, Dean peers inside his glass as if it's an aquarium and he's searching for marine life within its depths. Is he as gobsmacked by the intensity of that kiss as I am?

Wait. What am I doing? How is this productive? I'm looking for someone who's all in. Dean's the kind of man who prides himself on being all out. Encouraging anything other than platonic friendship with him would be the baddest of bad decisions. So it's obvious what I need to do here. Drawing a deep breath, I shake out my arms. "Thanks for the rescue, Chapman. I've got to hand it to you, that was *very* convincing. Your acting skills are improving by the day."

His thumb pauses on the glass, then he stands and raps on the bar counter twice. "Right. It helps that I'm a quick learner. Glad I could be of service." He doesn't even glance at me before he takes off. "Enjoy the rest of your night, Solange."

"Take care, Dean," I call after him.

Then I drop my head on the bar. That didn't feel good. Or right. But it felt safe. And when it comes to Dean, safe is what I'm aiming for. I want to get out of this arrangement unscathed. And if that means I need to pretend my and Dean's kiss was a means to an end rather than a tantalizing glimpse of how explosive we could be together, so be it.

DEAN

"What are you doing here? Didn't you see the No Loitering sign?"

When I get home from Sip City, Max is lounging on a bench in front of my building, wearing basketball shorts and a white T-shirt that's seen better days, as if he threw on whatever was on the floor of his bedroom to come over.

"This is a reconnaissance mission," he says, rising to his feet. "Solange isn't answering her text messages, so I've been ordered

215

to return with answers, and I mean to comply."

"Lina's issuing orders now? Where's your pride?"

He shrugs. "I'm whipped, man. And I couldn't care less what you think about it."

His moony expression tells only a tiny fraction of the story that led him to fall for his older brother's ex-fiancée. Not all of it was pretty, but I can't argue with the result: My best friend looks happy. I truly hope he stays that way.

Blowing out a breath, I stride past him and hold the door open. "You're not staying long. I need to go into the office tomorrow."

Max shakes his head. "On a Saturday? There's more to life than work, you know."

"Actually, right now, there isn't. I'll get to the good stuff later."

I've relied on myself for a long time. My job helped me buy this place. Allowed me to pay off my loans. Gave me something to do. Without it, I'm not sure where I'd be. Max's mother is also his employer; he can't possibly know what it's like to have a boss who doesn't care whether he succeeds or fails. So, yeah, I'm keeping my head down and focusing on the one thing that'll secure my place at Olney: partnership. Vacations, hanging out on the weekends, dating, starting a family — all of that will happen in due time.

We take the stairs rather than wait for the notoriously slow elevator.

"How are the fake dates going?" Max asks behind me as I open the door to my condo. "Is Solange dazzling them?"

I drop my keys in the bowl on the credenza, flip the lights on, and toe off my shoes. "She's amazing, man. Engaging and supportive. Gets along with the women. And best of all, Peter doesn't intimidate her." Max tries to walk past me, but I block him with my outstretched arm. "Shoes."

He grimaces while he removes them. "These new floors are making you an extra pain in the ass." Grumbling, he strides to the kitchen and pokes his head in the fridge. "Grapes, dude? Seriously? Where's the cake? The leftover pizza?"

"At the grocery store, you schmuck."

He sucks his teeth, then straightens. "So that's it? You're done fake dating Solange?"

I blow out a harsh breath. If only. "Nope, still two more dates to go. We're taking them to a party tomorrow. Some exclusive event in Adams Morgan."

He crosses the room and flops onto my couch. "Okay, then. You're almost there. Why aren't you happier about it?"

"Solange and I kissed tonight," I blurt out.

And I can still taste her lips on mine.

And I can still hear her breathy moans of encouragement.

And I can still feel her sensuous curves molding to my body.

She may as well be in this room. Fuck.

Max sits up, his expression blank. "Okay, and . . . ? You're pretending to be a couple. You both knew a peck on the lips would be a possibility, right?"

I fall back onto a kitchen stool and sigh. "It wasn't a peck, and it had nothing to do with fake dating. Some guy was hitting on her at the bar, so we played it off like we were together." I rake a hand through my hair. "Honestly, the kiss wasn't necessary. It's just . . . I wanted to, and so did she. But I'm worried that I overstepped. Or misread what was happening and now it's going to be awkward between us."

Max crosses his arms over his chest and studies me for a long moment. "You're being too hard on yourself, D. She's human, and so are you. You're doing couple shit. Being cozy. Touching each other here and there. Stuff like that can mess with your brain." He tilts his head and peers at me. Hard. "Wait. You're not catching feelings for her, are you?"

"Of course not."

But I can't say I'm totally unaffected.

"Good," he says, nodding. "Then pretend it never happened and make sure you limit your interactions with her for these next two dates. Don't be an asshole, of course, but don't go out of your way to be overly affectionate either. That should be easy enough, right?"

I lick my lips. Which immediately makes me think of hers. "Right."

Wrong.

He brings his hands together in a single clap and jumps up from the sofa. "Excellent. My work here is done, then. And since you don't have any good munchies, I'm gone."

"You bastard," I say, clutching the front of my shirt. "I always knew you were just using me."

"Glad we could finally get that out in the open," he says, wearing a smirk as he puts on his sneaks.

I stride to the door and point to the hall. "Out."

He stops in front of me, grabs my chin, and squeezes it. "When am I going to see this gorgeous face again? I miss it."

I roll my eyes and push him past the threshold. "Basketball. Thursday. Now go."

"Remember, it's fake dating. Be sure to keep it that way." Then he saunters down the hall and pushes open the stairwell door.

It's in my nature to give Max a hard time, but I appreciate the reminder. Because as much as I hate to admit it, I needed one.

CHAPTER FOURTEEN

DEAN

The party Saturday night kicks off with a dud. On the drive over, I get three texts in quick succession:

Kimberly: Hi Dean! Nia isn't feeling well so we're going to sit this one out. Karaoke got the best of her. Sorry for the late notice, but we'll see you on Wednesday for Career Day and dinner. Have fun!

Peter: Hey Dean. Molly found out my ex is hosting the party and flipped. Says I'll sleep on the couch for a month if I go. Staying home to keep the peace. Just use my name to get in. Give Kimberly and Nia my regrets. Tx.

Solange: be there in 5 mins

Well, shit. This changes everything. And makes it a thousand times harder to limit my remaining time alone with Solange as

221

Max suggested.

Since Kimberly's and Peter's texts aren't time sensitive, I respond to Solange first.

> *Me:* No need to rush. I'll explain when you get here.
> *Solange:* ok!

Funny how a tiny exclamation mark can make you feel better about seeing someone again. It tells me Solange and I are still on good terms. The alternative — that I caused irreparable harm to our budding friendship when I kissed her last night — is too unsettling to contemplate.

I take a moment to respond to Kimberly, then I send Peter a thumbs-up. It's petty, yes, but I'd like Peter to think we're having an excellent time; I'll tell him about the cancellation on Monday.

My Lyft driver pulls up to the address in the invite just as a few people are entering the only row home on the block with a front porch.

I add a sizable tip for the trip and climb out. "Thanks, man."

My otherwise quiet driver snickers. "No problem. Have a good time."

It's an odd thing to say — he doesn't know what I'm doing here — but I figure that's his standard farewell, or he meant to say "take care" in that same embarrassing way I always say "you too" when a server tells me to enjoy my meal.

I wait for Solange by the stoop, occasionally nodding at the other partygoers filing in. Most people are dressed in dark slacks or suits, as if they've come directly from work even though it's the weekend. Considering we're in DC, I'm sure that's the case for at least some of the folks passing by me.

Solange appears when she said she would, her cell phone pressed against her ear as she speaks to someone on the line. Her hair is fluttering around her shoulders, and her long strides are eating up the sidewalk as if it's a runway. Like me, she's dressed in black from head to toe. Unlike me, she's mesmerizing in a gauzy top and pants that cinch above her ankles. I clench my hands, then release them, my breath quickening the closer she gets. Probably residual nerves from the unexpected turn of events last night.

She stops a foot away from me and mouths, *Sorry,* as she points to her phone. I mouth, *No problem.* She doesn't seem to be concerned about my overhearing her conversation, so I simply wait for her to finish up.

"Mãe, I know," she says, crossing her eyes. "There's nothing to worry about. Of course we have clean sheets. Yes, yes, and coffee. Sugar too. Sure, bring towels if you want. Tá. Vejo você amanhã. Te amo!"

"What was that about?" I ask.

"Our cousins from Brazil are coming to visit next weekend. A couple of them are bunking with Brandon and me, and my mother wants to be sure we'll have everything they'll need."

"That's considerate of her."

Solange tucks her phone into her purse — a little crossbody number that probably can't hold more than a few items — then drapes the bag over her shoulder. "Dean, she asked if I had enough toilet paper for everyone to wipe their butts for at least three days. She's the most inconsiderate person I know."

"But you love her."

Wearing a wistful expression, she quickly agrees. "More than anyone else in the world." She scans my face and outfit, then curves her red-stained lips into a wide smile. "You look great, by the way."

"Not half as great as you."

She curtsies. "Why, thank you." Then she glances at the row home. "Where's everyone else?"

"Kimberly bowed out. Nia wasn't feeling well."

"And Peter?"

"Molly's pissed at Peter. They're not coming."

She sighs, then blows out a raspberry. "Wait. Are you telling me I could be lying on my couch in my sweats right now? Eating Cherry Garcia and watching *The Circle,* no less?"

I can't help grinning. She's nothing if not honest. A party like this one, attended by DC's elite and trading on its exclusive vibe, is the last place Solange would choose to go. Honestly, this isn't my bag either, but I regard it as a necessary evil of firm life. "I'd understand if you didn't want to bother going inside."

She sweeps her arms out to her sides. "Do you see this outfit? These shoes?" She points at her mouth. "This is Velvet Ribbon by Lisa Eldridge."

I purse my lips. "I don't know what that means."

"Neither do I," she says, her hands flailing. "But Natalia sure does. Point is, I made an effort tonight, and I expect to be rewarded with a nice glass of wine and decent hors d'oeuvres."

"Well then, let's go inside," I say, mimicking her flailing hands.

Her whole face lights up, and she slips her arm through mine. "Let's!"

The guy at the door looks as though he practices how to body-slam people as part of his daily exercise regimen. Everything about him is broad: chest, shoulders, thighs. He's a slab of granite large enough to custom-fit a sizable kitchen island. Why is he necessary?

"Hey," I say to him.

He looks me dead in the eyes and nods. That's it. No instructions. No information.

"Should we just go in?" I ask.

"You can't *just go in,*" he says. "Are you on the list?"

"We were told we would be."

He smiles. "Names?"

"Dean Chapman and Solange Pereira."

Behind me, Solange peeks her head out. "You're Bruce Banner's alter ego, I presume?"

Ah shit. That mouth is going to get us killed.

He grunts, then narrows his eyes at her. "Wrong."

She disappears just as quickly as she appeared.

Not-Hulk consults his clipboard again and nods. "Guests of Peter Barnum?"

"That's the one," I say.

"You're cleared. Enjoy."

I take a long look at my surroundings, my gaze immediately landing on the steel table situated in front of the stained glass double doors leading to the rest of the home. The area inside is illuminated in blues and reds, and I can hear the steady thump of music with a driving bass line playing inside. Solange grasps the back of my shirt, as if she's concerned about getting separated from me.

"Are you okay?" I ask over my shoulder.

"As long as I'm using you as a human shield? Sure."

Another slab of a man is standing by a second set of doors. As we approach, he reaches behind him and produces a plastic bin. "Evening, folks. You can place your personal belongings — keys, phone, whatever else — in here. We'll lock them up for you."

"What the hell?" I whisper to Solange. "Is this airport security? What's next, a body scan?"

A woman in line behind us laughs. "Psst, it's no big deal. It's just what some of these VIPs require. DC, you know?"

No, I *don't* know. And I'm not sure I want to spend an evening with any VIPs. I certainly don't want to give up my phone in some strange place. "Is there another option? One that will allow us to hang on to them?"

He nods without hesitation, as if he's been asked this question many times before. "What brand?"

"iPhones."

"I can change the settings to restrict your access to the camera app from the lock screen, then unlock the phones when you both come back out." He jiggles the plastic bin. "It's up to you."

I'd expect this level of gatekeeping in McLean, but a quiet side street in Adams Morgan isn't a magnet for people who consider themselves VIPs. Now I'm curious to know who's behind those closed doors.

I turn to look at Solange.

"I'm keeping mine with me," she says, giving the man a frosty look. "In case I need to make an emergency call."

"Yeah, let's change the settings." I unlock my phone and hand it to him; Solange does the same.

His expression bland, he fiddles with our phones, and in less than a minute, returns them to us. "Done. I'll unlock them when you leave."

"You won't forget the password you used?" I ask.

"I won't forget the password I used."

Once we're inside, it takes me a few seconds to adjust to the eerie glow cast by the overheads. People of all races, ages, and sizes are scattered about in clumps — drinking, laughing, dancing — and I'm reminded of the dozens of relatively innocuous law firm gatherings I've attended over the years.

"It's a regular shmegular party," Solange says, frowning. "So why the hell did they put us through that rigmarole?"

"No idea," I say, shrugging. "Maybe one of these people has a security detail."

"Well, I'm cautiously ready to haul ass if I need to. Just sayin'." She surveys her surroundings, then points at the bar across the room. "Why don't you get us something to drink while I scope out the bathroom. I need to adjust my underwear."

I'm trying to behave tonight, so I pretend I didn't hear that last part. "What would you like?"

"Water, for now. Until I have a better sense of what we're dealing with."

Solange trots down a long hall while I weave my way through the crowd. As I wait my turn at the bar, I check out the home's interior design, such as it is. The room's large and configured for lounging, with several couches and chaises positioned in different corners of the space. The terra-cotta walls are bare, which gives the home a newly moved-in feel. Whoever lives here hasn't settled in yet.

"What can I get you?" the bartender asks.

As I'm giving him my order, someone in the room rings a handbell. Excited chatter follows, and the energy in the room shifts. People sit, stand, and generally rearrange themselves in the space, their expressions charged with anticipation. Then the hand-bell rings again. A man behind me noncha-lantly unzips his pants, and the woman he was chatting with drops to her knees in front of him, reaching for his . . . dick.

My head snaps up, and I search the crowd. Everyone's either tugging off clothes, kissing, stroking someone else's body parts, or watching. What. The. Fuck?

I stumble forward, the shock of what's happening propelling me to abandon the line. I turn back to the bartender. "Bath-room?"

He points in the direction where I last saw Solange, and I sprint toward it, passing a sea of writhing bodies in various stages of undress. So. Many. Ponies. I can't unsee it. Solange opens the door just as I reach it.

"What's wrong?" she asks, a look of concern crossing her face when she sees my panicked expression.

I need a moment to regroup, so I pull her inside the bathroom and lock the door.

"Do we need to make a quick exit?" Solange asks as she tugs on the window frame and tries to pull up the pane. It only lifts a crack, and she growls in frustration, then throws up her hands. "What's going on?"

I brace my hands against the porcelain sink and meet her confused gaze in the mirror's reflection. "Holy shit, Solange, we're at a sex party."

SOLANGE

What? No, he *must* be punking me. "Dean, be serious for a minute."

"Solange, listen to me," he says as he paces the length of the surprisingly spacious bathroom. "I'm being one hundred percent serious. Does this sound like something I would lie about? *Me?*"

Oh. My. God. I kind of scream on the inside for a few seconds. This is bananas. All I can do is repeat his words. "We're at a sex party."

"Bingo. I'll take 'Oh, baby, the places I never thought I'd go' for one million, Solange."

"Shit. Are you telling me Peter wanted to bring a firm recruit *here*?"

"Now that I think about it, no, that's not what's going on," he says. "Peter wanted *me* to bring a firm recruit here. He didn't know that Kimberly and Nia had canceled. He just conveniently and suddenly decided that his marriage meant more to him than a very important assignment that could give him a leg up in his bid to become a firm partner. The sneaky, cutthroat, disloyal son of a bitch. Peter set me up. Or tried to."

"Are you sure that's what this is, though? Because I've read about sex clubs, Dean — just . . . uh . . . out of curiosity — and there's a whole process to this. Waivers, promises of confidentiality, rules."

"Well, I'm not an expert in these things, but a bell rang and suddenly people were having sex, and everyone in there seemed to know what was up. That sounds like a sex club to me."

It does to me too. *What the hell is wrong with Peter?* I pegged him as a sleazeball from day one, but this is beyond the pale. If Dean and I had consented to attending, I wouldn't blink twice at what's going on beyond these walls — okay, maybe I'd blink once, depending on the scene. But we *didn't* agree to this, which means Peter is a menace who must be stopped. My immediate priority, though, is to get us the hell out of here.

"So we should just leave, right?"

"Right," he says, raking his hands through his mussed hair. " 'When in doubt, get the fuck out' is my mantra. I'm sorry, Solange."

I raise a brow. "Sorry? What for? You didn't do anything."

"But you're caught up in all of this because of me."

"Dean, stop," I say, jumping in front of him and halting his incessant pacing. "Look at me."

He does the very opposite of that, his gaze bouncing from object to object in the space, until he lets out a harsh breath and finally returns my stare. Dean prefers to control his surroundings, so being thrust into an unexpected situation like this one must be unsettling.

I link our hands together and squeeze. "I take it from your reaction that you've never attended a sex party before?"

He snort-laughs, as if my question is ridiculous. "Uh, no. Never. Have you?"

"I have."

His gaze snaps to mine, and his eyes go wide. "Really?"

I clear my throat. "Really. Nothing like this, though. It was a gathering among friends in grad school. All this to say, I'm fine. I'm not freaking out. Sex between consenting adults isn't anything to be ashamed of."

"Of course," he says, slipping his hands out of mine and tugging on his shirt collar.

"It took you by surprise. I get it."

He blinks a few times, then puffs out his cheeks. Poor Dean. Going to a sex party was never in his life plan, I guess. After a moment, he takes a few steps back and sits on the edge of the claw-foot tub. "May I ask you a question about your experience?"

"Go ahead," I say, joining him.

Is it odd that I'm comfortable talking with him about this? I've never mentioned that party to anyone, not even Brandon, and yet here I am, ready to share the details with Dean. Maybe it's because I trust that he isn't interested in my answers for his own titillation; he's asking questions because he wants to understand.

He turns his head toward me. "Did you participate?"

"Depends on what you mean by 'participate.' I was there, so, yes, I participated. But I didn't have sex with anyone. I watched . . . and pleasured myself."

Dean's eyelids fall to half-mast, and a flutter zips through my chest. If I could choose a superpower in this moment, it would be the ability to jump to another location with just a snap of my fingers. We're confined in a bathroom, and a short distance away, people are doing delightfully dirty things to each other. The sex-starved lobe of my brain is regarding this as a plum opportunity to seduce him, while the rational part of my brain is warning me of the impending danger of listening to my inner hussy.

Dean puts out his hands and glances at them, then he raises his chin and pins me with a red-hot gaze. "Is that something you like? Watching?"

I grip the tub's edge. His voice is low and silky and glides over my body like a caress. He's ensnaring me in his net, and I suspect he doesn't even know it. I have no choice but to respond truthfully. "It's not something I've done often. But yes, the idea of watching people have sex turns me on . . . What about you?"

He leans over and rakes his fingers over the tops of his thighs, as if he's desperately trying not to stroke himself. "I'm turned on right now. Does that count?"

Jesus. He's killing me. And maybe he *does* know it. "Depends. Are you turned on by the idea of stepping outside this bathroom and watching other people have sex?"

He licks his lips and nods. "I am."

Coupled with the memory of last night's

masterful kiss, his admission leaves me breathless. "I am too." What neither of us is saying is that we're turned on not just by the setting but also by each other. I, for one, am not ready to take that leap. Still, I can help him explore a part of himself he may never have considered until now — and experience my own pleasure in the process. "Would you like to go out there and watch? With me?"

His nostrils flare, and his eyes flash with unbridled need. "I would."

I bite back a moan. Well, that escalated perfectly.

Chapter Fifteen

DEAN

Solange and I leave the bathroom, then she gestures for me to follow her. The home is lit in red, a set of pendant lights hanging from the ceiling creating a starburst effect on the walls. Now that I'm no longer in shock, I'm able to appreciate the seductive atmosphere, the ease with which people are reveling in their partners.

"Let's go down here," Solange says, jutting her chin in the direction of a long hallway. She weaves through the crowd, periodically turning back to make sure I'm still with her. At some point, we lose each other, but then she doubles back and places her hand in mine. She steadies me with her intense gaze and gives me a firm squeeze. I feel her touch all the way down to my toes, but I school my features. I'm consumed with the need to touch her. Desperate to be the one to give her pleasure. Still, Solange has consented to being here, nothing more, and I will *always* respect her boundaries.

We dip our heads in the first room that we come to and find naked people massaging and fondling one another as they engage in substantive conversations. I mean, one guy's talking about air fryer recipes. What the hell?

"So many PDEs," Solange observes, her gaze bouncing around like a ping-pong ball.

"Don't you mean PDAs?"

A corner of her mouth lifts before she explains: "No, I meant PDEs. Public Displays of Erections."

Welcome to Solange World, where the official languages are English, Portuguese, and Inventive Acronyms. If I'm not careful, I'm likely to be sporting my own PDE before this night is through. How the hell am I supposed to hide my arousal in a place like this? With this woman by my side? Brilliant plan, Dean. Just brilliant.

Seemingly impatient to move on, Solange tugs on my shirt and leads us to another room and . . . jackpot.

A woman is lying in the center of a platform bed. Her legs are spread out as two naked men kiss and caress her. She's wearing garters without stockings and nothing else, suggesting that we missed part of the disrobing.

Solange and I aren't the only observers, but we're the only people who appear to be together. We inch our way to an open spot, our bodies close but not touching because she slipped out of my loose grip as soon as we ventured inside.

"Is this okay?" I ask her.

She nods, her teeth pressing into her bottom lip until she releases it to speak. "This works."

One of the men slips a finger inside the woman, and she lets out a breathy moan. Fuck. My eyeballs were expecting to be eased into this, but nope, that's not happening. Beside me, Solange shifts. I turn and meet her gaze.

"My shoes," she explains in a whisper. "Taking them off isn't an option, though."

"Get in front of me, then," I say. "You can lean against me to take some of the pressure off your feet. You'll see better too."

"No, it's okay," she says, shaking her head. "It's not bad."

Someone at the other end of the room shushes us. We're plainly doing this wrong, and everyone knows it. I shake my head at her, and although she smirks at my expression of mild frustration, Solange accepts my offer and slips in front of me. Slowly, so slowly I can barely detect her progress, she rests her back against my chest and puts most of her weight on one hip.

I lean in and whisper my question near her ear. "Better?"

"Yeah." She angles her head to the side, as though she's signaling to me that her neck is fair game, and the impulse to suck on the skin there nearly makes my knees buckle. Fuck, I'm reading signals where there are none.

Trying to get a handle on myself, I focus on the exhibitionists on the bed, but it's a struggle. Solange is surrounding me on all sides: her touch, the faint scent of vanilla on her skin, the miniature clouds of hair filling my peripheral vision and tickling my jaw. Her presence so easily diverts my concentration that somehow the sensual scene in my line of sight is the distraction rather than the main attraction.

There's no use denying it: I want this woman so bad I can't think straight. For a man who prides himself on always keeping his wits about him, that's a serious problem.

SOLANGE

Is this really happening? Am I watching three people having sex in public as I lean against Dean's chest? *Yes, yes, I am.*

I wish I could pretend this is an out-of-body experience, but I am very much in my body, and said body is *very* aware of the man behind it.

The woman on the bed could be me, could be anyone, and I gather that's where my mind is meant to go. But I don't think I'm supposed to superimpose Dean's face on the two men pleasuring her. I've created a pair of Deans in my head, and oh my God, they're experts at bringing me to the brink and electrifying every inch of me.

What was it he said once? *I'm never dull when it counts.*

Not wanting to torture myself any longer, I squeeze my eyes shut and try to clear my brain. When I return my gaze to the scene, I make every effort to consume it as a spectator rather than a person wishing to be an active participant.

The men are what most people would consider conventionally attractive, both fit but not overly so. One of the men is Black, his skin a deep brown and enviably smooth. The other man is white, his eyes and hair dark as night. The woman appears to be a natural redhead, a smattering of freckles across her nose and cheeks her most arresting feature.

Until this point, the spectacle has largely

been a lesson in the many ways one can evoke pleasure simply through touch. But now the men are looking at each other, communicating their intentions, it seems, and despite the absence of a verbal exchange, they lie on the bed in a coordinated dance, each snaking an arm around one of the woman's legs. It's a tight fit, but the men manage to share the space between her thighs. She opens for them, and a wave of heat washes over me when one man slides two fingers inside her and the other kisses her clitoris.

In that moment, I want to be her. And I want one of the men to be Dean. Desperately.

The woman cries out, her voice piercing the bubble of silence among the onlookers. Startled, I stumble back, but there's nowhere to go except farther into the cocoon of Dean's body. He keeps me upright by placing his arm across my middle.

"I got you," he says, low and slow, each word sticking to the next one like honey.

My nipples tighten, the arousal in the air and the deepness of his voice working in tandem to heighten my reaction to the spectacle in front of me.

I grasp Dean's hand as if doing so will keep me steady, but I'm more unbalanced than ever, teetering on a seesaw in my head, unable to make sense of what's happening *to* me or *around* me. Somehow, I cut through the mental haze and register Dean's heavy breathing, an awareness that sizzles across my skin and settles between my legs.

Before me, the men switch places, one set of fingers sliding out, another set of fingers gliding in. A different tongue. More pleasure. Keening cries. They continue this pattern, taking turns as they drive her wild with their mouths and hands, until she arches her back high off the bed and screams through her orgasm.

I'm no longer grasping Dean's hand — I'm gripping it — and then our fingers are entwined, squeezing together almost painfully as we come down from whatever has us in its clutches. It occurs to me that we could make our way to a dark corner and fuck each other senseless, and no one would raise a brow; for a millisecond, I consider asking him if he'd like to. Without meeting his gaze, I turn into him, my forehead grazing his chin and my free hand fisting his shirt. Propelled by pure need, I rise on my toes.

"I can't help myself," he whispers above me. "Can you?"

My chest expands, and I melt against him,

ignited by his consent. "I can't either."

But before our lips can touch, reality returns as the room suddenly brightens, the stark white walls and flustered faces of the people around us revealed for all to see.

A man jumps away from a spot near the door, revealing the dimmer switch behind him. "Oh shit," he says, his cheeks pink from arousal or embarrassment or both. "Sorry about that. I hit the light by mistake."

A collective groan fills the room, and everyone quickly disperses, the evening interrupted by the clumsy person who killed the mood and saved me from myself.

"I think I'm ready to go now," I say to Dean, not daring to look at him as I step out of his embrace. "You?"

"Yeah," he says hoarsely. After clearing his throat, he tries again. "Yeah, let's get out of here."

CHAPTER SIXTEEN

DEAN

After the security guy unlocks our phones, Solange and I skip down the front steps of the sex lair masquerading as a quaint row home in the middle of Northwest DC.

"So, same time, same place, next Saturday?" I ask nonchalantly.

The tension in my chest eases when I catch the hint of a smile that appears on her dewy face. She looks as though she's recovering from a burst of physical activity. As if she's just taken a quick lap around the block and needs to catch her breath.

"Dream on, Chapman," she says, simultaneously waving me off and fanning herself. "Dream on."

I feel lighter on my feet knowing nothing's fundamentally different between us. Sure, I'm growing accustomed to my attraction to Solange. Doing something about it, though, would be game changing. It's a challenge,

245

but if I can withstand the temptation of being within inches of her at a sex party, there's literally no scenario I can envision that would break my resolve not to get thrown off course by Solange's allure.

She doesn't seem all that fazed by the encounter anyway. And it's entirely possible her reaction was nothing more than an indiscriminate response to being in a highly arousing situation. Admittedly, an extremely small and selfish part of me hopes that's not true, but that part of me can fuck right off.

"Did you drive?" I ask her once we reach the sidewalk.

"Yeah." She points up the street. "I'm a block over that way."

"I'll walk you to your car."

She nods, and we wordlessly stroll side by side, the air on this balmy evening in July adding weight to even the smallest physical movement.

"So, what are you going to do about Peter?" she asks, finally breaking the silence.

Peter deserves to suffer for this stunt, no question. Yet confronting him about it might provoke questions I'm not prepared to answer. If everyone canceled, why did we attend the party? And what did we see or do once we got there? I've never been a fan

246

of sharing my private business with colleagues, but this experience between Solange and me is superpersonal, and I don't intend on sharing it with *anyone,* let alone my dirtbag coworker who's obviously dead set on getting me fired. "I'm not sure. Still working out the possibilities in my head."

"Let's think about this for a minute." She narrows her eyes and twists her lips back and forth. It's her pensive expression. The one that tells me I'm about to get the benefit of her singular wisdom. I love that she wants us to work this out together.

Quickening her pace, she sticks an index finger in the air. "Scenario one: Peter didn't know it was a sex party. I bet lots of people hated him in law school. He's the guy everyone resented because he had a mean competitive streak and monopolized every class discussion. We had someone like that in grad school. So maybe this was all a prank, and he would have been just as surprised as you were. He'll assume you decided not to go and that's that."

"I wish it were that easy to explain, but knowing Peter, I doubt it is."

"Okay, fine, so let's consider the second scenario," she says, holding up two fingers. "Peter knew it was a sex party, and he was hoping Kimberly and Nia would be offended by the night's festivities and blame you for taking them. Once he discovers they canceled, what then?"

"The stunt becomes pointless."

"Exactly," she says, painting double check marks in the air. "Which means he won't say anything unless you do. If you think about it, not saying anything and keeping him guessing will secretly infuriate him. He'll spend weeks wondering if you're going to retaliate in some way."

I give her a devious smile. "That'll torture him."

She rubs her hands together. "It's deliciously vindictive. Beneath you, really. And yet it has the potential to be extraordinarily satisfying." Then she reaches into her purse and pulls out a set of keys with a fob. "This is me."

Well, one thing's clear: Solange isn't inclined to discuss the party. And I suspect her willingness to brainstorm how to tackle the Peter issue was meant to prevent us from even acknowledging what happened back there. Can't say that I disagree with her approach; maybe that's the best way to handle this anyway. Pretending *does* seem to be our fallback position.

I'm poised to watch her drive off, but as she's climbing into her pint-size cherry-red

Mitsubishi hatchback, her phone rings. With the door still open, she answers it and immediately tries to calm the caller. "Hang on, hang on. I can hardly understand you. Breathe."

"That's what I'm fucking trying to do," the person on the other end of the line — a woman — yells.

"Where's Paulo?" Solange asks.

She listens intently, then blows out a slow breath. "Okay, I'm coming to get you. Be there in twenty-five minutes, twenty if the stoplights cooperate." With the car door still open, she hunches over and rests her head on the steering wheel.

"What's the matter?" I ask.

She looks up at me, her expression anguished. "It's Natalia. She's going into labor, and her husband's stuck on the other side of the Bay Bridge in Maryland because he had a meeting out there."

Contending with Bay Bridge traffic is a way of life in the area. An accident or even heavy fog can leave commuters stranded for hours on the Eastern Shore. Depending on what's happened, Natalia's husband could very well miss his child's birth. "Is Natalia all right? The baby?"

"Oh, she's fine," Solange says flatly. "She

knows my car is reliable. Lina's might break down."

"Makes sense . . . but why the long face?"

She gives me an incredulous expression. "It's Natalia. She's having a baby. You don't know my cousin like I do. She's the kind of person who could make her childbirth experience go viral."

"*That* dramatic?" I ask.

"Oh, Dean. She's going to torment us all."

"What can I do to help?"

Solange tips her head to the side, her brows pinched together. "Trust me. You don't want any part of this experience."

I see what's happening here: She's boxing me out. Pretending to be her boyfriend in front of my colleagues is one thing; interacting with her family is quite another. But I'd like to think we're friends, and I wouldn't abandon a friend in a time of need. "C'mon, Solange. I'm a strapping young man. That may come in handy."

She considers me for a moment, then reaches for the inside door handle. "Okay, get in. But listen, whatever happens tonight, don't say I didn't warn you."

Damn, I'm not having the baby, am I? What the hell is she envisioning? If anything, I'd say Solange is the one being overdramatic here.

SOLANGE

As I hightail it to my cousin's place in Wheaton, Dean helps me triage the phone calls to the family network.

"You call Max and Lina first. They'll be able to keep her calm if need be. I'll call her mother at the store. She'll let the tias know what's going on."

I place Viviane on speakerphone. "Oi, Tia. O bebê vai nascer logo."

I hear Tia Viviane suck her teeth. "Sim, já estou sabendo."

Well, if she already knows, why isn't she scrambling to get to her daughter?

"I need to put my makeup on first," my aunt explains. "I can't go to the hospital without something on my face."

I glance at Dean before I return my attention to the road. He scrubs a hand down his face to hide his smile as he waits for Max to pick up. Yes, by the looks of things, he, too, is now fully aware of the depths of my family's wackiness.

"Just meet us at Natalia's," I tell Tia Viviane. "Where's Mãe and Tia Mariana?"

"They're getting themselves together," she says. "Don't worry. We'll be there soon."

I can't with them. Not now. Sure, they may miss the birth of Natalia's child, but at least they'll look cute when they eventually join us.

Twenty minutes later, Dean and I pound on Natalia's front door. She swings it open, her sweat-slicked face twisted in a grimace. "Hey, you two."

I immediately pull out my phone. "I'm calling 911. You need an ambulance."

"No," Natalia forces out through clenched teeth. "They'll figure out a way to charge us ten thousand dollars for a ride on a glorified ice-cream truck. Don't do it, Solange."

"Okay, so what do you want us to do?"

"I'll get in your car. Drive me to Holy Cross. My OB is on call there. The contractions are like six minutes apart, so we should be good."

"Fine. Let's get your stuff together." I turn to Dean. "We don't have time to wait for everyone. Can you call Max and Lina back and tell them to go directly to the hospital instead? Ask them to update the tias too."

He nods, his eyes softening as he lifts the phone to his ear. "On it, Captain."

I appreciate that he isn't offering suggestions or activating the mansplaining gene. Instead, he's patiently waiting for any instructions, and that in itself makes me less anxious about my limited role in the situation. I reach out and give his hand a squeeze. "Thanks for being here."

"Of course," he says with a wink. "Wouldn't want to be anywhere else."

"Honest?"

"Honest."

Natalia sucks her teeth. "Oh my gosh, you two. *I'm* the one having the baby. If you can get your heads out of each other's asses long enough, I might be able to get to the hospital to pop this monster out."

She waddle-stomps up the steps to the second floor of her and Paulo's townhome. I scurry after her, appreciating the excuse not to meet Dean's gaze.

In the bedroom, Natalia's muttering to herself as she double-checks the contents of her overnight bag.

I throw up my hands. "What do you need Sudoku for?"

"To pass the time," she says between breaths.

"Natalia, I think you're going to be a little too busy for Sudoku. And when the baby arrives, you'll be lucky if you have enough time to wipe your ass properly."

"Oh my God. Just shut up. *Shut up,*" she says, scrunching up her face and placing a hand on her lower back. "And here I thought *I* was the drama queen."

Wrapping her in a loose embrace from

behind, I rest my chin on her shoulder. "I'm kidding, prima. Just trying to distract you. You're doing great, and I'm in awe of your strength."

"Thank you."

"Now what else do you need?"

She squirms her way out of my arms and takes a slow spin around the room, her gaze bouncing around as she tries to gather herself. Her eyes grow wide when they land on a device in the corner. "Oh, the electric stimulator! I definitely need that."

I flinch my head back. "The what?"

She dons a devilish expression, then huffs and puffs. "Paulo and I took this New Age birthing class that encourages the partner who isn't in physical labor to experience simulated contractions. It's supposed to bring us closer together and teach him empathy. Supposedly it reduces my pain too."

"No shit!"

"Who knows?" she says, shrugging her shoulders. "But it's the least he could do considering he's the reason we're in this mess."

I can't help grinning at her ridiculousness. "Wait. Why is he to blame?"

"Because he makes me do things," she says, glancing furtively at the door, then lowering her voice to a whisper. "Things I'd never imagined doing. Like agreeing to a process that makes my vagina large enough for a watermelon to fit through it."

I mentally cross my legs. Ouch. "To be fair, some people can manage that outcome with their dicks alone."

She draws back. "Mulher, what kind of dicks have you been fraternizing with?"

"None, unfortunately," I grumble. "I hear stories, is all."

"Anyway," she says as she crosses the room to grab the stimulator, "if the contractions start coming faster, I may need you to strap on a few of these electrodes. I don't want to change anything else about my birthing plan. It's already bad enough that Paulo may not make it in time."

Yeah. No. I'm not doing that. "Dean!" I shout loud enough for my voice to reach the downstairs living room.

He appears at the door in a flash. "What do you need?"

"I'll explain on the way to the car."

He *did* say he's a strapping young man. That'll come in handy, indeed.

CHAPTER SEVENTEEN

DEAN

"Say what now? You want me to do *what*?"

I must have misheard them.

Solange lifts a device the size of an iPhone in the air as she unlocks her car. "This is an electric stimulator. It's actually for physical therapy, but you can use it to simulate the pain of contractions so a person can experience parts of the birthing process as their partner does."

"I'm sorry," I say, shaking my head. "Did you time travel and become a medical doctor when I wasn't looking?"

She rolls her eyes at me. "Natalia's the expert. She just filled me in."

With Natalia's overnight bag hanging from my shoulder, I rush to help the expectant mother into the passenger seat.

"It's no big deal, Dean," Natalia says. "You just attach these electrodes to your stomach, and I press a few buttons to mimic what I'm feeling. Bingo, bango, that's it."

"Why can't *you* do it?" I ask Solange, whose full-toothed grin isn't fooling me.

She rattles her car keys. "Can you drive a stick shift?"

"No."

She looks . . . relieved. "Well, there's your answer."

We climb into the car — me in the back and Natalia in the front because she needs the extra legroom — and Solange starts the engine.

Natalia settles into the seat, fastens her seat belt, then groans before turning her head to face me. "About the stimulator: It'll help me get through this, okay? But if you don't want to do it, no problem. I understand it may be daunting for some." She closes her eyes and breathes out. "That's another one. We should start timing them again."

I'm not a man who can be easily egged into a situation by the suggestion that I'm wimpy. So if that's Natalia's angle, it's a wasted effort.

She drops her head and whimpers. "God, I wish Paulo were here. This isn't how I thought this day would go."

Now *that's* the kind of sentiment I can't ignore. "Give me the device."

Natalia turns around again, her expression noticeably brighter. "You'll do it?"

"Yeah, I'll do it."

A few minutes later, I'm wearing four electrodes on my abdomen and two electrodes on my back; six wires tether me to the device in Natalia's lap, leaving me at her mercy. I've never met the man, but Paulo owes me big-time for this.

"Okay," Natalia says. "So the next time I have a contraction, I'll hit the dial. Let me know if you need me to stop. And, Dean?"

"Yeah?"

"This is already distracting me, so I'd say it's working."

"Glad I could help, Natalia," I say, sitting back.

"We'll be there soon, you two," Solange notes. "You're doing great."

"Here's the next contraction," Natalia says. "Dean, take a deep breath in as it starts, then slowly release and focus on a mental image of your body suspended in water."

The electrodes on my abdomen pulse against my skin and several currents zing through my body. I let out a few garbled sounds as I push through the discomfort. "This isn't pleasant. Forgive me, but if it goes any higher than this, I'm going to need to curse."

"Who gives a fuck," Natalia says. "After this, you're in the family."

"What do you need me to do?" Solange asks. "Anything?"

"Keep your eyes on the road," Natalia says. "Encouraging words are good. Shut up when I ask you to shut up. No music."

Solange nods. "Fair enough." She and I exchange a look through the rearview. *You okay?* she mouths. I give her a thumbs-up in response.

The next contraction is worse, though. Natalia shouts from the pain, and I jam my feet against the floorboards when she turns up the dial. "Goddamn . . . Almighty . . . fuck . . . That's it, Natalia, breathe."

"Look at you two," Solange says up front. "You're both amazing. Doing great."

Is it bad that I want to stuff a sock in her mouth? Yeah, I suppose that's bad. Why the hell did I insist on coming with her to Natalia's? I could be at home getting ready for bed. But noooo, I just *had* to spend a little more time with Solange. Well, who's the sucker now?

"Dean," Natalia says a few minutes later. "Just a warning: Another's coming, and they're getting more intense."

I wipe my brow with the back of my hand.

"Thanks for the heads-up. I'll be right there with you."

"Four minutes apart," Solange adds.

Suddenly Natalia leans forward and howls. Seriously. As though she's lost the rest of her pack and calling out to them is the only way to guarantee a reunion. "Oh God, oh God, oh God. Jesus Cristo! Shiiiiiiiiiiit."

The bad news is that she's in pain.

The good news is that she forgot to hit the dial on the device.

"Natalia," Solange says, her voice cutting through the panting and grunting in the car. "Sweetie, you forgot to hit the dial."

Where's a fucking spare sock when you need one?

"Oh!" Natalia says, looking as if activating the device has given her a new lease on life. "Here you go, Dean."

"Jesus. Fucking. Christ. What. The. Fuck?" This time the pain is so intense I unfasten my seatbelt and go horizontal, aligning the length of my body with the backseat and pressing the soles of my shoes against the window. My back spasms. "Make. It. Stop. Make. It. Stop." Literal tears stream down my face. I grab on to my hair and yank on it, hoping to transfer some of the discomfort elsewhere, but all that I manage to do is make myself feel like I'm on fire from head to toe. I curl up into a ball and mewl. Any minute now, I'm going to tap out.

The car jerks to a stop just as Natalia's cell phone rings.

"Paulo!" she exclaims as Solange runs around to open the door for her. "Where are you?" She and Paulo talk while I yank the electrodes off my body. Natalia, suddenly spry as hell, hoists herself out of the car, the phone at her ear. In the meantime, I'm still struggling to sit up.

The back door flies open, and Solange reaches for my arm. "C'mon, strapping young man. You were phenomenal, but I think your work here is done."

"Don't talk to me," I say, dodging her hands. "And don't snort either."

"Okay, okay," she says, backing away with a huge grin on her face, her hands up in the air in surrender. "I'm going to park the car."

An orderly with a wheelchair greets us in the circular driveway of the hospital's emergency entrance. I'm hunched over, a hand at my back and the birthing bag at my side as I try to support Natalia's slow climb up the cement incline.

"Who's the patient?" the jokester asks.

"Funny. She's the mom-to-be," I say.

The orderly helps Natalia into the wheelchair. Good thing, too, because I'm still catching my breath. With Natalia safely tucked away and ready for transport, her hands gripping the wheelchair's armrests and her bag hanging from the handles, the orderly rolls her inside.

I scan the hospital grounds for any sign of Solange and easily spot her hair bouncing in the air as she trots across the visitors' parking lot.

She's panting when she reaches me, her cheeks slightly flushed. "You, my friend, have gone above and beyond. You can definitely call it a night."

And miss this rare event? No way. I didn't grow up in a big family. My mother has no siblings, and she burned her bridges with her own parents even before I was born. For obvious reasons, I've never even met my grandparents on my father's side. Hell, I'm not even sure they know I exist. So this — mothers and aunts and cousins gathering around to celebrate the birth of their newest relative — is new to me. I'd like to experience this moment, even if it's second-hand. Besides, I don't want the night to be over just yet. I *like* Solange. As a person. And I can push aside my attraction if it means I get to spend more time with her. "Forget it, Pereira," I say as I massage my belly. "I'm in it for the long haul. Waiting-room pacing and everything."

She smiles, and it's as though the joy of hearing my statement is illuminating her from the inside and spreading a burst of brightness in every direction. All that damn pain was worth it to get to see her like this.

"Okay, well, let's go pace together," she says.

I like the sound of that. Us. Together. Maybe more than I have the right to. But I *can* be her friend and embrace wherever that takes me — even if it begins at a surprise sex party and ends with a simulated birth.

What's even wilder than my already wild night? I wouldn't change a damn thing about it, and if given the chance, I'd do it all over again.

After scoping out the hospital's private waiting areas — each with its own television, refrigerator, dinette set, and couch — Solange and I claim an empty one. We wipe most of the surfaces clean (my idea), then stand just outside the door so Lina and Max will easily find us when they get here.

An elevator down the hall dings, and when it opens, a group of people rush out, none of them Lina or Max. A tall, striking middle-aged Black woman with streaks of gray at her temples leads the charge as though she's poised for battle.

"That's Tia Viviane," Solange explains. "Natalia's mom and the eldest of the three sisters." As her aunt approaches, Solange shakes her head. "Nice lipstick. I'm sure the baby will love it."

Tia Viviane waves her hand as if she's flicking away an insect with the audacity to buzz around her, but there's a lift to her lips, suggesting she secretly appreciates Solange's perfectly timed wisecrack. "Onda ela está? Para onde eu vou?"

Solange points to the nurses' station. "Lá."

Clutching her purse, Tia Viviane strides to the nurses' station, then disappears behind the set of double doors leading to the delivery rooms.

Everyone else barrels inside our designated waiting area.

Solange's family doesn't just shift the energy in the room. No, they *are* the energy in the room — amped up to ten — and there are only five of us here. It's a tight space, yet everyone manages to pivot and sidestep in a perfectly boisterous and choreographed effort to make room for one another. Two middle-aged women stride to the counter by the fridge and pull out foil-wrapped containers from paper shopping bags while a burly dude with arms and thighs that put mine to shame sets two-liter soda bottles on the dinette table.

"That's my mother, Izabel," Solange says, leaning into me. "The other woman is Tia Mariana, Lina's and Rey's mom."

I can't help taking in a deep breath and savoring Solange's vanilla scent again. I'm a fiend for sugar cookies, so her fragrance makes me want to press my mouth against her neck and nibble on it. *Don't think about the party. Don't think about the party.* Struggling to focus, I somehow manage to string together a decent question. "Rey's the big guy, I take it?"

"Correct," she says, nodding as she watches them unpack. "I'll introduce you in a minute."

"Should we offer to help?"

She shakes her head. "This is a military operation. Unless you've been through boot camp, it's best to stay out of the fray when they're in setup mode."

"I wouldn't dream of interfering, then."

Solange gestures at the bags and containers. "What's all this anyway?"

"Food, obviously," her mother says. "We're going to need something to eat while we wait."

"Nothing too heavy," Lina's mom says.

"Sandwiches. A little salad. Some fruit."

Solange groans. "This isn't a cookout, for God's sake."

"Shhh," I tell her, gently smacking the top of her hand. "If they want to share their gifts with us, who are you to complain?"

Her mouth falls open, but her eyes are sparkling with amusement. "Did you just *hit* me?"

"It was a love tap, that's all." I cringe on the inside when the L word slips out. "I meant a friend tap, of course."

"Thanks for the clarification," she says, her voice dripping with sarcasm as she gives me an eye roll in excruciatingly slow motion.

"Who's this?" Mariana says pleasantly, her gaze landing on me.

"This is Dean," Solange says. "He's Max's best friend."

The descriptor bugs me. Is that all I am to her? A guy she's doing a favor for because he's *Max's best friend.*

Maybe she sees something in the set of my expression because she hastily adds, "And my friend too, of course. I'm helping him with a project at work, so he was around when Natalia called."

Mariana tilts her chin up. "Dean? Why does that . . ." Her eyes widen in recognition, then she crosses my hand. "How are yo

Rey, who's already food, shakes his head. " strong suit, Ma."

There's sympathy in sion, and suddenly I'm r sion to be here. It's ol about the canceled wed ....ough she didn't say so outright. It never occurred to me that anyone in Solange's family would know or care, but Lina helped plan the wedding, so it must have come up, even in passing.

"I'm fine," is all I can muster. I mean, what else is there to say?

Solange's mother places a hand on her hip and inspects my face; she's holding some kind of hors d'oeuvre. "Você precisa de comida, filho. Está muito magro."

"I'm sorry?"

She shakes her head as though she's silently chastising herself. "Food. You need food. You're too tall to be so slim." She puts out her free hand. "Come. We'll get you something to put more meat on your bones."

I glance at Solange, looking for guidance on how to respond.

"Just go with it, man," Max says from the

azilian elder's prerogative to
five pounds in a single sitting.
on't rest until you're as buff as I

uff, huh?" I ask, raising an eyebrow as I
Solange's mother guide me to the mini-
feast the sisters have prepared. "Is that what
they're calling it these days?"

Max's snide response gets swallowed by
the fresh round of excited chatter ushered
in by his and Lina's arrival. I can't help
grinning when Mariana pinches Max's
cheeks, then wraps him in a bear hug that
looks comical given her small frame.

"Any updates?" Lina asks.

We shake our heads, and before anyone
can say another word, she's walking out the
door — looking for answers, I'm sure.

Izabel hands me something encased in
foil. "Here."

I unwrap her offering, and the mouthwa-
tering smell of garlic and spices enters my
nostrils. "What's this?"

"Sanduíche de fraldinha na manteiga e
alho."

"Which is . . . ?"

Solange joins me at the table, standing
close enough that her arm brushes mine.
"It's a flank steak sandwich. Plenty of butter. Plenty of garlic. Squishy, yummy bread."

I waggle my eyebrows at her. "Say that again. Just once more. Slower this time."

Grinning, she bumps my shoulder. It's a small thing, but that show of familiarity seems just as meaningful as a hug. I'm surrounded by Solange and her family, and I truly feel a part of this gathering, as though I belong here. As though I'm taking up space in Solange's world, and she's okay with that. One of the upshots of always telling women precisely what they can expect of me is that I'm rarely invited to meet their parents. Until Ella. Who had her own reasons for letting me into her life. So, yeah, this is nice. But it doesn't escape my notice that none of the husbands are here, and I wonder whether it's because they're the kind of men who make promises they can't keep. Solange certainly believes her dad is one; maybe he'd still be in her life if he had been honest about his limitations.

"You don't want to try it?" Izabel asks, a dispirited expression on her face.

"He probably wants to wash his hands first," Solange says.

She's not entirely wrong, but the travel sanitizer in my front pocket is an adequate substitute; I quickly reassure Solange's mother as I rub it in. "Oh no, that's not it at all. Was just thinking about something." I take a bite of the sandwich, and after chewing a bit, make a chef's kiss gesture. "This is delicious. Truly, truly excellent."

Izabel beams at me, and it's as if I'm back in grade school, when all I ever wanted was to be the teacher's pet. My brain apparently wants nothing but gold stars from the Pereira women.

"Out the way, new guy," Rey says. "You're blocking access to my seconds."

As Solange and I wander to the couch, Lina returns, her forehead creased with worry. She begins pacing near the door.

"I don't understand how anyone can even eat at a time like this," she says, side-eyeing the rest of us.

Max rises from his seat and puts an arm around his girlfriend, effectively halting her progress. "Let's go get some coffee. That'll take your mind off this until we hear something." He gestures at the group. "Anyone else want a cup?"

"Definitely," Solange says.

"Me too," I add, settling my paper plate on my lap. "Cream and sugar for me. Black, no sugar, and superhot for Solange." When I look up, everyone's staring at me. "What?"

"That's very specific," Max says, giving me a shit-eating grin. "So noted."

As Max and Lina leave, Natalia's husband,

Paulo, appears at the door, panting as if he ran all the way from the Bay Bridge to get here. "Estou aqui!"

Solange's mom points down the hall. "Vá falar com a enfermeira, filho."

With his suit jacket hanging on his thumb and his tie in the other hand, he sprints away — in the wrong direction. Seconds later, he whizzes past the room again, a panicked expression on his face.

Rey chuckles. "Paulo looks like he doesn't know what hit him. I think he just realized his life will never be the same."

"In a good way, yes," Izabel says.

Rey twists his mouth to the side. "If you consider never getting a full night's rest again a good thing, then yes, that's exactly what I mean."

Mariana and Izabel exchange amused expressions and return to the business of doling out food — mostly to Rey.

"Remember, filho, they're not doing this alone," Solange's mother says. "They'll have us. And we're going to spoil the baby like it's ours." She glances at her daughter. "And that goes for anyone else in this family who has kids someday. It's what we do."

Solange, who's been happily noshing on her sandwich, freezes midchew but says nothing. Maybe she doesn't want children.

Or maybe she isn't keen on being pressured to have them. It's one of the topics we never discussed. And why would we? Still, I'll confess to being curious about her stance. It's just another piece of information I'd like to know about her.

"Well, don't look at me," Rey grumbles. "I can't keep a boyfriend past the two-week mark."

"Don't look at me either," Solange says. "It's kind of hard to take care of babies when you're traveling all over the country."

Well, there's part of the answer, I guess: Kids aren't in her immediate plans. But apart from that, it finally dawns on me that Solange is leaving at the end of the summer, and the first day of August is literally tomorrow. This is how it was always going to play out, right? So why does that *feel* like such a big deal? And isn't it a *big fucking deal* that it *feels* like a big deal? Holy fuck, someone bludgeon me, please.

The sound of a person's hurried footsteps saves me from drowning in my own mental quicksand. Within seconds, Paulo and Viviane appear at the threshold, both wearing hospital gowns and caps. "It's a boy!" they exclaim in unison.

Everyone gathers around the new dad and grandmother and fires off more questions than they can handle:

"How's Natalia?"

"Did she curse up a storm in there?"

"What's the baby's name?"

"Is the baby okay?"

"When can we see him?"

That last question comes from me. I'm just as excited as everyone else to see the newest member of the family. This has always been a part of my plan: to welcome a child into my life. I want to make new traditions. Provide them with a warm and safe place to rest their head. Nurture their dreams. Do silly shit like make blanket forts or leave cookies out for Santa. I didn't do much of that growing up. But my kid's childhood will be different from mine. I'll make sure of it.

Paulo puts up a hand to quiet everyone. "Natalia's doing great. She did brilliantly in there. The baby's name is Sebastian, and he'll be brought out to the nursery in a little bit." He scrubs a hand down his face, his expression turning serious. "Even though I couldn't get to Natalia fast enough, I never doubted she'd be okay because all of you were there for her. So thank you."

I can't help envying how Paulo has been embraced by this family. If I were in his place, I'm not sure many people would have risen to the occasion the way Solange and her relatives did tonight. My mother's a rolling stone, and if her latest adventure is any guide, she isn't changing course any time soon. Max would be there for me, no question — and I'm certainly grateful for his friendship — but seeing this family coalesce around Sebastian's birth reminds me that I have very few people in my corner. I look over at Solange, imagining what it would be like to count her among the people who'd have my back if I needed them.

As if she can sense my thoughts, Solange appears at my side, pulling me out of my internal pity party. "Hey there."

"Hey," I say, still watching Paulo and Viviane bask in the joy of the new baby.

"Let me know when you're ready to go, and I'll walk you out."

I give her a sidelong glance. "Trying to get rid of me, Pereira?"

"Moi?" she says, wide-eyed, the fingers of both hands fanned out over her chest. "Never."

"Good. Let's meet Sebastian before I go."

Solange and I don't have much time left together. I intend to make the most of it.

Chapter Eighteen

SOLANGE

"Isn't Sebastian precious?" I say, looking up at Dean dreamily as we wait for an elevator.

Dean nods, a faint smile teasing the edges of his mouth. "An excellent set of lungs too."

"I can already picture the screaming matches between him and Natalia. They're going to be epic."

Dean has said his goodbyes to everyone, and I've offered to walk him out to the lobby. One elevator has been idle since we got here, and the other started at the top and is stopping on every floor. When one finally arrives, it's crammed with people. *Of course.* I raise a hand in the general direction of the folks inside, all of whom are giving us the death glare for even thinking about jumping on. "We'll wait."

"Let's just take the stairs," Dean says. "After being twisted like a pretzel in your bumper car, I could use an excuse to stretch my legs."

I narrow my eyes at him, giving him my own death glare. "Need I remind you that you still need my help on Wednesday? Consider being nicer to the person saving your ass."

"You're right," he says, pulling me into his arms and steering me in the direction of the stairwell. "Consider me reminded and appropriately chastised." He holds me in a loose embrace, as if he's hugging a buddy, but after the night we've had my reaction to his touch is decidedly not friendly. God, why does he always smell so good, no matter the scent he's chosen to wear? With my face inches from his neck, I breathe in the smoky and sweet scents radiating off his skin, a heady combination that reminds me of toasted cinnamon sprinkled over warm apple pie. Mmm, Dean á la mode. Now *that* would be a yummy indulgence.

Happily basking in the warmth of Dean's body, I'm startled when he jumps away and holds the door open. "Oh wait," he says, wide-eyed, a theatrical performance looming. "I'm not supposed to be this close to you, right? You didn't use your safe word."

I should thank him for the reminder, but that would be hypocritical of me since I have zero interest in paying attention to it. I move past the threshold and look back at him. "Is this your way of telling me you'll only touch me if we're pretending? Good Lord, Chapman. That's no way to make a woman feel wanted."

I precede him down the stairs, and as I'm approaching the second-floor landing, he gently tugs on my sleeve, halting my progress. I don't turn back. I simply wait, a team of miniature gymnasts somersaulting in my belly.

"Is that what you think?" he asks. "That I don't want you?"

I was kidding, although it seems I missed the mark. I'd love to see his face, but I'm afraid to move. Is his expression as intense as his voice? Are his hazel eyes crystal clear, or are they cloudy with desire? *Damn, damn, damn.* What's the point of asking these questions? We should be going our separate ways so I can rejoin my family upstairs. When I spin around to tell him just that, *he's right there,* a single step above me, his back against the railing and his face close enough that I can see the exquisite details of his features. And yes, his expression is intense. And his eyes are most certainly clouded with desire. "Don't mind me, okay?" I don't meet his gaze as I explain. "It's been a long day, and I'm exhausted.

You probably shouldn't take anything I say to heart."

"And yet that's exactly what I'm doing," he says without hesitation. "At the very least I need to clarify that I want you so fucking much, I'm aching to touch you right now. But . . ." Instead of finishing the sentence, he squeezes his eyes shut. Still, it's not hard to figure out what he isn't saying.

But . . . we're not right for each other.

But . . . you're leaving.

But . . . if we act on our attraction, one of us will get hurt — and that person is you.

I'm gripped by the certainty that a big mistake is gaining momentum and barreling in my direction. Honestly, it would be great if someone slapped some sense into me, but I have a niggling suspicion that when it comes to Dean, I'm steadily moving past the point of logic and knowingly exposing myself to heartbreak. I'm smarter than this. I *know* I am. I'm not interested in being anyone's temporary diversion, and Dean's made it abundantly clear that romance isn't in his wheelhouse. So why is it so damn hard to listen to the warning signs?

Because you like him, a voice in my head says. *And you're attracted to him. And his transparency is disarming;you can't very well tell yourself he duped you if he's been honest*

Thinking back to everything that's happened tonight, from our interactions at the sex party to the physical discomfort he put himself through so Natalia could experience the labor she'd envisioned, it all reminds me that Dean has been open and honest and *present* for me in every way. And right now, in this dimly lit stairwell, after a chaotic night that still isn't over, I want his lips on mine once more. *Just* once more. So I move up to his step, then rest my hand against his stomach. "Shove all those thoughts out of your mind and do it, then. Touch me."

"Solange."

There's wonder in his voice, as if I've given him a gift he never expected to receive.

I drop my forehead to his chest. Suddenly his fingers are in my hair, leisurely massaging my head, until he lifts my chin so we're facing each other. "May I . . . kiss you?" The question breaks in his throat and shatters my last defenses.

"Yes."

He descends a step, then takes my hand and guides me to him, the change in position placing us centimeters apart. A kiss to Dean isn't just a meeting of mouths. No, it begins with a low drag of his thumb across my lower lip, transitions to a soft peck above my Cupid's bow, then continues with a brush of our cheeks as he breathes me in.

I wait and wait and wait, until I can't wait any longer, and soon I'm tugging him closer and assuming control. I bite his lip, not hard but strong enough to let him know I want more. Faster, fiercer, harder. *Give it to me,* I'm saying with my hands, my lips, my teeth. He obliges, his hand gripping my neck and his mouth setting a deliciously thorough yet frenzied pace.

"Touch me," I whisper when we come up for air. "Everywhere."

This close, I can see that his pupils are dilated and his eyes are so darkened by lust they appear brown. We stare at each other, our gazes bouncing from feature to feature as he lifts my shirt and slips his hand under the waistband of my pants.

I gasp, my mouth going slack in anticipation. Trembling with desire, I try to urge him with my eyes. *Yes, touch me there. Make me wet. Make me come.*

A finger glides over my underwear, along my cleft, then another finger joins in as the first retraces its steps.

"Please," I say against his cheek.

Those fingers delve under the fabric, and

finally, finally, settle on my clitoris, drawing torturously slow circles there. Oh God. It's both not enough and too much. I let out a long moan, my entire body tingling.

"Like this?" he asks, his breath feathering over my eyes.

"Yes, just like that," I whisper.

"Ah Jesus, Solange. You're so soft."

My skin's taut, the tension in my arms and legs stretching it to its capacity, the sensations evoked by Dean's touch having nowhere to go so they build and build and build inside me.

"Let me take you home," he says, his voice rough and urgent as his talented fingers dip inside my slick heat. "Spend the night with me."

The word *yes* hovers in the air, until the sound of someone pushing the metal release on a door above us echoes in the stairwell and yanks me out of the moment.

He draws his hand out of my pants and gingerly straightens my top. I blink my eyes open and try to focus on our surroundings. We're in a stairwell, not all that different from the one I was in when I discovered his fiancée *three weeks ago.* That parallel is the splash of cold water I need. "I should get back. They're probably wondering where I am. Let's just forget . . ." I gesture around

281

me as if to say *us*. Let's just forget *us*. As an idea. As a possibility.

He clears his throat, then nods once. "Yeah, I hear you." His face is flushed, and his lips are wet, and his hair is adorably mussed. Note to self: The more disheveled his appearance, the harder it is to resist him.

I brush off my pants for no reason whatsoever. "Well, one more get-together, and we're done, right?"

He raises a brow at that, though I didn't mean it to sound so final. I'm about to clarify, but my mother appears at the top of the landing.

What the hell?

How?

Why?

"Filha, are you leaving?" she asks, her gaze darting to Dean before it returns to me.

"No, I'll be up in a sec."

"Okay, good. I wanted to ask you if you still wanted to go to the community garden tomorrow."

"Yes, I do. And we can talk about it later. Because I'll be up in a sec, okay?" I widen my eyes, but she pretends not to understand that I'm asking her to make herself scarce, which immediately makes me suspicious of her motivation for being here.

"Oh, no problem." She winks at Dean.

"Nice to meet you, filho."

"You too, Ms. Pereira," he says, a hint of amusement in his tone.

Then my mother spins around, pushes open the exit door, and waltzes out of sight.

I shake my head. "I don't even know what that was about."

"A mother's prerogative, I think," he says, giving me a knowing smile.

"A mother's nosiness, you mean." I flick a thumb over my shoulder. "Anyway, I should get going. Talk to you soon."

"Bye, Solange," he calls after me.

"Bye," I say, giving him a seemingly carefree wave as I scurry up the stairs.

Sure, I can't change what just happened between us, but I *can* make sure *nothing else* happens. It'll be fine. Absolutely fine. We're only one outing away from being done with our fake dating arrangement, then Dean and I can move on with our regular lives.

Separately, of course.

Sunday afternoon, my mother and I meet up at the Lanier Heights Community Garden project site. Preparing four dozen plots of land, each measuring approximately fifty square feet, should be easy enough, but we're experiencing a crisis at the management level — specifically too many cooks and only one kitchen.

Cindy, a middle-aged white woman who thinks one can never wear enough animal prints, and Danilo, a young Filipino short-order cook who *still* hasn't sent me his supposedly world-famous chicken adobo recipe, have been debating the design for a half hour now.

Beside me, my mother sighs, then whispers into my ear: "The plots need to be separated with fencing or they're going to get contamination."

"Cross-contamination, you mean?"

"Yes. And using patio stones would be too hard on everyone's knees when they're gardening. Grass is better."

"Why don't you say something, then?"

She shrugs. "This isn't my garden. I'm just here to help you."

That's what she thinks. She's here to be inspired. And hopefully to reinvigorate her interest in flowers and plants. But so far, she isn't moved by the discussion, and I can't say that I blame her. Cindy's and Danilo's voices are rising, and a third volunteer, whom I don't know, looks as though he's about to enter the fray. Enough.

I clear my throat to get their attention. "So as I understand it, regardless of the plot setup, we need to turn the soil, right?"

They all nod.

"Can my mother and I work on that while you continue chatting about this?" I peek at my watch. "Because we'll need to get going soon."

And we're tired of standing around.

"Okay, yes," Cindy says. "We can use everyone's help with that." She points at the far-right corner of the garden. "You can find compost over there."

"Great. We'll get started."

Ten minutes later, Mãe and I have dispersed a layer of compost over our chosen area and are flipping the soil with handheld spades. The repetitive task allows us to engage in conversation with relative ease.

"Viviane can't stop talking about Sebastian," my mother says with a smile. "She's so happy."

"We're all happy. He's the first baby of the next generation. It's a big deal."

"I hope he gets to grow up with his cousins, like you did. I can see myself spoiling all of them. Wouldn't that be nice?"

"Hmm, yeah," is my reply, partly because I don't think she'd appreciate anything else I'd say about this subject. Her question, though, only reinforces what I already suspected: Staying in DC probably isn't the best decision for either of us. I need to chart my own course, and she needs to redefine herself as more than someone's mother. Even now, she's waiting for me to return home so she can step into the only role she's ever known. She's sacrificed so much and for so long that I don't think she knows how to do or be anything else. She had dreams, though. Before my father. Before me. Before her sisters convinced her that opening the shop would help provide for us all. Now she's stuck. And if my mother continues to use our relationship as her lodestar, I'm afraid she won't ever reach for her dreams again. She deserves her own life. Her own happiness too. I want this for her more than anything else.

Yes, my mother and her sisters built the familial village my cousins and I grew up in, and I'm grateful for what they did for us. But Viviane and Mariana fully expect that they'll eventually pass the leadership to us, whereas my mother appears reluctant to relinquish her caretaking role. And sure, raising kids, whether biological or adopted, isn't out of the question, but I'm in no rush, and I certainly don't expect my mother to devote the lion's share of her time to looking after them.

"Tell me about Dean," she says, not meeting my eyes as she deftly changes the subject. "He seems sweet."

"He's a friend," I say flatly. "That's it, Mãe. Don't get any ideas."

She draws back and rests her hands on her lap. "So defensive, filha." She crinkles her nose. "What's the project you're working on together?"

"It's a long story."

"We have a lot of composto."

I can't help snorting. "Touché." I give her the rundown of my and Dean's exploits, and her mouth gapes in the same way mine did when Dean first proposed his scheme. When I'm done, she shakes her head. "Wow, wow, wow. Que confusão!"

"Believe me, I know."

"So why can't he pretend to be your boyfriend when Cláudia comes next weekend? Instead of Brandon?"

I shake my head like a testy parrot. "No, no, no. We have one more date left, then I need to move on."

"Because you like him," my mother says as she studies my reaction to her statement.

"Because there's no point in prolonging the inevitable. I'm leaving soon. Maybe."

She seizes on the word *maybe* and perks up. "What do you mean 'maybe'? Did you hear something from the school?"

I wish I could lie to my mother, but every time I fix my mouth to do so, it rejects the attempt, as if my brain has figured out how to make it physically impossible. "Yes, they gave me a permanent offer." I drop the spade and put up my hands. "But please wait, wait, wait, because I'm ninety percent certain I'm not going to take it."

"Why?" she asks on a huff.

"Lots of reasons, Mãe. I'd be committing to staying in DC, and I'm not sure this is the best place for me. Plus, they want me to implement a new curriculum, and what if it doesn't work out? Or the students don't stick with the program? I don't want to find myself stuck if this turns out to be a bad decision."

She knits her brows, and a line appears between them. "So you're going to assume all of those bad things will happen and that's it?"

I groan. Now we're both frustrated. "It's just that I don't want to make a bad decision and find myself wondering how the hell I got off course."

She looks down at her hands and flexes them. "That's what you think happened to me."

Her voice is soft and laced with hurt, and now I want to smack myself with the spade.

"Mãe, no, I couldn't be prouder of you than I already am. But you gave up enough, and I worry that you're waiting for me to fix my life so you can know what to do with yours."

"I'm your *mother,*" she says, exasperated.

"Of course, Mãe. But that's not *all* you are. Remember you said you wanted to grow flowers?" Florticulture, she called it once. She even spent summers working at the Jardim Botânico in Rio when she was young to cultivate that interest.

She whips her head around and laughs, recognition dawning on her face. "Is that what we're doing here?"

"I just thought it would be a way to help spark your interest in growing flowers again. Maybe as a career." I drop my head. "But I can see I just made a mess of things."

"No, this was kind of you." She takes my hand. "But, filha, I didn't give up anything I wasn't willing to give up. I had you, and I did what I needed to do because I love you with all my heart. I don't regret a single day." Her voice is fierce, as if it's important that I understand the strength of her conviction on this point. "And listen, I'm not going to tell you what to do with your life, but please let me worry about mine."

"But I'm your *daughter,*" I say, mirroring her exasperation from moments ago.

"See that?" she says, squeezing my chin. "That's how I feel about you!"

Ugh. She's too damn smart for her own good.

"Let me ask you something," she says. "Did you tell Dean about this offer?"

"No. Why would I?"

"Ah, the better question is, why wouldn't you?"

Shit. My mother's blowing my mind today. I've had plenty of opportunities to tell Dean about the offer, but I chose not to. Because what if the possibility of exploring a relationship with Dean factors into my decision-making, and that, too, turns out to be a bad choice on my part? I mean, there's no *what if* about it. That *would* be a bad decision on my part.

When I don't respond to her rhetorical question, she adds, "You know, I think the more something's important to us, the more we feel we'll lose if it doesn't work out. So we convince ourselves not to want the thing. That goes for your job, and maybe Dean too." She points at her feet. "These sneakers? They're old. Feio. It was easy to choose them this morning because I didn't care if they got messed up. But if I only had nice shoes? The decision about which ones to wear would have been much harder."

"I'm not following," I say, shaking my head. "Dean's a nice pair of shoes?"

"Something like that," she says with a grin.

I pick up the spade again and plunge it through the dirt in frustration. Even now, I'm wondering what Dean's doing. Is he at work on a Sunday? Probably. Or is he cooking in his meticulously well-kept kitchen? Reading a brief? Dammit, this is a problem. So yeah, Dean's something, all right. I just don't know what — and my gut tells me it's best if I keep it that way.

Chapter Nineteen

DEAN

I'm more nervous about speaking at Career Day than I usually am about appearing in court. For starters, Kimberly and Nia are in the audience, so I'm mindful that I should still be in recruitment mode. And, of course, I'm talking to a bunch of teenagers, none of whom are white and all of whom have different life experiences than mine as a result. I'd like to add value to their education, not detract from it. Most of all, I don't want to let Solange down. She's put a lot of thought into her work here, and I'd hate to bomb the assignment.

The good news is, Solange refused to invite Peter — "I'm not subjecting these sweethearts to that prick," she explained — and I'm taking some small comfort in his absence, particularly because he's been extra annoying of late. Earlier in the week, when Henderson asked about the party, I told him the group canceled its plans, so Peter probably thinks he's in the clear and will be insufferable at dinner later. *Chin up, Dean. You're almost done. But first, you need to speak to these kids.*

So I tell the class about college and law school and my path to becoming a litigator. My entire spiel doesn't take long, and the picture I paint of my life isn't all that interesting or appealing; it comes across as uninspired. Damn, when did I become this sterile? Not surprisingly, several students are spacing out; a few don't even try to mask the boredom in their expressions.

Solange strides to the front of the room — to save me, probably. "Thank you, Mr. Chapman. I think this would be a great time to open the floor for questions. Remember what we talked about, everyone: nothing too personal."

"Where'd you grow up?" a kid in the back asks.

"My mom and I moved around a lot," I say. "Spent the longest time in Delaware, though."

"Delaware?" another student asks as if I just announced that I lived on Mars.

I glance at Solange, who has returned to the back corner of the room and is smiling behind her hand. "Yeah, it's an actual, honest-to-God state. The president and the First Lady live there when they're not at the White House."

"The first state to ratify the U.S. Constitution," Layla says. "Right, Ms. Pereira?"

Solange winks at her, then nods proudly. "Right, Layla."

Man, the teacher's pet in me can easily spot another teacher's pet. Layla is Solange's.

"Ever had anything funny happen to you in court?" This from a kid who was nodding off just a few minutes ago.

I think about it for a moment, then chuckle. "Yeah. A couple of years ago, my best friend, Max, he tells me he wants to see me in action and shows up for my first trial ever. It was a small case. No jury, just the judge. And the plaintiff in the case was representing himself. Max sits right up front, in the second or third row, maybe. He looks like a proud father, all eager to hear me try this case. Later, I'm cross-examining a witness, and the sound of loud snoring fills the courtroom. Like, loud-loud."

"No way," a student says, collapsing onto his desk and shaking his head. "Max fell asleep, right?"

"Right. But what's worse is that the judge

stopped the trial to scold him. Said something like, 'Spectators are advised that they should be paying attention to the proceedings, or the court will have to remove them.' So, yeah, Max is banned from seeing any more of my trials."

A kid who's as tall as me and whose name tag reads "Héctor" jumps in next. "What would you do if you couldn't be a lawyer?"

"Great question, Héctor," Solange says. "If you'd asked me that ten years ago, I would have said 'be a professional swimmer and compete in the Olympics,' but I think it's too late for that. I can cook, though. Been doing it since I was a kid. So maybe I'd study to be a chef."

A few students nod. This isn't so bad. They seem interested. Engaged, even. They're not cackling like they were during Nia's presentation, but I'm holding my own.

"What's your favorite part of your job?" Layla asks.

"My pro bono work, no question," I respond.

"What's that?" the student behind Layla asks.

"*Pro bono* comes from the Latin phrase *pro bono publico,* which means 'for the public good.' Basically, it's the part of my job that lets me represent people for free

295

when they need my help but can't pay my fees. I make sure people can stay in their homes. I'm telling you, there's no better feeling than winning a case for a client facing eviction or dealing with a shady landlord."

Kimberly, who's leaning against a desk on the right side of the room, clears her throat, then raises her hand.

I sit up straight. "Yes, Ms. Bailey?"

"Can you tell us something you *don't* like about your job?" she asks. "Like, what's the thing that sticks in your craw?"

"Your *craw*?" one student asks, looking confused.

"The thing that's hard to swallow," Kimberly clarifies.

Hmm. This is a tough one. I could say something trite — the long hours are at the top of my con column and don't necessarily reflect poorly on the firm — but I promised to be honest about my experiences, and I'm not changing course now. If Kimberly's going to be my colleague, I'd want her to have a full understanding of what she's getting into, and it occurs to me that I've been giving her a skewed version of the firm simply because I've been sidestepping anything unpleasant. So I tell her — and them — the truth. "Being an associate is a challenge.

We're always proving ourselves. And the partners dangle the promise of partnership in front of our eyes to keep us in line. I wish they cared about us. As people. But I don't think they really do. In the end, it's just business." I raise a finger in the air. "But it *does* pay well. And for a kid who had to put himself through college and law school, that counts for a lot."

Is it enough, though? I'm not so sure anymore. I've been putting one foot in front of the other for so long, it never dawned on me to consider whether I'm heading down the right path. Or maybe I've purposefully avoided considering it. Because for better or worse, this job is an anchor, and without it, I'd just be bobbing around. Adrift and aimless.

I look up and meet Solange's gaze. She tips her head and smiles, the warmth in her expression going straight to my heart. I'd like to think Solange is saying she's proud of me. Because if that were the case, I'd consider this day a success no matter what else happens.

SOLANGE

Once Career Day's over, we meet Peter and Molly at Jaleo, a Spanish restaurant in Penn Quarter. Our group is on time for the reservation, but our table isn't ready.

"We're so sorry for the wait, folks," the harried host says. "It's been a hectic night. We'll do our best to get you seated as soon as we can. In the meantime, you're welcome to sit in the lounge."

Peter huffs and appears ready to fuss and complain, but Molly places a hand on his arm and subtly shakes her head. Surprisingly, he relents. Peter's mellowing the longer I'm in his presence, or maybe I'm just getting used to him; the latter's a scary thought.

Taking the host's suggestion, we drift to the lounge and find a circular seating arrangement large enough to accommodate our group.

Dean and I choose to sit on a high-backed padded bench, and I cozy up next to him, hoping to convey the natural ease between us. He picks up on my cue and settles a hand on my lap. It's an act, a simple arrangement of our bodies meant to convey our familiarity with each other. But to me, it's infinitely more complicated than that, because in that moment, with Dean's finger gently circling the top of my thigh, I imagine what it would be like to be his true partner, to absorb tiny intimate touches like this one as if they were commonplace.

My brain's got a lot of explaining to do.

Peter lifts a menu off the table and skims it for a few seconds. "Solange, any advice on what to order?"

Bless you, Peter. Just the kind of question to get me out of my head. But also: *Go to hell, Peter.* It's a Spanish restaurant. Why would I be an expert on the menu? "Not really. I've never been, so I can't really recommend anything."

"Oh," Peter says, frowning. "I just thought since some of the food descriptions seem to be in Spanish that you'd have some insight."

"Brazilians speak Portuguese," I say matter-of-factly. "Different colonizer."

Someone snorts, but I refuse to look anyone else in the eye. If Peter's expression were captured in a photograph, it would be captioned "Damn you to hell."

"Have you ever been to Brazil, Solange?" Kimberly asks.

I nod, grateful for the redirect. "Several times. We usually travel to Rio as a family and plan one big reunion when we get there."

"Nia and I vacationed there after college graduation," she says. "It was the best gift we've ever given ourselves."

"Where'd you go?" I ask.

"A week in Rio, a few days in São Paulo,

and a week in Salvador da Bahia. It was a whirlwind, but we had a blast. The people were so lovely. I'd read about Bahia, about the heavy African influence there, but seeing it firsthand was a different thing entirely."

Nia nods enthusiastically. "And can we talk about the food? Amazing!" She turns to Kimberly. "Remember that little place in Rio? The one just a few minutes from our hotel? It had the most amazing bread and these little snacks I couldn't get enough of."

Oof. She's making me hungry just talking about them. "You're probably thinking of salgadinhos. Fried dough stuffed with vegetables or meat or cheese? Sometimes all three?"

"Yes!" Nia says, pointing her finger in agreement. "That's it! I could eat those all day every day."

"Solange knows where you can get them close to here," Dean says, waggling his eyebrows. "Her mother and aunts own a Brazilian grocery store and café in Wheaton, and let me tell you, the tias know how to cook."

Dean's a mess. He's met my mother and aunts once; now he's calling them "the tias"? Oh, wait. I see what he's doing. *Catch*

300

up, Solange. You're fake dating him, remember?

"I've never been to Brazil," Molly says on a wistful sigh. "But I hear so much about the food. I'd love to try it sometime."

Peter snaps his fingers. "I have a great idea. Seeing as this place still doesn't have a table for us, how about we ditch it and head over to . . . What's it called, Solange?"

I gulp before answering. "Rio de Wheaton."

"Right," Peter says, his smile slick and slimy. "Rio de Wheaton. I'm sure *the tias* would love to see you and Dean, and then we can get some of those salgaritas —"

Eek. He's an oaf. "*Salgadinhos,* you mean."

"Sure, sure," he says. "What do you think?"

Nia bounces in her seat and claps her hands. "Can we? That would be an excellent way to top off this trip."

Oh my Lord, this is the stuff of nightmares. We're *this close* to successfully ending the charade; a visit to Rio de Wheaton, though, risks so many potential land mines, we're likely to be swallowed whole by the resulting crater.

I glance at Dean, trying to gauge whether he's aware of the danger. Goodness, is that sweat on his forehead?

He removes his hand from my lap and sits up. "I don't know. The traffic might not be great out that way."

Molly, who typically doesn't contribute all that much to our conversations, suddenly pipes up. "I go out to UMD for research every Wednesday, and I can get us there in no time. I'll just tell our driver to take Sixteenth Street and head out on 97." Now she's an expert in DMV traffic patterns?

Think, Solange. Think. "Well, it's late in the day, so I'm not sure they'll have a good selection. But we could try a place in —"

With his phone at his ear and his eyes boring into mine, Peter speaks to someone, probably Tia Mariana, on the line. "Yes? Hello? Is this Rio de Wheaton? Yeah, I'm wondering if you have salgaritas —"

"Salgadinhos," Molly snaps, her nose flaring before she adopts a serene "so help me" expression.

Peter smiles hard. "Yeah, salgadinhos. You do? Fresh from the oven too? Excellent, excellent. Thank you!" He shoves his phone in his pants pocket and rubs his hands. "So we're doing this?"

I glance at Dean. He's eyeing the exits as if he's seriously considering a quick escape.

"Dean, what do you say?" Peter asks.

302

"Sure, if it's okay with everyone else, it's okay by me."

Peter throws up his hands in vindictive glee. "Yes! I'll arrange for a seven-passenger. We're going on an adventure!"

Indeed, we are. Problem is, I don't think it's going to be fun at all.

I grab my phone as soon as we're in the Lyft.

> **Me:** shit this is NOT GOOD
> **Dean:** I know but what choice did we have.
> **Me:** Peter wants to catch us so bad
> **Dean:** Probably going to get his wish too.
> **Me:** fuck that. i'll text Lina and get her to prep the tias
> **Dean:** It's worth a shot.

"Everything okay, you two?" Peter asks from the front passenger seat.

"Totally fine," I say cheerfully. "Just checking some old messages."

And planning your long-overdue demise, you little shit. But first, Lina.

> **Me:** MAYDAY. MAYDAY. headed to Rio. got cornered into taking the group there.

Tias need to pretend Dean's my boyfriend. can you give them the heads-up?

The three dots appear immediately, then nothing. *Not now, Lina. I need you.*

Lina: Had to get Jaslene to cover a client meeting. On my way. But I can't stay. You're on your own after I'm gone.

Done. As simple as that. People sometimes ask me what it's like to be an only child, and I tell them I wouldn't know. My cousins *are* my siblings, and they'd ride-or-die with me any day.

As I envision the countless ways this evening still could go wrong, Molly and Kimberly chat about the pros and cons of living just outside DC. Airports nearby. Proximity to Baltimore. More space. Unfortunately, I can't summon enough focus to take part in the conversation; it's all background noise to me.

Minutes from our destination, Dean slips his hand in mine and threads our fingers together. He gives me a sweetly encouraging smile, and the churning in my belly settles. His touch is a reminder that I'm not doing this alone. A reminder, too, that he's probably more nervous than I am — although he's doing a much better job of masking it. I send up a silent prayer that this excursion isn't a catastrophe in the making.

The Lyft stops in front of Rio de Wheaton, and everyone climbs out.

Kimberly and Nia are thrumming with excitement. I hope the experience doesn't disappoint. If nothing else, I want them to have a good time.

"This is going to be so great," Nia says to me. "I can't wait to meet your family."

"Me neither," Peter says. He looks up at the door. "They even have a little shop bell."

Tia Viviane says she bought it because it reminded her of the bell above the bookshop in *You've Got Mail.* If Peter says anything snide about it in Tia Viviane's presence, we may need to carry him out of here on a stretcher.

Mentally making the sign of the cross, I usher everyone into the store.

My mother, Tia Viviane, and Tia Mariana are standing side by side behind the counter, three wide-eyed owls wearing overly bright smiles.

"Solange and Dean," Tia Mariana says grandly. "Wow. We *never* expected to see you two here. How may we help you?"

Oh dear. The cringe factor is strong with

305

this one. We're never going to pull this off.

I turn to our guests. "Why don't you take a spin through the aisles." To Kimberly and Nia, I say, "Maybe you'll recognize a few products on the shelves?"

They nod with enthusiasm and wander off as if they're skipping through their own personal playground.

"We'll find a place to sit," Molly says.

Considering the café consists of three tables and maybe twice as many chairs, the search won't take very long. Still, I'm grateful for the reprieve because I need to speak to my mother and aunts.

Dean and I rush over to them.

"Relax," I say through gritted teeth.

"You're one to talk," Tia Viviane says. "What's wrong with your mouth?"

"Nothing. Try to act natural, okay? Right now, you all look constipated."

"Constipation *is* natural," my mother says. "Just the other day —"

I put out a hand to cut off whatever she's planning on saying next. "Mãe, no. Please."

"I'm sorry to draw you into this mess," Dean tells them, his tone conveying a mixture of amusement and nervousness. "Hopefully we won't be too much of a bother. We'll try a few things and be out of here in no time."

"Filho, don't worry about it," my mother says, her eyes soft and kind. "You've been through so much. We're here for you too."

Yes, yes. So tragic. But we don't have time for this. I flap my hands, unsure what else to do. "Maybe you should make yourselves look busy. That way, Peter won't be able to ask any questions."

Lina's mother agrees. "One of us should bring a bunch of salgadinhos to the table. That'll occupy them for a little while."

"Don't ask me to do it," my mother says. "I'm a terrible liar."

"Viviane should do it," Tia Mariana suggests. "She doesn't know how to make small talk anyway."

Tia Viviane frowns at her. "Shut up, Mariana. See? There's your small talk."

Tia Mariana punches her fist into her elbow joint and raises her other fist in front of her face, a move she normally reserves for heated political discussions. "Take that, Viviane."

My mother shushes them. "Stop it. We're supposed to be *helping,* remember?"

Tia Mariana, apparently fed up with the lack of progress on our part, takes it upon herself to begin placing various salgadinhos in a baking dish, then places the dish in the oven. "Someone should offer them drinks."

"I'll do it," I say. "We should minimize your exposure to them anyway. All of you stay here. Dean, you ready?"

He nods, his eyes darting everywhere as though he's searching the store for any and all exit points. "Ready."

Dean and I stride over to the table, then I pretend to be holding a pad and paper in my hands. "Welcome to Rio de Wheaton, friends. Can I start you off with a beverage?"

Everyone agrees to a round of Guaraná Brazilia, and Dean and I grab the soft drink cans from the fridge. Minutes later, our group is huddled around a tiny table, a warm batch of salgadinhos in the center, thanks to Tia Mariana, who skedaddled away to the back as if she were Remy from *Ratatouille* and a health inspector had just walked in.

Nia bites into one of the coxinhas and slaps her hand on the table. "Yes! Yes! Yes!"

"Goodness, Nia," Kimberly says, her eyes twinkling in amusement. "You're giving us Meg Ryan fake-orgasm-in-the-diner vibes."

"I'm not faking it, though!" Nia says, dabbing the sides of her mouth with a napkin. "But I do love that movie."

Dean chuckles. "I know that scene. Everyone does. But I've never seen the entire movie."

Nia's eyes nearly pop out of her head. "You haven't? Oh, you need to fix that, *stat*. *When Harry Met Sally* is a classic for a reason."

"I'll put it on the list for our next movie night," he says.

For a few seconds, I actually believe Dean's going to do just that. As if movie night isn't a mythical event that exists only in the context of our phony relationship. *Snap the hell out of it, Solange. After today, you're going to steer clear of this man.*

Molly hums her approval. "Nia's right. I'm in heaven."

I steal a glance at Peter, who's watching the tias behind the counter. As long as I keep him away from them, we should be okay. Satisfied that Dean and I are off the hook for now, I grab an empadinha de camarão and take a bite. The buttery flakes of the mini pot pie crumble in my mouth, and I moan my appreciation.

"Someone's giving Sally a run for her money," Nia says, winking at me.

Gaining confidence that we'll survive this fiasco with each passing minute, I offer Dean a taste. "Want to try?"

His eyes flickering with interest, he opens

his mouth — just as the bell above the door chimes and my cousin Rey's voice fills the store. "What's up, meu povo! No one told me about the party!"

Oh God, oh God, oh God. I grab Dean's thigh under the table. Unless Lina's a magician, which isn't entirely outside the realm of possibility, Rey has no clue what's going on.

Dammit, Rey, don't come this way. Don't come this way.

A line etched between his brows, Rey scans the table, tilts his head, then walks over to us. "This is a surprise. Solange, I thought —"

Before Rey can finish, Tia Mariana reappears, tackles her son, and stuffs a coxinha in his mouth, almost toppling the only empty chair in the café. As she drags Rey away, she smiles at our group. "He's been harassing me about using this new recipe. I wanted him to try the results as soon as he got here. Hope you're enjoying the food!"

Peter grins. "Everything's great. Thank you!"

Maybe Peter's finally given up. Maybe he can be a decent person when he wants to be. Maybe Mercury's no longer in retrograde. Whatever it is, I'll take it.

But then the bell chimes again, and two

middle-aged people walk into the store. The woman isn't a stranger, but I'm having trouble placing her.

"Cláudia!" my mother exclaims from behind the counter, her voice high and tight. "What are you doing here?"

Oh shit. I think I may have tinkled in my underwear. Can this really be happening? Of course it can. It's my life after all. Cursed. Every damn cell in my body is cursed.

"Oi, família!" our cousin Cláudia says. "I know I said to expect us on Friday, but Rodrigo and I decided to surprise you!"

The doorbell chimes yet again, and a man and a woman laughing and jostling each other stumble inside.

"And here's my daughter and her husband!" Cláudia says proudly.

I lean over to Dean, throw my arm over the back of his chair, and press my mouth against his ear. "Remember that IOU?"

He swallows audibly, the gulp in his throat sounding like a boulder hitting the surface of a lake. "Yeah."

"I'm calling in my debt right now."

CHAPTER TWENTY

DEAN

San Antonio, we have a problem.

If I'm understanding Solange correctly, we're now trapped in a fake dating mashup that's going to tie us together for just a bit longer. Are we tempting disaster by prolonging this pretend relationship? Of course. Am I going to do it anyway? For Solange? Hell yes.

Solange's mom and aunts gather around the newcomers, and everyone talks excitedly with one another. As the group drifts away from the door, the younger of the two women waves at our table, crouches between Solange and me, then gives Solange a peck on the cheek.

"Oi, prima," she whispers. "Is this the new boyfriend?"

"Oi, Ana," Solange says, looking down and rubbing an eyebrow. "He's the one."

The woman winks at me, then straightens.

"Can't wait to talk later."

My "girlfriend" lightly squeezes my thigh and stands. "Excuse us, everyone. Our cousins are visiting from Brazil. Dean and I should go say a quick hello."

"Hang on," Kimberly says, her hand hovering over the table to stop us. "We don't want to monopolize your time any more than we have, so let's just say our goodbyes now." She gives us a warm smile, then places her hand in Nia's. "This has been so much fun, and we really appreciate your giving us a taste of the DMV. You've been gracious hosts, and we're excited to make the big move. I'll be singing your praises when I speak with the firm's partners next week."

Kimberly isn't revealing whether she'll accept a position with the firm, but I didn't expect her to; she's been up-front from the beginning that Olney & Henderson is one of three firms she's considering. I've tried my best to be honest about Olney, pointing out its strengths *and* its weaknesses; the rest is up to Kimberly. I know one thing, though: If she decides to go elsewhere, it *won't* be because Peter and I failed to do our part.

"We appreciate the kind words," I tell her. "And if there's anything else we can share, you know how to reach us."

Kimberly nods. "Absolutely."

"But tell the truth," Peter says, swinging a thumb between him and me, his smug grin in place. "Which one of us would you say is going to make the more lasting impression?"

Kimberly stares off into the distance before responding. "I'll remember you both. For different reasons." She scrunches her nose. "Let's just leave it at that, okay?"

"Deal," I say, smiling as I rise from my chair.

"Can I get a to-go box, though?" Nia asks sheepishly.

Solange laughs. "One to-go box, and if it's okay with you, two great big hugs, coming up." The women exchange hugs, then Solange strides to the counter.

"We did good," Peter tells me, his hands stuffed into the pockets of his chinos. "I never would have imagined it, but we make a great team."

"No one's more surprised than I am."

He leans in so only I can hear what he says next. "I'll admit, I thought you and Solange were faking this relationship. And make no mistake, I was ready to sing like a canary when I confirmed it. For whatever reason, Henderson's really got a bug up his ass about you. But seeing as I couldn't trip you up, I'll finally concede it's legit."

"How big of you. The truth is, our relationship may have started under atypical circumstances, but I care about her a lot."

It's the first honest statement I've made about Solange and me since forever, and it feels good to say it out loud.

Peter gives me a friendly tap on my arm. "I'm happy for you, then."

"Thanks, man."

I'm *this close* to asking Peter about the sex party — whether he knew what he was getting us into, specifically — but this isn't the time or place, and I'm not sure it matters anyway. We did what needed to be done. Opening up a new can of worms isn't wise.

Our group says its goodbyes, and after the Olney contingent leaves, Solange draws me into the circle of people getting reacquainted with Cláudia and her family.

She places an arm around my waist and pulls me close. "This is Dean, my boyfriend."

"He's a liar," Solange's mother adds. Beside me, Solange stiffens, then her mother's eyes bug out. "I mean, he's a *lawyer.*"

"No, you were right the first time," Rey says with a smirk.

Oh, yeah. We need to lock Tia Izabel away somewhere for the duration of their stay; if not, she's liable to confess everything under the slightest duress. And Rey? He's a damn jokester.

"So good to meet you, Dean," Cláudia says.

"Likewise, ma'am."

Cláudia leans toward Solange. "Ele é bonito."

Solange covers her mouth with a fist and laughs into her hand. "She thinks you're cute."

"I like her already," I whisper loud enough for everyone to hear.

Rodrigo shakes my hand. "Sorry we showed up early. One of my colleagues mentioned that seeing the DC tourist attractions this weekend would be a nightmare, so we decided to switch around our itinerary and head to New York City on Saturday instead." He points at his wife. "And she thought it would be fun to surprise everyone."

Beside me, Solange's mother grumbles and talks to her sisters under her breath. "I bet she wanted to catch us with a dirty house. Humph."

Oblivious to Izabel's suspicions, Rodrigo adds: "And thanks for letting Ana and Carlos stay with you while we're here. We appreciate your hospitality."

I flinch slightly, then catch myself. *Poker*

face, Dean. Poker face. What's this about Ana and Carlos staying with us? I turn to Solange for an explanation, making every effort not to broadcast the panic coursing through my body.

"Just a few days, remember?" she says, curling into me and patting my chest. "Because we have two bedrooms." She drops her voice to a whisper when she addresses Cláudia and Rodrigo. "He's so busy. Sometimes I think whatever I say goes in one ear and out the other."

Oh shit. She did mention some of her cousins would be bunking with her and Brandon. But now that I'm reprising my role as her fake boyfriend, they're bunking with *me.* I'm going to need cue cards or a teleprompter to pull this off. "Sorry, you're right." I fake a forgetful gesture. "It slipped my mind, but we're happy to have you."

Ana gives her husband a saucy wink before she returns her gaze to Solange and me. "It'll be nice to give my parents some space. We're all sharing a hotel room in New York, so a little privacy now would be nice."

Carlos waggles his brows at his wife.

Ah damn, they're definitely planning to have sex in my home. Unfortunately, my walls are thin. And Solange and I will be stuck together in my bedroom. Let's hope that Ana and Carlos keep the dirty talk to a minimum and that Solange is a heavy sleeper.

Solange taps my chest again. "Oh! Just in case this slipped your mind, please don't forget we're having dinner at the tias' place Friday night." She turns to Cláudia and Rodrigo. "We're still on for that, right?"

"Shouldn't be a problem," Rodrigo says. "We're leaving for New York early Saturday morning."

"Great," I say. "And no, sweetie, I didn't forget." I raise our clasped fingers and kiss the front of her hand. "Wouldn't miss it for the world."

Solange gives me a coquettish smile. Damn, she's good.

Cláudia taps Solange on the arm. "If you two are living together, does this mean a wedding will happen soon?"

"Nope," Solange says matter-of-factly. "Marriage isn't for everyone. Besides, a piece of paper isn't going to change how I feel about Dean. We're in love, and we're committed to each other. That's enough for us."

If that were true, Solange and I could be a real couple. But she's pretending, and so am I. *You must remember this, Dean.* I look over to Solange's mother. "Izabel, can we get a few boxes of Pilão? We're running out, and we're going to need some for the morning."

Izabel looks at me with hearts in her eyes. "Of course." She takes my hand. "Come, filho. I'll help you gather a few things to make sure your guests have a nice stay."

Now that I think about it, faking a relationship around Solange's family is going to be infinitely easier than faking a relationship around my colleagues. I just need to be charming, treat Solange like a queen, and keep any inappropriate thoughts to myself.

This is going to be a breeze.

This isn't, in fact, a breeze.

For two people who've been doing a decent job of pretend dating thus far, we're flubbing it now — big-time.

As soon as we walk through the door of my condo, Solange switches on an as-yet-unseen HGTV mode in her brain. Problem is, it in no way suggests she's ever seen my place, let alone *lived* here.

"Wow," she says, her eyes widening in wonder. "These floors are gorgeous. Ash-gray hardwood is *such* a unique touch."

I chuckle and flick my gaze up to the ceiling. "C'mon, Solange. Stop fishing for compliments about our flooring. I'm sure

Ana and Carlos are so tired they couldn't care less."

Solange straightens and shakes her head as if to clear it. "Right. Of course." She gives them a rueful grin. "Sorry to blab about *our* décor. That I helped pick out."

Ana and Carlos park their suitcases by the door and wander through the kitchen and living area.

"It's a great place," Carlos says. "Spacious too."

"Yeah," I say proudly. "I lived in a unit a few floors down, but then this two-bedroom became available a couple of years ago, and I jumped on it."

"*We* jumped on it, honey," Solange says, forcing a smile. "And I'm *pretty sure* I was the one who found the listing."

"Yeah, how could I forget about that." I gesture as if my head's too full of information. "So much to remember."

"Yes, well," Ana says, yawning. "We're pretty exhausted. Would it be okay if we turned in early?"

"Absolutely," Solange says. "I'll make sure to have coffee ready in the morning. Dean leaves at the crack of dawn —"

No, I don't.

"— so you probably won't see him until tomorrow evening."

"Sounds good," Ana says. "Can one of you show us to our room?"

Solange bounces on her toes. "Sure!"

Okay, then.

She leads Ana and Carlos down the hall and turns left — toward *my* bedroom.

"There's no need to show them our room first, Solange!" I call after her. "We can give them the tour tomorrow." I drop my head on the counter and silently cry-laugh. Witnessing Solange fall apart is the most adorable thing ever.

"Right," she yells back, pivoting midstep and striding to the guest bedroom. "It's just *such* a neat room. I get excited to show it to people."

My phone buzzes in my pocket. When I check my texts, I see a message from Max:

Max: We heard. Lina rushed over to Solange's and put together a few things. Going to leave the stuff outside your door in five mins. Up to you to get it inside.

Me: Thanks.

Max: Be smart.

Me: Always am.

When Solange returns, I put my index finger over my lips and show her the text.

"That's *excellent* news," she whispers.

"But why is he telling you to 'be smart'?"

I shrug. "I think he's just worried that you're going to take advantage of the situation."

She tilts her head and stares at me.

"I'm kidding," I say, holding my hands up. "He thinks Lina will be pissed if I cross any lines with you."

"I'm twenty-eight years old, not twelve, and it's none of their business." She snaps to attention. "Not that I'm suggesting I *want* something to happen. It's just not their concern if something *does* happen."

"Exactly. Yeah. I know what you mean." I don't want to say anything else. Not about crossing lines, at least. Soon, we'll be going to my bedroom, where we'll spend the night together — me on the floor, probably — and I don't want her to feel any more uncomfortable than she's already feeling. "Your things should be outside by now."

Solange tiptoes to the hall and gives me a thumbs-up, which I suppose is my cue to drag her bag inside. Once that's done, we creep to my bedroom, where she immediately catalogs her belongings.

"Lina's the *best,*" she says. "Seriously, cousins who get you are priceless. She even included a romance novel." She pulls out two neatly folded items of clothing. "If it's

322

all right with you, I'd love to take a shower."

"Solange, you're not a guest here. You're my . . . friend. Do whatever you want."

Truth is, I want her in my room. I want her to use my things. I want her not to think of herself as my guest. Using my shower is a step in that direction. Which sounds ridiculous, but it's true. All of this over a damn shower. What the hell is wrong with me?

"I won't be long," she says, her clothes and toiletry bag in hand. "Five-minute showers are the norm."

She closes the door, and I heave a deep sigh. It's going to be a rough night.

Minutes later, Solange emerges from my bathroom. She's wearing terry shorts and a tank top, and her hair is piled high on the top of her head. Her cheeks are dewy, and beads of moisture dot the bridge of her nose. And fuck if my heart doesn't start beating wildly just because we're alone in the same room together.

I take a deep breath and blow it out slowly. Solange is in my life as a test. That *must* be it. There's no other rational explanation. Since meeting her, I've been questioning goals that have guided my decisions for years. Whether my job is the right fit for me. Whether I have the kind of support network that would help my eventual partner and me to raise a child. Whether it would be so bad to make the kinds of promises that would keep a woman like her in my life. This is terrifying stuff, but then I remember: A plan isn't solid unless it can handle the occasional curveball. There's no need to panic, and there's no need to upend my world. *One foot in front of the other, Dean. You've got this.*

"Do you need anything?" I ask while I gather my own sleep clothes.

She massages her neck, a light touch that draws my eye to her collarbones and shoulders. I want to rest my head in that space and fall asleep there. *Fuck. Maybe you don't got this, Dean.*

"I'm fine," she says. "Are you going to take a shower now?"

I swallow and nod. It's the best I can do.

"Then I think I'll go out to your kitchen and get my bearings. You won't be around during the day to steer me in the right direction when I get lost."

"Good point."

She places her phone in its charging dock and slips out of the room.

After showering, I find Solange sitting in the armchair in the corner of my room, a paperback in her lap. She sits up and nibbles on her lip. Damn, I hate this air of unease between us.

"I'm happy to take the floor," I say, pointing at the bed. "But there's plenty of space for us both, and I changed the sheets this morning. Whatever you want. Really. What matters to me most is that you feel comfortable."

We stare at each other for several beats, then Solange slips under the comforter without a word. I climb in too.

"You own fitted sheets. And a headboard. Amazing." She buries her face in my pillow and takes a deep breath. After a few seconds, she lifts her head. "And you use fabric softener?"

"Bingo. Downy lavender and vanilla bean. Max once accused me of giving him bedding that smelled like a woman's perfume. I was so insulted."

She flops onto her back. "An unsophisticated nose, he has."

"Right? He's uncouth as hell."

We're lying side by side, both of us staring up at the ceiling. It's an unexpected end to our evening, but when I'm spending time with Solange, unexpected is my new normal.

"What a fiasco, huh?" she says.

That's the understatement of the decade. "There's never a dull moment when I'm with you. Must be a day ending in Y."

She laughs. "Cute."

"So tell me why we're doing this."

"This?"

"Faking a relationship for your relatives."

She turns on her side, and I do the same. This is intimate as hell, and yet it feels right. We're not strangers. Not anymore. I've shared details about my life with her that only a few others know. If she asked, I answered. Because I thought it had some bearing on what we needed to accomplish. Now I realize Solange knows more about me than most people in my life do.

And, sure, she's shared pieces of herself too. And I can order her a cup of coffee just the way she likes it. But I want to know everything. Or as much as she'll tell me.

She inhales, then breathes out slowly. "I don't know all the particulars, but my mother and aunts feel like Cláudia looks down on them because they were all single mothers when they raised their kids."

"That sounds like a reason to look up to them."

"I agree. Tia Viviane and Tia Mariana aren't pressed about it, I don't think, but it's a sore spot for my mother. Before the visit, Cláudia made a remark suggesting that I'd never settle down. My mother, annoyed but also feeling uncharacteristically petty, bragged that I was in a relationship and that it was getting *very* serious."

"Ah, so this is where Brandon comes in."

"Yeah."

"Is Cláudia right about you? Are you destined never to settle down?"

She lifts her head a bit and peers at me. "I'll settle down eventually. Where and when it makes sense to."

I don't say anything. Right now, all I want to do is listen — and be here for her.

After a minute of silence, she says, "My mother thinks I avoid making big decisions because I'm afraid I'll end up being sucker punched by them. She's not entirely wrong, but she's not entirely right either. I just think I owe it to her to be smart about my choices. To not fall into the same traps that she fell into."

"You're referring to your father?"

"That's the main one, yeah. But it's other stuff too."

"Where's your father now?"

"No clue," she says. "The last time we talked he promised to attend my high school graduation. He didn't show. The worst part is that my mother tried to warn me against relying on my father. She didn't tell me not to connect with him, but she cautioned me not to expect too much. She was right. I was wrong. Lesson learned."

"He's never tried to contact you as an adult?"

She closes her eyes. "Not even once."

The ache in my throat prevents me from responding as quickly as I'd like to. It's inconceivable to me that a person wouldn't want Solange in their life in some way. Being a part of her circle is a prize we should all want to win. "Are you angry with him? Resentful?"

"As to me, not at all. Because that would suggest that I was missing something by not having him in my life. Or that my mother didn't do enough, and that's very much not the case. My mother was my mom *and* my dad. She made up for his absence a million times over. But as to her, I'm livid. He had no business saddling her with a kid if he didn't want to hang around."

"I'm sure your mother never thought of you as a burden," I say gently. "The love between you two is unmistakable."

"Still, I can't help thinking about what might have been if she hadn't gotten pregnant with me." She shrugs. "Sometimes we feel things we know aren't rational, but we still feel them."

I treasure her honesty. Appreciate that she's willing to be vulnerable with me. She deserves the same. "I don't know my dad. At all . . . He and my mother had a fling."

"Does he know about you?"

"My mother claims he does."

She reaches over and squeezes my arm. "Then it's *his* loss, Dean. I hope you know that. You're an amazing guy, and anyone who can't appreciate that isn't worth your time."

A part of me wants to believe her. But I can't help wondering why my father never looked for me. Why I didn't matter. Then again, if he's anything like the men my mother dated when I was a kid, maybe I'm better off without him. "I wish you weren't leaving so soon. I'm going to miss talking to you."

"I'll be one text or phone call away. Besides, you'll be too busy doing whatever partners do."

I can picture it now. Being a partner at Olney. Working my ass off seven days a week. Ditching my pro bono work because it doesn't align with the firm's priorities. Coming home to an empty place. Sounds . . . fan-fucking-tastic.

For a moment, I pretend I'm living a different life. One in which Solange and I make sense. One in which I come home to her every night. To this bed. "Can I hold you?" I manage to say, my voice uneven. "*Just* hold you."

"You're a spooner," she says, a hint of amusement in her voice.

"Yeah, I'm a spooner."

She turns over. "Hold me, then."

I don't hesitate to mold my body against hers and pull her in tight. The back of her head is resting against my chest, a few of her curls tickling my neck. Taking in a deep breath, I let her freshly bathed scent fill my nostrils. As of tonight, vanilla is my new aphrodisiac.

"Better?" she asks, snuggling into my embrace.

"This is perfect," I whisper.

She stiffens in my arms, but then her muscles loosen quickly, as though she knows her response to my words revealed too much.

I don't wait for her to say anything in return. Instead, I disentangle us just enough for me to turn off the lamp on my nightstand. Within seconds, I'm gathering her in my arms again. Her breathing's steady, so I close my eyes and simply marvel at the fact that Solange is here.

Before I drift off to sleep, her voice fills the air. "Dean?"

"Yeah?"

"I'm glad I crashed your wedding."

My instinct is to pin this statement to a board and dissect it for educational purposes. What does she mean exactly? Is she happy we met? Glad I didn't get married? Asking her to explain is precisely what I *shouldn't* do.

But Solange surprises me and answers the very questions rattling around in my head. "I'm glad you didn't marry Ella. She wasn't the right person for you."

I don't want to be another guy in her life who makes promises he can't keep. Empty declarations are just as meaningless to me as they are to her. So I settle on the truth. I can always give her that. "I'm glad you crashed my wedding too. And . . ."

"And what?" she whispers.

"And I'm so glad you're in my life."

I hope that's enough. Judging by the way she squeezes my hand, I think it is.

Chapter Twenty-One

SOLANGE

I wake up momentarily disoriented, the first rays of sunlight casting a golden glow over my surroundings. Oh hey, this is nice. I'm still in Dean's arms. I could very much get used to being here. But a persistent knocking pulls me out of my pleasantly languid state.

"Dean," I say, trying to tap him awake. "Someone's knocking on your door."

"No one's knocking on the door," he says behind me, not a trace of grogginess in his voice.

"Then what's that . . . *oh.* How long have they been at it?"

"Not sure. They're getting louder, though, so maybe it'll be over soon?"

Louder doesn't quite capture what's going on here. They're shouting. As if they're two gladiators going head to head in a sex match. Penis loaded. Tits drawn. A fight to the (little) death. Awkwardness lodges in my chest and prepares to rest there permanently. "Um, your walls are super thin."

"I suspected as much, but this confirms it."

"Should we put on music or something? Maybe get up and move around so they know we're stirring?"

"Good idea."

He rolls away from me and stumbles out of bed. It's my first true opportunity to see the way Dean looks before he transforms into Clark Kent — bedhead and all — and I can't help sneaking a peek.

Well, the view is glorious. A veritable feast for my greedy eyes. Now I know Dean's hair goes haywire overnight, and his already plump lips become even puffier in his sleep. As if that weren't enough, his pajama shorts have the nerve to sit low on his hips, and he appears to be sporting morning, afternoon, *and* evening wood. This isn't information I can just tuck away for safekeeping. No, this is mind-bending stuff here.

When I look up to examine his face, he's staring at me. I'm so fucking busted, and I can't even pretend otherwise. "Sorry."

He scrapes his bottom lip with his teeth. "Don't be. Honestly, I like the way you look at me."

Before I can turn that statement inside out and upside down, our guests amp up the volume yet again, as if they're providing the soundtrack for Anitta's next hit, and it's a banger:

Não para, amor.

Isso! Isso! Isso!

Assim mesmo, isso.

"Can you understand them?" Dean asks, his sleepy eyes alight with mischief. "They *must* know we can hear what's going on."

"Bits and pieces," I say, making a so-so gesture. "They're enjoying it, if that helps."

He smiles as he stretches, the hem of his T-shirt lifting so I can see a dusting of hair on his toned belly. "You don't need to understand Portuguese to figure *that* out."

When he drops his arms, we grin at each other like goofballs.

"I'm going to use the bathroom, then get some coffee going. Any specific instructions for making your super-special brew?"

I jump up and bend at the waist — not because I'm actually interested in stretching but because it's an effective way to hide my morning nipples. "You don't have to do that. You're doing *me* a favor. I can take care of my cousins while they're here. Just do what you need to do to get yourself off to work."

"There's no rush," he says nonchalantly as he rummages through his dresser. "I'll get there when I get there."

That's a phrase I never expected to hear from him. Naturally, I resist the temptation to presume his lack of urgency has anything to do with me. "You *must* be a clone. What have you done with the real Dean?"

He puts up a finger. "Hold that thought." Then he disappears inside the bathroom. When he returns — in jeans and with only morning and afternoon wood this time — his hair is freshly combed.

"It's all yours," he says, gesturing behind him. "Going to make the coffee and check in with the office." He taps me on the nose. "And if you must know, I'm not in a rush to leave because I want to spend more time with you."

The flutter in my belly is hunger. I'm sure of it. But then we brush against each other as we stride in different directions, and another flutter zips through me. I can't even lie to myself anymore. The extent of my attraction to Dean is threatening to break me. Good thing my cousins are visiting. No telling what would happen without them here as a buffer.

After freshening up and throwing on one of my favorite T-shirt dresses, I join Dean out in the kitchen.

He silently hands me a steaming cup of coffee and rests his elbows on the kitchen island, waiting for my reaction to his efforts.

I take a sip and moan. "That's good. Really good. Would you consider a position as my personal barista?"

He winks at me as he straightens to his full height. "I'll submit my application by close of business today."

Is he flirting with me? Am I reading too much into that wink? Why would it matter? The safest course is to ignore it. Because good sex is *always* welcome, but I want an emotional connection too, and Dean isn't prepared to give that to *anyone*. And yet, to reiterate, good sex is *always* welcome, and I haven't had any in a *really* long time.

Unfortunately, I can't parse my feelings further because Ana and Carlos, fully dressed and apparently ready to go, stroll into the kitchen and plop onto the counter stools next to mine.

"Mãe just called," Ana says. "Your mother's cooking us breakfast before the tias open the store, and then we're going sightseeing. Want to join us?"

I shake my head. "Can't. I need to prepare for work this afternoon." Plus, the idea of hitting all the DC tourist spots on a Thursday in August holds as much appeal as walking on hot coals — feels similar too.

Dean places two coffee cups and a tray of sugar and cream in front of them. "Did you sleep okay?"

Ana and Carlos grin at each other as they prepare their coffee.

"We did, thank you," Ana says. "Hey, can I ask how long you two have been living here?"

I'm too tired to perform math, so I throw out an answer that's vague enough not to get us in trouble. "Sure. As roommates, about two years. As a couple, not long."

"Ah, that explains it," Ana says.

"She thinks it looks like a place for a single person," Carlos adds.

I gulp. It *does* match Dean's sleek and functional aesthetic perfectly. "Like a bachelor pad, you mean?"

"Yes, that's it," Ana says. "Even little things, like the single-cup coffeemaker."

"Well, he lived alone before me, so he bought some of this stuff on his own," I tell them. "Besides, we don't like to put too much on our counters. For space-saving reasons."

Dean clears his throat. Is that a poke at my and Brandon's counters? He's going to pay for that one.

337

"Anyway, it's a wonderful place," Ana says as she rises from her counter stool. "It's just a thing I noticed." She looks at her phone, then turns to Carlos. "Eles vão nos encontrar lá embaixo. Ready?"

He stands and takes a last sip of coffee. "Ready."

They're almost out the door before Ana turns back. "Oh, do you want to give us your keys? That way, you won't have to worry about letting us in? Maybe yours, Solange?"

I gulp. "Mine?"

"If it's a problem, we can just call you when we're close."

"Oh, it's not a problem." I pat down my pockets as if a set of keys to Dean's place might materialize if I wish for it hard enough. "I just don't know where I put them. I'm always misplacing things."

Dean digs inside a drawer near the fridge and pulls out a set of keys. "They're right here, silly. You put them there last night."

"Right," I say, clearing my throat, then smacking my forehead. "How could I forget? Anyway, have fun, you two!"

"Take lots of pictures," Dean says, waving like a pageant queen.

When the door shuts after them, I collapse against the counter. "Faking a relationship is exhausting."

"I don't know," Dean says with a shrug. "I think it's been kind of fun."

I stare up at him, my mouth agape. "Yeah, you're definitely a clone. How are you not stressed about this?" I'm seconds from full-on whining, and I want to slap myself.

He arches an eyebrow and tilts his head. "Oh, I'm stressed about this, all right. But probably not for the same reason you are."

"What's your reason, then?"

"It's hard to pretend to be your boyfriend and not want to hold you. For real."

God, I know the feeling. But we're supposed to be burying it deep inside our psyches, where it can't do us any harm. He's not sticking with the program. Damn him. "I think the stress is finally getting to me."

He rounds the island and opens his arms, silently coaxing me to fall into his embrace. In that moment, it's what I want most in this world, so I rise from the stool and erase the space between us, my arms sliding around his waist and my hands settling on his back. Grounded. That's what being in Dean's arms does to me. It's as though he's steadying my body *and* my mind. Whatever happens next, tomorrow, and beyond, I will always remember the perfection of being hugged in this way. Never mind that the person doing the hugging is Dean. Never mind that I'm definitely not supposed to be enjoying this to the extent that I am.

Too soon, he loosens his hold on me. I don't let go, however. No, I want to hang on as long as I can.

Dean pushes a few curly strands away from my face, and I look up at him.

"You okay now?" he asks, his voice soft and comforting.

"Yeah, thanks." I shake my head. "You must think I'm a mess. Would you be willing to erase the last few minutes from your memory?"

He shakes his head. "Sorry, can't. I'd have to forget what you feel like in my arms."

"Then why'd you pull away?" I ask.

His eyes narrow, as though he's assessing whether I'm being serious.

I totally am, Dean. I totally am.

After a beat of heavy silence, he says, "The other night . . . at the hospital . . . you ran out of that stairwell like your life depended on it. I figured you'd decided to pump the brakes."

"You're taking your cues from me, then?"

He steps away and rakes a hand through his hair. "Always. I don't want any misunderstandings between us."

There won't be any — so long as I keep

my expectations in check. Yes, I'm terrified that Dean could one day be my worst mistake, but that would only happen if I asked for more than he's willing to give. Whether I leave DC or not, it would be foolish to want anything more from Dean than to explore this physical attraction between us — and I'm no fool. I only need one promise from him: that he'll continue to be honest with me, no matter what. "If we take this step, for however long it lasts, I need to know that you're not going to blow smoke up my ass about your feelings."

He stares at me, then falls over in laughter. "That was *not* what I thought you were going to say."

I stamp my foot, though I'm grinning so hard right now. "I'm serious, Dean."

His expression sobers. "Okay, seriously: I won't play games with your heart. Ever. And we're going into this with open eyes. Enjoying it for what it is. Agreed?"

This is it. I'm jumping in. "Agreed."

His nostrils flare, and he pins me to the spot with a blistering gaze. "May I touch you?"

"Yes."

We stare at each other, a breathless moment of indecision on his part the only delay, then he tugs me close, his fingertips ghosting over my jaw before he tilts my chin up so our mouths can meet. "Thank fucking Christ."

My entire body shudders when his lips touch mine. Our hands tangle as they cross paths, each of us seeking to explore the other, to fit our bodies together in a way that evokes the most pleasure. Dean slides his hands to my ass while mine meander underneath the hem of his T-shirt. He flinches, as if I've singed him, and that small reaction sparks my curiosity.

What will happen if I lick the seam of his lips? I have my answer within seconds: He moans, filling the room with a low, melodic tone that makes his hunger palpable. And what if I rub my breasts against his chest and create enough friction to make my nipples tighten? Oh yes, that elicits a hiss, and the heightened evidence of his need ratchets up my own. I'm hot everywhere, achy with want, dizzy from all the unspent desire building inside me.

He dips his head and burrows his face against my neck, trailing kisses there until he nips at me in frustration. Then, in just a few steps, he walks us back to the wall that separates his foyer from the living area, and the change in location flips a switch in my brain. This isn't *maybe we will;* it's *we absolutely are* — right now.

"Give me a sec," he says. "I need to grab protection."

"Hurry," I whisper, my voice tight and urgent.

He's gone in a flash and returns just as quickly, a look of intense concentration on his handsome face as he crowds me. "Where were we?"

"I was going to touch you," I say.

"Christ, touch me as much as you want."

I don't hesitate to take him up on his offer, and I'm not subtle about my intentions either. I unsnap the top button of his jeans and pull his zipper down. "May I?"

"Hell yes, you may."

I reach into his boxer briefs and run my hand along his rigid cock, my gaze never leaving his. Dean's stance falters, and he squeezes his eyes shut as though he's experiencing the very definition of exquisite torture and wants to block everything else out so he can focus on nothing else.

Eyes still closed, he bends his knees and kisses me, and I use that opportunity to switch places and guide him so that *his* back is pressed against the wall.

When we come up for air, he stares at me, his eyes drowsy with lust.

"You're so hot," I whisper, stroking his

thick erection with a firm grip. "And so hard. I can feel you pulsing against the palm of my hand. I can't wait to get you inside me."

"Holy shit, Solange," he growls. "You're going to make me combust even before that happens."

"Well, we can't have that, can we?"

"No, we can't." His big hands travel up the outsides of my thighs, taking the soft fabric of my dress with them, until he stops at my hips and massages me tenderly. The faster I stroke, though, the more frantic his touch gets. Seconds pass before his legs collapse under him, and he slides to the ground, using the wall to break his fall. I'm right there with him, clumsily sinking to my knees, then straddling him, a flimsy swatch of lace and his jeans the only material between us.

I put out my palm, the anticipation of being fully seated on his cock almost too much to bear. "Condom."

He pulls one from his back pocket and gives it to me, then he helps me shove his pants down, twisting and turning every which way as we struggle to free him. Oh God, we're almost there. A quick tug of his briefs and I'll finally be able to fuck him. When his underwear is gone and the condom's on, I pull the crotch of my panties to the side with one hand and take his dick in the other, guiding him inside me with much less finesse than I'd prefer. His erection presses against my channel as though it's designed precisely and specifically for me. "Dean, this is . . . I can't believe . . . I need it all."

He easily obliges, thrusting all the way in, then he freezes me in place with two words. "Don't. Move."

It's the hottest command ever even though I have no intention of complying with it.

"What's wrong?" I ask, my voice breathy and unsure and barely audible to my own ears.

"I need a distraction," he says. "Or else . . ."

I reach for the hem of my T-shirt dress and pull it over my head. The bra comes off next.

Dean cups my breasts, his fingers grazing the nipples in maddeningly slow circles. "This works."

"Can I move now?"

"No," he says sternly.

His response registers far and wide and sets my nerve endings ablaze as if he's struck a match to them. "You're not being —"

He leans forward, closing his mouth over a nipple and sucking gently. And just like that, I can't even remember what I was going to say. But if Dean believes that's going to stop me from riding his cock, he's got another think coming. And an orgasm too.

"Dean, I need to move."

He leans back, his mouth still affixed to my breast, then he slowly pulls away, lengthening my nipple to twice its usual size before he lets it go with a soft pop of his lips. "Now you can move," he whispers. "I appreciate your patience."

His smile is smug as he says this, as if he's a customer service representative at the local DMV and knows I'm at his mercy. Dean's in for a surprise, however. I don't want anything about this morning to be polite. Because my mission is simple — to get him out of my system — and failure is *not* an option.

CHAPTER TWENTY-TWO

DEAN

I'm inside Solange, and the feeling is *unreal.*

She rocks on top of me, her thighs slapping against mine. I alternate between caressing and gripping her ass, content to let her steer this ship as I revel in the silken feel of her squeezing my shaft.

"Yes, Dean, that's it," she says, her voice ragged and needy as her lips graze my temple. More urgently, she says, "Keep doing that." It's the closest she's come to begging me for anything, and I'm hell-bent on giving her exactly what she needs.

I thrust upward, meeting her each time she bears down.

"Perfect," she says, her smoky brown eyes pinning me with their intensity.

The way she rides me is so damn glorious I want to bottle it and take it everywhere I go. But that isn't all. I want Solange. Her sounds. Her touch. Everything that comes with *this.*

I can't stop touching her either. She's strong and soft, and I'd happily make massaging her my only pastime if she'd let me. I also wish I could do this all day. But I can't. I really can't. To ward off my impending orgasm, I resort to an old and rarely necessary standby: mumbling a piece I've committed to memory.

She pulls back, a sex-drunk expression on her face. "Are you humming?"

I blurt out, "Reciting something."

"Why?" she says, her voice tinged with amusement.

"Helps me last."

Grunting my responses is all I can do; the fewer words the better.

"Let me hear it," she says. "I grind. You rhyme."

"Later. I promise. Just . . . It's probably more than you need to hear."

"I'm going to hold you to it," she says, collapsing against me. Now our chests are pressed together, and her head is resting on my shoulder. The warmth of her skin, the coconut scent in her hair, it's an intoxicating combination that heightens the pleasure of being inside her.

We're a tight fit, and she knows just when to contract around me to make the fit even tighter. "Hang on, I just . . . fuck, Solange."

She draws back, her eyes so heavy they're almost closed, then she takes my hand and pulls it between her legs. "I need you to finish what you started in that stairwell."

The thought of touching her there and making her come against my hand makes my heart race even harder. Without hesitation, I massage her folds, then tease her with a featherlight pass over her clit. She tenses and chases the sensation, desperate for more, but I don't want us to get to the punch line just yet, so I skim her opening, tracing a finger over the places where my cock meets her pussy.

She lets out a long moan, and it's as though the sound is vibrating against my dick.

"You're deliciously wet," I tell her, my lips drifting over her neck and jaw. "I wish I could taste it."

"Oh God, yes," she says as she wriggles on my lap. "I want that too."

"We have plenty of time. But for now, I want to play with this pussy. I didn't get to do it justice last time." I press the pad of my thumb against her clit, watching her closely to gauge her reaction.

Solange jolts. "*Yes,* Dean. *Please.* Rub me there."

I rub back and forth, then trace a circle over her clit, repeating the sequence because she appears to like this more than anything. She parts her lips, and her moans grow louder. And fuck, she's contracting around me so tightly I'm going to detonate any minute now.

The faster I rub, the harder she rides. My damn toes are curled, and I'm sweaty and so fucking hard. Breathing is optional. It really is. It's just Solange and me and this feeling I want to savor all night.

I squeeze my eyes shut, summoning the concentration necessary to bring her to orgasm with my fingers. Solange's moans and breathy sighs are all the encouragement and direction I need. But then I feel her hands running through my hair, and I lose focus. Seconds later, I'm sucker punched by an even stronger swell of emotion when she leans forward and kisses my forehead. I don't have a name for it, nor do I want one. Still, I can see why an experience like this would prompt someone to blurt out their feelings, to trot out a litany of promises they can't keep. But that's not me. That's *never* been me.

"Dean, I'm so close," she says. "And I want to come *so* bad."

I groan. Her honesty in this moment is

disarmingly sexy. I want this to be good for her. I want to surpass her expectations. I want her to carry the memory of this morning with her into tomorrow and next week.

"Touch yourself," I say. "I need my hands free."

She dips her hand between her legs while I withdraw. Then I grab on to her ass and move her up and down my cock again and again. My arms are burning, but I'm not stopping until we're both wrecked.

"Yes, Dean. Yes. That's it. Oh God. Please, please, *please* don't stop."

The base of my dick is tingling, and my orgasm is so close I can practically taste it. "Fuck, Solange. What do you need?"

"I need you to do exactly what you're doing," she says, her breasts pushed together as she continues to stroke herself. "I'm *right* there."

I gather all the energy left in my body and pump with abandon. I'm on fire. Unstoppable. My only task in life is to make her come.

She cries out my name. "Dean! Yes!" Then, with her eyes squeezed shut, she shudders uncontrollably, her thighs trembling from the force of the orgasm. And holy shit, within seconds of that, I come so hard my vision blurs and my head spins. In a daze, I just repeat her name as I ride it out. "Solange, Solange, Solange."

She laughs as she comes down from her high. "I'll admit you were right."

"How's that?" I ask as I work to slow my breathing.

"You're never dull when it counts."

I place a hand around her neck and gently draw her down for a tender kiss, one that ends with a scrape of my teeth against her jawline. "Rumor has it I can be even more interesting in an actual bed."

She waggles her eyebrows. "How about you let me be the judge of that?"

"Out with it, Chapman. Don't think I forgot."

Solange's torso is draped across me like the softest, most decadent blanket ever, and she's lazily circling her fingers across the expanse of my chest.

"Forgot what?"

Yes, I'm feigning ignorance. Revealing this could change her perception of me. And I'm a firm believer that certain things aren't meant to be shared.

"You promised," she says, her lips going all adorably pouty.

I blame that on being fully immersed in the heat of the moment. Solange's presence is all-consuming, so it's hard to think of anything else when she's around, and when she's focused on you, that task is doubly hard. Shit, I would have signed over the deed to my home had she pressed for it.

"Please, Dean," she says, her eyes twinkling. "Whatever it is, it'll be our little secret."

That gets me. That *really* gets me. The idea of sharing secrets other than the ones required to pull off our fake relationship is far too tempting to resist. I may never live this down, but it's worth it for that reason alone. And since she asked so sweetly, I clear my throat and oblige her:

I love little pussy
Her coat is so warm
And if I don't hurt her
She'll do me no harm.
So I'll not pull her tail
Nor drive her away
But pussy and I
Very gently will play.

"Oh my God," Solange says, her eyes lighting up in mock wonder. "Is that an original?"

"Nah, it's a nursery rhyme called 'I Love Little Pussy.' Discovered it by accident in

353

college, during an all-nighter in the library. Written in the seventeen hundreds, I think, author unknown, and it had a profound effect on my sexual development."

"You know it's about a cat, right?" she says on a laugh.

"I'm not so sure, but it doesn't matter. That nursery rhyme helped me to establish a positive relationship with pussies. Taught me to treat them with the care and respect they deserve."

"Well, as a recent beneficiary of that positive relationship, I very much approve."

I'm itching to dole out additional benefits, but I don't want to overstep my bounds. Maybe she isn't interested in more. Maybe this was meant to be a two-and-done, never to be repeated. Solange and I know we have no future together, so what now?

"You're overthinking this," she says, lightly tapping my chest. "We had sex. Really, *really* great sex, but in the end, it doesn't have to mean anything more than that. Stop trying to figure out where I fit into your life plan. I don't. And that's okay."

I sit up, easing her upright along with me, and stumble my way through a decent response. "Oh, yeah, I absolutely know that. I just wanted to be sure we're still on the same page."

"Same page, huh?" she says, adjusting the sheet to cover her torso. "If by 'same page' you mean the attraction between us was bound to boil over, but our baseline is and will always be that we're friends, then yes, we're on the same page. This isn't the beginning of our love story. We both know that."

I nod. "Of course."

She peers past me. "Isn't it time for you to head into the office?"

"I was thinking I could work from home today. Maybe spend a little more time with you before you leave for class this afternoon. If you're cool with that."

She swallows, then smiles. "I'm cool with that. On one condition."

"Anything."

"I'd like you to demonstrate how much you love little pussy again."

Hell yeah. With fucking pleasure.

I slide down the bed and roll onto my stomach, adjusting my body so I can accommodate the hard-on that inevitably followed Solange's tantalizing request. "Drop the sheet and let me in between your thighs, then."

Her breath hitches, and her eyes go cloudy. Slowly, she tugs the sheet down, teasing me as she reveals her breasts — first the tops, then the brown puckered nipples, then the soft undersides. Finally, goddamn finally, she pushes the sheet out of our way, her completely bare body splayed against my bed as though she were put on this earth to make my wettest dreams come true. My stomach clenches from the anticipation of pressing my mouth to her core and licking my way inside. I'm so turned on I can't help grinding my cock against the mattress to chase a bit of friction for myself. "Open up for me, Solange. *Please.*"

She closes her eyes. As if she's absorbing the barely contained desperation in my voice. Then she spreads her legs, bending her knees and digging her heels into the bed for support.

I breathe Solange in. *Yes.* This all-consuming lust makes sense to me. Attraction. Pheromones. The dopamine hit that goes along with being horny. It's biology, plain and simple. My only job here is to drive her wild. I won't stop until I make her come with my tongue. I needn't worry about anything else. As she rightly pointed out, this isn't the start of our love story. We're just two people making each other feel good.

Best thing is, we're in agreement on that.

CHAPTER TWENTY-THREE

SOLANGE

Thursday afternoon, I arrive at Victory Academy earlier than usual, not because I'm a particularly punctual person but because I need a quiet place to think. A quiet place to put my time with Dean in proper perspective. Far from his piercing gaze. Far from Brandon's smug expression (which, fair, considering I came home with a dazzling just-fucked glow that left little doubt about the nature of my morning activities).

I sit at my desk and stare out at the rows of empty chairs. Every class is a new opportunity to reach someone. To give them the boost they need to shoot for the stars. To remind them that life presents us with a host of opportunities, and it's up to us to decide which ones are worth pursuing.

It stands to reason, then, that I should heed my own advice and accept the obvious: Dean isn't worth pursuing. Dammit, I *know* this. And yet I'm imagining a scenario in which a man I'm totally incompatible with becomes the person I need.

Someone who isn't driven by a single-minded desire to attain professional success.

Someone who doesn't approach dating as if it were a job interview.

Someone who wants to love their partner to distraction for the sake of that soul-deep connection and nothing more.

Someone who isn't so fixated on never deviating from their life plan and can appreciate the freedom in exploring all their options until they land on the right one.

Dean isn't that person, and he isn't interested in becoming that person either. So I should just let him be. That's easier said than done, though.

Get Dean out of my system? Hardly. Instead, he's wormed his way into every nook and cranny of my psyche, and try as I might, I can't kick him out of here. Worse, I'm premenstrual, so I'm extra grumpy about the situation. As if all that weren't enough, now I need to put on a happy face and teach my students how our government works in theory when they damn well know how it works in practice. Might as well call this session Intro to Fairy Tales rather than

Intro to Civics.

The sound of shuffling footsteps draws me out of my musings. It's time to shut off the Dean compartment of my brain and focus on my class. After everyone's settled, I glance at the empty desk where Layla usually sits. I shouldn't have favorites, but I'll confess to having a soft spot for her. She wants to be a paralegal. I even connected her with Lina, who was one herself before she became a wedding planner, so Layla could get the real scoop on her dream profession. "Has anyone seen Layla?" Most of the students shrug.

This isn't like her. She's punctual. And uber responsible. If she's going to be late to class, she sends an email. She's never missed a class altogether. I look up to find the rest of the students staring at me expectantly. "Sorry, everyone. Turn to page one-forty-six in your study guides. We're going to talk about capitalism today. But first, let's begin with a question: Can anyone tell me what Biggie Smalls meant when he said, 'Mo money mo problems'?"

After class, I check email on my laptop, still distracted by Layla's absence. Sure enough, a new message from her sits in my inbox. *That's my girl.* It reads:

Hello, Ms. Pereira:

I'm sorry I missed class today. I wanted to tell you this in person, but I don't think I'll be able to get out there anytime soon. A job opportunity fell into my lap, and I had to take it. Unfortunately, it means I won't be able to attend your class anymore. It's just Mom and me, so I really don't have a choice. I hope you understand.

Thank you so much for making school fun again. If I'd had you as a teacher in high school, I probably would have finished.

Sincerely,
Layla

I stare at the words for a minute or two before they truly sink in. There's nothing earth-shattering about the news, but the casual finality of it guts me for some reason. Her explanation is perfectly reasonable: A job, particularly in this economy, isn't a small matter. But I'd gotten ahead of myself and imagined seeing Layla pass her GED, attend community college, study to become a paralegal. In my head, I would be serving as her mentor, even if I decided not to accept a permanent position with Victory Academy. Just like that, the scenario I

360

envisioned is no longer a possibility. It's a timely reminder that relationships can often be one-sided. Making space for someone in your life doesn't guarantee they'll make space for you in theirs.

"I'm ready for my lesson, Ms. Pereira."

I startle at the sound of Dean's deep voice. It's tinged with humor — and matches the half smile he's wearing as he leans against the door frame. His unbuttoned suit jacket allows me to see the sinewy muscles straining against his dress shirt.

"What are you doing here?" I ask, ignoring his attempt at flirtation.

His smile vanishes, replaced by a look of concern. "I thought we could catch a ride home together. Show up to my place at the same time. I think it would be awkward if I were alone with your cousins, and I didn't want you to have to scramble if they asked you for something and you couldn't find it."

I should be grateful he's thinking ahead, but I'm growing tired of the subterfuge. It isn't Dean's fault, though, so I muster a smile and slowly rise to my feet. "Good idea."

He steps inside, then shuts the door behind him. "Hey, what's wrong?"

Because Dean's my friend, it never occurs

to me to tell him anything but the truth. "I got some unexpected news today. About one of my most promising students. It left me a bit deflated."

"Are they okay?"

"I think so. But they've dropped the class. For a good reason, I'm sure. I suppose I was getting attached, and I didn't even realize it."

"That's a sign of a good teacher. You care." Dean holds out his hand. When I take it, he tugs me forward and draws me into his arms. Neither of us says anything. I don't know that there's anything for us to say anyway. He's providing comfort. Being supportive. This is precisely what I need right now, and somehow Dean gets that.

"Ready to head home?" he asks, his breath feathering over my ear.

"Sure, I'm ready to head to your place."

Home. His place. There's a difference. And no matter how comforting it is to be wrapped in his arms, I can't lose sight of that fact.

DEAN

My brilliant idea to arrive at my condo together was pointless; Ana and Carlos aren't even here, and Ana texted to let us know they won't be arriving anytime soon.

362

"Is there anything else bothering you?" I ask.

Having fed Solange my signature bachelor meal of spaghetti and salad, I'm standing next to her at the kitchen counter as we dry the last of the dishes. She looks drained, the usual life in her eyes conspicuously missing. I can't help wondering if I've done something to upset her.

She sighs, then sits on a stool. "I didn't expect I'd ever have to explain this to you, but my period is coming, which means I'll be grumpy for a bit. It's not a fun time. I get terrible premenstrual cramps for several days, and they sap me of my usual strength. Happens like clockwork, unfortunately. I can borrow the electric stimulator from Natalia if you'd like to experience it for yourself."

"Uh, no thanks." There's no way I'll willingly strap on those nodes ever again. "So, given how you're feeling, is it safe to be around you?"

She narrows her eyes.

Shit. I'm fucking toast. I back up a few steps just in case.

"Here's a life tip, ol' pal of mine," she says. "There are certain things you don't get to talk about. Not without negative consequences. And only people who get periods can talk about the attitude that goes along with them. I don't make the rules; that's just the way it is."

"I can live with those rules," I say quickly. "Permission to change the subject, then?"

"Smart man. Granted."

I pull her off the stool, take her place, and draw her across my lap so we're facing each other. "Okay, I want to know something about you that wasn't in your dossier. A fact others would find surprising. And you need to make it good." I waggle my eyebrows. "Extra points if it's incriminating stuff."

She rests her shoulder against mine and thinks about my question for a bit, then puffs out her chest as though she's putting on a brave face and pushing through her discomfort. "Okay, here's something: I throw one-person fashion shows in my apartment. And I don't mean trying on clothes in front of a mirror. No, it's an event. Makeup. Lights. Hairstyle changes. Brandon plays the emcee."

It's easy to picture them doing this together. I mean, Brandon would be the perfect hype man. "I bet he's excellent at it too."

She nods. "He is."

I study her face and watch the life return to her eyes. This is an activity Solange obviously enjoys. But then she grimaces, and I wish there were something I could do to make her feel better.

"Want to throw a show here?" I ask.

Where the hell did that suggestion come from?

"I don't have any clothes," Solange says on a laugh. "I wish I . . ." Her voice peters out as she considers me. "Oh, but you do, don't you? Is that what you were suggesting? That you'd be the model, and I'd narrate?"

"Honestly, the thought just popped into my head, so I have no damn clue what I was suggesting. My mouth occasionally disobeys my brain and goes rogue. But yeah, we could do that if you want."

"I want!" She jumps off my lap, wobbles a bit, then places a hand on the counter. "Whoa. Too fast."

I'm at her side in seconds. "Come sit on the couch and relax. I'll take care of everything." She leans on me as I guide her across the room, accepting my help as if it were an ordinary occurrence.

Once Solange has taken Tylenol and is safely ensconced in a comforter, a glass of water within reach, I shuffle back to my bedroom and lay a few outfits on my bed. Hopefully my antics will lighten Solange's mood. Regardless, I'll get to experience what it's like to be a part of her inner circle.

After I settle on the runway order, I reenter the living area, move the coffee table out of the way, then reposition the floor lamp to act as a spotlight.

"You're taking this seriously," Solange says, grinning.

"I'm a professional through and through." I leave without another word. Then, after my first outfit is squared away, I stroll down the hall. "Ready or not, here I come."

"Wait," Solange shouts back. "I need a mic!"

"Use the remote!"

"That works. Okay, ready."

I glide down the hall, slowing my pace when I get to the living area's entryway.

Smiling wide, Solange tucks her legs under her butt and raises the remote in front of her mouth. "Next, we have our most popular model of the evening, Dean Chapman. He's wearing an expensive suit made by a designer I can't name —"

"Tom Ford," I say.

"Okay, then," she continues. "He's wearing a Tom Ford suit that probably costs at least a few months' rent, but since I've seen him wear it twice in the time that I've known him, I won't make any snide comments about his excess. Yet."

"Focus, woman," I say, rolling my eyes. "We won't ever get to the good stuff at this pace."

"Fine, fine. It's a navy blue three-piece suit that highlights Dean's classic style."

With a wink, I spin around and lift my jacket.

"Scratch that," Solange adds. "The suit shows off his very fine ass."

"That's more like it," I say before striding back to my bedroom.

The plan is to put on progressively more casual clothes and end with the pièce de résistance: my very fine *naked* ass — if Solange is up for it. And if *that* doesn't distract her from feeling shitty, nothing will.

When I come out, Solange's expression melts into one of undisguised desire. Her mouth parts a fraction, and her breath hitches.

"Nothing to say?" I ask.

She shakes her head. "Oh. Right. Chapman's latest ensemble is irreverent and simple. Men's casual wear at its finest. The gray sweatpants sit just below his waist and emphasize his enticing happy trail. Correction: That trail is fucking ecstatic."

I swing my hips from side to side in a slow

roll. "Notice anything else worth mention-ing?"

Her gaze lands on my crotch. "The beauty of the fit is that underwear is optional, ap-parently. Either Chapman is freeballing or he's carrying a baguette in his pants."

Solange's comment makes me miss a step.

"Yep," she adds. "He's definitely freeball-ing."

I raise one finger in the air. "Hang on. I have one more outfit."

"Chapman."

I turn back. "Yes?"

"I do hope you're going to wear even less for the next round."

"Great minds, Solange," I say, puckering my lips. "Great minds."

She throws a pillow my way. "Get to it, then."

A minute later, I return wearing . . . noth-ing. Just in case our wires have crossed, I hold the sweatpants against the front of my body.

Solange gestures at me. "Drop them, Chapman."

I happily comply.

She whoops and circles her fist in the air. "Yesssss. That's what I'm talking about."

My plan is to make a slow revolution so she can enjoy my very fine ass, but the doorbell rings and I freeze instead.

Solange springs to her feet and takes a giant hop in my direction.

"Who could that be?" she whispers.

"Not sure," I whisper back.

Outside, a voice says, "Dean, Solange, it's Ana and Carlos. We were going to use the key, but then we heard a . . . scream . . . and uh, we just wanted to be sure it's okay to come in."

No, we aren't having sex, but I *am* buck naked.

Solange, without any regard for my dignity or safety, spins me around, slaps my ass, and propels me down the hall. "It looks even better when it bounces," she whispers.

"Oh, man, you're going to pay for that," I whisper back before scrambling out of sight. *I gua-ran-tee it.* It's a shame we were interrupted, but I'm already envisioning an encore.

A half hour later, Solange and I are in bed. She's reading a novel; I'm reviewing my notes for a hearing in one of my pro bono cases. But nothing's sinking in. Because I can't stop thinking about the woman beside me. I can easily imagine our being together this way each night. Even when Ana and Carlos are no longer here. But that's ridiculous, right? Solange and I already agreed this isn't that kind of party.

After a period of comfortable silence, she drops the book onto her lap. "What are you reading over there?"

"I have a hearing in a landlord-tenant case on Tuesday. I'm preparing a cross-examination."

"That's when you question your opponent's witness?"

"Yeah. This time it's the landlord."

Solange turns on her side, snuggles into the blanket, and rests a hand against my chest. "Can you tell me what the case is about?"

For a moment, all I can do is stare at her. She's looking up at me, her dark eyes alert and curious, her lips parted as she waits for me to respond. She's so damn lovely. And she's interested in my work. And I'm interested in her. And holy shit, my pulse is racing, and my brain is fuzzy right now.

"Dean?" she prompts.

I rub my temples, then take a calming breath. "Sorry. It's a typical scenario. Landlord claims he gave proper notice that my client violated the lease by handing the notice to my client's teenage son. Which was impossible since the kid was at an orientation for his new job at the time."

"Oh, wow. The landlord flat-out lied. Will

the hearing be open to the public?"

"Should be. Why?"

"Would it be okay if I told my students about it? I keep thinking of ways to make the class more interesting. Maybe seeing you in action would do that. Or would that be too embarrassing for you?"

I'm touched, actually. Solange has never seen me in the courtroom, yet she has enough confidence in me that she assumes it won't be a disaster. "I wouldn't mind at all. I'll send you the hearing info. I can even chat with them if they find me afterward. So long as they promise not to snore in the courtroom, that is."

She grins. "Thanks for being receptive to it. I mean, I'm not sure anyone will show up, but I'd like to offer it as an option. They'd be doing it on their own time."

"And I'm sure they'll appreciate it. It never goes unnoticed when someone goes the extra mile. Your students are lucky to have you."

"If not me, it would be someone else. With the right curriculum, another person could do what I do in their sleep."

The notion that this woman can be easily replaced by someone else strikes me as ludicrous. But Solange wants to believe it. Or maybe she *needs* to believe it — because

371

it'll make it easier for her to leave the academy at the end of the summer. "You know, I bet your students would disagree. They're going to miss you, Solange."

Hell, I'm going to miss her too. And in that moment, I realize something else: I want this woman in my life. Forever. As a friend, of course, but still. I'd like to be a part of her village; I'd like her to help me build mine. My chest tightens, and my breathing grows shallow. Damn, what the hell is wrong with me today? Maybe I just need a good night's rest.

I turn off the lamp on my nightstand, and we settle in for bed.

"Need me to rub your belly?" I ask. "Would that help?"

"You're the sweetest. Sure."

"Get on your side, then."

The sheets rustle as she positions herself. Once she's still, I blanket her body from behind, snake my arm over her waist, and place my hand on her stomach. I rub in circles, hoping the sensation will distract her. "Is that good?"

"Yeah," she whispers.

A minute later, she covers my hand with hers and draws our entwined fingers inside her drawstring pajama pants. "But here's where I really need it," she says, dragging my hand across her lower belly.

I scoot back, afraid that I'll grow hard and that she'll think I'm doing this for me. This is for her. Only for her.

It's so quiet I can hear every breath she takes, each contented sigh. But then the unmistakable sound of wailing fills the room, and I jerk my hand out of her pants as if I've been scalded.

"Oh God," Solange says, pulling the pillow out from under her head and covering her face with it.

"Jesus, it's like we're right there with them."

She turns toward me and peeks out from under the pillow. "I know."

"I think I can get them to stop," I tell her.

"How?"

"Well, if they heard *us,* maybe they'd realize how thin the walls are."

Her eyebrows snap together. "Good try, buddy, but no. I'm *not* having sex with you so they can listen to us."

"You won't have to. I'll just fake it like Sally."

She draws her head back and leans up on her elbows. "Who?"

"You know. Harry. Sally. When she faked an orgasm."

"Oh, Lord," she says, raising her gaze to

373

the ceiling. "*This,* I must hear."

"It won't embarrass you?"

She gives me a deadpan expression. "You know me better than that."

Right. Solange doesn't embarrass easily — if at all. As I sit up and arrange my pillow behind me, I begin to moan. "Oh, *that's it,* Solange."

She shakes her head. "If we were actually having sex, you'd be *much* louder than that."

Fair point. I narrow my eyes at her, picturing the way she owned my body just this morning. Channeling the energy I felt when she rocked against me earlier, I try again. "Yes, yes, *motherfucking* yes."

"That's better," she says, her expression smug.

"What's that, baby? I'm too big to fit?"

Her eyes go wide, and she grits her teeth. "Too big to fit, my ass," she grumbles.

"Don't worry, Solange," I exclaim, panting heavily in between each word. "It's not. Too big. To fit your ass."

"Ew. You sound like William Shatner." She punches me in the shoulder. "And anyway, that is *not* what I meant."

"Oh, sorry," I say, grinning sheepishly. "I didn't hear the comma."

She cackles on the inside, her mouth open and her chest heaving from the effort not to laugh out loud.

"Oh, fuuuuuuuck," I say, pounding my hands on the mattress.

After a few more expletives, I ask, "Are you trying to insult me?"

"No, why would you say that?" she whispers.

"We're supposed to be having sex, and you haven't made a peep."

"Oh, right." She rolls onto her knees, grabs the headboard, then starts rattling it as if it were a fence. "Yes, yes, yes! Big Daddy, yes."

"Big Daddy, eh?"

"Just go with it, Chapman," she says, then she screams, "Ooh, right there. Yes. That. Is. Motherfucking. It."

"Damn, I'm better in your fantasies than I am in reality."

"True, true."

I tackle Solange to the bed and tickle her until tears are streaming down her face. Eventually, I help her up as I listen for any sounds from our guests. It's quiet again, so I assume Ana and Carlos got the hint . . . or finished.

Solange and I give each other a high five, then I kiss her forehead. I can't recall ever being this silly with any person I've dated in the past. *Not* that Solange and I are dating.

She's a friend. A friend I have sex with. A friend I have fun with. And I can't forget that she'll be leaving town for who-knows-where in just a few weeks. My brain wants to skip over that part, though.

She makes a big production of rearranging the pillows and comforter just the way she likes them, which is to say she hogs them, then she drops onto her back and lets out a satisfied sigh. "Now we'll be able to sleep. And think about it: All we have left is dinner with the family tomorrow night, and then I'll be out of your hair."

I guess that's supposed to be good news. My stomach dips when I realize it isn't.

CHAPTER TWENTY-FOUR

SOLANGE

After a delicious buffet-style dinner courtesy of the tias, the family's sitting around the dinner table drinking cafezinhos and eating Tia Mariana's house-famous flan.

Cousin Cláudia lifts her plate to her nose and sniffs the dessert before trying it. "Do you serve the pudim at the store?"

"No," Tia Mariana says, beaming. "We thought about it, but I make it for the kids. It's my special gift to them."

By "kids," she means Lina, Rey, Natalia, and me, and I never realized until now that she kept her flan off the menu because she didn't want to share it with anyone else. I feel a pang in my chest remembering the many ways the tias have showered us with affection over the years.

"I think that's smart," Cláudia says. "It's good for home but maybe not the right thing to sell."

Jesus, Cláudia needs better manners. If she makes one more judgy comment tonight, I'll slap a muzzle on her myself. It's not even that she's said any one jaw-dropping thing. No, she's doing that shit I despise: dishing out insults by a thousand tiny paper cuts. I relax the muscles of my face into a blank expression and look across the table at Lina. She's in neutral mode too, her head tilted as she stares back at me.

Are you hearing this? I ask with my eyes.

Lina shakes her head ever so slightly, as if to warn me to let it go. She knows the tias wouldn't want to start a squabble, so she's not inclined to engage. Natalia, the person most likely to raise a ruckus, is resting at home. Tia Viviane, the second most likely person to raise a ruckus, is spending the night there to help the new parents. The upshot: I'm seething alone.

Max and Rey, meanwhile, can't seem to get enough of the flan; Max is hunched over his plate as if he's feeding from a trough, and Rey's licking the caramel sauce off his spoon.

"This is *so* good," Max tells Tia Mariana. "I'd eat this any day."

"Thank you, filho," she says proudly. "I'm glad you like it."

Beside me, Dean squeezes my hand, then

leans over to whisper in my ear. "We're almost done here. You're doing great."

Those few words say so much. He's not oblivious to Cláudia's occasional jabs, and he recognizes that I'm trying not to make a scene. I can't recall any other boyfriend being this attuned to me, and Dean's only faking the role. I squeeze his hand back. "From your lips . . ."

Unfortunately, our brief exchange catches Cláudia's attention, and she turns her body in our direction. "Tell me, Solange, how did you two meet?"

Oh shit. Dean and I never bothered to work out a story. Must tread carefully here. "We met at a wedding."

Dean snorts. "Seems so long ago."

I gaze at him tenderly. "Feels like it was yesterday."

Cláudia nods. "And you're living together, but you don't want to get married. What about kids?"

I want to counter with my own questions: *Why do you care? How is this your business?* But I tamp down the urge to cause a clash. "As far as I know, getting married isn't a prerequisite for having kids."

She snaps her brows together. "But wouldn't you want to get married before you have a baby?" She glances over at Ana and Carlos. "Like they're planning to do."

This feels like a setup. As if she's gearing up to insult my mother in a roundabout way. Dean throws an arm around my chair, probably to remind me that he's here — or to hold me back if I suddenly lunge across the table.

I shrug. "I haven't given it a lot of thought. I'm only twenty-eight. But anyway, I don't think you need to be married to have kids. And I don't think you even need a partner to have a child."

Her eyes grow wide as saucers. "But your mother didn't *choose* to be a single mother, you know. Even she knows a baby needs his mother *and* his father."

Rodrigo scowls at his wife. "Cláudia, não fala mais sobre isso."

Bless his heart; he should get a medal for trying to get her to pipe down. But it's too late; I'm done letting her take potshots at my mother. I breathe in through my nose and count down in my head. *Five, four, three . . .*

Dean clears his throat. "Forgive me for butting in, but I was raised by a single mother too, so I *have* thought about this a lot. The way I see it, a baby needs someone to care for them. Someone to give them food. To provide them with a safe place to rest their head. Someone who'll encourage their dreams. But most of all, a baby needs love. And all kinds of families can raise a child." He gestures with his hands. "I mean, look around us. Families come in different shapes and sizes. The ones you're born into; the ones you find later in life. They may have one parent, or two, or a bunch of people who pitch in like the tias did here. There may be two mothers or two fathers, two grandparents, whatever works. But being a single parent? That's a challenge all its own. I never gave my mother enough credit for doing it alone, and I should have. Now these women? I'm in awe of what they did. Coming from Brazil to an unfamiliar place and raising their kids together. Giving their children the guidance to become the wonderful people they've become. Building a thriving business. Could you imagine doing that? Could you imagine the strength and devotion they had to have to accomplish those things? So, yeah, since Solange is Izabel's daughter, I don't doubt for a minute that all that strength and devotion will be second nature to her too. Solange will be fine, whatever she decides."

Cláudia purses her lips, a nod the only indication she's at all moved by what Dean said.

I sneak a glance at my mother. She looks like one of those cartoon characters with flashing hearts doubling in size and popping out of her eyes. Well, Dean can plan on a lifetime's supply of free food from Rio de Wheaton after that monologue.

Ana throws her clasped hands on the table. "That is *so* nice." She looks over at me. "I'm happy for you, prima. You found a good man."

"She did, didn't she?" Lina says, her curious gaze swinging between Dean and me.

"The *best,*" Max adds, grinning.

My ears are burning, and my face *must* be flushed. Am I going to hyperventilate? Yeah, I think I'm going to hyperventilate. I blink back tears. Dean didn't just defend me. He defended *my mother.* My heart's pumping hard in my chest, asking for direction: *It's this guy, right? We want him, yes? Please tell me he's the one.* Except Dean doesn't want to fall in love, so I need to tell my heart it's a false alarm. And God, it would be *so* easy to meet him where he needs to be. To tell him that he doesn't need to love me. That being with him would be enough. But I know doing so would be a mistake. I can feel it in my gut.

Desperately needing air and space, I jump to my feet. "Dean and I should get going.

We have . . . stuff to do."

"I just bet," Lina says under her breath.

"Places to go. *People to do,*" Rey singsongs with a smirk.

Dean stands as well. "Yeah, she's right. Always working, you know. Um, Tia Izabel, do you think we could get some food to go? The picanha, especially?"

Seriously? Asking a Brazilian elder if you can take home seconds is like asking them if the Earth's round. The answer's yes. Always yes. Is he trying to ingratiate himself with my family? Has he no shame?

"Of course, filho," my mother says, slowly rising from her chair. She holds out her hand. "Come, we'll get you everything you like."

Ana appears at my side. "Hey, we're going to stay here for a little bit more, okay? Rey said he would drop us off at your place later. And since we're leaving for New York very early, you should give me a hug now."

I pull her into my arms for a tight embrace. Her mother may be a pain, but Ana's a gentle soul — who just so happens to be super vocal during sex. I'm a big fan of her energy. "Take care, prima."

"Next time, we'll leave Mãe at home," she whispers.

"I'm counting on it," I whisper back.

After Dean and I say our goodbyes to everyone (Cláudia only gets a lukewarm wave), we leave the family home and climb into my car. Dean's packed into the front passenger seat so tightly his knees nearly touch his chin, but he's kind enough not to complain about it, probably because there are two plastic bags filled with food in the backseat.

"Are you okay?" he asks.

"Yeah. That was exhausting, though."

"I hear you, but *we did it,* Solange," he says, his eyes brimming with excitement. "We convinced everyone we're dating, and we didn't get caught."

I throw up a weak fist. "Yay."

He rolls his eyes at me. "I'm not going to let you kill my buzz. This is an accomplishment, and we should celebrate it."

"Okay, okay," I say. "What did you have in mind?"

"Let me make you dinner tomorrow night. We can hang out at my place. Watch a movie. Spend the evening together. Whatever."

Because putting our relationship in proper perspective seems crucial to my self-preservation, I give him a saucy grin. "Have sex too?"

He surveys me with a heated gaze that

electrifies me from head to toe. "If that's what you want."

It's the least of what I want, but I'm not ashamed to say I still want it. "I do."

Dean's phone buzzes, and he pulls it out, grimacing at the interruption. "Huh," he says on a chuckle a few seconds later.

"What's going on?" I ask.

"It's a text from my mother. A photo of her with her new boyfriend. Mountains in the background. Says he's taking her to meet his children. I'll show you later."

"Meeting the family. That's a big deal."

Shrugging, he says, "Maybe." He draws in a long breath, then reaches over and squeezes my shoulder. "Anyway, just think, Solange. We're done pretending. And by tomorrow morning, we'll be home free."

Well, no, that's not precisely true. *He'll* be home free. As for me? Considering that I'm starting to fall for this man, I'm still facing a high probability of heartbreak.

Lina calls as I'm heading to Dean's Saturday night. Because parking is always at a premium in both of our neighborhoods, I'm opting to take a Lyft there.

I pick up on the first ring. "Hey, hang on. I'm getting a ride." I throw my overnight bag in the backseat, greet the driver, then confirm Dean's address. Once I'm settled, I get back to Lina. "What's up, mulher?"

"Don't 'what's up' me. I've been trying to reach you all day."

"Why? What's going on?"

She sucks her teeth. "Really, Solange? You're trying this with me?"

She's right. There's no point in being evasive with Lina. She'll hound me until she gets the answers she's looking for. "In my defense, I truly was busy. I helped Dean clean up his place after Ana and Carlos left this morning, and then I hung out with Brandon. But, uh, I'm headed back to Dean's now."

When she doesn't immediately respond, I tease her instead. "What's the matter? Max got your tongue?"

"Heh. I'm processing, okay? Because I thought the fake dating caper ended last night."

"Technically, it did."

Lina clears her throat. "So . . ."

"So we're just hanging out."

"Hmm, a summer fling before you leave DC. I'm not mad at you."

I wish it were that simple. I really do. But if a summer fling is all I can expect from Dean, what other choice do I have than to enjoy it for what it is? "One thing, though. I may not be leaving DC."

Lina's voice goes up several octaves. "What?!? When did you decide that?"

"I haven't decided anything, but the school did make me a permanent offer, and I'm considering it."

"Congrats, Solange. I'm so happy for you!"

"Hang on, Lina. I'm considering the position in Ohio too. And I don't want to feel pressured by anyone or anything as I figure this out."

That applies to Dean too. I can't let my feelings for him steer me in the wrong direction when it comes to my career. If I'm going to make this choice, I need to make it independently, free of his influence, and without regard for what I *wish* would happen between us if I were to stay, especially when all signs point to my never getting my wish in any case.

"I understand," she says, her voice softening. "But I'm here if you want to talk about it."

"I know."

"And I'll see you tomorrow for Sunday dinner at Natalia and Paulo's?"

"Wouldn't miss it for the world."

"Excellent. Now, before I let you go, inquiring minds want to know: This thing with Dean, it's a fling no matter what?"

"Yeah, it has to be. We're heading in different directions."

"Then, woman, climb that man like a tree. I mean, good Lord, he's fine."

"That's what I'm trying to do, mulher! Bye!"

Dean opens the door to his condo, and his eyes go wide. "Wow."

Exactly the reaction I'd hoped for. Wanting to bask in his appreciation a bit, I twirl so he can see the tight black dress I'm wearing from every angle.

"Double wow," he says as he steps aside to let me in.

"Can you grab that for me?" I ask sweetly, pointing at my weekender bag, which is still in the hall.

Dean grunts as he lifts it. "Are you moving in? What the hell's in here?"

I use my fingers to tick off a list of the goodies inside. "Gummy bears, kettle chips, ingredients for caipirinhas — enough for several, actually — sweatpants and fluffy socks for later. You know, movie-watching essentials."

"So there's an order to the evening?"

I wink at him. "Not really, no. I'm ready for just about anything."

He looks down at his own clothing. "I'm sorry I didn't dress up for the occasion."

He's wearing a heather-gray T-shirt and a pair of black sweat shorts, the latter sitting low on his trim hips. This outfit is just as appealing as the three-piece suits he wears to work every day, maybe even more, because it's a peek around the curtain of perfection he's so fond of hiding behind. Instead of telling him all of that, I relax into a sultry expression. "The important point is that we're both dressed for easy access."

"Right," he says, his head tilted as if he's not sure what my deal is.

Honestly, I'm not sure I know what my deal is either. In my head, I'm chanting, *Summer fling, summer fling, summer fling.* But I'm being ridiculous. I don't need a personality transplant to keep things casual between us. I just need to remember not to fall for him.

Dean drops my bag next to his entryway table and takes my hand, pulling me into the living room. "I made lasagna. And a salad. There's wine too." He snakes a hand around my waist and draws me close, his head dipping so he's at my eye level. "I'd like to feed you. Listen to your beautiful voice as we talk. Where it goes from there is your choice."

"Sounds like the perfect evening," I say.

There's a beeping noise, then Dean rounds the counter, throwing on an oven mitt as he rushes to the stove. "Perfect timing. You hungry?"

"Depends," I tell him as I approach and peek at the dish he's pulling out of the oven. "On?"

"Whether you're expecting me to eat it directly off the peninsula like that trend I saw the other day. TikTok is the devil."

He hip-bumps me out of the way. "I thought you knew me better by now. Just for that, I'm depriving you of seconds."

We talk through dinner (delicious, thanks to Dean) and the kitchen cleanup (meticulous, also thanks to Dean), and then I enlist his help juicing the limes for the caipirinhas. *Lots* of limes. Dean puts his whole body into the task, giving my eyes a lot of surface area to study. I'm particularly drawn to the way the corded muscles in his forearms strain against his skin as he twists the limes along the reamer. I'm tempted to keep handing him citrus all night.

"Why am I doing all the work?" Dean asks on a huff.

"The acidity tends to irritate my skin."

"Really?"

"No."

He stops twisting the lime and stares at me.

I give him a teasing grin and put out my hand. "My turn."

We switch off. Rather than sitting at the counter as I did, Dean remains behind me, inches away from touching my back, giving off a wall of heat that makes it difficult to concentrate on the relatively simple job before me.

"You're just going to stand there and watch?"

He slides a finger under the spaghetti strap that's fallen off my shoulder and slowly drags it back into place. "I'd like to."

"Well, while you're at it, why don't you make yourself useful and lift my dress."

He makes a noise — a deep-throated moan that ends in a soft hiss — then the cool air kisses my skin as he grasps the fabric and slides it upward, his warm fingers skimming the backs of my thighs. "Fuck."

"What's wrong?" I ask innocently, well aware that he's discovered I'm not wearing any underwear.

"Nothing's wrong. Everything's right." He steps closer, his arms caging my body as his hands hit the counter, then he pushes forward, his broad chest and the rigid line of his erection holding me in place. His breath ghosts over my ear. "The limes can wait."

"Wait for what?"

It's a game, of course. I know exactly what he's going to say: The limes can wait for us to have sex — or something else in that vein. And I couldn't agree more. But when he finally speaks, Dean says, "For me to make love to you like my next breath depends on it. Because honestly, Solange, I think it does."

"You're breathing now," I say, my tone playful even though his statement has kicked my lust into overdrive and turned my insides to jelly.

He grinds his dick against my ass. "Just barely, though."

Oh God. This man is dangerous any day. But now? With his desire for me at a fever pitch? He's downright lethal. I'd make all kinds of deals with unsavory characters to keep him in this altered state. "Let's move this into the bedroom, then."

I try to tug Dean in that direction, but he resists.

"What's going on?" I ask.

He opens his mouth, then closes it, his nostrils flaring a touch as he breathes through his nose.

"Dean, say what you need to say. I'm a

big girl. I can handle it."

He grasps the hem of my dress and tugs me back a step. "I'd like you to keep this above your waist and walk ahead of me. Would you do that for me?"

In answer, I lift the skirt of my dress to my waist and saunter toward his bedroom, staring at him over my shoulder as I go. "You coming?"

"I'm planning on it," he says, his voice laced with amusement.

For good measure, he does the scraping-his-teeth-over-his-bottom-lip thing.

Oh boy. I'm going to rock this man's world tonight. Doing so will put me fully in my element. All the other stuff — cozying up together, watching movies together, eating together — is secondary to sex. It has to be.

When we reach his room, Dean sits on the bed and pulls me between his legs. He trails his fingers across my collarbones and slips them under the straps of my dress. "They've been falling down all evening. It's been such a distraction." He meets my stare, his eyes blazing with need. "May I?"

"Yes," I say, my voice barely above a whisper.

He coaxes the straps down, and the bodice of the dress falls to my waist. "Damn, Solange. You're beautiful. It's like I'm seeing you for the first time." He grunts his approval, then leans forward and brushes his lips against my belly, caressing my breasts so lightly that I press into his touch, aching for more.

"Dean, please," I beg.

It's a vague request, sure, but he has to know I'm dying here.

"Please, what?" he asks, his voice tight and commanding.

Goose bumps dot my arms. Dean *likes* to be bossy in the bedroom. Knowing this about him is a huge turn-on. Still, I can't have him thinking I'm a pushover. "Can we move this along?"

"No problem. Step out of your dress."

I shimmy the fabric to my ankles and kick it off. "Done."

Now I'm naked and horny, and this gorgeous man is just staring at me.

Slowly — far too slowly for my taste — he rises off the bed, then shucks off his own clothing in three easy steps. Instead of touching me, he sits back down and strokes himself, as though he doesn't have a care in the world or a bare woman at the ready.

"This is called delayed gratification," he says. "You've probably come across the term in your travels."

I refuse to respond. The more I engage, the longer he'll draw this out.

"Do you see what you've done to me?" he says as he fists his dick and strokes it. "Just by asking me to lift your dress. This is because of you. All you."

I can't help staring at the way his big hand grips his cock. The way he slides his fingers down to the root, draws on his balls, and tightens his hold as he meanders back up to the crown. God, I want him in my mouth. "May I taste it?"

He squeezes his eyes shut and widens his legs. "Fuck, yes."

I drop to my knees and rest one hand on his thigh.

"Hang on," he says, opening his eyes and reaching for the clip securing my ponytail. "I want your hair brushing against my body."

Once my curls tumble to my shoulders, I draw him inside my mouth.

"Solange," he breathes out. "Yes, baby. Yes."

I lick my way up his length and slide my tongue over the head. Dean grabs a section of his comforter and clutches it as if it'll help him remain grounded. With the other hand, he pushes my hair to the side, ensuring himself a clear view of my ministrations.

I'm just as greedy to see the evidence of his pleasure, so I catalog his features and note that each time I apply a tiny bit of pressure at the base, he clenches his jaw and flinches.

He caresses my cheek and watches me with an intensity that drives me to take him deeper, to suck him harder. "Fuck, Solange, your lips sliding over my dick is the most amazing thing I've seen in ages."

Those words travel to my sex and settle there, a steady throb that makes me squirm in frustration.

Dean notices. "You need my tongue too, don't you?" He pats the bed. "Come on up here."

I release him and climb onto the bed.

"Stay on your hands and knees, please," he says as he rises to his feet.

I stop midcrawl and wait — but not for long. Soon, Dean's massaging my ass, and not long after that, he gently pushes my torso down so my face is resting on the bed. When he licks my pussy from behind, I nearly jump out of my skin. "Oh God, oh God, oh God." Other words follow, but I'm not making any sense. My muscles tighten, as if doing so will help me isolate and heighten the sensations between my thighs.

His mouth leaves me, and I whimper a

soft protest.

"Don't worry," he says. "I'm not done."

As far as I'm concerned, he could bury his face between my legs for eternity and it wouldn't be enough.

"Turn around, Solange."

I do.

"Now scoot all the way up," he instructs.

I do that too.

Dean then lies on the bed and settles his face against my thighs. "You're so plump and pretty down here." He grazes my clit with his thumb. "It's swollen. So deliciously swollen. And I can't wait to lick you here."

I'm undulating on the bed now, shamelessly trying to draw his mouth closer to my core. "Please, Dean."

"Would you like my fingers?" he asks.

"I'd like your fingers. Your mouth. Your tongue. Give me everything. *Please.*"

What follows is a riot of sensation that's both dizzying and disorienting. Dean's hands and mouth seem to be everywhere — stroking, sucking, kneading. My brain can't process everything he's doing, but my body registers the pleasure just fine. At one point he raises his head. "Tell me when you're close."

"I've been close since we started," I say.

After putting on a condom, he crawls up

the bed and coaxes me onto my side, positioning himself behind me. "Can I fuck you this way?"

"Dean, you can fuck me any way," I say, reaching back to caress his jaw.

In response, he grips my hip and nudges against my ass until he finds my sex and slowly guides himself inside. We're so close, I can feel his heat, inhale our mingled scents, and hear his ragged breathing.

"Yes, yes, yes," I chant as he enters me completely. "So good, so fucking good."

"You like the way I fill you?" he whispers against my ear.

"Oh God, yes."

"Let's see if moving inside you feels even better." With that warning shot issued, he presses his chest against my back, eliminating even a centimeter of space between us, and fucks me from behind as if the orgasms of our lives depend on it. "Solange, squeeze my cock. Take it each time. It's yours as long as you fucking want it."

His declaration sounds almost like a promise. Almost. But I know better. I don't just want his cock. I want his heart too. I grind my ass against him in frustration, meeting his thrusts, until he snakes an arm around my waist and centers two fingers over my clit.

"You want this?" he asks against my ear. "Do you need it?"

"Yes, oh God, yes."

He fucks me and strokes me in tandem, and I don't know which way is up, or whether I'll ever stop wanting to claim Dean as my person. Minutes later, we come together, our bodies freezing and shuddering as we shout our release. Once my breathing evens out, I turn over to face him, and he pins me with a questioning gaze.

"What?" I ask.

"That was better than average, right?" he says, panting. "Tell me it's not just in my head."

"It's not."

In fact, it's so not that it's disconcerting. I can't remember the last time a man asked me what I needed in bed — and gave it to me so eagerly. Dean didn't assume he had the answers; instead, he asked the questions. And shared what he needed for his own pleasure too.

"Okay, good. In that case, I think we should do it again. When you're ready. After all, practice makes perfect."

I know he's teasing, but as my eyes grow heavy, I'm struck by how close to perfect that truly was. Worse, I'm forced to face the inescapable truth: I planned to rock his

world; instead, Dean's steadily upending
mine.

CHAPTER TWENTY-FIVE

DEAN

Solange lays her head on my chest, draws the comforter to her chin, then lets out a satisfied sigh. I'm watching a favorite memory materialize right before my eyes. Wanting to complete the picture, I stroke her hair and twirl a curl. Yeah, this is perfect. Addictive, actually.

For the first time in forever, I'm considering the possibility of dating for dating's sake. No agenda. No endgame either. Who the hell am I?

I'm a person with a plan. Someone well on his way to securing the stability he's been chasing all his adult years. And fresh out of a relationship that was supposed to end in a long-lasting commitment. But maybe I should stop pedaling the life cycle and hit the pause button. Continue to focus on my career. Resume the multistep to-do list a little later. In the meanwhile, I can spend

time with Solange on an exclusive basis —
for as long as she'll have me. I'd even travel
to Ohio to see her if she wanted. Given how
busy we'll both be, maybe a long-distance
relationship is the solution. Would she want
that, though?

Solange groans as she snuggles farther
into my embrace. "You're doing it again. I
wish you'd stop."

"Stop doing what?"

"Overthinking. The surgeon general warns
against it."

Is this what it's like to have someone know
you well enough that they can guess what's
going on inside your head? I like it. A lot.
"You're right. We need a reset. So how
about that movie?"

She disentangles herself from my arms
and rests on her elbows. "Which one did
you have in mind?"

When Harry Met Sally. I shrug. "It just
feels like it should be our thing."

"*Our* thing?" she asks, her lips jutting out
as if she's skeptical of the phrase. "We have
'*things*' now?"

"Yeah," I say, tapping her nose. "It feels
like our inside joke. Or it should be. Something that's only between us."

She shakes her head and pretends to
grimace. "I don't know, Dean. Are you feel-

ing okay? Because that sounds kind of romantic."

It does, doesn't it? And I bet she doesn't appreciate the mixed messaging. "Well, you and Brandon have 'things,' right?" I say, making air quotes. "And you two are friends."

She swallows. "We do, and we are."

"So this is the same idea."

"Riiiight," she says, shaking her head. "You're absolutely right. Got it."

"Okay, then," I say, sitting up. "Let's move this party to the living room, where surround sound and high resolution await you. We're doing this."

"Be right back," she says. After planting a soft kiss on my lips, she slips out of the bed and walks her naked ass out of my room.

She returns less than a minute later, her bag in one hand. "It's a lot lighter now that it's no longer holding enough contents to serve an entire bar."

A bunch of stuff happens at breakneck speed: She dashes into the bathroom; emerges in a cropped tee and sweats; drops onto the bed to throw on socks; and gathers her hair into a messy bun, then jumps up. It's a dizzying scene.

I crawl out from under the comforter. "You're a damned tornado."

"And you're a slowpoke. I'll meet you out there. Going to finish the caipirinhas."

Minutes later, I enter the living area and pull up short as I watch Solange carry two cocktail glasses over to the coffee table. I take in her sweet expression, her vibrant presence, the way she settles on my couch in anticipation of watching a film that she's already seen, probably dozens of times.

As soon as I settle in next to her, she drapes a throw blanket over our legs, presses play on the remote, and leans against my side.

I try to ignore the way the moment mirrors what I've always envisioned for a regular Saturday night. Belonging. Belonging to someone, more specifically. For years, it was an idea. But now I'm experiencing the reality, and it is so much better than anything I could have imagined. Because it's Solange.

Okay, so it turns out I'm a liar. I don't just want to watch a movie with her. I don't just want us to have "things." And I don't just want to casually date her. I want her in my life. Only problem is, I don't know how we can possibly make this work, especially since I'm not sure either of us is equipped to give the other what they need.

So I settle for watching the movie —

because remaining in this happy place is easier than figuring my shit out.

"Billy Crystal's voice is annoying as hell," I say as I munch on the kettle chips Solange brought with her.

She hands me the bag. "Keep it. I'm full."

"Meg Ryan's cute, though."

"Mmhm."

"Harry's hair is a mess. Is that how they wore it in the seventies?"

"Based on pictures I've seen, yes."

"They're going to drive eighteen hours together? That's a recipe for disaster." I set the bag next to me and rub my hands together. "Oh, is this the diner scene? This is going to be good."

"No, that one comes later. After college. When they're much older."

"Oh, embarrassing herself in diners is a thing in this movie, I guess."

Solange lunges for the remote, presses pause, and whacks me with a pillow, all within the space of seconds. "Are you incapable of being quiet during a movie? Because you haven't stopped talking since the moment I hit play."

I snatch the pillow away and give her a sheepish grin. "I'm sorry. It's just . . . I like it when you're around, and I'm trying to get in all the words as if we have a time limit."

Her eyes soften. "We don't. I'm spending the night, remember? And I'll still be here when you wake up."

"I meant, you won't be in DC much longer."

Her gaze darts to mine as she fiddles with the remote. "Ah. Well, carry on with your gibberish, then."

"No, you're right. I'm being a pain. I'll shut up so we can enjoy the movie."

Unfortunately, my cell phone rings just when we're ready to press play again, and a quick glance at the screen indicates the caller is using the condo's intercom system. "Hello?"

"Dean, it's your mom. Can you let me up, son?"

My stomach drops. Melissa Chapman isn't one for surprise visits. She's supposed to be across the country. In a motor home. With Harvey. I glance at Solange, who's frozen in place, then place a hand on her thigh. "Hey, Mom. Are you alone?"

My mother doesn't immediately respond. I suspect my choice of words isn't helping. Finally, she says, "Yes, I'm alone."

"Hang on. I'm in two oh six."

"I know," she says on a laugh. "I send you

Christmas cards, don't I?"

She sure does. Sometimes a card and a few phone calls make up the extent of our contact in any given year. Sighing, I type in the numbers that will unlock the front door, then slowly rise from the couch.

Solange follows suit. "We can always watch *When Harry Met Sally* another time." She waves a thumb behind her. "I'm going to gather my stuff. It's probably best if I make myself scarce."

Seconds ago, I couldn't contain my excitement about spending time with Solange. Now, it's as if my mother's arrival has drained me of even an ounce of energy. I pull Solange toward me. "Let's play it by ear. See what's going on first. For all I know, she could be dropping off a souvenir from her trip."

Solange taps my chest. "I'm going to get my stuff together just in case. And I'll give you two a few minutes to talk. In the meantime" — she winks at me — "I'll just be perusing your medicine cabinet."

I watch her jog out of the living room, then brace myself for whatever has brought my mother to DC. While I'm waiting, I glance at my phone notifications and see a recent text from Max among them. It says:

You sly dog. Lina filled me in. I'm not so sure

about this, but I got your back. My advice? Convince Solange to accept the offer in DC. Worry about the rest later.

Offer in DC? What's he talking about? It takes only a few seconds for me to grasp the gist of Max's message: Victory Academy must have offered Solange a permanent position. And she didn't tell me.

Disappointment courses through my body, a heavy weight cementing me to the spot. Either she didn't want me to know about the job, or she's already decided to decline it. Neither possibility suggests that she's tying herself in knots the way I am. Wondering if we can make us work. Envisioning something more. And sure, it's not like we've made any promises to each other, but we're friends, right? Considering everything else Solange has shared with me, it's telling that she never mentioned the possibility of staying in DC.

Rather than admit I didn't know about the offer, I text Max a thumbs-up and set my phone on the kitchen counter. Seconds later, Melissa Chapman is at my door.

Despite the cheeriness I first heard in my mother's voice when she was downstairs, the red-rimmed eyes, runny nose, and splotches of pink on her chin and cheeks tell a different story.

"Is everything okay?" I ask as I stand aside to let her in, my gaze moving past her into the hall to confirm that she's not bringing anyone else along.

"I'm fine," she says, rolling a duffel bag on wheels behind her.

"Do you need something? A drink? The restroom?"

She repeats herself, louder this time: "I'm fine."

"So what's going on?"

She parks her bag in a corner and spins around, her shoulders slumped in defeat. "Harvey and I had a fight. The plan was to drive to Massachusetts to meet his kids before heading back to Delaware."

"And . . . ?" I say, eyeing her shoes. I can't fucking help it.

She rolls her eyes, then toes them off while she explains. "And it was clear he'd never told them about me. I was angry. He was confused. And when I shouted that it only seemed right that he would mention the woman he was going to be living with to his children, he balked. Apparently, sharing his home with me wasn't in the plans. It blew up from there, so I asked him to take me to the closest train station, and now I'm here."

"Why not take a train home to Delaware?"

She swallows before she responds. "I

didn't renew my lease."

"Because you thought you'd be moving in with Harvey."

"Yes."

I don't know how she can stand it. Every new man who comes into her life is "the one." She gets all warm and fuzzy, then, when they inevitably disappoint her, it's as if she's starting at zero again. As a kid, I watched it happen time and time again. Still, part of me secretly hoped Harvey would be different. "You can stay here, of course. For as long as you need to. And I'll help you find a new place."

"Thank you."

She opens her mouth, then closes it.

"What?"

Sighing, she shrugs her shoulders. "I thought he was my soul mate. I thought he was it for me."

Christ. I hate this so much. My mother isn't a bad person. She deserves better than to be let down by every man she dates. Then again, she scoffed at me when I told her that warm, fuzzy feeling wasn't reliable. Maybe she's finally ready to accept that I have a point. I bridge the distance between us and wrap my arms around her. "I'm sorry it didn't work out."

"Turns out he was just as shitty as the others. Well, he was good in bed, I'll give him that."

"I could have done without that mental picture, thank you." Looking around us, I add, "Let me get you set up in the guest bedroom."

My mother takes a moment to survey my place. She widens her eyes when her gaze lands on the caipirinhas Solange made. "Oh shoot. Am I interrupting something?"

"A friend's here," I say, my mouth suddenly going dry. "She wanted to give us privacy."

My mother gives me a devilish grin. "Wow, my son works fast."

"It's not like that," I whisper.

"What's it like, then?" she whispers in reply.

I grind my teeth and glare at her. "We're not having this conversation right now."

For at least two reasons. One, Solange is in my bedroom, and it doesn't feel right to talk about her in this way. Two, I have no fucking clue what I'd say. It's been a month since she crashed my wedding. If I hinted that Solange and I are anything other than friends with benefits, a barrage of questions would follow. I'm not an impulsive person. Telling my mother I have feelings — *serious feelings* — for a woman I met last month

411

would raise all kinds of red flags in her mind. She knows that's not my MO. Because it's hers, and we couldn't be more different if we tried.

Shit, comparing myself to my mother throws what's been going on between Solange and me into sharp relief. Now that I think about it, what the hell am I doing? This isn't me. At all. Instead, I'm taking a page from Melissa Chapman, and that's the clearest sign that I've gone astray from where I need to be.

She puts up her hands. "Okay, okay. May I take a shower at least? I have seven hours' worth of high-speed-train germs on my body."

Before I can respond, the click of the door to my bedroom snags my attention and Solange enters the living room, her bag slung over her shoulder.

"Hello," she says to my mother. "I'm Solange. Dean's . . . friend. I was just leaving."

My mother steps forward and, as they shake hands, says, "I'd never forget your face. Made quite the splash at the wedding. Well, it's nice to finally meet you, sweetheart."

Solange swallows. "Same." She looks at

me, then pokes my stomach. "Walk me out?"

I'm sure I resemble a bobblehead as I swivel around. "Of course." I'm struggling to process everything cycling through my brain: the idyllic time I spent with Solange earlier; the implications of my mother's unexpected visit; the revelation about Solange's job. Hell, it's a struggle just to figure out what to do with my hands. My natural inclination is to put one of them at Solange's lower back, but my mother's watchful gaze prompts me to slip them into the pockets of my shorts instead.

I turn back to my mother. "Make yourself at home. Sheets are changed. Towels are in the closet." She mouths, *Thank you,* then I shut the door behind me.

We walk in silence to the elevator bank. There, Solange presses the call button, turns to me, and rests a hand on my stomach. "Is everything all right? With your mom, I mean?"

"Not really," I say, rubbing the back of my neck. "She broke up with her boyfriend. The aftermath isn't always great."

"Is there anything I can do to help?"

Her question doesn't surprise me. Because even though Solange lives and breathes sarcasm and cynicism, she's also an incredibly giving person. "No, I don't think so. Short story: She gave up her apartment, and now I need to help her find a new one."

"Will she be okay?"

"Only time will tell. It's been a while since I've been around when one of her relationships imploded." I shrug. "We'll see. But just a heads-up: That means I'm probably not going to be available much. Between work and my mother being here, I won't have time to spare."

She furrows her brow and steps away from me; it's like watching an alley cat hunch its back in defensive mode. "I don't recall asking for your time."

"No, you didn't," I say, shaking my head. "But I also don't want you to think I'm ghosting you. It's just . . . the circumstances." My chest tightens. What the hell am I saying? I need a moment to breathe and figure out what the fuck I'm doing, but Solange is staring at me as if she's seeing me in a new light — and it's not a good one either. I forge ahead even though I probably shouldn't. "You asked me not to blow smoke up your ass, remember, so I won't. The truth is, I think I've been stuck on fantasy island, and as soon as my mother showed up, I realized playtime is over."

"I have no idea what any of that means,"

she says, crinkling her nose.

Why should she? I'm doing a terrible job of explaining myself — and probably pissing her off in the process. I clench and unclench my fists at my sides and try again. "I think all of this pretend dating messed with my head. I started to imagine that we could work as a couple. For real. But tonight, I remembered the reasons that isn't a good idea. I need a sense of security. Normalcy. Order. It's what I've been working toward my whole life. I have a plan —"

"And I don't fit into it," she says, scowling. "Got it." She gives me a dismissive wave, as if she's over this conversation — over me, too. "You've got every single one of your remaining days on God's green earth mapped out. Where the hell do I get off interfering, am I right?"

"Oh, c'mon, Solange. You don't even *want* to be a part of my life plan."

"What makes you so sure of that?" she asks, her face tilted as she lasers me with those damn bottomless eyes.

"Well, if you thought there was a possibility of a future for us, you would have been up-front with me. Can you truly say that's the case?"

"Who are you? The Riddler?" she asks, folding her arms over her chest. "You obviously have something on your mind. Just spit it out."

"Fine," I say gruffly, the muscles in my jaw tensing. "Why didn't you tell me about your offer from Victory Academy?"

She scoffs, then begins to pace the hall, and it's like I'm watching a snowball gather force as it covers more ground and picks up speed. "Because I haven't decided one way or the other yet, and I need to do this on my own. And okay, yes: I *don't* want you to be a factor in my choice. Because that would be a mistake, wouldn't it? You refuse to fall in love, and I refuse to be with someone who won't love me. You're not wired for romance, remember?"

"Can you blame me?" I say, pointing at my door. "Solange, without me, she'd be out on the streets because she thought he was 'the one.' Listen, I know firsthand how volatile relationships can be. One day you're in love. The next day, you're not. You have expectations, and when someone doesn't meet them, you're disappointed. Gutted, even. Why *wouldn't* I want to take all of that out of the equation?"

She tugs on my wrists, as if she wants to shake some sense into me. "Because then you're just existing. Is that what you want? To go through life being physically present

416

and emotionally absent?"

I don't answer quickly enough for her liking, so she charges ahead. "Well, that's a cop-out, Dean, and it's lazy. You want the trappings of being in a committed relationship, but you don't want to roll up your sleeves and do the work necessary to be worthy of it."

"That's been my point all along: We define committed relationships differently." I blow out a deep breath. "Look, I'm not trying to hide the ball here. When Ella and I parted ways, I was fine. Picked myself back up, no problem. That wouldn't happen with you, and that terrifies me." My vision blurs. Fuck, this is hard. "I'd always be worried that you're on the verge of leaving. Because you're not tied to anyone or anything. I'm not saying that's wrong — you should go out there and explore your options — but that's not right for me. And I know you want more. Shit, I'd be the first person to admit you *deserve* more. You deserve *everything*. Sadly, I can't be the one to give it to you. We just don't line up the way we should."

A tear slips down her cheek, and it feels as though someone's slammed me to the ground.

"Don't cry," I say.

She steps forward and rests her forehead against my chest. "Too late."

I run my hands up and down her back as we stand together in silence.

Her head still down, she eventually says, "I'm not upset because you're wrong. I'm upset because you're right. It's true that I'm still figuring my shit out, and I'm good with that. What I know, though, is that I need someone who's all in. And maybe that's just not in the cards for me. Not now, anyway." She wipes her eyes dry. "So what? This is it? You don't even want us to be friends anymore?"

I take her hand and brush a thumb across it. "That's not what I'm saying at all. I want us to reach a point where we both feel comfortable being in each other's lives. Wherever the hell you end up."

She hiccups on a laugh, then jabs me in the stomach. "I'm going to hold you to that, asshole."

I wrap my arms around her and press my mouth against her forehead. Everything between us is so astonishingly civilized. Makes me wonder if we're making more of our differences than we need to. But no, there isn't any point in wavering. Solange and I are puzzle pieces that simply don't fit; trying to force us together is only going to frustrate us both.

The elevator car arrives, and Solange backs into it, her dull gaze never straying from mine. We're still holding hands, neither of us quite ready to let go. After a long moment, she takes a deep breath and pulls away. Then the doors slide shut, and she's gone.

A part of me wants to run down the stairs, stop her in the lobby, and kiss her senseless. But Solange isn't the person for me; pretending otherwise is only going to lead to the kind of heartache my mother's experiencing at this very moment. I'll reach out to Solange in a few days. Make sure she knows that I genuinely want us to remain friends. Anything else would be impractical — no matter how much I wish that weren't the case.

CHAPTER TWENTY-SIX

SOLANGE

Natalia answers the door, a sleeping Sebastian wrapped in a blanket and cradled in her arms. "It's about time you came to see me!" she yells.

I gesture at the baby. "Shh. You'll wake him."

"Don't shush me, bitch." Spinning around, she adds, "I have a very important job these days."

I follow her into the house. "Yes, I get it, but how is speaking more quietly going to interfere with that?"

She gives me a "duh" expression. "This kid needs to get used to his very loud mother. So I'm starting him out young. All of the parenting guides say if you make your home unnaturally quiet, a baby will respond to every little thing and —"

"Obviously that isn't going to happen here," I mutter.

"You're lucky I'm curious about the contents of that bag," she says, pointing at my shopping tote. "Otherwise, I'd tell you to turn right around and come back when you learn how to respect your elders."

Ah, yes. The "respect your elders" refrain. To Natalia, our two-year age difference means I'm young enough to be her daughter. It's ridiculous, but I've come to accept that, just as there are dog years, there are cousin years too. I've also come to ignore it. Besides, today I have a far more important matter monopolizing my attention: the little bundle in my cousin's arms.

As I stare at Sebastian, I can practically feel my heart expanding to accommodate the extra love for this newest member of our family. "He's beautiful, Natalia. Congrats to you and Paulo, and may he always be happy, healthy, and safe."

"Thanks, Sol," Natalia says, beaming as she looks down at her son. "Paulo and I are still pinching ourselves."

A chorus of laughter erupts in the kitchen. "The gang's all here, huh?"

"Yeah," Natalia says. "They've cleaned the house, started the laundry, organized Sebastian's nursery, and prepared enough food to sustain us through the apocalypse. Dinner should be ready soon." She leans forward and lowers her voice to a whisper. "Tia Vivi-ane even purchased condoms. For later, she said. But I swear, the only penis I'll be see-ing for the foreseeable future is Sebastian's when I bathe or change him."

"Is there anything that could possibly fall into the category of TMI for you?"

"You mean, like the fact that Paulo and I regularly use butt plugs to spice up our sex life?"

Jesus. "Yes. Like that."

"Nope," she says matter-of-factly.

Shaking my head, I guide her down the hall. "C'mon, I want to show you the good-ies I brought."

When we enter the living area, a cacoph-ony of voices greets us. Lina and Jaslene are prepping food in the kitchen, my mother and aunts are lounging on the couch, and Rey is sitting in an armchair, his eyes fixed on the TV screen.

Natalia doesn't even let me present the gifts — massage vouchers for the grown-ups, ridiculously adorable clothes for Sebas-tian, and a white noise machine for his room. She simply grabs the bag and heads upstairs, (loudly) explaining over her shoul-der that she needs to put Sebastian down for a nap.

I cross the room to my mother and kiss

her forehead. "Oi, Mãe."

"Oi, filha," she says without losing her place in her conversation with her sisters.

I kiss Tia Mariana and Tia Viviane, then round the island to join Lina and Jaslene.

"There you are," Lina says, a cutting board of diced onions and whole tomatoes on the counter in front of her. She dabs her eyes with a tissue, then grabs a knife. "We were wondering if you'd show up. Your mom said you passed on gardening today."

"Wasn't in the mood," I say, shrugging. "Still tired from all the fake dating with Dean. We're finally done, though."

"In more ways than one, I hear," Lina says, narrowing her eyes. "Want to fill us in on what happened?"

It figures that Lina would already know Dean and I are no longer spending time together. Dean tells Max everything, and Max tells Lina everything. Together, the three of them could supply Page Six with a year's worth of gossip. Not wanting to discuss Dean, I ignore Lina's remark and focus on the food they're preparing. "What are you two making, by the way?"

"Picadillo," Jaslene says. "Lina's been literally begging me for the recipe for my empanadas, and I didn't want her to embarrass herself any longer, so I caved. The filling's almost ready."

I lean in and take a whiff. "Smells delicious."

Jaslene plucks a spoon from the dishwashing rack, dips it into the picadillo, and presents it to me. I open my mouth, but before I can snag a taste, Lina lowers Jaslene's outstretched hand.

My eyes snap up to my cousin's. "What?"

"I'll repeat my question: Want to fill us in?"

Jaslene sets the spoon down and claps. "*Oh,* bring on the bochinche."

"No, no, no," I say, shaking my head. "We're not gossiping about what should remain between Dean and me. All I'm going to say is that we went beyond the fake part, then decided we wouldn't work as a real couple."

Natalia appears at the foot of the stairs, just a few feet away. "Wait. You and Dean stopped pretending and hooked up for real? Why am I just hearing about this?"

Until now, my mother and aunts have been chatting with one another, seemingly oblivious to my conversation with Lina and Jaslene. But Natalia's big mouth alerts them that there's a more interesting discussion to be had. I know this because their voices grow quieter — so they can talk among themselves *and* listen to us at the same time. Latinx mothers have superhuman hearing that can detect both gossip and children behaving badly at vast distances and beyond concrete walls.

Unsurprisingly, the migration begins soon thereafter. Tia Viviane drifts over and pretends to be looking for something. Tia Mariana offers to roll out the dough for the empanadas. My mother locates the cleaning wipes and focuses on ridding the counters of crumbs.

"I'm not doing this with y'all," I say, unable to temper the exasperation in my voice.

The tias glance at each other, then, as if they're some sort of Brazilian outpost of the Avengers team, they assemble in the living room and motion for me to join them. This is an interrogation — and an intervention, possibly.

My gaze bounces between my mother and her sisters.

"You don't look happy, filha," Tia Viviane says. "Do we need to hurt Dean?"

It warms my heart that she cares. Truly. I couldn't ask for a better support network than these women. Add in my cousins, who learned their "família primeiro" mantra from the sisters, and I'm blessed with all the backup any person could ever need.

"No need to inflict bodily harm on Dean," I tell them.

Tia Mariana paces in front of the sofa as she studies me, her head tilted and her lips pursed. It's not difficult to guess where Lina gets her detective skills from. "Then what's going on?"

I wish I had a succinct answer, ideally one that would whittle down what happened between us into a few words and shut down this conversation. Dean and I are so much more than a sentence or two, however, and these women are relentless. "It would take forever to explain, but in the end, we're not a good match. I'm looking for love. Dean isn't. He wants someone who fits into his perfectly ordered life, and I certainly don't. It's as simple as that."

"Nothing's ever that simple," Tia Viviane says. "Emotions are complicated, sweetheart. You don't always get to choose how you feel about someone. Sometimes your heart makes the decision for you."

I return her steady gaze. "I get it, Tia. But sometimes your heart doesn't know what's best for you, and it's your job to steer it in the right direction. Choosing to give your all to someone is no small thing. It needs to be absolutely right. If it isn't, you're destined for disaster."

426

My mother sighs. "You know what your problem is?"

"I wasn't aware I had a problem," I say under my breath.

"You do," my mother replies bluntly. "Solange, you're scared to make a bad decision because you think it will change the course of your life. But, filha, think about it: Making *no* decisions can change your life too." She snags the space between Tia Viviane and me and takes my hand. "I'm not talking about which shoes you're going to wear. Or what you're going to eat for breakfast. I'm talking about the important stuff: what you want to do with the gifts you have, who you want to spend your time with, where you want to plant roots. You told me the other day that you don't want to wake up one morning and discover that you're stuck." Mãe squeezes my hand. "I'm sorry to tell you, but —"

I know what she's getting at, and she's right: "But I'm already spinning my wheels, aren't I?"

She nods. "Your father changed my life, yes. But not in the way you think. Filha, he gave me you, and you are the *farthest* thing from a mistake that I can think of. I'm not trapped, or stuck, or anything else. I'm satisfied with my choices. Can you say the same?"

All I can say is that I'm tired of treating every opportunity or person as a potential booby trap.

"I'll tell you something else," my mother continues. "Castle Florists in Rockville offers a floral design class in the fall." She winks at me. "I'm thinking about taking it."

My heart swells. Just the thought of my mother doing something entirely for herself brings tears to my eyes. I raise our clasped hands and kiss her palm. "You're amazing, and I'm so blessed to be your daughter."

My mother stands and lightly bops me on the nose. "Yes, I know I am the bomb, as you kids say."

"No one says that," Rey adds, remaining motionless in the armchair but plainly eavesdropping.

We ignore him. It's our shared superpower.

"Okay, enough of this," Tia Mariana says as she walks to the kitchen. "While you figure out your life, I'll be frying empanadas. Who's helping?"

Tia Viviane gives her thighs a forceful pat, then stands. "I am."

The flurry of activity is comforting. When everyone's busy, no one's paying attention to me. I prefer it that way. Because I don't have any answers. Just feelings. Lots and lots of confusing feelings.

As Jaslene and the tias work in the kitchen, Natalia and Rey set the table. I'm poised to join them, but Lina blocks my path.

"You want to hear my take?" she asks.

"I'm sure you're going to tell me even if I don't."

She pushes me away playfully. "Well, smartass, *I* think you operate as a one-woman show." She sweeps her arm in an arc. "But look around you, prima. Every person in this room would catch you if you fell. So go big, make mistakes, and learn from them. I certainly did, and I'm doing okay."

I draw back. "Are we talking about Dean or Victory Academy?"

"Could be both," she says, shrugging. "But I'll say this: You have a whole-ass family that adores you here. You have ideas you want to implement at Victory. You have students waiting for your guidance. Where's the impasse?"

Although my instinct is to challenge her observations, I say nothing as I watch her walk away. In my mind, self-preservation means you avoid making the kinds of mistakes that will break your heart. But my

429

mother and Lina are right: Being so afraid to make a mistake has led me to build a life that's hollow in the places that matter the most.

Rey lumbers over and motions for me to join him on the couch. Oh God, what now?

I've always regarded Rey as a big brother, a role he eased into over the years as his own self-confidence grew, but sometimes he tries to elevate that role to father-figure status, and it's cringey. I'm mentally praying this isn't one of those times.

"I couldn't help but overhear," he says.

"Don't tell me you have advice too," I mutter.

"No, I was just wondering if you'd be willing to give me Dean's number." Rey waggles his eyebrows. "He seems more promising than the average white guy. Since you're not interested in him in that way, I figured —"

"Shut up, Rey," I say flatly.

He smirks at me. "So stingy with your booty calls."

I'm tempted to wrestle Rey to the ground and make him cry uncle, but he's built like a man who can kick anyone's ass, and I'd probably sprain something in the process. "Don't disrespect him like that. Dean's *not* a booty call."

"With all this hand-wringing, I can tell,"

Rey says, his expression smug and knowing. "As one of the most prolific poets of our time, Lin-Manuel Miranda, once wrote, '*Fucking* is easy, young man, *loving* is harder.' "

I puff out my cheeks. Should I even claim this person as a relative? "He never wrote that."

"Did too."

I reach over and squeeze Rey's hand. "You're a mess, and I love you for it, but leave the advice to Lina and the tias. Please."

Besides, they've given me enough to think about. Now I just need to figure out how to move forward.

CHAPTER TWENTY-SEVEN

DEAN

After an overlong networking lunch with a prospective client, I return to Olney & Henderson and find Michael sitting in a guest chair in my office.

"Make yourself comfortable, why don't you?" I bark out as I round my desk and take a seat. I'm cranky, and I have no idea why.

"Don't be an ingrate. I come bearing news."

My gaze snaps to his; the new emails in my inbox can wait. "Good news?"

"Promising news. It's about Kimberly Bailey."

I've been on the edge of my seat wondering whether she'll accept the firm's offer. "Promising" doesn't sound like she did. "What can you tell me?"

"Basically, she's down to two firms: us and Gibson Connolly. She had questions for us

— about long-term compensation and her path to partnership — and she was up-front in saying she's asking the same questions of GC. So we're in a holding pattern, but we're not out of the running."

"You're right. That *is* promising."

"That's not all, either. Your name came up — in a good way. And given that Henderson's been your biggest detractor, I'd say your efforts to reel in Bailey have helped you clear a major hurdle. Henderson even pointed out that you'd stepped up to the plate despite the recent setback in your personal life."

Is that how they see my breakup with Ella? I suppose in the grand scheme of things it technically is, but if it hadn't happened, I never would have spent so much time with Solange. I'd hardly consider that a setback. "Did they mention Peter?"

"They did. Henderson's a fan. That's all I'll tell you."

Which means he isn't telling me everything. And that's fair. I appreciate that Michael is willing to share this much. Above all else, I'm relieved. My mother doesn't share much about her personal finances, but high school teachers are notoriously underpaid, and finding and furnishing a new apartment is going to take cash she probably doesn't have. The jump in salary that comes with partnership would allow me to give her what she needs. "So, in other words, keep my head down, bring in a new client or two, and double up on work for paying clients."

"The student has become the teacher." Michael grins as he rises from my guest chair. "Just sit tight. If I hear anything about Kimberly Bailey, I'll let you know."

"Thanks, man."

After Michael leaves, I close my eyes and take a rare moment to just sit with the fact that partnership is within my grasp. It's an achievement, for sure, but I can't help thinking that the past month has dulled its shine. I should be proud of myself. I should be anticipating what's to come. More clients. More cases. More responsibility. Honestly, though, I'm thinking about the practical effect of it and nothing else. Partnership isn't going to change my life; it's going to keep it stable.

I return my attention to the emails waiting in my inbox. The sooner I can finish my work for the day, the sooner I can get home to my mother. If she's alone for too long, I'm confident she'll get wrapped up in the breakup. At least when I'm there, I can keep her occupied. Yesterday, we demolished the leftovers from the dinner for Cláudia and her family, took virtual apartment tours, and caught up on each other's lives. She didn't mention Harvey once; I thought about Solange only half my waking hours. Staying busy helped us both, apparently.

My phone buzzes. As if I've conjured her, Solange's name pops up on the screen.

Solange: hey. sorry to bother you, but I think I left my bc pills in your bathroom
Me: bc?
Solange: birth control
Solange: I missed a dose yesterday so I need to get them asap
Me: got it. want to stop by tonight to pick them up?
Solange: can't. have class. can I pick them up now? still have the key.
Me: my mother's there. is that ok?
Solange: sure. I'll leave the keys with her.
Me: cool. will let her know you're coming.
Solange: be there in 15 mins. thanks.

I toss my phone on the desk, and it clatters to the edge. The way Solange and I interacted in that text exchange, as if we mean absolutely nothing to each other, was

435

probably the least genuine moment in our entire relationship, even including the period when we were faking one. Solange and I only pretended to date, yet somehow I'm experiencing a damn breakup anyway. And fuck, there's this ache in my chest whenever I think about her. *Not good.*

I stand abruptly and snatch up the phone.

My mother picks up within two rings. "Hello?"

"Hey, it's me. Just wanted to give you a heads-up that Solange needs to pick up something from my place. She'll be there soon."

"Solange?" she asks, a tinge of humor in her voice.

She's doing this on purpose, and I don't have the patience for it. "The woman you met Saturday night."

"Oh yes, the woman who crashed your wedding. Such a pretty lady."

I can barely hold back the growl in my throat. "Just don't harass her, okay? Let her get in and get out. No twenty questions."

"Of course."

"Thank you."

"I'll shoot for nineteen." Then she hangs up.

My gut's telling me this isn't going to end well; the mile-high stack of files on my desk and a three o'clock team meeting are telling me I can't do shit about it.

SOLANGE

Well done, Solange. You powered through those texts like a champ.

As I begin the walk from my apartment to Dean's, I applaud myself for holding it together. There's no use denying it: Distancing myself from him isn't going to be easy. Even now, I want to be near him. Talk to him. Kiss him. But Dean isn't my person, nor does he want me to be his. I knew this from the outset. Yet I got sidetracked by our chemistry, his willingness to wear his vulnerability on his sleeve, the way we played the role of lovers so skillfully that it began to feel real.

Silly me. Dean was never anything more than a diversion. I likely served the same function for him. No harm, no foul, right?

Wrong, Solange. It doesn't even sound convincing in your own head.

Here's hoping my and Brandon's trip to Vegas will yank me out of this funk.

I trudge up the short walkway to Dean's building, then square my shoulders before pushing open the outer door. In the box-size vestibule, I pull his keys from my purse, unlock the wrought iron security gate, and

437

head straight for the elevator.

When I arrive at Dean's condo, I take a deep, steadying breath and ring the bell. With any luck, Dean's mother won't engage me in conversation, and I'll be able to slip in and out with no fuss.

Melissa Chapman opens the door with a flourish. She's an attractive woman. The resemblance between her and Dean is striking. Same hazel eyes. Same dirty-blond hair, hers styled in a shoulder-length bob. Dressed in relaxed jeans and a cream linen top, she could easily be mistaken for his older sister.

"Solange, come in, come in."

"Sorry to bother you, Ms. Ch—"

"Please. Call me Melissa."

"Right," I say, stepping inside. "Sorry to bother you, Melissa. I just need to grab something I left the other day. I'll be out of your hair in no time."

"It's no bother. Do what you need to do."

I keep my head down, stride to Dean's room, and find my floral birth control case next to his toothbrush holder. The bathroom's spotless. No surprise there. I take a moment to scan Dean's bedroom. The bed's made, the window shades are drawn on each side at precisely the halfway mark, and Dean's house slippers are lined up together in the only empty corner. A small stack of files rests on the nightstand; on top, a bowl of peppermints serves as a paperweight. The devil on my shoulder is whispering in my ear, encouraging me to leave his pristine sanctuary in disarray, but I mentally flick the suggestion away. This place is so quintessentially Dean, I don't want to mess with it. Enough of this. It's time to bounce.

When I return to the living room, Melissa grabs the remote and turns off the TV.

"Well, I'm all good to go." I jingle the keys in my hand. "I'm just going to drop these on the counter." I don't know why, but I keep my hands visible and creep to the kitchen — as if one false move will set off a chain of events I'm not prepared for — then I place the keys near Dean's coffeemaker.

Melissa watches me, her lips curved into a half smile. "Solange, please don't leave yet. It's been a while since I've had the opportunity to meet any of Dean's friends." She points at the armchair facing the sofa. "Sit with me a bit?"

Dammit. Here we go. I slowly lower myself onto the chair, then look at her and wait.

"How is he?" she asks. "Really, I mean. He says he's fine, but just a month ago, he was going to marry Ella. I'm hoping you know more."

"He seems" — I shrug — "okay?"

What else can I say? Dean and I didn't talk about Ella that much. We just talked about everything else. And laughed a lot. And gave each other toe-curling orgasms. And blurred the line between fiction and reality even though we both claimed we never would.

She studies me curiously. "How'd you two meet, by the way?"

My chest contracts like a collapsed soufflé. I have no idea whether Melissa liked Dean's bride. Will she turn hostile once she knows Dean and I were complete strangers when I stopped his wedding? Does it matter? She's Dean's mother; of course it does. "Um, I crashed his wedding."

Her eyes go wide, and she falls forward. "*That* was the first day you two met?"

Okay, good. She doesn't seem upset. Instead, she appears to be amused by the revelation, and I fall a little bit in love with her right then. I sit up in the armchair. "It was."

"Well done, my dear." Her expression sobers. "Is he . . . getting over Ella?"

"Honestly, I don't think there was much to get over. It sounded like they'd convinced themselves a modern-day marriage of convenience made sense. I suspect in hindsight they're relieved they didn't go through with it."

Or Ella is. I'm not so sure about Dean.

After letting out a long sigh, she says, "I did this to him."

"Did what?" I ask, frowning.

"Made him wary of falling in love," she says, picking at the nonexistent lint on her sleeves.

"Forgive me, but I doubt that's true. We're all informed by our experiences, but how we react to them is partly on us."

"Then I exposed him to the experiences that led him to be wary of love. Better?"

I'm torn. One the one hand, I'm practically rabid for any additional insight into Dean's psyche. On the other hand, maybe I shouldn't try to dissect Dean's worldview any more than I already have. Not surprisingly, I cave. "Tell me why you think so."

"Dean's grandparents stopped communicating with me shortly after his birth. The *why* isn't important. By then, his father had already abandoned us, so after the fallout with my parents, I was completely alone in the world. *Twenty-five* and alone. With a young child. I tried to find that missing stability in my relationships with men. Still do. But the reality is, my relationships were never healthy, and I ended up turning myself inside out to avoid being alone again."

She grimaces as she considers her next words. "Dean bore the brunt of that. With age comes clarity, you know. We moved around a lot so I could remain close to whichever latest boyfriend I'd sworn my heart to. Which meant Dean didn't really have a place he could call home. When a relationship ended, we were usually the ones moving out."

Now I understand Dean's dedication to working with clients having problems with their landlords. He relates to their need for security — because he's been chasing the same thing his whole life.

"Dean heard the promises these men made," Melissa continues. "And he was there to pick up the pieces when a relationship went south. At some point, I'm guessing he started to think those promises were meaningless. Or he didn't want to turn himself inside out for love the way I did. And I think it's more complicated than even Dean realizes. When all is said and done, Dean doesn't believe anyone will ever put him first, because I didn't. So he's fashioned a life for himself that ensures no one will ever have to. If Dean looks out for Dean, he'll be fine. Or so he thinks."

So when I didn't mention the job offer, I only underscored what he believes: that people won't consider him a priority. But no one's going to prioritize Dean if he isn't willing to reciprocate. If he isn't willing to risk that his life won't always go according to his grand plan. *That's* the impasse.

Melissa stares off into the distance, then stretches out her legs in front of her, settling her hands between her thighs. "Did he ever tell you he wanted to be a swimmer?"

"He did."

She nods knowingly. "When Dean was fourteen or fifteen, I can't remember precisely when, he tried out for his school's swim team. Came home all excited about it. I came home excited too. Because I'd been dating a guy I met at a work conference, and he'd asked us to move in with him."

A weight settles on my heart. I can picture a young Dean barreling through the door, his bright eyes dancing with excitement. "Let me guess, the guy lived somewhere else."

Melissa nods. "Pennsylvania. We lived in Delaware at the time. I didn't understand the effort Dean had put into getting on the team. He did it all on his own. So when we

443

relocated to Pennsylvania, he was sullen. Moody. Way more than usual. I thought he was just adjusting to a new place, a new school, and he was. But he was also dealing with the loss of one of his childhood dreams. Now, maybe nothing would have come of his swimming career, but the point is, my choices made it impossible for him to even try."

If Dean were here, I'd tuck him against me and just hold him. For however long he wanted. We're a lot alike, actually. We both want to guarantee only positive outcomes in our lives. But that's not how any of this works. Not by a long shot. "Why are you telling me all of this?"

She leans forward and takes my hand. "Because I saw his face when you left on Saturday. And I've seen his face each time I ask about you. He clams up. But there's *something* in his eyes. He cares about you, Solange. Maybe enough to give himself permission to fall in love. But he's terrified that he won't figure into your life in the same way he'd like you to figure into his."

I don't like this conversation. At all. It's giving me hope. Making me want things I thought were out of reach. And Dean's mother is contradicting the very statements her son made just two days ago. I jump to my feet. "I appreciate the insight, Melissa. I really do. Dean's a wonderful guy. There's no doubt in my mind about that. But there are numerous parts to this equation, and I think Dean and I have maxed out on where our relationship can go. Thanks for chatting with me."

She drops her head and sniffles.

"What is it?" I ask, alarmed by the abrupt change in her demeanor.

She hiccups through her response. "It's just . . . I hate being here . . . alone. And Dean won't be home for a while." She waves her hands in my general direction. "Don't worry about it, dear. This is all on me."

Ah jeez. She sounds so tragic that I'm hesitant to leave her like this. But what am I supposed to do? I can't understand her aversion to being alone; half the time I don't even want to talk to my own damn family.

Oh.

That's it.

She needs to meet the tias.

If anyone can show Dean's mother there's no shame in being alone, it's them.

"Hey, Melissa, my mother and aunts own a small Brazilian grocery and café in Wheaton. It's a bit of a hike, but it'd be worth it. You game for heading over there with me?"

She jerks her head up, then wipes away her tears. "Is that where Dean got all of that glorious food we ate yesterday?"

"No, that was a home-cooked meal. They only sell breads and bite-size snacks at the shop. Everything's delicious, though."

"Well, in that case, I'd love to!"

I send Dean a text to let him know my plans.

Me: I'm taking your mother to Rio de Wheaton. she's bored.

Dean: seriously?

Me: no, jokingly

Dean: cute. this is great actually. I could use a couple more hours at work. thanks.

Me: no problem

Dean: promise you two won't get into any trouble?

Me: I never make promises I can't keep. tchau.

Me: psst. isn't it freeing to let go of all those punctuation marks?

Dean: not really but I'm trying

Now *that* exchange felt better. Maybe we're not doomed to be estranged after all.

I drop my phone into my crossbody and slip back into my shoes by the door. "Ready?"

"Sure! Can't wait!" Melissa says.

Oddly enough, there's no sign of the tears she shed literally a minute ago. Whatever. The tias will know what to do with her.

CHAPTER TWENTY-EIGHT

SOLANGE

"Melissa, this is my mother, Izabel, and her two sisters, Viviane and Mariana. Mãpara sua casa. Issoe. Tias. This is Melissa, Dean's mother. She's visiting from Delaware."

My mother and aunts widen their eyes, then nod in understanding.

"Nice to meet everyone," Melissa says cheerfully. She surveys Rio de Wheaton's aisles and adds, "This place is wonderful. Cozy and charming. And it smells *so good* in here."

"Would you like to try something?" Tia Mariana asks, taking on the hostess role as usual. "A cafezinho to start, maybe?"

"That would be wonderful," Melissa says.

I'm glad I brought her here. Staying cooped up in Dean's apartment all day couldn't have been good for her mood. She needs to be around people. Having fun. Forgetting what's-his-name.

After Melissa and Tia Mariana drift off together toward the counter, Tia Viviane nudges me in the direction of the small café section on the left side of the store.

A lone man sits at a table watching futebol, his eyes drooping and occasionally widening as he struggles to stay awake.

Tia Viviane kicks at his chair. "Vá para sua casa. Isso não é um hotel."

The man rises to his feet and stumbles out the door, sufficiently scolded by my aunt for using the store as his motel room.

"Okay," Tia Viviane says, her lips barely moving so Melissa can't overhear. "What's going on? Why is she here?"

"Be nice, all right?" I say. "She just broke up with her boyfriend. I'm trying to cheer her up."

My mother sidles over and slips into the conversation. "What are we supposed to do about that?"

I shrug. "Not sure, exactly. I just thought she'd appreciate seeing all three of you. Single women. Controlling your own destinies. Prospering. Living well."

"*Not* having sex," Tia Viviane says, her lips curled in disgust.

My mother covers her face with her hands. "Viviane, precisa ser tão vulgar?"

"Sim," Tia Viviane says without further

explanation.

"It's fine, Mãe. I *do* know what sex is."

She gasps, but she's also holding back a grin.

Tia Viviane raises a brow. "You and Dean are back together, then?"

"There's no Dean and me," I say, shaking my head.

My mother tilts her head. "So why are you babysitting his mother?"

Damn, these women are relentless. I sidestep the question. "Look, all I'm asking is that you be yourselves and get to know her. Is that doable?"

Tia Viviane lifts her nose in the air before answering. "I suppose I can do that."

"Me too," my mother adds.

I let out a sigh that sounds like an equal mix of relief and exasperation. *"Thank you."*

They shuffle back to the counter and join Dean's mother and Tia Mariana. Melissa pulls out her phone and displays her screen, prompting all four women to gather closer together. If I had to guess, I'd say she's sharing photographs of her trip out west. Will that be Lina, Natalia, Rey, and me someday? A generation of filhos de brasileiros keeping this place going after the tias are gone? No, I'd rather not think about that. Not just yet. Thankfully, the bell above the door rings, and I turn my attention to our newest arrivals. Not so thankfully, I recognize them immediately.

"Molly and Peter, this is a surprise!" I say, trying to act unfazed and struggling to get past the frog in my throat. *Shit, shit, shit. Why, why, why?*

Molly smiles. "It's a rare day off for us both, and we decided to treat it as a mini-date." She points a thumb at Peter, her expression flirty and playful. "This one couldn't stop talking about the salgadinhos we had the last time we were here. Figured we'd buy a few to take home."

"Oh, that's great. Well, let me take care of that for you!" My body's gone haywire and won't stop moving from side to side. To an outside observer, I probably look like the least talented member of a fifties doo-wop band. "Want to grab a table while I put together a to-go box?"

Peter tilts his head and waggles his eyebrows. "Nah, looking through the display case is part of the experience, right?" He rubs his hands together in good-natured anticipation. "Besides, I don't know the names, but I can recognize my favorites."

Behind us, the tias and Dean's mother are tittering as if they're old friends sitting on a stoop and gossiping about their neighbors. I suspect they haven't even noticed Molly and Peter's arrival since they're hunched over Melissa's phone, presumably looking at photographs on the screen.

"Well, why don't you grab yourselves a drink while I wash my hands and get set up behind the counter," I say.

If Molly and Peter are distracted, I might have just enough time to fire off a discreet warning shot to Melissa and the tias. Fortunately, Molly and Peter turn in the direction of the fridge. But then Melissa and the tias wander off together down an aisle, and I'm forced to scurry to the back to wash my hands. Heart pounding, I return within seconds and pluck the tongs from the holder. "Ready when you are," I call out to Peter and Molly.

They hurry over, and Peter bends down to get a better look at the selection. "What's that one over there?" he asks, pointing at the case.

"Bolinho de bacalhau. Salted cod croquettes. Want those? How about a dozen. Coming right up!"

Still bent over, Peter taps the top of the case. "Whoa, whoa, whoa. Not so fast, Solange. Let me get my bearings. Hmm. And that one?"

I crouch down to see which type of salgadinho he's pointed to. "That's —"

"Oooh, those are delicious," Melissa says behind Molly. "My son just loved them to death. Highly recommend! In fact, I'd love to take some home for Dean if you can spare a few."

Peter pops up, a big smile on his face. "Oh, hey! You wouldn't happen to be talking about Dean Chapman, eh? I'm his colleague."

"Oh, how nice," Dean's mother says. "It's great to meet you."

No. It is *not* great to meet him, Melissa. He's a terrible, no-good man. "Um, Peter, how about I get you two of everything in the case?" I grab a box and slide two coxinhas de frango inside.

He tilts his head back and forth. "Uh, that's probably too much, but let me try one of those." He turns back to Melissa. "So, about the wedding. Wild, huh? I'm guessing you're happy about the outcome, though?"

Melissa gestures around her head as if the memory of that day is too much for her to handle. "Can you imagine? A stranger crashes your wedding? And turns out to be a sweetheart?" She moves in closer, as if she's only talking to Peter, but her next words are plainly meant for my ears too.

"Just between us, I'm still hoping that Dean and Solange will get together. Wouldn't that be the *best*?"

Peter's gaze snaps to mine, and he narrows his beady eyes. "Indeed, it would be."

I'm sinking into quicksand. With no one around who can possibly pull me out of the mess this moment will make of Dean's life. Peter may be bowled over by my family's food, but he's a vindictive asshole to his core, and now he has just enough information to sabotage Dean's career. I'm about to curl into a ball right on the fucking floor of this shop. But I owe it to Dean to try to clean this up. Maybe I can still signal to Melissa that Peter's a threat.

"Melissa, this is Peter. He and Dean aren't *close* or anything. And this is his wife, Molly."

Peter ignores the introductions. He's a viper going in for the kill. "So Solange and Dean aren't dating, huh?" Peter asks this on a chuckle, as if he and Melissa are old chums shooting the breeze.

"Well, I wouldn't say that, exactly," Melissa says, grinning. "But they didn't start out that way, and I'm just loving the idea that their relationship may turn into something more."

"Right, right," Peter says, nodding.

With her skin mottled and her expression pinched, Molly swings her gaze between Peter and me.

Her husband raps his knuckles on the display counter. "On second thought, Solange, go ahead and give us two of everything. I think a celebration's in order.

"Molly," he calls over his shoulder. "We need to head out soon. I have a few texts to send after this."

"I'm sorry," Molly says softly, a hand pressed to her throat as she looks at me in sympathy.

My stomach is caving in on itself, and my heart is beating as if it's being powered by the drums of a thousand bateristas. "It's okay," I say, my voice barely above a whisper.

Before I can flee, Melissa lays a hand on my forearm. "Is everything okay?"

"No, not really. I need to speak with your son."

DEAN

As Priya, a junior associate, updates the team on the status of her document review, I try to picture what's happening at Rio de Wheaton. The image that materializes, one in which Solange is offering my mother fresh coffee and warm bread, brings a smile to my face.

Henderson, the only partner present, clears his throat, and my gaze snaps to his. Right. Happiness is frowned upon here. What a fucking joke.

"All right, thanks for your hard work, Priya," Henderson says. "What about you, Dean? Where are we with witness interviews?"

I begin to outline the schedule, focusing on the people with potentially critical testimony. A minute into my report, however, Henderson hunches over and commences to type with urgency, his fingers flying across the screen of his iPhone. At one point, he raises his head, stares at me with a glazed look in his eyes, then drops his chin so he can resume texting, or emailing, or whatever. I flub my words, momentarily thrown off by Henderson's uncharacteristically engaged behavior; he's the most disinterested lawyer I know, yet his attention's plainly been captured by *who the hell knows what.*

"Everything okay?" I ask.

He shoots out of his chair. "Actually, let's end early and reconvene another time. Something's come up."

"Sure, no problem," I say.

Priya and I watch him go, then shrug at

each other.

"You did great earlier," I tell her.

"Thanks," she says, her shoulders relaxing now that Henderson's gone. "I'm glad you're on the team." She hurries to pack up her papers. "It's been helpful having someone who doesn't bite my head off when I ask questions."

I remember the feeling. Navigating law firm life can be like running a Hunger Games gauntlet with no protective gear, no special skills, and no weapons. If I can make the experience better for those who come after me, maybe together we can slowly change the culture. "That's why I'm here," I say, strolling to the conference room door. "Use me as a buffer anytime."

When I return to my office, I notice a string of texts from Solange that came in during the team meeting. The last one asks me to call her as soon as possible, so that's precisely what I do.

"Oh, thank goodness," she says hoarsely.

"Are you okay?" I ask, my heart ratcheting up at the possibility that she's in trouble.

"Yes, yes."

"Is my mother okay?"

"Yes, she's okay too. It's . . ."

"Solange, *breathe.* Whatever it is, it'll be fine."

"It's Peter and Molly. Well, Peter really. He was here. At Rio de Wheaton."

"Okaaay."

"They met your mother, and somehow it got out that we're not really a couple. I don't know. He asked her about the wedding. Said it was wild. And then it spiraled from there. It's a mess."

"So Peter knows it was all a lie?"

"Yes," she chokes out. "I'm *so, so* sorry."

My vision swims, and I can't stop blinking. Fuck. This is a nightmare. I'd bet my life that Henderson was texting Peter during the meeting just now. "It's not your fault, Solange."

"Still." She lets out a heavy sigh. "I'm going to take your mother home and head to my place. I'll be around if you need me."

I wish I could reassure her, but I'm too dazed and confused to be persuasive at the moment. Besides, Henderson just appeared at the threshold of my office, so I can't say anything of consequence anyway.

"Thanks for letting me know," I tell Solange. "I'll take it from here."

Henderson regards this as his cue to close the door. Wearing a smug expression, he drops into one of my guest chairs. "As you may already know, I received a disturbing text from Peter this afternoon. Although there's no explanation that wouldn't make me question your judgment, I thought I'd give you a chance to say your piece before I go to my partners."

His condescending attitude saps me of the energy to go toe-to-toe with him. I'm just . . . tired. I mean, utterly and truly depleted. This man has never wanted me to succeed here. I don't bring in enough business. I spend too much time volunteering. I'm not cutthroat enough. Worst of all, some of our clients prefer me to him. And just when he was going to have to swallow his resentment and vote for my promotion, Peter gave him the gift he's always wished for: a valid excuse to fire me. So I'm fucking done. "Let's cut the bullshit, Henderson. Will anything I say make a difference?"

"I need to know that my colleagues are trustworthy. Honesty is the lifeblood of our trade, as you know. So in my mind, the answer's a definite no."

His canned response isn't surprising, but it still hits me like a punch to my chest. Eight fucking years. Over. In a matter of minutes. If I thought I had enough strength to lift my damn desk, I'd chuck it across the room. "Well then, do what you need to do."

He springs to his feet. "With pleasure, Dean. With so much pleasure." Before he leaves, he fires the kill shot: "You want to know the real kicker here? All your machinations didn't even amount to anything. Kimberly Bailey passed on our offer this afternoon. I'll make one last push, just to be sure she didn't decline because of something you did, but in any case, it's not looking good for you, kid."

Henderson closes the door behind him, the click of the lock reminding me that he's the firm's gatekeeper, a power he relishes wielding whenever he can.

I stagger backward and collapse into my chair. My heart's racing like a thoroughbred, and the tips of my ears are burning. I suppose I should have begged for his mercy. Instead, I let my frustration get the best of me. Leaning over, I place my hands on my knees and take small sips of air in a desperate attempt to calm down. It's no use, though. Fuck, fuck, fuck. I think I just shit-talked myself out of a job.

What the hell do I do now?

CHAPTER TWENTY-NINE

DEAN

"They fired me," I say, my voice sounding brittle and weak.

Solange pulls me inside her apartment, immediately drawing me into her warm embrace. "Oh, Dean. I'm so sorry."

Today may have rocked me to my core, but being enveloped in Solange's arms makes me feel grounded. There was never any question that I'd come to her. I respect her opinion. Value her perspective. She knows I've been chasing partnership for years and understands how devastating this is.

Solange draws back and grabs my shoulders, her worried gaze roving over my face. "What happened? Tell me."

"Henderson ate it up and ran with it," I say, my voice just above a whisper. "Technically, I'm resigning. Said it was the least they could do to thank me for my eight

461

years of service to the firm."

"Bastards," she says, scowling. "They were looking for a reason to do this."

"I'm sure you're right. Unfortunately, I handed them one on a silver platter."

She squeezes her eyes shut, as if she's willing herself not to cry. "Shit. None of this would have happened if it weren't for me. I took your mother to the shop, and it went downhill from there."

I place a hand on her chin and lift it gently. "Look at me, Solange."

She stares at me, her eyes glistening.

"This isn't your fault," I continue. "Everything that's happened is one hundred percent on me. *I* chose to lie to the firm. *I* convinced you to lie on my behalf. Now I need to accept the consequences of my actions. End of story."

She gives me a small nod. "Even so, I feel awful about it."

"Because you care. I appreciate it more than I can say."

We drift to the couch and sit side by side, our thighs pressed together. She strokes my hair, and I lean into her, desperately seeking her calming touch. I'm still agitated, though, and I doubt this feeling will be going away anytime soon. How the hell did everything go south so fast? Or is this how it was always going to play out? Did I miss the signs? Or did I ignore them?

I let out a harsh breath and drop my head. "You know, I'm seriously questioning if partnership was ever on the table. Maybe they would have promoted me eventually, but I don't think they really wanted to. I didn't bring in enough clients. Spent too much time on pro bono. Couldn't even land Kimberly Bailey." I draw back and meet her gaze. "I suppose the writing was on the wall, but I refused to see it."

"Well, they don't deserve you," she says fiercely. "And one day, they're going to regret letting you go."

My heart swells. If there's a scrap of joy I can salvage from this crap day, it's that Solange and I are going to be okay.

"So what's next?" she asks.

"I need to figure out what to do about my pro bono cases. I don't want to abandon my clients, but who knows if the firm will help me through the transition. As for money, I have enough saved to cover my expenses for the rest of the year. Being a planner has its advantages."

Still, I need to find a job. Help my mother get a new place. Figure out what the hell I'm going to do with my life now that being a partner at Olney & Henderson is no longer an option.

Solange takes my hand in hers. "You know, I think it's telling that your first concern was your pro bono work. My mother once told me the things we value the most are the things we're most afraid of losing. Keep that in mind as you sort out what to do next."

I appreciate her insight, and I'll take that into consideration as I overthink my life in the days ahead. But right now, I want to hear about her. "Tell me what's going on with you. Have you decided what to do about Ohio? Or about your offer here?"

She nods. "I think so, and ironically, your firing is what's giving me the final push. You've worked so hard for so long and still didn't get the reward you've been chasing. Meanwhile, I'm being offered the opportunity to use my heart and talents at a place that's already demonstrated it values me. Plus, I get to stay close to family and remain a part of the village that has supported me since forever. I'm kind of mad at myself that it took me this long to get my head out of my ass." She studies my face. "I probably shouldn't have said any of that out loud. The timing is terrible."

"Are you kidding?" I say, cocking my head. "When life gives me lemons, you make lemonade for yourself. It's part of your brand."

With her face contorted in a playful grimace, she pretends to stab a dagger through her heart.

"But seriously," I say, squeezing her hand, "I want you to be happy. And if this decision makes you happy, I'll be in your corner one hundred percent."

"Thanks," she says, her expression sobering. "But enough about me. Do me a favor and focus on yourself today, okay?"

I take in a deep breath and expel it slowly. "Yeah, I should let my mother know what's going on. She sounded pretty distraught on the phone."

"Go easy on her, Dean. She feels just as bad as I do."

"She's probably blaming herself, but I'm not interested in putting any of this on her. I'd rather find a way for us to support each other. My childhood may not have been perfect, but she was there for me. It's time to let go of the past and build a relationship with her based on the present."

"I'm glad you think so."

Solange walks me to her apartment door and draws me in for another hug. "You're going to be all right," she says softly. "I'm confident of that. Now go do what you need to do."

"Thanks for listening," I say, caressing her cheek.

Closing her eyes, she burrows into my touch for a moment, then she steps back and opens the door. "I'm here for you, Dean. Always." She gestures behind her. "None of the other stuff is going to interfere with our friendship."

"That means a lot, Solange. Probably more than you'll ever realize."

As I walk down the hall, I can't shake the feeling that I'm headed in the wrong direction. That I should be moving toward Solange, not away from her. But I plod ahead anyway. I've made my choices. Now I need to live with them.

SOLANGE

I'm taking a page from Dean's playbook and making my own plan to get "unstuck." One of the first steps is to meet with my former student Layla.

Not long ago, I convinced myself that Layla's departure was further proof that committing to Victory would be a mistake; now I realize I was using it as an excuse to avoid making critical decisions about my future. No more. Layla's important to me, and if I'm going to plant roots here in DC, I can't think of a better person to be a part of my new village.

I watch Layla stride up the sidewalk; she's wearing a cream blouse and a pair of black slacks. "Wow. Don't you look stylish."

She takes the chair opposite me. "Your wardrobe came in handy after all."

We're meeting at an outdoor café near her new job as a receptionist for a small accounting firm in Georgetown. She's on a lunch break, so we don't have much time. The server quickly takes our orders and sprints away to another (demanding) table.

"Poor guy," I say.

"I couldn't do it," Layla says, shaking her head. "I'd be fired the first week."

"I'd be fired the first day."

She laughs, squinting against the sun's rays. "So, what did you want to see me about?"

I twist my hands on my lap. I'm making too much of this, and if I don't speak up soon, I'll probably weird her out. *Just go for it, Solange.* "The class misses you."

"Aww, I miss them too," she replies, smiling. "Even big-head Darius."

"I'll pass along the message," I say on a chuckle. "So listen, I know you need this job, and I totally support that, but I'd like us to stay in touch. I'd be happy to tutor you for the GED outside of school and give you career advice and be a general sounding board whenever you have an issue." I wave my hands around. "Whatever you're comfortable with. What do you say?"

She nibbles on her bottom lip as she studies me. "What about Victory? Will you still be working there?"

I haven't formally accepted the offer, but I plan to later this afternoon.

"Yes," I say. "I'm going to be working at Victory for the foreseeable future. It's breaking news, though, so don't tell anyone just yet."

"I'm glad you're staying, Ms. P. And I'd love for you to be my mentor. I could use all the help I can get."

I give her a playful wink. "Well, now you'll have mine."

The waiter arrives with our entrées — salmon for me and a salad for Layla — and we dig in.

After a few bites, Layla takes a sip of water, then clears her throat. "Does being my mentor mean I can ask personal questions?"

"You can always ask. But I reserve the right not to respond. Depends on the question."

"Whatever that means," she mutters.

"Go ahead and ask your question," I say, holding back a smile.

"That guy who came to class. The lawyer. What's up with him?"

She doesn't have enough time for this story. Besides, I wouldn't share too much about Dean anyway. "His name's Dean, and he's just a friend."

It's the best answer I can give her, but it doesn't sound right to my ears. I suppose I'm still getting used to the idea of putting our relationship in that specific box.

I'll get there, though. Slowly. Surely. Eventually.

"That's a shame," Layla says.

My eyes go wide. "*Watch it,* Ms. Young."

She giggles and holds up her hands. "He's a cutie. I'm just sayin'."

He's so much more than that, but yeah, she has a point. Thinking about Dean isn't part of my getting-unstuck plan, though. "When would you like to get started on tutoring?"

"I'm ready when you are," she says. "How about this weekend?"

"Ooh, sorry. I'm heading to Vegas to celebrate my roommate's birthday."

Layla drops her shoulders, then tilts her head as she gazes at me dubiously. "Are you going to be a shady mentor?"

"What?" I say, grinning. "No. I just have plans, that's all. I'll be at your disposal any other weekend."

She gives me a toothy grin. "I'm just kidding. I know you won't let me down."

She's right. I won't.

It feels good not to be floundering anymore.

CHAPTER THIRTY

DEAN

I wake up to someone sprinkling water on my face and jump up from the couch as though an intruder's on the scene. I'm ready to rush the person — until I realize it's Max.

"You're so damn slow," he says, chuckling.

"And you're a creepy stalker," I say as I massage my chest and take stock of my surroundings. The sun's setting, and my place looks like trash. "How the hell did you get in here?"

"Mr. Donatelli in three oh seven let me in downstairs. He's seen us together enough times to know where I was headed."

"That doesn't explain how you entered my unit."

He stalks my way and glowers at me. "Your damn door was open. So what the hell's going on?"

I step back and give him an honest answer.

471

"I don't even know."

It's been a few days since I officially became unemployed. A few days of not knowing how to get my life plan back on track. A few days of mostly wishing Solange were here. Thankfully, my mother's settling into her new apartment in Delaware.

As I watch Max rifle through my fridge, I realize he's wearing athletic gear, which means I must have missed our standing basketball meetup. "Shit. I'm sorry I didn't show."

He waves off my apology and moves away from the fridge, a cold beer in hand. "Figured something must have happened when I couldn't reach you. You went on do-not-disturb mode?"

I nod and drop onto the couch. "Yeah. Everyone except my mom."

"This is serious, then."

I frown at him, unsure what he's referring to. "This?"

"This thing with Solange."

"That's not what *this* is about."

Max slips me a dubious glance and folds himself into the armchair facing the couch. "Dude, you didn't show up for basketball. You put your phone on do-not-disturb. You left your door unlocked while you slept. Your hair looks like it's being held up by static electricity. You have the beginnings of a five o'clock shadow. There's stale popcorn on the coffee table." He turns to the movie on pause on my TV screen. "And you're watching *When Harry Met Sally*. You're not only watching a rom-com, but you're also acting as if you're starring in one. This has I'm-in-my-feelings-about-Solange written all over it. Am I right?"

I can't argue with the facts. "Yeah, you're right."

Max holds up his hands. "I'm not here to tell you I told you so."

"Good."

"I'm here to sing it instead." And true to his word, he singsongs the damn words like a four-year-old. "I *told* you so. I *told* you so. La-la-la-la-la. I *told* you so."

I can't help laughing. I know my best friend. He's only acting like a fool because he wants me to get out of this funk. And I should. But it isn't easy. I can't just snap my fingers and erase everything I experienced with Solange. Plus, I'm terrified. I don't even have the security of my job to fall back on. "Yeah, you did warn me, and I had my own reservations. Instead of listening to my instincts, I convinced myself we made sense together. I was kidding myself."

"Let me ask you this," Max says. "Would

you prefer that the last several weeks had never even happened?"

I don't need to think about it. The answer is no. Undoubtedly, unreservedly, unequivocally hell no. I shake my head. "I'd do it all over again in a heartbeat if I could. Except the getting-fired part."

"It was a rhetorical question. Just hoping to clear your head a bit. And let me ask you something else: When you learned you'd been fired, who's the first person you told?"

I blow out a breath. "Solange." Max wants to ascribe some significance to that fact, but there's a reasonable explanation. "She wanted to help me get a promotion. I thought it was only fair that I tell her it didn't pan out."

Max shakes his head as if he's disappointed in me. "If that's what you want to believe, fine. But you're never going to be happy until you figure out *why* you were chasing partnership like life depended on it. News flash: It doesn't."

"This is all I know, okay? My career has always been solid. It gives me clothes. Food. A roof over my head. A fucking purpose."

"Dean, a job is not a personality. It's not a life either. Somehow you need to figure out how to make a life for yourself that *includes* your work but also gives you space

474

for the people and things that make you happy."

That all sounds great on paper, but the reality isn't as easy or rosy. "So what are you suggesting? That I chase after someone who won't stay put? Someone who doesn't know what she'll want next week, let alone next year? If I let myself love her and Solange wakes up one day and decides I was just a phase in her life, I'd only have myself to blame. Knowing what I know about her, it doesn't make sense to put myself out there like that. No, Solange was a detour, and honestly, I think she prefers it that way."

"Here's the thing about detours, though: Sometimes they become the destination."

My head snaps up, and I look at him askance. "What the fuck does that mean, Yoda?"

Max puts his hands together and bows. "When you figure it out, you will have achieved your true purpose."

"Get the hell out of here with that shit." I throw a pillow at him for good measure. "I need to start calling in favors with law school classmates." Damn, I also need to pick up my personal belongings at the firm — with a security guard watching over me, I'm sure.

"The big picture is that you can't change

what's happened. You can only move forward. It's time to get your shit together and figure out your next steps." He scans my face and outfit. "You need to shower and shave. Put a comb and some fucking gel in your hair, because I've never seen it look like that and I'm worried whatever's happening on the top of your head is permanent." He gestures at the TV screen. "And stop watching all of these damned movies. They're only going to depress you in your current state. Although I'll admit *Always Be My Maybe* was hilarious."

"You're right," I say, sitting up and rolling my shoulders. "I'll do all that . . . tomorrow. But for now, I'm going to watch clueless people fall in love."

Max drops his head and sighs. Yeah, I'm a disappointment. Fuck if I care.

He pulls out his phone and taps on the screen at warp speed. It buzzes a few times as he texts with someone, Lina presumably, then he places the phone on the side table. "Okay, I'm yours."

"Excuse me?"

He groans. "Dean, I recognize a cry for help when I hear one. Sure, I'll stay over and watch rom-coms with you. Clearly, you need to get your mind off Solange, and I'm the right person for the job."

"But I didn't ask —"

"You'll thank me later," he says, jumping up from the couch, then opening and closing several kitchen cabinets. "A movie marathon is the perfect distraction." He returns with an unopened bag of chips under his arm. "This'll work out just fine. I can sleep in my gym clothes."

"How convenient," I mutter under my breath.

"What's that?" he says as he rips the bag of chips open.

"Nothing."

"So, what are we going to watch first?"

He's determined to stay, and I'm determined not to be ungrateful. "I was thinking about *When Harry Met Sally.* Solange and I never got around to finishing it, but one time we . . ." I smile at the memory of our fake sex session when Ana and Carlos were visiting.

Max socks me in the face with a pillow. "Wrong answer. Let's watch *Always Be My Maybe.* Don't tell Lina, but Ali Wong is my celebrity crush."

"I don't even know who that is," I say, honestly.

"Oh, you'll know by the end of this movie. Adorable. Smart. Grumpy. Reminds me of Lina."

"Or we could watch something you haven't —"

"It's fine," Max says, getting settled on the couch. "I don't mind."

I grab the remote and queue up the movie. I'm willing to do whatever it takes to drown out the thoughts that would take up residence in my brain if he weren't here. Once the opening credits appear, I tap Max on the arm. "Thanks for doing this."

"No problem. You'd do the same for me."

"Actually, I wouldn't."

He smirks at me. "Fuck off and watch the movie."

Yes, that's excellent advice. I can deal with the rest of my chaotic life tomorrow.

Friday morning, I exit the elevator holding a single sad banker's box with the few personal belongings I kept at Olney & Henderson. I surrender my employee badge to the building security guard, Harold, a middle-aged white guy with pythons for biceps. For the past eight years, Harold was often the first person I saw in the morning, a friendly face amid the hustle and bustle, a neighborhood reporter who always told me what to expect when I got upstairs.

"Henderson's pissed today."

"Olney's running late, and she spilled coffee

on her blouse."

"Must be a partner meeting this A.M. A gang of 'em just went up."

I see now that he took care of me, in his own understated, gossip-prone way.

"Take care of yourself, Big Dean," he says, the grooves at the outside corners of his eyes deepening as he gives me a wide smile. "Won't be the same without you coming in here every damn day of the week."

I set the box down on the reception desk and pull him in for a hug. "Make sure they give you a retirement party, okay?"

Harold chuckles as he draws back. "They're too selfish. Everyone knows that." He whispers a parting comment: "And you're too good for this place."

I'd like to think that's true, but I don't know up from down anymore.

"Dean?" a voice behind me asks.

I spin around to see Kimberly Bailey a few feet away.

"Kimberly. What are you doing here?"

She wrings her hands as she talks, a pinched expression on her face. "I was hoping I'd catch you, but I'm primarily here to see Olney and Henderson."

It's unclear what business she still has with them considering she declined the firm's offer. That, along with my lying to the

479

partners about dating Solange, is why I'm leaving this building for the last time.

She points to a bench to the left of the elevators. "Can we chat for a minute?"

"I'll watch your box," Harold says.

Once we sit, Kimberly takes a calming breath. "So I'm just going to come out and say it: Nia and I are best friends."

I'm not surprised. They're completely in sync, and it's apparent to anyone who sees them that they treasure each other as people first. "Some of the most successful romantic relationships are founded on friendship."

Kimberly fiddles with the thin platinum band on her left hand. "No, what I mean is we're best friends" — she turns to meet my gaze — "and nothing else."

Oh.

Oh.

What?

"You mean —"

Kimberly lets out a heavy sigh. She's going to chafe if she continues to slide that ring up and down her finger. "Nia and I faked our relationship, and after I dug around a little, Peter finally admitted that you were fired for doing essentially the same thing. So I knew I had to set the record straight, first with the partnership, and then with you."

I can't fathom that Kimberly and Nia aren't a romantic couple. The affection in their eyes. Their intense chemistry. The ease with which they touched each other. It was all an act? "Why did you feel the need to lie?"

"It is absolutely true that Nia is considering artist-in-residence programs in the DC area. We're roommates. Met in college. Have lived together ever since. And when I realized she was leaving Atlanta, I panicked. Wanted to curl up and cry. I just" — she drops her head, her shoulders sagging — "couldn't imagine my life without her. It was in that moment, when she told me we wouldn't be roommates anymore, that it became clear ours wasn't a platonic relationship. For me, that is. I decided I'd move here to be with her."

Most days, I probably would have figured out the punch line by now, but I'm emotionally drained, and my brain isn't firing on all cylinders. "So why the ruse?"

"C'mon, Dean. You know how it is. Try explaining why an eighth-year associate is leaving the only firm she's ever worked for to relocate to DC. People assume you weren't going to be made a partner and your bosses are letting you go gracefully. Nia became my valid reason."

"But she agreed to fake the relationship, right? So she must have understood why you did it."

"I didn't tell her. Instead, I claimed I wasn't happy with my current situation. Said this would be the perfect opportunity for us both to try something new."

"Kimberly," I say, leaning closer and meeting her eyes. "You need to tell her how you feel."

She shakes her head. "I don't think I can. What if she doesn't reciprocate? What if telling her changes our relationship forever? What if we grow apart because of it? I'd rather have her in my life in some way than not at all. The alternative — not being able to spend time with her, not seeing her when I get home from work, not sharing my hopes and dreams with her — I can't even imagine it."

The fucking pounding in my chest nearly causes me to hunch over. What Kimberly is describing, what sounds a lot like love, is precisely how I feel about Solange. And I was perfectly prepared to give it up because I'm terrified that I don't matter to her as much as she matters to me, or that she'll run off somewhere, and I'll be worse off when she's gone. It's the reason I acted like an ass when I found out she was contemplating leaving DC even though she'd been offered an opportunity to stay.

But I see it now: That feeling I've been chasing for over a decade — a feeling of rightness, of belonging, of being secure in who I am — I won't be able to fully achieve it without Solange in my life. And fuck, I essentially told her the exact opposite. I said she deserved everything, but I couldn't be the person to give it to her.

I take Kimberly's hand. "We need to tell them how we feel."

"We?" she asks cautiously.

"Yeah, *we.* You need to take that risk with Nia, and I need to take that risk with Solange. We both could be missing out on the one person in this world who's meant for us. Not because it makes sense on paper, or in our heads" — I place a hand over my heart and tap it a few times — "but because it makes sense in here."

"I don't know if I'm ready to do that," she says, her eyes glistening. "It could go sideways real fast."

"Promise me you'll think about it?"

She nods. "Okay, I will."

"One other thing."

She jerks to attention, plainly still working through her own dilemma. "What's up?"

"If you need to come clean to Olney &

Henderson for your own peace of mind, you obviously can, of course. But don't do it for me. I don't need a second chance. No, actually, I don't *want* a second chance. I'll find another way to achieve my goals."

"I thought making partner *is* your life goal."

Yeah, I thought so too. But for the wrong reasons. "That's just it. That's not a life goal. That's a career goal. There's a difference. Now I'm ready to work on building the future I want; Olney & Henderson won't be a part of it."

Kimberly rises from the bench, and I follow suit.

"You know, I think we were meant to meet," she says, her small smile growing broader.

"I do too. And I truly mean that."

"Can I walk you outside?" she asks.

"Sure."

Suddenly that banker's box Harold's holding for me doesn't seem so sad anymore. I stride over to the desk, give him a final fist bump, and grab the box that now represents a new beginning. Kimberly holds the door open, and I take the deepest, most cleansing breath I've ever taken in my life.

Outside, a Black man in a sharp three-piece suit is leaning against a slate-gray

SUV; he looks up, sees Kimberly, and smiles. I've seen him before. When he argued a case before the DC federal court trying to get a reporter's press pass restored. He was brilliant, and the court sided in the reporter's favor.

"That's your dad, isn't it?" I whisper.

She chuckles. "Don't be so awestruck. He's just a regular guy. C'mon, I'll introduce you."

Kimberly walks up to her father and clips him on the shoulder. "Hey, I'll explain later, but I'm not going up."

I can't see his eyes behind the aviators he's wearing, but the rest of his expression turns grim. "Are you sure?"

"I am," she says, nodding as if the words further her resolve. "Anyway, I wanted you to meet someone." She turns to me and puts out a hand with a flourish. "This is Dean Chapman, the lawyer I mentioned. Dean, meet my father, Larry Bailey."

"Good to meet you, sir. You're a legend in the legal community."

He folds his newspaper in half and wedges it under his arm before accepting my outstretched hand. "Too bad I'm not a legend to my own daughter."

"Sorry?" I ask.

He rolls his eyes. "She wants nothing to

do with Baxter Media, a fact that breaks my heart."

"I'd have to be a glutton for punishment to work with you," she says with a smile. "Hard pass." Then she tilts her head as though she's working through an idea. "But I have it on good authority that there's an amazing lawyer in DC who's both skilled at media work and a champion for pro bono service. Sounds like someone you might want to consider adding to your staff." She winks at me. "Just a thought."

Larry Bailey swings his gaze between Kimberly and me, glances at the box at my feet on the pavement, then purses his lips as if the suggestion isn't entirely preposterous. "Despite your current situation, a recommendation from my daughter means a lot. She rarely gives them. And given what my daughter did, I'd be the last person to say that lying about a relationship is necessarily disqualifying." He pulls the newspaper out from under his arm and slaps it against his thigh. "Send me your résumé. We'll talk." Then he rounds the hood of the SUV and climbs into the driver's seat.

"Take care, Dean," Kimberly says, her hand on the passenger-side door latch. "Maybe I'll see you again soon."

"Stranger things have happened," I say.

"Most of them in the last month."

She gives me a two-finger salute before she enters the SUV, then lowers her window to wave goodbye. "Good luck with Solange. I hope you get the answer you're hoping for."

"So do I, Kimberly. So do I. And good luck with Nia," I tell her. "I hope you get the answer you deserve."

Meanwhile, I'm mentally ditching my old life plan. Solange is it for me. Once I make amends with her, everything else will fall into place. Or not. Thing is, if I'm destined to stumble, I'd rather do it with Solange by my side. So as soon as she returns from Vegas, I'll tell her exactly how I feel and beg her for another chance.

CHAPTER THIRTY-ONE

SOLANGE

"We're such a disappointment," I tell Brandon as I snuggle into the comforter in our double room at the Mirage. "We should be on the casino floor playing slots or something. I even went to the bank and got two rolls of quarters."

Brandon barks out a laugh. "What the hell are you going to do with two rolls of quarters?"

"Spend within my means, is what I'm going to do."

"We'll go down in a minute," he says. "We need to get lit first." Whistling, he flips his suitcase open — and unveils several large bottles of vodka and whiskey and a mind-blowing assortment of travel-size liqueurs.

Slack-jawed, I spring out of the bed and peer inside his bag. "Holy shit, so that's why you needed to check it at the airport."

"Exactly," he says, wearing a self-satisfied

smile. "I'm not drinking watered-down liquor for my thirtieth birthday."

"You brought Solo cups too," I say, my voice rising an octave as I take in Brandon's level of preparedness. Bartending is his partial vocation; it figures he wouldn't rely on someone else's drinks to achieve his long-anticipated birthday buzz.

We transfer the alcohol from his suitcase to the top of the executive desk, which Brandon has pulled to the center of the room. He stands behind his makeshift bar counter as if he's poised to make magic. "Any requests?"

"Surprise me."

And boy, does he. I take a sip of the drink he's made me and choke. "Good God. Is this grain alcohol?"

He places a hand over his chest and drops his chin. "You wound me."

"I'm a lightweight, my friend. My inability to handle liquor has nothing to do with your skills."

"In any case, we're toasting to the day I was born, and you're going to drink it as if it's yummy and delicious and you can't get enough of it."

I nod. "Got it." Then I raise my red plastic cup in the air. "To Brandon. You're one of the sweetest, gentlest, funniest, and most talented men I know."

"One of?"

"Yes, I know others. Lots of 'em, in fact, so it's not like you're special. Don't interrupt again." I take a deep breath and resume my toast. "You, my friend, deserve every single good thing that happens to you, and I know your light is only going to grow brighter in the coming years. Cheers."

"And cheers to the new job. Breaking in a new roommate would have been a nightmare." We clink plastics, then he knocks back the entire contents of his cup and pounds his chest.

I follow suit, and this time, the alcohol goes down smoothly, the simmering heat settling in my belly like a warm hug. "Another!"

After a few cocktails, Brandon and I move the party to our respective beds. We're lying on our sides, facing each other, a foot of space between us. Despite the distance, I can smell the alcohol on his breath from here. He's at the pity-party stage of inebriation.

"I'm a mess, Solange," he says. "Still chasing dreams I should have put to rest years ago. What person in their right mind wants to date a struggling actor who bartends on the side? Maybe I'll find a boyfriend or

490

girlfriend once I'm in a groove. But in the meantime, the occasional date or hookup is good enough."

"You deserve more than good enough," I say.

"Just like my future partner deserves me at my best," he counters. "I'm not there yet." Then he laughs.

"What?" I ask.

"Remember when we used to joke that if we hadn't found 'the one' by the time I turned thirty, we'd just marry each other?"

I seem to remember a drunken conversation or two along those lines, sure. Is he suggesting what I think he's suggesting? If he is, things are about to get very awkward between us.

He shifts to lie on his back. "Even if I still wanted to do something like that — and I'm *definitely* not saying that I do — we wouldn't be able to."

"Why the hell not?" I ask, defensive for no good reason.

"Because you already found the one, mama."

I swing my legs off the bed and sit up. Could Brandon be right? My brain cycles through my experiences with Dean these past few weeks. I want more of those days. More of his kisses. More of just being

491

around him. Teasing him. Talking to him. Doing everything *with* him. It's a simple calculation: I'd rather give Dean my love and embrace the *probability* that he'll be one of the best things to ever happen to me than protect myself from the *possibility* that he'll be my worst mistake. "Oh God, I think I'm in love with Dean." I fan my face, then drop my head between my thighs. "And I think I'm going to hyperventilate."

"Well, I'd bet my life savings that Dean feels the same way."

"Two whole dollars?" I say, still hunched over. "Now *that's* a high-stakes wager."

He lobs a pillow at me, but I swat it away.

"Seriously, though," Brandon says as he sits up. "He needs to know that he's going to miss out on a good thing if he doesn't get his act together."

I jump to my feet. "You're right!"

Brandon rises to his knees on the mattress. "You're a fantastic woman, and any person would be lucky to have you!"

"Exactly!" I say, pacing between the beds.

"And remember, no matter what, Solange, you'll always have me."

"You're the best hype man," I say, throwing my arms around his shoulders. "But it's going to take some effort to convince him."

Brandon falls onto his back again, his eyes

narrowing in mischief. "That can be arranged."

I'm not exactly sure what he has in mind, but when I open my mouth to ask him to elaborate, I lose my train of thought. "I should call Dean!" I say, plucking at individual strands of my hair and staring at them. Perhaps it's time for highlights. Or a Brazilian blowout. Ooh, a Brazilian wax too. Or a Brazilian butt lift. Now wait a minute . . .

"That's the alcohol talking."

"Yes. It's making me braver than I would be otherwise. Just go with it."

He waves me away, as though he's granting me permission to make an ass of myself. "Knock yourself out. But can we head downstairs first? I want to take some pictures in the casino, then walk the streets a bit. You game?"

"For you? Of course!"

"Cool. Don't forget to tell Dean everything we just talked about. He needs to hear it too."

DEAN

My cell phone rings, pulling me out of my stupor. Setting aside the Chinese takeout I'm eating out of the carton in bed, I lean toward the nightstand and glance at the screen.

Solange.

The phone is in my hands in seconds, and I sit up as I answer, readjusting the pillow behind me. "Hey, is everything okay?"

We're three hours apart, and it's just past six o'clock in the evening here. Time is pointless to me these days, though. I'm in this mental netherworld where getting ready for bed before sunset is perfectly appropriate.

The first thing I hear is music. Very loud music. Then shuffling of some kind. "Solange, are you there?" I ask.

"Hey, Dean, sorry to bother you, but I'm in Vegas, and I just wanted to say hello."

Her speech is slow — not slurred — which means she's probably tipsy.

"Hello to you too. What's going on?"

"Well, here's the thing. I've been thinking about what you said the last time we were together."

Shit. This isn't a conversation I want to have over the phone. I have declarations to make, assurances to give. They aren't going to land the same way if we do this now. "Don't worry about it. I said a lot of things that day, and not all of them are true. We can talk about it when you get back from Vegas if you want."

"Well, okay, but I wanted to tell you that

494

I'm an amazing woman, and you're missing out on a good thing. And any person would be lucky to have me as their partner." She lowers her voice and speaks to someone on her end of the line. "What?" she says to them. "Oh, yeah. I'll tell him that too." Then to me, she says, "But you know what? It'll be okay. I'll always have Brandon."

I rake a hand through my hair. She isn't making any sense, and I can't do shit about it. I want to be able to state my case, but I need to be in her presence, look in her eyes, hold her. "When can I see you? Can I meet you at the airport when you get back?"

She laughs, but it peters out as if it's too tiring for her to do anything else. "That airport's a mess." She yawns. "I'm exhausted."

"Solange, where are you?"

"At the bar," she says. "Brandon's . . . around. Where are you?"

"In my bed, which is where you should be. I mean, if you're exhausted, *you* should be in *your* hotel bed."

"Can't. Brandon's got plans for us. He's in this weird, introspective mood."

If the incessant ringing is any guide, she's in a casino. And if I were Brandon, I wouldn't leave her side even for a second. "Solange, do me a favor: Send me a thumbs-up when you're in your room, okay? Promise?"

"Will do," she says. "Farewell, Dean. Don't let the bed rugs bite."

"Bedbugs, Solange. You mean bedbugs."

"Yeah. That."

I hear a click, and the music blaring in the background is no more.

What the hell is going on over there? I pull the pillow from behind me and smother my face with it. I need a damn nap.

The insistent buzz of my cell phone forces me awake. I shoot out my hand and grab the offending object for the second time.

"Hello?"

"Dean, it's me."

It's Max, and his voice is strained.

"Everything okay?"

"Have you been on Instagram lately?" he asks.

At first blush, it sounds like a random question, but the undercurrent of agitation in his voice suggests it's not random at all.

"IG? Not lately, no," I say on a yawn. "I don't make a regular habit of going on there. What time is it?"

"Just after seven in the evening. Why the hell are you sleeping already?"

"Don't ask."

"Whatever. I'm going to send you a pic. Call me back when you see it."

The photo arrives in a text. My eye travels over everything: the image, the username, the accompanying message. The pic shows the façade of a steel-gray building with a scripted sign indicating that it houses the Marriage License Bureau. The username is @BrandonTheThespian, and the message says: "Going to the chapel and we're going to get married . . . in the morning."

I pull back the covers, spring out of bed, and call Max. "What the hell? Is this a joke?"

He blows out a breath. "I can't be sure. Lina just showed it to me, and she says Solange isn't answering her phone."

I never pick at my nails, but I'm gnawing on them now. This can't be happening. No fucking way. I brace my neck and stomp through the unit as I try to make sense of what's going on. Brandon once warned me that Solange was one bad relationship away from never dating again and marrying him instead. Is Solange really contemplating this? Is this why she said she'll always have Brandon? "What should we do?"

"We?" Max barks out. "Oh no, buddy. The question is, what are *you* going to do about it? I'm here for moral support only. The two

of you need to work this out amongst yourselves."

"I need to stop this wedding," I say, my
heart pounding in my chest.

"Yes, you need to stop this wedding."

"Because I want to be with Solange, and
she needs to know that before she does
something she can't easily undo."

"Holy shit," Lina says in the background.

"Is Lina eavesdropping?" I ask Max.

"She's wrapped around my body like a
koala. It can't be helped."

I smile at the picture he's painted. "Tell
her Solange is upending my life in the worst
way, and I'm loving every minute of it."

"I assure you she heard that. My adorable
curmudgeon is grinning so hard."

"Okay," I say, already running through the
unit gathering what I'll need for the trip.
"I'm getting off the phone. I have a plane to
catch — at the crack of dawn, probably."

"Whoa. Now I know you're in love."

I stop short. "How's that?"

"Because you're voluntarily heading to
DCA on the weekend. I can't stand that
airport; it's going to be a nightmare."

"She's worth it."

"Glad you think so. We'll keep trying to
reach Solange, and I'll monitor their IG for
any clues as to where they are. If you get to

498

them first, let us know what's going on, okay?"

"Will do."

"Good luck, man."

I'd intended to invite Solange to dinner and share my feelings then. Should have known that was entirely too ordinary for Ms. Pereira. Now I'll be the one crashing Solange's wedding. Assuming I can find her, and I'm not too late, that is.

CHAPTER THIRTY-TWO

DEAN

Early Saturday morning, I make my bleary-eyed way through the plane's cabin and let out a huge sigh of relief. *Made it.* Blessedly, the plane isn't full. I'm in the aisle, and my seatmate, a broad-chested white guy with massive thighs, has the middle seat.

"This is promising," I say to him, pointing to the crew members preparing for takeoff. "Looks like we'll be able to spread out."

He swings his gaze from the window seat to me. "Nah. I prefer the middle." Then he tips his head back and places his red Nationals baseball cap on his face.

What a jackass.

I wipe down my seat and tray table, then settle in for the trip. As one of the flight attendants hands out earphones, I call Max. "Hey, any news? Has Lina talked to her?"

"No, she's still not answering, but Brandon tagged Oasis Wedding Chapel, and the caption said 'Morning plans.' Nothing else, though."

"That's good enough. I'll head straight there from the airport." A commotion near the cockpit draws my attention. "I've got to go. I'll check in with you when I land. We're supposed to get in just after eight thirty A.M. local time."

"Sounds good. I doubt they'd schedule a wedding before nine anyway. Be safe."

I tuck my phone in my pocket and try to get a better look at what's going on up front. I mentally pray to the gods of the friendly skies: *Please, please, please don't do anything to delay this flight.*

"Mariana, *go* already," a throaty voice says, and when the next group of boarding passengers appears at the cabin entrance, I see Tia Viviane inching her way up the aisle, with Tia Mariana and Solange's mom, Izabel, following closely behind her.

What the hell?

Izabel spots me first. "Dean! There you are, filho!"

"Izabel. Mariana. Viviane. Uh, this is a surprise."

"We heard about Brandon and Solange," Izabel says as she hands me her bag. "And if I need to be there to talk some sense into my daughter, then that's what I'll do. Can you put that away for me?"

"Of course."

I end up stowing bags for all three women.

Viviane looks at her ticket. "Oh, I'm right here in your row, Dean."

Nationals guy grunts and stands, letting her in, though it's plain from his serious expression that he was hoping the window seat would remain empty. So damn strange. Mariana takes a seat in the row behind Nationals guy, and Izabel takes the aisle seat directly across from me. Essentially, I'm surrounded by the three sisters and one guy who thinks his dick is so big he can't close his legs.

"You want to switch with her?" I ask my neighbor, pointing at Tia Viviane.

"Nah, I'm good."

Tia Viviane flares her nostrils and glares at him. Oh, she's pissed. Any minute now, Nationals guy is going to regret his decision not to switch seats with her.

Once we're in the air, Tia Viviane proceeds to dig into her bag and remove a five-course meal. She hands Tia Mariana an item wrapped in foil, then asks me to pass another item covered in plastic wrap to Izabel. Tia Viviane isn't bothering to limit her movements either. Instead, she's using her full range of motion, her arm sweeping across Nationals guy's face and almost clipping him on the nose as she purposefully prolongs the process of distributing the food. That'll teach him.

I get a whiff of garlic, and my stomach rumbles. "Is that a sanduíche?"

"Yes," Tia Viviane says, smiling at me for the first time. "Want one?"

"You have enough?"

"We always pack extra."

"Yeah, I'd never turn one down."

Tia Viviane makes a production of handing over my sandwich, cautioning that it's hot and slathered in butter and might spill. Tia Mariana pulls on Nationals guy's seat back as she gets comfortable. Unable to resist joining in on the fun, I pass wipes and hand sanitizer to Tia Viviane. As expected, Nationals guy grunts, straightens in his seat, and hits the call button. The flight attendant glides to our row within seconds.

"How may I help you, sir?"

He removes his cap, then shoots daggers at Tia Viviane and me. "I'm kind of a big guy. Wondering if it might be possible to snag a less congested row somewhere so I can spread out."

She gives him an understanding smile. "All we have available is the very last row, near the restroom."

"I'll take it," he says as he puts up his tray table.

I try to cover my grin, but then I catch Tia Viviane's wicked expression and decide not to bother. After Nationals guy gathers his belongings, I slip into the aisle to let him out, then wave goodbye as he lumbers to the back of the plane.

"Okay," Izabel says, turning toward me as if driving away Nationals guy was only the first order of business. "So what's the plan?"

For a man who prefers to be prepared for even the most minor event, I'm embarrassingly bereft of any good ideas. What am I going to say to Solange? Will she even care that I want to be in a relationship with her? I was pretty adamant that I would never be able to love her the way she deserves to be loved. Will she believe that I've changed my mind? My head's going to explode.

I bite into the bread and moan my appreciation. I may not know how to tell someone I love them, but I damn well know how to eat a delicious flank steak sandwich.

"Dean," Izabel snaps. "You can talk and eat at the same time, no?"

"Yes, yes. I'm just gathering my thoughts. I mean, as wild as this may sound, I'm in love with your daughter. I'm going to start with that and just speak from the heart."

Her eyes soften. "Okay," she says, nodding. "Now we're getting somewhere."

Whether I'll get anywhere with Solange, though, remains to be seen.

A full belly and a four-and-a-half-hour nap dramatically improve my mood. Not long after I wake, we're touching down on Nevada ground, and I'm up and out of my seat as soon as the plane parks at the gate.

I scowl at a man who's barreling through the aisle and refusing to wait his turn, then I help the tias get their bags from the overhead compartments. After a stop at the restroom, the tias and I follow the signs for ground transportation.

"There are slot machines in the airport?" Tia Mariana asks rhetorically. "Who thought that was a good idea?"

At ground transportation, I pull up the address for the Oasis Wedding Chapel. According to Google, it's on the Vegas Strip and should only be a short trip from the airport. Once we're all settled in the cab, I try my luck reaching Solange. To my surprise, someone picks up after the first ring.

"Hey, Dean," Brandon whispers. "We can't talk right now. We'll call you back in a half hour or so."

"Brandon —"

He hangs up before I can say another word.

I growl in frustration, then remember I'm not alone. "Sorry about that, everyone. I'm stressed."

Izabel pats my forearm. "It's okay, Dean. We understand."

"How can you be so serene about this?" I say, bracing my neck. "Aren't you worried Solange is making the biggest mistake of her life?"

She shrugs. "I have faith everything will work out in the end. Deus sempre encontra um caminho."

Tia Mariana leans over. "God will always find a way."

"And who knows?" Solange's mother continues. "Maybe Brandon and Solange are meant to be. I just need to see this with my own eyes."

Yeah, no. I don't need to see shit with my own eyes. If Solange is meant to be with anyone, it's abso-fucking-lutely me. I meet the driver's curious gaze in the rearview. "Listen, we need to be at Oasis Wedding Chapel as soon as possible. Can you make that happen?"

"I'll do my best," he says. "Going to a wedding?"

"Yes," I say, nodding. "But with any luck,

we'll be stopping it."

The driver grins and steps on the gas. I get the fare and a sizable tip ready and spend the rest of the trip doing deep-breathing exercises to calm my nerves. My experience simulating childbirth wasn't all for naught.

Twenty minutes later, I'm still not calm, but I'm ready for showtime anyway. As soon as the cab pulls to a complete stop, I rush to the trunk and unload everyone's bags. After surveying the complex, I blow out a harsh breath. I expected a small white chapel, like the ones I've seen in countless movies. What I get instead is a maze of small gray and blue buildings and immaculately landscaped grounds in the middle of a glittery concrete town. Thankfully, one of the buildings is marked with an "Enter Here" sign. I point it out to the tias. "Over there."

Izabel places a hand on my arm. "You go ahead first, Dean. I'm not sure it would be good for us to show up together. We'll come in after. Good luck!"

"Thanks," I say, sprinting away. "I'm going to need it." A minute later, I push open the double doors and jog to the front desk. There, a woman wearing a friendly smile and a blue wig dances in her seat by way of greeting.

"Oooh, getting married today, sweetheart?" she asks in a heavy Southern accent.

Even though I'm short of breath, I manage to eke out a response. "No. I'm here to . . . uh . . . witness a wedding, and I think I'm going to be late."

"Only one wedding on the books this morning. Down the hall and to the right. Maybe you can catch the last few seconds. Enjoy."

"Can you watch my bag?" I ask, panting.

"Sure, sugar, set it right here," she says, pointing to the area behind her.

I drop the bag without regard for any of the contents inside and sprint down the hall as though I'm a wide receiver making their last appearance in the Super Bowl. When I get to the doors of the chapel, I throw them open and rush inside.

SOLANGE

"So, Brandon, has your curiosity been piqued?"

That was a sweet wedding, but I'm beat, and Brandon dragged us here before we could eat breakfast. Now that the newlyweds are retreating back up the aisle, I drop into the pew and stretch my calves. Brandon's cocktails are potent, so even after a decent night's rest, I'm existing in a mental haze that makes everything look overexposed.

"Yeah, yeah, thanks for humoring me," he says. "I can finally say I've witnessed a Vegas wedding. One more item off my bucket list."

"You're a weirdo," I say, bumping his shoulder.

Brandon studies his phone screen. Which reminds me.

"Don't let me forget to check in with the hotel's lost and found. I *know* I had my phone when we were sitting at the bar. Not having it is totally disorienting. Hopefully someone turned it in."

"Hopefully," Brandon says as he types away. Out of the blue, he stands and grabs my hand. "C'mon, I'm going to ask the officiant to take a picture of us for posterity."

I don't resist, but I do trudge to the altar because I'm just so damn tired.

"Okay, you two," the officiant says. "One quick pic coming up. On three, say cheese."

Brandon and I stand next to each other and smile for the camera. Before the officiant begins the count, Brandon turns to face me and interlaces our fingers.

"One, two —"

Suddenly the doors of the chapel swing open, and Dean bursts inside. "Wait! Solange, don't do this!"

I gasp, and my heart thuds in my chest. What is he doing here? "Dean, I'm not —"

"Let him speak, Solange," Brandon says, his eyes glinting with mischief. "There's no reason we shouldn't hear what he has to say."

Honestly, I wish I had some popcorn. Because this? This is riveting. I'm tempted to launch myself into Dean's arms, but I resist the urge, partly because I don't know exactly why he's here. Still, something tells me he wouldn't have traveled across the country to reiterate that we're never going to be a couple.

So I just stare at him and wait. God, he's a sight for my lovesick eyes. His hair's a glorious mess, and the faded jeans he's wearing sit perfectly on his hips. My instinct isn't to look at him and say *Mine, mine, mine.* All I can think is, *Baby, I'm yours, yours, yours.*

Dean takes small steps down the aisle and stops a foot away from me. He looks at Brandon, his expression somber. "I'm sorry to interrupt, but this needs to be said."

Brandon gestures as if he's giving Dean the floor. "Go right ahead. I want her to be absolutely certain about this."

Dean returns his gaze to me, his hands clenched into fists at his sides.

"For years, I've clung to a view about love that boils down to this: It isn't worth it. I never doubted that it existed or that people experienced it. But I regarded it as a weakness. One that would leave me vulnerable and insecure. I need stability, I told myself. And giving my heart over to someone would make me weak, would surrender my future to their whims, would only leave me disappointed. So I focused on securing all the trappings of stability I could think of: a well-paying job, a home, a partner with the same ambitions as mine. And I was fine."

I take a step in his direction, a glimmer of hope propelling me forward. "Until?"

He takes a deep breath and expels it slowly. "Until you."

Oh God. I'm giddy and weightless, and I may never return to earth. So *this* is what euphoria feels like.

Dean's not done, though.

"I once tried to explain to you how I envisioned my future, and it was so far off from what I actually want and need, it's laughable." He chuckles, then drags his fingers through his hair. "Solange, at this very moment, I have no idea what my job will be, whether I'll be able to afford my mortgage much longer, or whether I'll ever get married and have kids. And you know what? I'm not terrified. Why? Because if there's *any* chance that you'll be a part of my life, I can handle all of the other unknowns, even if that means we can't be in the same place right now."

He steps closer, his hands clenching and unclenching at his sides. "And this isn't about jealousy or wanting what I can't have or anything like that. It's really that over the course of the weeks I've known you, I've gotten glimpses of what it would be like to be your person. I've gotten a taste of what it would be like to be the one loving you. And it kind of feels like an honor. Like maybe I don't deserve you. But I want to try to earn a place in your heart." He chokes up a bit before continuing. "I want to try so damn much. These feelings you've inspired in me make me feel reckless and impulsive and disoriented in the best way. And I'm sorry that I once told you I couldn't love you. Because that isn't true. I already do."

I tilt my head and smile at him. "It's that damn warm, fuzzy feeling, isn't it?"

His mouth twitches, then he smiles wide, affection glowing in his eyes. "Yes, damn you, *yes.*" He straightens and looks at Brandon as though he's just remembered Brandon's still here. "I'm really sorry about this, but Solange and I have unfinished business."

"I was never in the picture," Brandon says. "No worries at all."

Dean's brows snap together. "So . . . you're not getting married?"

Brandon shakes his head. "Nah. That was just a ruse to get you here." He digs into his pocket, pulls out my *missing* phone, then tosses it my way. "I had a little help too."

As if on cue, my mother and aunts shuffle to the front of the chapel. Tia Viviane's wiping her eyes with a tissue.

"Mãe, tias, what are you doing here?"

"We were giving Dean a little push," she says. "And sending Brandon updates so he knew when to expect us."

"Diabolical," I say. "Every one of you."

Dean shakes his head in wonder. "Indeed."

"Hang on," I say to Brandon and my family. "Could you excuse us? Dean and I need a minute." I link arms with him, then draw him to an alcove on the right side of the chapel. Taking his hands in mine, I summon the courage to make some promises of my own. "You have no idea how much it means to me that you came here and fought for us. Because that's what I'm prepared to do too. For so long, I have been resistant to committing to anything, claiming I was being careful, never overselling myself, avoiding mistakes that could change my life forever. I was stuck, Dean. But now I realize that by never choosing anything, I was choosing not to live the life I deserve."

After taking a fortifying breath, I continue: "So today, I choose you, Dean. You. I'm not expecting easy. I'm expecting fireworks. And bumps in the road. And sweet moments. And mind-blowing sex. And hair-pulling conversations when we forget how to use our words. But I want it all. Every moment, whether it's messy, tender, maddening, or sublime. I only want that with you."

He tugs me close and wraps his arms around me. If I could, I'd remain in this moment forever. But too soon, several throats clear, demanding our attention.

"Is everything okay over there?" Tia Viviane asks. "There's a show at noon we want to see."

I flinch my head back slightly. "A show? Which one?"

Tia Mariana mumbles her answer; my mother drops her head and covers her face.

I cup my ear. "What? I can't hear you."

Tia Viviane steps forward, her chin raised as if she's daring anyone to challenge her. *"Magic Mike Live."*

514

Dean snorts. I just shake my head.

"Go," I tell them. "We'll meet at the hotel later."

"C'mon, ladies." Brandon puts his arm around Tia Viviane and waltzes up the aisle. "I'll make sure you get there on time."

Minutes later, Dean and I are finally alone.

"Now I need to ask you something," he says, his mouth curved into a smile that fills me with pure, unadulterated joy.

"What is it?"

He holds my hands and squeezes. "Will you, Solange Pereira, take me as your boyfriend, to have and to hold, through sickness and in health, through the good times and bad, as long as we both shall share a Netflix account?"

I hold back a laugh and nod. "Throw in Apple TV+, and we've got a deal."

"Done."

I rise to my tiptoes and tug him close. Then we kiss. And it's magic. The start of something special. A moment that could only happen between us.

EPILOGUE

ONE YEAR LATER

SOLANGE

Dean bends to my level and plants a soft kiss on the back of my neck. "Baby, we can't be late for this."

"I know," I say, my fingers flying across the keyboard as I prepare for a virtual chat with Layla. "This'll only take a few minutes, and then we'll go."

He sighs. "I'll believe that when it happens."

Dean has a point. Layla and I do tend to lose track of time during our weekly calls.

When I start my video, Layla's already in the meeting room, and I wave wildly at the camera. "Tell me everything. How'd it go? Were you nervous? What kinds of questions did they ask? When will they make the decision?"

"Slow down, Solange," she says on a laugh. "I'll never be able to remember what I'm supposed to tell you."

"You're right," I say, grimacing apologetically. "Let's try this again. How'd it go?"

Layla has her GED now. Yesterday, she interviewed for a pilot program that would pay her to shadow a paralegal. She's in it for the long haul, and so am I.

She fills me in, explaining that she expects to hear back from the program by the end of next week.

I clap effusively. "Eeep! Please don't wait until our regular Saturday morning call to tell me the news. Send me a text as soon as you know."

"I will," she says, her eyes bright and hopeful. "Thanks for telling me about the opportunity. And for always being my sounding board."

"Of course, Layla. It truly is my pleasure."

I absolutely mean that too. My role as her mentor. My role at Victory Academy. These are responsibilities I don't take lightly, and I'm honored that I get to guide these wonderfully deserving young people. It isn't always easy, but even when I experience a hiccup, I never second-guess my decision to align my future with theirs.

Out of the corner of my eye, I track Dean's movements in the kitchen. He's dressed in a gray three-piece suit, and his hair is still wet from the shower he took minutes ago. Muttering to himself, he searches the cabinets.

"It's in the one above the dishwasher," I tell him before I return my attention to Layla. To her, I say: "Okay, my dear, I need to go. The wedding's due to start in an hour."

Layla gives me a thumbs-up, then blows me a kiss. I mimic her farewell and close the Zoom app. As soon as I do, Dean presses the power button on the handheld blender I gave him last Christmas, and its god-awful whirring noise fills the room.

I wait for him to finish before I speak. "What are you —"

The noise resumes, then stops.

"What are you making —"

Again with the whirring. Which he's plainly doing on purpose.

I look up and narrow my eyes at him. "Oh my God, are you a toddler?"

"I'm happy," he says, his smile broadening so wide I want to drag him into the bedroom. For a few seconds, I contemplate a quickie. Something in my eyes must give my thoughts away, because he sets the blender down and leans against the counter, as if he knows I'm bound to join him.

He's right.

As I slink across the room, I catalog his

appearance, taking special note of the wicked curve of his smile and the way the cut of his vest complements his lean frame.

This man is my partner. Pinch me, someone.

That warm, fuzzy feeling he was so averse to when we first met? It's a constant in my life these days. He stirs it in me; I stir it in him.

"I'm making us smoothies to go," he says, his expression wary as he watches me approach.

"I can see that," I say, crowding his personal space. Unable to resist, I settle my thumb at the corner of his mouth and draw it across his lips.

He moans into my hand, his hazel eyes sparking with heat and promise. "Solange, we're going to be late. And you'll mess up my hair."

I reach up to touch his carefully arranged locks, but he slaps my hand away.

"Don't," he says, his voice quivering dramatically. "It took me forever to get it to behave."

I can't help snorting. "Okay, you win. For now. When we get home tonight, though . . ."

His eyelids fall to half-mast, and he pulls me close. "Have I told you lately how much

I enjoy hearing you call this your home?"

Pretending to think about his question, I tap my chin and study the ceiling. "Only every day since I moved in."

I made the leap three months ago. Officially, that is. During the nine months prior to that, we basically spent every night together, either at his place or mine. But Vegas didn't change just us. It changed Brandon too. When he returned to DC, he decided that it was finally time for him to move to New York and focus on his acting career. Dean and I inspired him, he says. He even signed with Julian Hart, a Black agent making a name for himself in Hollywood. I'm rooting for my friend to grab hold of his dreams and soar. And maybe one day he'll find his person too.

So with Brandon gone, I needed another roommate — or another place to live. Dean offered both. And I'm so glad he did. Neither of us is perfect, but we don't need to be. We're us. A perfectly imperfect couple figuring life out together. All real. Absolutely no faking.

"Ready to head out?" he asks, his arms outstretched as he holds our smoothies.

I kiss him. Sweetly. Softly. "With you? Always."

DEAN

We arrive at the Cartwright Hotel with only twenty minutes to spare, and two smartly dressed ushers immediately guide us to the gardens.

"Is it strange being here?" Solange asks, her hand squeezing mine.

"Not at all. Feels like a million years ago."

In fact, it's cathartic in a way. I was never meant to marry Ella in this place, or any-place else for that matter. And it's extra special that I'm finally returning with the woman I love beside me.

Before we can even snag seats, Jaslene marches up the aisle, her head lowered as she speaks into the microphone attached to her headset.

When she reaches us, she points at So-lange. "Listen, I know your history. Don't even think about opening your mouth dur-ing this ceremony."

Solange rolls her eyes. "Ha, ha. I'm not saying a word."

"Good," she says, pointing two fingers at her eyes, then at Solange's. *I see everything,* she mouths.

"You've outdone yourself," I say to Jaslene, interrupting their banter. "And you should be proud."

"Agreed," Solange adds. "Lina would be

proud too."

"Speaking of which," Jaslene says. "Have you heard from her?"

Solange shakes her head, but she's bouncing on her toes, and her eyes are dancing with excitement. "Nothing yet."

Lina and Max are at Surrey Hall Farms for a couple's retreat this weekend. Lina's expecting bonding exercises; Max is planning to pop the question in a field of tulips on the outskirts of the farm. He's promised the tias a photographer will capture it all. I look down at my watch. "Should be any minute now."

Jaslene shimmies her shoulders. "Okay, I need to make sure the trains are running on time. See you after the ceremony."

Solange and I continue down the aisle until we reach Larry Bailey, now my boss.

He immediately rises and puts out his hand. "Good to see you, Dean. Thanks for coming."

"I wouldn't miss this for the world, sir."

"Son, when are you going to start calling me Larry?"

I give him a sheepish grin. "Never?"

He chuckles, then looks around him. "You two should have a special place of honor somewhere considering you definitely had a hand in getting them together."

Solange playfully scoffs at the notion. "Nonsense. Kimberly and Nia were in love before we met them. They just didn't know it yet."

She may be right, but Kimberly herself admits that when Solange told her about my attempt to crash the wedding that never was, she, too, mustered the courage to confess her feelings to Nia. Now we're moments away from watching them walk down the aisle and pledge their love to each other.

Mr. Bailey smiles. "You're probably right, Solange. Anyway, we'll talk more during the reception." He points at me. "By the way, I read your proposal about the pro bono program, and I'm fully on board."

My proposal, which I sent to him just yesterday, recommended that each of the lawyers in the legal department take on a minimum number of pro bono hours in addition to their regular duties and that the department as a whole commit to handling one high-impact pro bono case per year. I'm both stunned and thrilled that he's read it this quickly and wants to proceed. "That's great news, sir."

"Well, I should clarify. I'm on board so long as you call me Larry."

"Then that's great news, Larry."

"One other thing," he says, raising his

index finger in the air. "We've got a team from Olney & Henderson coming in next week. Sam Henderson and Peter Barnum. They're making a pitch to be our outside law firm. I plan to be called away unexpectedly, so I'll need someone to cover for me and run the meeting." He twists his lips to the side, his expression wily and conspiratorial. "You can be the one to tell them we've decided to go in a different direction. If you want to, that is."

I should be the better person and politely decline the opportunity — but I won't. I'm only human, after all. Mirroring Larry's grin, I dip my head. "I'll be there."

Solange pulls me by the tie. "All right, you two. Enough about business. It's a wedding, for goodness' sake."

Solange and I find our seats, and minutes later, a quintet begins to play a jazz tune. The guests rise and face Kimberly and Nia, who are holding hands at the entrance to the gardens, Kimberly in a white pantsuit and Nia in a long flowing white gown.

The women stare at each other with love in their hearts and affection in their expressions. I know the feeling. Jesus, do I know the feeling. I never imagined I would, and yet here we are. Perhaps sensing that I'm overcome with emotion, Solange hugs me, her eyes glistening. I tear my gaze from hers, wanting to be respectful of Kimberly and Nia's special day, but damn, it's difficult not to just bask in Solange's loveliness. More than a year ago, this woman, whom I adore more than words can say, crashed my wedding, then pretended to be my girlfriend. Look how far we've come.

Max once told me that the detour sometimes becomes the destination. He's right. Solange and I took a detour, and now we've reached our destination together. The place where we're the happiest, the place at which we're the most content and secure, is in each other's arms.

There's absolutely *nothing* fake about that.

Revised Step Three: Find the love of my life.

Status: Completed.

THE END

ACKNOWLEDGMENTS

So we meet again, Acknowledgments. You're a relentless bitch.

I'm kidding.

Because the true relentless bitch was the manuscript that eventually became this book.

Folks, it put me through a lot. The experience didn't make me stronger. Nor did it inspire me to reach new heights in my career. No, it made me bitter. Honestly, I'm still salty about it.

Again, I'm kidding.

Or am I?

Seriously, though, this book is for you, my lovely readers. As many of you know, its predecessor, *The Worst Best Man,* released one month before our world was forever changed by the Covid-19 global pandemic. Since then, I've received countless messages from readers in the United States and abroad telling me that *TWBM* helped them through a difficult time. Those messages fueled me. And served as a powerful reminder that my stories, though funny and flirty and, yes, a little dirty, *can* make a difference in people's lives.

Although none of us can predict what the world will look like when this book releases, my wish for how it will be received won't change: I hope it gives you a much-needed respite from whatever challenges you may be facing.

Oh, one more thing: I hope it makes you laugh. That's the *least* this bitch should do, right?

Okay, so now I need to express my deepest gratitude to the people who helped me get this book in your hands.

To my husband: You have always been my biggest cheerleader, and, boy, did I need a lot of cheering this time around. Thank you for having my back and for loving me unconditionally. No fictional hero will ever hold a candle to you.

To my daughters: You are the sweetest and wittiest girls I know. I still occasionally pinch myself when I think about the joys of being your mother. Thank you for checking on me, bringing me coffee, and encouraging me whenever I needed an extra boost. I love you the mostest.

To my mother: You were always enough

and so much more. Thank you for everything. Eu te amo muito.

To my dear friend Tracey Livesay: Thank you for being my hype person; I'm honored to be yours. I quite literally could not have finished this book without you. Your uplifting advice and helpful counsel gave me the push I needed. Picture our favorite GIF from *The Color Purple* here.

To Sarah Younger: Your agenting skills are unmatched, and your support is priceless. Thank you for assuaging my fears, silencing the doubts, and continuing to believe in me and my stories. I'm glad we're on this journey called publishing together.

To Nicole Fischer: Until this book, I don't think I *truly* understood the careful balancing act you have to play in your role as a book editor. Somehow, you managed to steer me in the right direction without stifling my ideas or my voice. I'm so grateful for your insights and expertise (and for the LOLs in the margins).

To my beta readers (Susan Scott Shelley, Soni Wolf, and Ana Coqui): Each of you brings a different perspective to the table, and I appreciate them all so much. I can't thank you enough for your kind and honest critiques and for helping me tell a better story than I would on my own.

To the writer friends, new and enduring, who offered valuable feedback (Adriana Herrera, Sabrina Sol, Gabriela Graciosa Guedes, and Olivia Dade): I'm so thankful that you each took the time to read parts of this book and settle my nerves. Besos, beijos, and kisses, ladies!

To Kristin Dwyer of LEO PR: Thank you for jumping on this roller coaster of a journey with me. You're the consummate professional, and I'm happy to say that your poise is contagious. To Daniela Escobar of LEO PR: I'm delighted to have you on the team.

To my Romancelandia compatriots, especially my 4 Chicas posse (Alexis Daria, Priscilla Oliveras, and Sabrina Sol), my #BatSignal crew (Michele Arris, Nina Crespo, Priscilla Oliveras, Tif Marcelo, and Tracey Livesay), and my #LatinxRom amigas (Adriana Herrera, Alexis Daria, Angelina M. Lopez, Diana Muñoz Stewart, Liana De La Rosa, Lydia San Andres, Natalie Caña, Priscilla Oliveras, Sabrina Sol, and Zoraida Córdova): I'm so lucky to be surrounded by such wise, talented, and caring people. Thanks for listening and for inspiring me to be the best version of myself.

To Victoria Colotta of VMC Art & Design: You're a sweet and gifted soul. Thanks for allowing me to step away from Canva.

And finally, to all the wonderful people at Avon/HarperCollins who have championed and continue to champion my books: Thank you for helping me share my stories. Special shout-outs go to Nathan Burton for illustrating another fun and flirty cover and to the production team for working your magic.

Until we meet again, Acknowledgments. You're still a relentless bitch.

ABOUT THE AUTHOR

USA Today bestselling author **Mia Sosa** writes funny, flirty, and moderately steamy contemporary romances that celebrate our multicultural world. A graduate of the University of Pennsylvania and Yale Law School, Mia practiced First Amendment and media law in the nation's capital for ten years before trading her suits for sweatpants. Born and raised in East Harlem, New York, she now lives in Maryland with her college sweetheart, their two book-loving daughters, and one dog that rules them all.

The employees of Thorndike Press hope you have enjoyed this Large Print book. All our Thorndike, Wheeler, and Kennebec Large Print titles are designed for easy reading, and all our books are made to last. Other Thorndike Press Large Print books are available at your library, through selected bookstores, or directly from us.

For information about titles, please call:
  (800) 223-1244

or visit our website at:
  gale.com/thorndike

To share your comments, please write:
  Publisher
  Thorndike Press
  10 Water St., Suite 310
  Waterville, ME 04901